T0144800

Madame Midas

Madame Midas

Fergus Hume

MINT EDITIONS

Madame Midas was first published in 1888.

This edition published by Mint Editions 2021.

ISBN 9781513278360 | E-ISBN 9781513278827

Published by Mint Editions®

 MINT
EDITIONS

minteditionbooks.com

Publishing Director: Jennifer Newens
Design & Production: Rachel Lopez Metzger
Project Manager: Micaela Clark
Typesetting: Westchester Publishing Services

Contents

PROLOGUE

Cast Up by the Sea

A wild bleak-looking coast, with huge water-worn promontories jutting out into the sea, daring the tempestuous fury of the waves, which dashed furiously in sheets of seething foam against the iron rocks. Two of these headlands ran out for a considerable distance, and at the base of each, ragged cruel-looking rocks stretched still further out into the ocean until they entirely disappeared beneath the heaving waste of waters, and only the sudden line of white foam every now and then streaking the dark green waves betrayed their treacherous presence to the idle eye. Between these two headlands there was about half a mile of yellow sandy beach on which the waves rolled with a dull roar, fringing the wet sands with many coloured wreaths of sea-weed and delicate shells. At the back the cliffs rose in a kind of semi-circle, black and precipitous, to the height of about a hundred feet, and flocks of white seagulls who had their nests therein were constantly circling round, or flying seaward with steadily expanded wings and discordant cries. At the top of these inhospitable-looking cliffs a line of pale green betrayed the presence of vegetation, and from thence it spread inland into vast-rolling pastures ending far away at the outskirts of the bush, above which could be seen giant mountains with snow-covered ranges. Over all this strange contrast of savage arid coast and peaceful upland there was a glaring red sky—not the delicate evanescent pink of an ordinary sunset—but a fierce angry crimson which turned the wet sands and dark expanse of ocean into the colour of blood. Far away westward, where the sun—a molten ball of fire—was sinking behind the snow-clad peaks, frowned long lines of gloomy clouds—like prison bars through which the sinking orb glowed fiercely. Rising from the east to the zenith of the sky was a huge black cloud bearing a curious resemblance to a gigantic hand, the long lean fingers of which were stretched threateningly out as if to grasp the land and drag it back into the lurid sea of blood; altogether a cruel, weird-looking scene, fantastic, unreal, and bizarre as one of Dore's marvellous conceptions. Suddenly on the red waters there appeared a black speck, rising and falling with the restless waves, and ever drawing nearer and nearer to the gloomy cliffs and sandy beach. When within a quarter of a mile of the shore, the speck resolved itself into a boat, a mere shallop, painted a dingy white, and much battered by the waves as it tossed lightly on the crimson waters. It had one mast and a small sail all torn and patched, which by some miracle held together, and swelling out to the wind drew the boat nearer to the land. In this frail craft were two men, one of whom was kneeling in the prow of the boat shading his eyes from the sunlight with his hands and gazing eagerly at the cliffs, while the other sat in the centre with bowed head, in an attitude of sullen resignation, holding the straining sail by a stout rope twisted round his arm. Neither of them spoke a word till within a short distance of the beach, when the man at the look-out arose, tall and gaunt, and stretched out his hands to the inhospitable-looking coast with a harsh, exulting laugh.

"At last," he cried, in a hoarse, strained voice, and in a foreign tongue; "freedom at last."

The other man made no comment on this outburst of his companion, but kept his eyes steadfastly on the bottom of the boat, where lay a small barrel and a bag of mouldy biscuits, the remnants of their provisions on the voyage.

The man who had spoken evidently did not expect an answer from his companion, for he did not even turn his head to look at him, but stood with folded arms gazing eagerly ahead, until, with a sudden rush, the boat drove up high and dry on the shore, sending him head-over-heels into the wet sand. He struggled to his feet quickly, and, running up the beach a little way, turned to see how his companion had fared. The other had fallen into the sea, but had picked himself up, and was busily engaged in wringing the water from his coarse clothing. There was a smooth water-worn boulder on the beach, and, seeing this, the man who had spoken went up to it and sat down thereon, while his companion, evidently of a more practical turn of mind, collected the stale biscuits which had fallen out of the bag, then, taking the barrel carefully on his shoulder, walked up to where the other was sitting, and threw both biscuits and barrel at his feet.

He then flung himself wearily on the sand, and picking up a biscuit began to munch it steadily. The other drew a tin pannikin from the bosom of his shirt, and nodded his head towards the barrel, upon which the eater laid down his biscuit, and, taking up the barrel, drew the bung, and let a few drops of water trickle into the tin dish. The man on the boulder drank every drop, then threw the pannikin down on the sand, while his companion, who had exhausted the contents of the barrel, looked wolfishly at him. The other, however, did not take the slightest notice of his friend's lowering looks, but began to eat a biscuit and look around him. There was a strong contrast between these two waifs of the sea which the ocean had just thrown up on the desolate coast. The man on the boulder was a tall, slightly-built young fellow, apparently about thirty years of age, with leonine masses of reddish-coloured hair, and a short, stubbly beard of the same tint. His face, pale and attenuated by famine, looked sharp and clever; and his eyes, forming a strong contrast to his hair, were quite black, with thin, delicately-drawn eyebrows above them. They scintillated with a peculiar light which, though not offensive, yet gave anyone looking at him an uncomfortable feeling of insecurity. The young man's hands, though hardened and discoloured, were yet finely formed, while even the coarse, heavy boots he wore could not disguise the delicacy of his feet. He was dressed in a rough blue suit of clothes, all torn and much stained by sea water, and his head was covered with a red cap of wool-work which rested lightly on his tangled masses of hair. After a time he tossed aside the biscuit he was eating, and looked down at his companion with a cynical smile. The man at his feet was a rough, heavy-looking fellow, squarely and massively built, with black hair and a heavy beard of the same sombre hue. His hands were long and sinewy; his feet—which were bare—large and ungainly: and his whole appearance was that of a man in a low station of life. No one could have told the colour of his eyes, for he looked obstinately at the ground; and the expression of his face was so sullen and forbidding that altogether he appeared to be an exceedingly unpleasant individual. His companion eyed him for a short time in a cool, calculating manner, and then rose painfully to his feet.

"So," he said rapidly in French, waving his hand towards the frowning cliffs, "so, my Pierre, we are in the land of promise; though I must confess"—with a disparaging shrug of the shoulders—"it certainly does not look very promising: still, we are on dry land, and that is something after tossing about so long in that stupid boat, with only a plank between us and death. Bah!"—with another expressive shrug—"why should I call it stupid? It has carried us all the way from New Caledonia, that hell upon earth, and landed us safely in what may turn out Paradise. We must not be ungrateful to the bridge that carried us over—eh, my friend?"

The man addressed as Pierre nodded an assent, then pointed towards the boat; the other looked up and saw that the tide had risen, and that the boat was drifting slowly away from the land.

"It goes," he said coolly, "back again to its proper owner, I suppose. Well, let it. We have no further need of it, for, like Caesar, we have now crossed the Rubicon. We are no longer convicts from a French prison, my friend, but shipwrecked sailors; you hear?"—with a sudden scintillation from his black eyes—"shipwrecked sailors; and I will tell the story of the wreck. Luckily, I can depend on your discretion, as you have not even a tongue to contradict, which you wouldn't do if you had."

The dumb man rose slowly to his feet, and pointed to the cliffs frowning above them. The other answered his thought with a careless shrug of the shoulders.

"We must climb," he said lightly, "and let us hope the top will prove less inhospitable than this place. Where we are I don't know, except that this is Australia; there is gold here, my friend, and we must get our share of it. We will match our Gallic wit against these English fools, and see who comes off best. You have strength, I have brains; so we will do great things; but"—laying his hand impressively on the other's breast—"no quarter, no yielding, you see!"

The dumb man nodded violently, and rubbed his ungainly hands together in delight.

"You don't know Balzac, my friend," went on the young man in a conversational tone, "or I would tell you that, like Rastignac, war is declared between ourselves and society; but if you have not the knowledge you have the will, and that is enough for me. Come, let us make the first step towards our wealth;" and without casting a glance behind him, he turned and walked towards the nearest headland, followed by the dumb man with bent head and slouching gait.

The rain and wind had been at work on this promontory, and their combined action had broken off great masses of rock, which lay in rugged confusion at the base. This offered painful but secure foothold, and the two adventurers, with much labour—for they were weak with the privations endured on the voyage from New Caledonia—managed to climb half way up the cliff, when they stopped to take breath and look around them. They were now in a perilous position, for, hanging as they were on a narrow ledge of rock midway between earth and sky, the least slip would have cost them their lives. The great mass of rock which frowned above them was nearly perpendicular, yet offered here and there certain facilities for climbing, though to do so looked like certain death. The men, however, were quite reckless, and knew if they could get to the top they would be safe, so they determined to attempt the rest of the ascent.

"As we have not the wings of eagles, friend Pierre," said the younger man, glancing around, "we must climb where we can find foothold. God will protect us; if not," with a sneer, "the Devil always looks after his own."

He crept along the narrow ledge and scrambled with great difficulty into a niche above, holding on by the weeds and sparse grass which grew out of the crannies of the barren crag. Followed by his companion, he went steadily up, clinging to projecting rocks—long trails of tough grass and anything else he could hold on to. Every now and then some seabird would dash out into their faces with wild cries, and nearly cause them to lose their foothold in the sudden start. Then the herbage began to get more luxurious, and the cliff to slope in an easy incline, which made the latter part of their ascent much easier. At last, after half an hour's hard work, they managed to get to the top, and threw themselves breathlessly on the short dry grass which fringed the rough cliff. Lying there half fainting with fatigue and hunger, they could hear, as in a confused dream, the drowsy thunder of the waves below, and the discordant cries of the sea-gulls circling round their nests, to which they had not yet returned. The rest did them good, and in a short time they were able to rise to their feet and survey the situation. In front was the sea, and at the back the grassy undulating country, dotted here and there with clumps of trees now becoming faint and indistinct in the rapidly falling shadows of the night. They could also see horses and cattle moving in the distant fields, which showed that there must be some human habitation near, and suddenly from a far distant house which they had not observed shone a bright light, which became to these weary waifs of the ocean a star of hope.

They looked at one another in silence, and then the young man turned towards the ocean again.

"Behind," he said, pointing to the east, "lies a French prison and two ruined lives—yours and mine—but in front," swinging round to the rich fields, "there is fortune, food, and freedom. Come, my friend, let us follow that light, which is our star of hope, and who knows what glory may await us. The old life is dead, and we start our lives in this new world with all the bitter experiences of the old to teach us wisdom— come!" And without another word he walked slowly down the slope towards the inland, followed by the dumb man with his head still bent and his air of sullen resignation.

The sun disappeared behind the snowy ranges—night drew a grey veil over the sky as the red light died out, and here and there the stars were shining. The seabirds sought their nests again and ceased their discordant cries—the boat which had brought the adventurers to shore drifted slowly out to sea, while the great black hand that rose from the eastward stretched out threateningly towards the two men tramping steadily onward through the dewy grass, as though it would have drawn them back again to the prison from whence they had so miraculously escaped.

PART I

I

The Pactolus Claim

In the early days of Australia, when the gold fever was at its height, and the marvellous Melbourne of to-day was more like an enlarged camp than anything else, there was a man called Robert Curtis, who arrived in the new land of Ophir with many others to seek his fortune. Mr. Curtis was of good family, but having been expelled from Oxford for holding certain unorthodox opinions quite at variance with the accepted theological tenets of the University, he had added to his crime by marrying a pretty girl, whose face was her fortune, and who was born, as the story books say, of poor but honest parents. Poverty and honesty, however, were not sufficient recommendations in the eyes of Mr. Curtis, senior, to excuse such a match; so he promptly followed the precedent set by Oxford, and expelled his son from the family circle. That young gentleman and his wife came out to Australia filled with ambitious dreams of acquiring a fortune, and then of returning to heap coals of fire on the heads of those who had turned them out.

These dreams, however, were destined never to be realised, for within a year after their arrival in Melbourne Mrs. Curtis died giving birth to a little girl, and Robert Curtis found himself once more alone in the world with the encumbrance of a small child. He, however, was not a man who wore his heart on his sleeve, and did not show much outward grief, though, no doubt, he sorrowed deeply enough for the loss of the pretty girl for whom he had sacrificed so much. At all events, he made up his mind at once what to do: so, placing his child under the care of an old lady, he went to Ballarat, and set to work to make his fortune.

While there his luck became proverbial, and he soon found himself a rich man; but this did not satisfy him, for, being of a far-seeing nature, he saw the important part Australia would play in the world's history. So with the gold won by his pick he bought land everywhere, and especially in Melbourne, which was even then becoming metropolitan. After fifteen years of a varied life he returned to Melbourne to settle down, and found that his daughter had grown up to be a charming young girl, the very image of his late wife. Curtis built a house, went in for politics, and soon became a famous man in his adopted country. He settled a large sum of money on his daughter absolutely, which no one, not even her future husband, could touch, and introduced her to society.

Miss Curtis became the belle of Melbourne, and her charming face, together with the more substantial beauties of wealth, soon brought crowds of suitors around her. Her father, however, determined to find a husband for her whom he could trust, and was looking for one when he suddenly died of heart disease, leaving his daughter an orphan and a wealthy woman.

After Mr. Curtis had been buried by the side of his dead wife, the heiress went home to her richly-furnished house, and after passing a certain period in mourning, engaged a companion, and once more took her position in society.

Her suitors—numerous and persistent as those of Penelope—soon returned to her feet, and she found she could choose a husband from men of all kinds—rich and poor, handsome and ugly, old and young. One of these, a penniless young Englishman, called Randolph Villiers, payed her such marked attention, that in the end Miss Curtis, contrary to the wishes of her friends, married him.

Mr. Villiers had a handsome face and figure, a varied and extensive wardrobe, and a bad character. He, however, suppressed his real tastes until he became the husband of Miss Curtis, and holder of the purse—for such was the love his wife bore him that she unhesitatingly gave him full control of all her property, excepting that which was settled on herself by her father, which was, of course, beyond marital control. In vain her friends urged some settlement should be made before marriage. Miss Curtis argued that to take any steps to protect her fortune would show a want of faith in the honesty of the man she loved, so went to the altar and reversed the marriage service by endowing Mr. Randolph Villiers with all her worldly goods.

The result of this blind confidence justified the warnings of her friends—for as soon as Villiers found himself in full possession of his wife's fortune, he immediately proceeded to spend all the money he could lay his hands on. He gambled away large sums at his club, betted extensively on the turf, kept open house, and finally became entangled with a lady whose looks were much better than her morals, and whose capacity for spending money so far exceeded his own that in two years she completely ruined him. Mrs. Villiers put up with this conduct for some time, as she was too proud to acknowledge she had made a mistake in her choice of a husband; but when Villiers, after spending all her wealth in riotous living, actually proceeded to ill-treat her in order to force her to give up the money her father had settled on her, she rebelled. She tore off her wedding-ring, threw it at his feet, renounced his name, and went off to Ballarat with her old nurse and the remnants of her fortune.

Mr. Villiers, however, was not displeased at this step; in fact, he was rather glad to get rid of a wife who could no longer supply him with money, and whose presence was a constant rebuke. He sold up the house and furniture, and converted all available property into cash, which cash he then converted into drink for himself and jewellery for his lady friend. The end soon came to the fresh supply of money, and his lady friend went off with his dearest companion, to whose purse she had taken a sudden liking. Villiers, deserted by all his acquaintances, sank lower and lower in the social scale, and the once brilliant butterfly of fashion became a billiard marker, then a tout at races, and finally a bar loafer with no visible means of support.

Meantime Mrs. Villiers was prospering in Ballarat, and gaining the respect and good opinion of everyone, while her husband was earning the contempt of not only his former friends but even of the creatures with whom he now associated. When Mrs. Villiers went up to Ballarat after her short but brilliant life in Melbourne she felt crushed. She had given all the wealth of her girlish affection to her husband, and had endowed him with all kinds of chivalrous attributes, only to find out, as many a woman has done before and since, that her idol had feet of clay. The sudden shock of the discovery of his baseness altered the whole of her life, and from being a bright, trustful girl, she became a cold suspicious woman who disbelieved in everyone and in everything.

But she was of too restless and ambitious a nature to be content with an idle life, and although the money she still possessed was sufficient to support her in comfort, yet she felt that she must do something, if only to keep her thoughts from dwelling on those bitter years of married life. The most obvious thing to do in Ballarat was to go in for gold-mining, and chance having thrown in her way a mate of her father's, she determined to devote herself to that, being influenced in her decision by the old digger. This man, by name Archibald McIntosh, was a shrewd, hard-headed Scotchman, who had been in Ballarat when the diggings were in the height of their fame, and who knew all about the lie of the country and where the richest leads had been in the old days. He told Mrs. Villiers that her father and himself had worked together on a lead then known as the Devil's Lead, which was one of the richest ever discovered in the district. It had been found by five men, who had agreed with one another to keep silent as to the richness of the lead, and were rapidly making their fortunes when the troubles of the Eureka stockade intervened, and, in the encounter between the miners and the military, three of the company working the lead were killed, and only two men were left who knew the whereabouts of the claim and the value of it. These were McIntosh and Curtis, who were the original holders. Mr. Curtis, went down to Melbourne, and, as previously related, died of heart disease, so the only man left of the five who had worked the lead was Archibald McIntosh. He had been too poor to work it himself, and, having failed to induce any speculator to go in with him to acquire the land, he had kept silent about it, only staying up at Ballarat and guarding the claim lest someone else should chance on it. Fortunately the place where it was situated had not been renowned for gold in the early days, and it had passed into the hands of a man who used it as pasture land, quite ignorant of the wealth which lay beneath. When Mrs. Villiers came up to Ballarat, this man wanted to sell the land, as he was going to Europe; so, acting under the urgent advice of McIntosh, she sold out of all the investments which she had and purchased the whole tract of country where the old miner assured her solemnly the Devil's Lead was to be found.

Then she built a house near the mine, and taking her old nurse, Selina Sprotts, and Archibald McIntosh to live with her, sank a shaft in the place indicated by the latter. She also engaged miners, and gave McIntosh full control over the mine, while she herself kept the books, paid the accounts, and proved herself to be a first-class woman of business. She had now been working the mine for two years, but as yet had not been fortunate enough to strike the lead. The gutter, however, proved remunerative enough to keep the mine going, pay all the men, and support Mrs. Villiers herself, so she was quite content to wait till fortune should smile on her, and the long-looked-for Devil's Lead turned up. People who had heard of her taking the land were astonished at first, and disposed to scoff, but they soon begun to admire the plucky way in which she fought down her ill-luck for the first year of her venture. All at once matters changed; she made a lucky speculation in the share market, and the Pactolus claim began to pay. Mrs. Villiers became mixed up in mining matters, and bought and sold on 'Change with such foresight and promptitude of action that she soon began to make a lot of money. Stockbrokers are not, as a rule, romantic, but one of the fraternity was so struck with her persistent good fortune that he christened her Madame Midas, after that Greek King whose touch turned everything into gold. This name tickled the fancy of others, and in a short time she was called nothing but Madame Midas all over the country, which title she accepted complacently enough as a forecast of her success in finding the Devil's Lead, which idea had grown into a mania with her as it already was with her faithful henchman, McIntosh.

When Mr. Villiers therefore arrived in Ballarat, he found his wife universally respected and widely known as Madame Midas, so he went to see her, expecting to be kept in luxurious ease for the rest of his life. He soon, however, found himself mistaken, for his wife told him plainly she would have nothing to do with him, and that if he dared to show his face at the Pactolus claim she would have him turned off by her men. He threatened to bring the law into force to make her live with him, but she laughed in his face, and said she would bring a divorce suit against him if he did so; and as Mr. Villiers' character could hardly bear the light of day, he retreated, leaving Madame in full possession of the field.

He stayed, however, in Ballarat, and took up stockbroking—living a kind of hand-to-mouth existence, bragging of his former splendour, and swearing at his wife for what he was pleased to call—her cruelty. Every now and then he would pay a visit to the Pactolus, and try to see her, but McIntosh was a vigilant guard, and the miserable creature was always compelled to go back to his Bohemian life without accomplishing his object of getting money from the wife he had deserted.

People talked, of course, but Madame did not mind. She had tried married life, and had been disappointed; her old ideas of belief in human nature had passed away; in short, the girl who had been the belle of Melbourne as Miss Curtis and Mrs. Villiers had disappeared, and the stern, clever, cynical woman who managed the Pactolus claim was a new being called "Madame Midas".

II

Slivers

Everyone has heard of the oldest inhabitant—that wonderful piece of antiquity, with white hair, garrulous tongue, and cast-iron memory,—who was born with the present century—very often before it—and remembers George III, the Battle of Waterloo, and the invention of the steam-engine. But in Australia, the oldest inhabitant is localized, and rechristened an early settler. He remembers Melbourne before Melbourne was; he distinctly recollects sailing up the Yarra Yarra with Batman, and talks wildly about the then crystalline purity of its waters—an assertion which we of to-day feel is open to considerable doubt. His wealth is unbounded, his memory marvellous, and his acquaintances of a somewhat mixed character, comprising as they do a series of persons ranging from a member of Parliament down to a larrikin.

Ballarat, no doubt, possesses many of these precious pieces of antiquity hidden in obscure corners, but one especially was known, not only in the Golden City, but throughout Victoria. His name was Slivers—plain Slivers, as he said himself—and, from a physical point of view, he certainly spoke the truth. What his Christian name was no one ever knew; he called himself Slivers, and so did everyone else, without even an Esquire or a Mister to it—neither a head nor a tail to add dignity to the name.

Slivers was as well known in Sturt Street and at "The Corner" as the town clock, and his tongue very much resembled that timepiece, inasmuch as it was always going. He was a very early settler; in fact, so remarkably early that it was currently reported the first white men who came to Ballarat found Slivers had already taken up his abode there, and lived in friendly relations with the local blacks. He had achieved this amicable relationship by the trifling loss of a leg, an arm, and an eye, all of which portions of his body were taken off the right side, and consequently gave him rather a lop-sided appearance. But what was left of Slivers possessed an abundant vitality, and it seemed probable he would go on living in the same damaged condition for the next twenty years.

The Ballarat folk were fond of pointing him out as a specimen of the healthy climate, but this was rather a flight of fancy, as Slivers was one of those exasperating individuals who, if they lived in a swamp or a desert, would still continue to feel their digestions good and their lungs strong.

Slivers was reputed rich, and Arabian-Night-like stories were told of his boundless wealth, but no one ever knew the exact amount of money he had, and as Slivers never volunteered any information on the subject, no one ever did know. He was a small, wizen-looking little man, who usually wore a suit of clothes a size too large for him, wherein scandal-mongers averred his body rattled like a dried pea in a pod. His hair was white, and fringed the lower portion of his yellow little scalp in a most deceptive fashion. With his hat on Slivers looked sixty; take it off and his bald head immediately added ten years to his existence. His one eye was bright and sharp, of a greyish colour, and the loss of the other was replaced by a greasy black patch, which gave him a sinister appearance. He was cleaned shaved, and had no teeth, but notwithstanding this want, his lips gripped the stem of his long pipe in a wonderfully tenacious and obstinate manner. He carried on the business of a mining agent, and knowing all about the country and the intricacies of the mines, he was one of the cleverest speculators in Ballarat.

The office of Slivers was in Sturt Street, in a dirty, tumble-down cottage wedged between two handsome modern buildings. It was a remnant of old Ballarat which had survived the rage for new houses and highly ornamented terraces. Slivers had been offered money for that ricketty little shanty, but he declined to sell it, averring that as a snail grew to fit his house his house had grown to fit him.

So there it stood—a dingy shingle roof overgrown with moss—a quaint little porch and two numerously paned windows on each side. On top of the porch a sign-board—done by Slivers in the early days, and looking like it—bore the legend "Slivers, mining agent." The door did not shut—something was wrong with it, so it always stood ajar in a hospitable sort of manner. Entering this, a stranger would find himself in a dark low-roofed passage, with a door at the end leading to the kitchen, another on the right leading to the bedroom, and a third on the left leading to the office, where most of Slivers' indoor life was spent. He used to stop here nearly all day doing business, with the small table before him covered with scrip, and the mantelpiece behind him covered with specimens of quartz, all labelled with the name of the place whence they came. The inkstand was dirty, the ink thick and the pens rusty; yet, in spite of all these disadvantages, Slivers managed to do well and make money. He used to recommend men to different mines round about, and whenever a manager wanted men, or new hands wanted work, they took themselves off to Slivers, and were sure to be satisfied there. Consequently, his office was nearly always full; either of people on business or casual acquaintances dropping in to have a drink—Slivers was generous in the whisky line—or to pump the old man about some new mine, a thing which no one ever managed to do. When the office was empty, Slivers would go on sorting the scrip on his table, drinking his whisky, or talking to Billy. Now Billy was about as well known in Ballarat as Slivers, and was equally as old and garrulous in his own way. He was one of those large white yellow-crested cockatoos who, in their captivity, pass their time like galley-slaves, chained by one leg. Billy, however, never submitted to the indignity of a chain—he mostly sat on Slivers' table or on his shoulder, scratching his poll with his black claw, or chattering to Slivers in a communicative manner. People said Billy was Slivers' evil spirit, and as a matter of fact, there was something uncanny in the wisdom of the bird. He could converse fluently on all occasions, and needed no drawing out, inasmuch as he was always ready to exhibit his powers of conversation. He was not a pious bird—belonging to Slivers, he could hardly be expected to be—and his language was redolent of Billingsgate. So Billy being so clever was quite a character in his way, and, seated on Slivers' shoulder with his black bead of an eye watching his master writing with the rusty pen, they looked a most unholy pair.

The warm sunlight poured through the dingy windows of the office, and filled the dark room with a sort of sombre glory. The atmosphere of Slivers' office was thick and dusty, and the sun made long beams of light through the heavy air. Slivers had pushed all the scrip and loose papers away, and was writing a letter in the little clearing caused by their removal. On the old-fashioned inkstand was a paper full of grains of gold, and on this the sunlight rested, making it glitter in the obscurity of the room. Billy, seated on Slivers' shoulder, was astonished at this, and, inspired by a spirit of adventure, he climbed down and waddled clumsily across the table to the inkstand, where he seized a small nugget in his beak and made off with it. Slivers looked up from his writing suddenly: so, being detected, Billy stopped and looked at him, still carrying the nugget in his beak.

"Drop it," said Slivers severely, in his rasping little voice. Billy pretended not to understand, and after eyeing Slivers for a moment or two resumed his journey. Slivers stretched out his hand for the ruler, whereupon Billy, becoming alive to his danger, dropped the nugget, and flew down off the table with a discordant shriek.

"Devil! devil! devil!" screamed this amiable bird, flopping up and down on the floor. "You're a liar! You're a liar! Pickles."

Having delivered himself of this bad language, Billy waddled to his master's chair, and climbing up by the aid of his claws and beak, soon established himself in his old position. Slivers, however, was not attending to him, as he was leaning back in his chair drumming in an absent sort of way with his lean fingers on the table. His cork arm hung down limply, and his one eye was fixed on a letter lying in front of him. This was a communication from the manager of the Pactolus Mine requesting Slivers to get him more hands, and Slivers' thoughts had wandered away from the letter to the person who wrote it, and from thence to Madame Midas.

"She's a clever woman," observed Slivers, at length, in a musing sort of tone, "and she's got a good thing on in that claim if she only strikes the Lead."

"Devil," said Billy once more, in a harsh voice.

"Exactly," answered Slivers, "the Devil's Lead. Oh, Lord! what a fool I was not to have collared that ground before she did; but that infernal McIntosh never would tell me where the place was. Never mind, I'll be even with him yet; curse him."

His expression of face was not pleasant as he said this, and he grasped the letter in front of him in a violent way, as if he were wishing his long fingers were round the writer's throat. Tapping with his wooden leg on the floor, he was about to recommence his musings, when he heard a step in the passage, and the door of his office being pushed violently open, a man entered without further ceremony, and flung himself down on a chair near the window.

"Fire!" said Billy, on seeing this abrupt entry; "how's your mother!— Ballarat and Bendigo—Bendigo and Ballarat."

The newcomer was a man short and powerfully built, dressed in a shabby-genteel sort of way, with a massive head covered with black hair, heavy side whiskers and moustache, and a clean shaved chin, which had that blue appearance common to very dark men who shave. His mouth—that is, as much as could be seen of it under the drooping moustache—was weak and undecided, and his dark eyes so shifty and restless that they seemed unable to meet a steady gaze, but always looked at some inanimate object that would not stare them out of countenance.

"Well, Mr. Randolph Villiers," croaked Slivers, after contemplating his visitor for a few moments, "how's business?"

"Infernally bad," retorted Mr. Villiers, pulling out a cigar and lighting it. "I've lost twenty pounds on those Moscow shares."

"More fool you," replied Slivers, courteously, swinging round in his chair so as to face Villiers. "I could have told you the mine was no good; but you will go on your own bad judgment."

"It's like getting blood out of a stone to get tips from you," growled Villiers, with a sulky air. "Come now, old boy," in a cajoling manner, "tell us something good—I'm nearly stone broke, and I must live."

"I'm hanged if I see the necessity," malignantly returned Slivers, unconsciously quoting Voltaire; "but if you do want to get into a good thing—"

"Yes! yes!" said the other, eagerly bending forward.

"Get an interest in the Pactolus," and the agreeable old gentleman leaned back and laughed loudly in a raucous manner at his visitor's discomfited look.

"You ass," hissed Mr. Villiers, between his closed teeth; "you know as well as I do that my infernal wife won't look at me."

"Ho, ho!" laughed the cockatoo, raising his yellow crest in an angry manner; "devil take her—rather!"

"I wish he would!" muttered Villiers, fervently; then with an uneasy glance at Billy, who sat on the old man's shoulder complacently ruffling his feathers, he went on: "I wish you'd screw that bird's neck, Slivers; he's too clever by half."

Slivers paid no attention to this, but, taking Billy off his shoulder, placed him on the floor, then turned to his visitor and looked at him fixedly with his bright eye in such a penetrating manner that Villiers felt it go through him like a gimlet.

"I hate your wife," said Slivers, after a pause.

"Why the deuce should you?" retorted Villiers, sulkily. "You ain't married to her."

"I wish I was," replied Slivers with a chuckle. "A fine woman, my good sir! Why, if I was married to her I wouldn't sneak away whenever I saw her. I'd go up to the Pactolus claim and there I'd stay."

"It's easy enough talking," retorted Villiers crossly, "but you don't know what a fiend she is! Why do you hate her?"

"Because I do," retorted Slivers. "I hate her; I hate McIntosh; the whole biling of them; they've got the Pactolus claim, and if they find the Devil's Lead they'll be millionaires."

"Well," said the other, quite unmoved, "all Ballarat knows that much."

"But I might have had it!" shrieked Slivers, getting up in an excited manner, and stumping up and down the office. "I knew Curtis, McIntosh and the rest were making their pile, but I couldn't find out where; and now they're all dead but McIntosh, and the prize has slipped through my fingers, devil take them!"

"Devil take them," echoed the cockatoo, who had climbed up again on the table, and was looking complacently at his master.

"Why don't you ruin your wife, you fool?" said Slivers, turning vindictively on Villiers. "You ain't going to let her have all the money while you are starving, are you?"

"How the deuce am I to do that?" asked Villiers, sulkily, relighting his cigar.

"Get the whip hand of her," snarled Slivers, viciously; "find out if she's in love, and threaten to divorce her if she doesn't go halves."

"There's no chance of her having any lovers," retorted Villiers; "she's a piece of ice."

"Ice melts," replied Slivers, quickly. "Wait till 'Mr. Right' comes along, and then she'll begin to regret being married to you, and then—"

"Well?"

"You'll have the game in your own hands," hissed the wicked old man, rubbing his hands. "Oh!" he cried, spinning round on his wooden leg, "it's a lovely idea. Wait till we meet 'Mr. Right', just wait," and he dropped into his chair quite overcome by the state of excitement he had worked himself into.

"If you've quite done with those gymnastics, my friend," said a soft voice near the door, "perhaps I may enter."

Both the inmates of the office looked up at this, and saw that two men were standing at the half-open door—one an extremely handsome young man of about thirty, dressed in a neat suit of blue serge, and wearing a large white wide-awake hat, with a bird's-eye handkerchief twisted round it. His companion was short and heavily built, dressed somewhat the same, but with his black hat pulled down over his eyes.

"Come in," growled Slivers, angrily, when he saw his visitors. "What the devil do you want?"

"Work," said the young man, advancing to the table. "We are new arrivals in the country, and were told to come to you to get work."

"I don't keep a factory," snarled Slivers, leaning forward.

"I don't think I would come to you if you did," retorted the stranger, coolly. "You would not be a pleasant master either to look at or to speak to."

Villiers laughed at this, and Slivers stared dumbfounded at being spoken to in such a manner.

"Devil," broke in Billy, rapidly. "You're a liar—devil."

"Those, I presume, are your master's sentiments towards me," said the young man, bowing gravely to the bird. "But as soon as he recovers the use of his tongue, I trust he will tell us if we can get work or not."

Slivers was just going to snap out a refusal, when he caught sight of McIntosh's letter on the table, and this recalled to his mind the conversation he had with Mr. Villiers. Here was a young man handsome enough to make any woman fall in love with him, and who, moreover, had a clever tongue in his head. All Slivers' animosity revived against Madame Midas as he thought of the Devil's Lead, and he determined to use this young man as a tool to ruin her in the eyes of the world. With these thoughts in his mind, he drew a sheet of paper towards him, and dipping the rusty pen in the thick ink, prepared to question his visitors as to what they could do, with a view to sending them out to the Pactolus claim.

"Names?" he asked, grasping his pen firmly in his left hand.

"Mine," said the stranger, bowing, "is Gaston Vandeloup, my friend's Pierre Lemaire—both French."

Slivers scrawled this down in the series of black scratches, which did duty with him for writing.

"Where do you come from?" was his next question.

"The story," said M. Vandeloup, with suavity, "is too long to repeat at present; but we came to-day from Melbourne."

"What kind of work can you do?" asked Slivers, sharply.

"Anything that turns up," retorted the Frenchman.

"I was addressing your companion, sir; not you," snarled Slivers, turning viciously on him.

"I have to answer for both," replied the young man, coolly, slipping one hand into his pocket and leaning up against the door in a negligent attitude, "my friend is dumb."

"Poor devil!" said Slivers, harshly.

"But," went on Vandeloup, sweetly, "his legs, arms, and eyes are all there."

Slivers glared at this fresh piece of impertinence, but said nothing. He wrote a letter to McIntosh, recommending him to take on the two men, and handed it to Vandeloup, who received it with a bow.

"The price of your services, Monsieur?" he asked.

"Five bob," growled Slivers, holding out his one hand.

Vandeloup pulled out two half-crowns and put them in the thin, claw-like fingers, which instantly closed on them.

"It's a mining place you're going to," said Slivers, pocketing the money; "the Pactolus claim. There's a pretty woman there. Have a drink?"

Vandeloup declined, but his companion, with a grunt, pushed past him, and filling a tumbler with the whisky, drank it off. Slivers looked ruefully at the bottle, and then hastily put it away, in case Vandeloup should change his mind and have some.

Vandeloup put on his hat and went to the door, out of which Pierre had already preceded him.

"I trust, gentlemen," he said, with a graceful bow, "we shall meet again, and can then discuss the beauty of this lady to whom Mr. Slivers alludes. I have no doubt he is a judge of beauty in others, though he is so incomplete himself."

He went out of the door, and then Slivers sprang up and rushed to Villiers.

"Do you know who that is?" he asked, in an excited manner, pulling his companion to the window.

Villiers looked through the dusty panes, and saw the young Frenchman walking away, as handsome and gallant a man as he had ever seen, followed by the slouching figure of his friend.

"Vandeloup," he said, turning to Slivers, who was trembling with excitement.

"No, you fool," retorted the other, triumphantly. "That is 'Mr. Right'."

III

Madame Midas at Home

Madame Midas was standing on the verandah of her cottage, staring far away into the distance, where she could see the tall chimney and huge mound of white earth which marked the whereabouts of the Pactolus claim. She was a tall voluptuous-looking woman of what is called a Junoesque type—decidedly plump, with firm white hands and well-formed feet. Her face was of a whitish tint, more like marble than flesh, and appeared as if modelled from the antique—with the straight Greek nose, high and smooth forehead, and full red mouth, with firmly-closed lips. She had dark and piercing eyes, with heavy arched eyebrows above them, and her hair, of a bluish-black hue, was drawn smoothly over the forehead, and coiled in thick wreaths at the top of her small, finely-formed head. Altogether a striking-looking woman, but with an absence of animation about her face, which had a calm, serene expression, effectually hiding any thoughts that might be passing in her mind, and which resembled nothing so much in its inscrutable look as the motionless calm which the old Egyptians gave to their sphinxes. She was dressed for coolness in a loose white dress, tied round her waist with a crimson scarf of Indian silk; and her beautifully modelled arms, bare to the elbow, and unadorned by any trinkets, were folded idly in front of her as she looked out at the landscape, which was mellowed and full of warmth under the bright yellow glare of the setting sun.

The cottage—for it was nothing else—stood on a slight rise immediately in front of a dark wood of tall gum-trees, and there was a long row of them on the right, forming a shelter against the winds, as if the wood had thrown a protecting arm around the cottage, and wanted to draw it closer to its warm bosom. The country was of an undulating character, divided into fields by long rows of gorse hedges, all golden with blossoms, which gave out a faint, peach-like odour. Some of these meadows were yellow with corn—some a dull red with sorrel, others left in their natural condition of bright green grass—while here and there stood up, white and ghost-like, the stumps of old trees, the last remnants of the forests, which were slowly retreating before the axe of the settler.

These fields, which had rather a harlequin aspect with their varied colours, all melted together in the far distance into an indescribable neutral tint, and ended in the dark haze of the bush, which grew over all the undulating hills. On the horizon, however, at intervals, a keen eye could see some tall tree standing boldly up, outlined clearly against the pale yellow of the sky. There was a white dusty road or rather a track between two rough fences, with a wide space of green grass on each side, and here and there could be seen the cattle wandering idly homeward, lingering every now and then to pull at a particularly tempting tuft of bush grass growing in the moist ditches which ran along each side of the highway. Scattered over this pastoral-looking country were huge mounds of white earth, looking like heaps of carded wool, and at the end of each of these invariably stood a tall, ugly skeleton of wood. These marked the positions of the mines—the towers contained the winding gear, while the white earth was the clay called mulloch, brought from several hundred feet below the surface. Near these mounds were rough-looking sheds with tall red chimneys, which made a pleasant spot of colour against the white of the clay. On one of these mounds, rather isolated from the others, and standing by itself in the midst of a wide green paddock, Mrs. Villiers' eyes were fixed, and she soon saw the dark figure of a man coming slowly down the white mound, along the green field and advancing slowly up the hill. When she saw him coming, without turning her head or raising her voice, she called out to someone inside,

"Archie is coming, Selina—you had better hurry up the tea, for he will be hungry after such a long day."

The person inside made no answer save by an extra clatter of some domestic utensils, and Madame apparently did not expect a reply, for without saying anything else she walked slowly down the garden path, and leaned lightly over the gate, waiting for the newcomer, who was indeed none other than Archibald McIntosh, the manager of the Pactolus.

He was a man of about medium height, rather thin than otherwise, with a long, narrow-looking head and boldly cut features—clean shaved save for a frill of white hair which grew on his throat up the sides of his head to his ears, and which gave him rather a peculiar appearance, as if he had his jaw bandaged up. His eyes were grey and shrewd-looking, his lips were firmly compressed—in fact, the whole appearance of his face was obstinate—the face of a man who would stick to his opinions whatever anyone else might say to the contrary. He was in a rough miner's dress, all splashed with clay, and as he came up to the gate Madame could see he was holding something in his hand.

"D'ye no ken what yon may be?" he said, a smile relaxing his grim features as he held up a rather large nugget; "'tis the third yin this week!"

Madame Midas took the nugget from him and balanced it carefully in her hand, with a thoughtful look in her face, as if she was making a mental calculation.

"About twenty to twenty-five ounces, I should say," she observed in her soft low voice; "the last we had was fifteen, and the one before twenty—looks promising for the gutter, doesn't it?"

"Well, I'll no say but what it micht mean a deal mair," replied McIntosh, with characteristic Scotch caution, as he followed Madame into the house; "it's no a verra bad sign, onyhow; I winna say but what we micht be near the Devil's Lead."

"And if we are?" said Madame, turning with a smile.

"Weel, mem, ye'll have mair siller nor ye'll ken what to dae wi', an' 'tis to be hoped ye'll no be making a fool of yersel."

Madame laughed—she was used to McIntosh's plain speaking, and it in no wise offended her. In fact, she preferred it very much more than being flattered, as people's blame is always genuine, their praise rarely so. At all events she was not displeased, and looked after him with a smile in her dark eyes as he disappeared into the back kitchen to make himself decent for tea. Madame herself sat down in an arm-chair in the bow window, and watched Selina preparing the meal.

Selina Jane Sprotts, who now acted as servant to Mrs. Villiers, was rather an oddity in her way. She had been Madame's nurse, and had followed her up to Ballarat, with the determination of never leaving her. Selina was a spinster, as her hand had never been sought in marriage, and her personal appearance was certainly not very fascinating. Tall and gaunt, she was like a problem from Euclid, all angles, and the small quantity of grey hair she possessed was screwed into a hard lump at the back of her head. Her face was reddish in colour, and her mouth prim and pursed up, as if she was afraid of saying too much, which she need not have been, as she rarely spoke, and was as economical of her words as she was of everything else. She was much given to quoting proverbs, and hurled these prepared little pieces of wisdom on every side like pellets out of a pop-gun. Conversation which consists mainly of proverbs is rarely exhilarating; consequently Miss Sprotts was not troubled to talk much, either by Madame or McIntosh.

Miss Sprotts moved noiselessly about the small room, in a wonderfully dextrous manner considering her height, and, after laying the table, placed the teapot on the hob to "draw", thereby disturbing a cat and a dog who were lying in front of the fire—for there was a fire in the room in spite of the heat of the day, Selina choosing to consider that the house was damp. She told Madame she knew it was damp because her bones ached, and as she was mostly bones she certainly had a good opportunity of judging.

Annoyed at being disturbed by Miss Sprotts, the dog resigned his comfortable place with a plaintive growl, but the cat, of a more irritable temperament, set up and made a sudden scratch at her hand, drawing blood therefrom.

"Animals," observed Selina, grimly, "should keep their place;" and she promptly gave the cat a slap on the side of the head, which sent him over to Madame's feet, with an angry spit. Madame picked him up and soothed his ruffled feelings so successfully, that he curled himself up on her lap and went to sleep.

By-and-bye Archie, who had been making a great splashing in the back premises, came in looking clean and fresh, with a more obstinate look about his face than ever. Madame went to the tea-table and sat down, for she always had her meals with them, a fact of which they were very proud, and they always treated her with intense respect, though every now and then they were inclined to domineer. Archie, having seen that the food on the table was worth thanking God for, asked a blessing in a peremptory sort of manner, as if he thought Heaven required a deal of pressing to make it attentive. Then they commenced to eat in silence, for none of the party were very much given to speech, and no sound was heard save the rattling of the cups and saucers and the steady ticking of the clock. The window was open, and a faint breeze came in—cool and fragrant with the scent of the forest, and perfumed with the peach-like odour of the gorse blossoms. There was a subdued twilight through all the room, for the night was coming on, and the gleam of the flickering flames of the fire danced gaily against the roof and exaggerated all objects to an immense size. At last Archie pushed back his chair to show that he had finished, and prepared to talk.

"I dinna see ony new bodies coming," he said, looking at his mistress. "They, feckless things, that left were better than none, though they should hae been skelped for their idleness."

"You have written to Slivers?" said Madame, raising her eyes.

"That wudden-legged body," retorted McIntosh. "Deed and I have, but the auld tyke hasna done onything to getting me what I want. Weel, weel," in a resigned sort of a manner, "we micht be waur off than we are, an' wha kens but what Providence will send us men by-and-bye?"

Selina looked up at this, saw her opportunity, and let slip an appropriate proverb.

"If we go by by-and-bye lane," she said sharply, "we come to the gate of never."

This being undeniable, no one gave her the pleasure of contradicting her, for Archie knew it was impossible to argue with Selina, so handy was she with her proverbial wisdom—a kind of domestic Tupper, whose philosophy was of the most irritating and unanswerable kind. He did the wisest thing he could under the circumstances, and started a new subject.

"I say yon the day."

"Yon" in this case meant Mr. Villiers, whose name was tabooed in the house, and was always spoken of in a half-hinting kind of way. As both her servants knew all about her unhappy life, Madame did not scruple to talk to them.

"How was he looking?" she asked, smoothing the crumbs off her dress.

"Brawly," replied Archie, rising; "he lost money on that Moscow mine, but he made a fine haul owre the Queen o' Hearts claim."

"The wicked," observed Selina, "flourish like a green bay tree."

"Ou, ay," retorted McIntosh, drily; "we ken a' aboot that, Selina—auld Hornie looks after his ain."

"I think he leads a very hand-to-mouth existence," said Madame, calmly; "however rich he may become, he will always be poor, because he never was a provident man."

"He's comin' tae see ye, mem," said Archie, grimly, lighting his pipe.

Madame rose to her feet and walked to the window.

"He's done that before," she said, complacently; "the result was not satisfactory."

"Continual dropping wears away a stone," said Selina, who was now clearing away.

"But not iron," replied Madame, placidly; "I don't think his persistence will gain anything."

Archie smiled grimly, and then went outside to smoke his pipe, while Madame sat down by the open window and looked out at the fast-fading landscape.

Her thoughts were not pleasant. She had hoped to cut herself off from all the bitterness and sorrow of her past life, but this husband of hers, like an unquiet spirit, came to trouble her and remind her of a time she would willingly have forgotten. She looked calm and quiet enough sitting there with her placid face and smooth brow; but this woman was like a slumbering volcano, and her passions were all the more dangerous from being kept in check.

A bat flew high up in the air across the clear glow of the sky, disappearing into the adjacent bush, and Madame, stretching out her hand, idly plucked a fresh, dewy rose off the tree which grew round the window.

"If I could only get rid of him," she thought, toying with the flower; "but it is impossible. I can't do that without money, and money I never will have till I find that lead. I must bribe him, I suppose. Oh, why can't he leave me alone now? Surely he has ruined my life sufficiently in the past to let me have a few years, if not of pleasure, at least of forgetfulness." And with a petulant gesture she hurled the rose out of the window, where it struck Archie a soft and fragrant blow on the cheek.

"Yes," said Madame to herself, as she pulled down the window, "I must get rid of him, and if bribery won't do—there are other means."

IV

The Good Samaritan

Is there anyone nowadays who reads Cowper—that charming, domestic poet who wrote "The Task", and invested even furniture with the glamour of poesy? Alas! to many people Cowper is merely a name, or is known only as the author of the delightfully quaint ballad of John Gilpin. Yet he was undoubtedly the Poet Laureate of domesticity, and every householder should possess a bust or picture of him—placed, not amid the frigid splendours of the drawing room, but occupying the place of honour in his own particular den, where everything is old-fashioned, cheery, and sanctified by long usage. No one wrote so pleasantly about the pleasures of a comfortable room as Cowper. And was he not right to do so? After all, every hearth is the altar of the family, whereon the sacred fire should be kept constantly burning, waxing and waning with the seasons, but never be permitted to die out altogether. Miss Sprotts, as before mentioned, was much in favour of a constant fire, because of the alleged dampness of the house, and Madame Midas did not by any means object, as she was a perfect salamander for heat. Hence, when the outward door was closed, the faded red curtains of the window drawn, and the newly replenished fire blazed brightly in the wide fireplace, the room was one which even Cowper—sybarite in home comforts as he was—would have contemplated with delight.

Madame Midas was seated now at the small table in the centre of the room, poring over a bewildering array of figures, and the soft glow of the lamp touched her smooth hair and white dress with a subdued light.

Archie sat by the fire, half asleep, and there was a dead silence in the room, only broken by the rapid scratching of Madame's pen or the click of Selina's needles. At last Mrs. Villiers, with a sigh of relief, laid down her pen, put all her papers together, and tied them neatly with a bit of string.

"I'm afraid I'll have to get a clerk, Archie," she said, as she put the papers away, "the office work is getting too much for me."

"'Deed, mem, and 'tis that same I was thinkin' o'," returned Mr. McIntosh, sitting bolt upright in his chair, lest the imputation of having been asleep should be brought against him. "It's ill wark seein' ye spoilin' your bonny eyes owre sic a muckle lot o' figures as ye hae there."

"Someone must do it," said Madame, resuming her seat at the table.

"Then why not get a body that can dae it?" retorted Archie; "not but what ye canna figure yersel', mem, but really ye need a rest, and if I hear of onyone in toun wha we can trust I'll bring him here next week."

"I don't see why you shouldn't," said Madame, musingly; "the mine is fairly under way now, and if things go on as they are doing, I must have someone to assist me."

At this moment a knock came to the front door, which caused Selina to drop her work with a sudden start, and rise to her feet.

"Not you, Selina," said Madame, in a quiet voice; "let Archie go; it may be some tramp."

"'Deed no, mem," replied Archie, obstinately, as he arose from his seat; "'tis verra likely a man fra the warks saying he wants to go. There's mair talk nor sense aboot them, I'm thinkin'—the yattering parrots."

Selina resumed her knitting in a most phlegmatic manner, but Madame listened intently, for she was always haunted by a secret dread of her husband breaking in on her, and it was partly on this account that McIntosh stayed in the house. She heard a murmur of voices, and then Archie returned with two men, who entered the room and stood before Madame in the light of the lamp.

"'Tis two men fra that wudden-legged gowk o' a Slivers," said Archie, respectfully. "Ain o' them has a wee bit letter for ye"—turning to receive same from the foremost man.

The man, however, did not take notice of Archie's gesture, but walking forward to Madame, laid the letter down before her. As he did so, she caught sight of the delicacy of his hands, and looked up suddenly with a piercing gaze. He bore the scrutiny coolly, and took a chair in silence, his companion doing the same, while Madame opened the letter and read Slivers' bad writing with a dexterity only acquired by long practice. Having finished her perusal, she looked up slowly.

"A broken-down gentleman," she said to herself, as she saw the easy bearing and handsome face of the young man; then looking at his companion, she saw by his lumpish aspect and coarse hands, that he occupied a much lower rank of life than his friend.

Monsieur Vandeloup—for it was he—caught her eye as she was scrutinising them, and his face broke into a smile—a most charming smile, as Madame observed mentally, though she allowed nothing of her thoughts to appear on her face.

"You want work," she said, slowly folding up the letter, and placing it in her pocket; "do you understand anything about gold-mining?"

"Unfortunately, no, Madame," said Vandeloup, coolly; "but we are willing to learn."

Archie grunted in a dissatisfied manner, for he was by no means in favour of teaching people their business, and, besides, he thought Vandeloup too much of a gentleman to do good work.

"You look hardly strong enough for such hard labour," said Mrs. Villiers, doubtfully eyeing the slender figure of the young man. "Your companion, I think, will do, but you—"

"I, Madame, am like the lilies of the field that neither toil nor spin," replied Vandeloup, gaily; "but, unfortunately, I am now compelled by necessity to work, and though I should prefer to earn my bread in an easier manner, beggars,"—with a characteristic shrug, which did not escape Madame's eye—"cannot be choosers."

"You are French?" she asked quickly, in that language.

"Yes, Madame," he replied in the same tongue, "both my friend and myself are from Paris, but we have not been long out here."

"Humph," Madame leaned her head on her hand and thought, while Vandeloup looked at her keenly, and remembered what Slivers had said.

"She is, indeed, a handsome woman," he observed, mentally; "my lines will fall in pleasant places, if I remain here."

Mrs. Villiers rather liked the looks of this young man; there was a certain fascination about him which few women could resist, and Madame, although steeled to a considerable extent by experience, was yet a woman. His companion, however, she did not care about— he had a sullen and lowering countenance, and looked rather dangerous.

"What is your name?" she asked the young man.

"Gaston Vandeloup."

"You are a gentleman?"

He bowed, but said nothing.

"And you?" asked Madame, sharply turning to the other.

He looked up and touched his mouth.

"Pardon him not answering, Madame," interposed Vandeloup, "he has the misfortune to be dumb."

"Dumb?" echoed Madame, with a glance of commiseration, while Archie looked startled, and Selina mentally observed that silence was golden.

"Yes, he has been so from his birth,—at least, so he gives me to understand," said Gaston, with a shrug of his shoulders, which insinuated a doubt on the subject; "but it's more likely the result of an accident, for he can hear though he cannot speak. However, he is strong and willing to work; and I also, if you will kindly give me an opportunity," added he, with a winning smile.

"You have not many qualifications," said Madame, shortly, angry with herself for so taking to this young man's suave manner.

"Probably not," retorted Vandeloup, with a cynical smile. "I fancy it will be more a case of charity than anything else, as we are starving."

Madame started, while Archie murmured "Puir deils."

"Surely not as bad as that?" observed Mrs. Villiers, in a softer tone.

"Why not?" retorted the Frenchman, carelessly. "Manna does not fall from heaven as in the days of Moses. We are strangers in a strange land, and it is hard to obtain employment. My companion Pierre can work in your mine, and if you will take me on I can keep your books"—with a sudden glance at a file of papers on the table.

"Thank you, I keep my own books," replied Madame, shortly. "What do you say to engaging them, Archie?"

"We ma gie them a try," said McIntosh, cautiously. "Ye do need a figger man, as I tauld ye, and the dour deil can wark i' the claim."

Madame drew a long breath, and then made up her mind.

"Very well," she said, sharply; "you are engaged, M. Vandeloup, as my clerk, and your companion can work in the mine. As to wages and all that, we will settle to-morrow, but I think you will find everything satisfactory."

"I am sure of that, Madame," returned Vandeloup, with a bow.

"And now," said Madame Midas, graciously, relaxing somewhat now that business was over, "you had better have some supper."

Pierre's face lighted up when he heard this invitation, and Vandeloup bowed politely.

"You are very kind," he said, looking at Mrs. Villiers in a friendly manner; "supper is rather a novelty to both of us."

Selina meanwhile had gone out, and returned with some cold beef and pickles, a large loaf and a jug of beer. These she placed on the table, and then retired to her seat again, inwardly rebellious at having two tramps at the table, but outwardly calm.

Pierre fell upon the victuals before him with the voracity of a starving animal, and ate and drank in such a savage manner that Madame was conscious of a kind of curious repugnance, and even Archie was startled out of his Scotch phlegm.

"I wadna care aboot keepin' yon long," he muttered to himself; "he's mair like a cannibal nor a ceevalized body."

Vandeloup, however, ate very little and soon finished; then filling a glass with beer, he held it to his lips and bowed again to Madame Midas.

"To your health, Madame," he said, drinking.

Mrs. Villiers bowed courteously. This young man pleased her. She was essentially a woman with social instincts, and the appearance of this young and polished stranger in the wilds of the Pactolus claim promised her a little excitement. It was true that every now and then, when she caught a glimpse from his scintillating eyes, she was conscious of a rather unpleasant sensation, but this she put down to fancy, as the young man's manners were really charming.

When the supper was ended, Pierre pushed back his chair into the shadow and once more relapsed into his former gloom, but Vandeloup stood up and looked towards Madame in a hesitating manner.

"I'm afraid, Madame, we disturb you," he murmured vaguely, though in his heart he wished to stay in this pleasant room and talk to such a handsome woman; "we had best be going."

"Not at all," answered Madame, graciously, "sit down; you and your friend can sleep in the men's quarters to-night, and to-morrow we will see if we can't provide you with a better resting-place."

Vandeloup murmured something indistinctly, and then resumed his seat.

"Meanwhile," said Mrs. Villiers, leaning back in her chair, and regarding him fixedly, "tell me all about yourselves."

"Alas, Madame," answered Vandeloup, with a charming smile and deprecating shrug of his shoulders, "there is not much to tell. I was brought up in Paris, and, getting tired of city life, I came out to India to see a little of the world; then I went over to Borneo, and was coming down to Australia, when our vessel was wrecked and all on board were drowned but myself and this fellow," pointing to Pierre, "who was one of the sailors. We managed to get a boat, and after tossing about for nearly a week we were cast up on the coast of Queensland, and from thence came to Melbourne. I could not get work there, neither could my friend, and as we heard of Ballarat we came up here to try to get employment, and our lines, Madame,"—with another bow—"have fallen in a pleasant place."

"What a dreadful chapter of accidents," said Madame, coolly looking at him to see if he was speaking the truth, for experience of her husband had inspired her with an instinctive distrust of men. Vandeloup, however, bore her scrutiny without moving a muscle of his face, so Madame at last withdrew her eyes, quite satisfied that his story was true.

"Is there no one in Paris to whom you can write?" she asked, after a pause.

"Luckily, there is," returned Gaston, "and I have already sent a letter, asking for a remittance, but it takes time to get an answer, and as I have lost all my books, papers, and money, I must just wait for a few months, and, as I have to live in the meantime, I am glad to obtain work."

"Still, your consul—" began Mrs. Villiers.

"Alas, Madame, what can I say—how can I prove to him that I am what I assert to be? My companion is dumb and cannot speak for me, and, unluckily, he can neither read nor write. I have no papers to prove myself, so my consul may think me—what you call—a scamp. No; I will wait till I receive news from home, and get to my own position again; besides," with a shrug, "after all, it is experience."

"Experience," said Madame, quietly, "is a good schoolmaster, but the fees are somewhat high."

"Ah!" said Vandeloup, with a pleased look, "you know Heine, I perceive, Madame. I did not know he was read out here."

"We are not absolute barbarians, M. Vandeloup," said Madame, with a smile, as she arose and held out her hand to the young man; "and now good night, for I am feeling tired, and I will see you to-morrow. Mr. McIntosh will show you where you are to sleep."

Vandeloup took the hand she held out to him and pressed it to his lips with a sudden gesture. "Madame," he said, passionately, "you are an angel, for to-day you have saved the lives of two men."

Madame snatched her hand away quickly, and a flush of annoyance spread over her face as she saw how Selina and Archie stared. Vandeloup, however, did not wait for her answer, but went out, followed by Pierre. Archie put on his hat and walked out after them, while Madame Midas stood looking at Selina with a thoughtful expression of countenance.

"I don't know if I've done a right thing, Selina," she said, at length; "but as they were starving I could hardly turn them away."

"Cast your bread on the waters and it shall come back after many days—buttered," said Selina, giving her own version of the text.

Madame laughed.

"M. Vandeloup talks well," she observed.

"So did HE," replied Selina, with a sniff, referring to Mr. Villiers; "once bitten, twice shy."

"Quite right, Selina," replied Mrs. Villiers, coolly; "but you are going too fast. I'm not going to fall in love with my servant."

"You're a woman," retorted Selina, undauntedly, for she had not much belief in her own sex.

"Yes, who has been tricked and betrayed by a man," said Madame, fiercely; "and do you think because I succour a starving human being I am attracted by his handsome face? You ought to know me better than that, Selina. I have always been true to myself," and without another word she left the room.

Selina stood still for a moment, then deliberately put away her work, slapped the cat in order to relieve her feelings, and poked the fire vigorously.

"I don't like him," she said, emphasizing every word with a poke. "He's too smooth and handsome, his eyes ain't true, and his tongue's too smart. I hate him."

Having delivered herself of this opinion, she went to boil some water for Mr. McIntosh, who always had some whisky hot before going to bed.

Selina was right in her estimate of Vandeloup, and, logically argued, the case stood thus:—

Some animals of a fine organization have an instinct which warns them to avoid approaching danger.

Woman is one of these finely-organized animals. ERGO—

Let no woman go contrary to her instinct.

V

Mammon's Treasure House

At the foot of the huge mound of white mulloch which marked the site of the Pactolus Mine was a long zinc-roofed building, which was divided into two compartments. In one of these the miners left their clothes, and put on rough canvas suits before going down, and here also they were searched on coming up in order to see if they had carried away any gold. From this room a long, narrow passage led to the top of the shaft, so that any miner having gold concealed upon him could not throw it away and pick it up afterwards, but had to go right into the searching room from the cage, and could not possibly hide a particle without being found out by the searchers. The other room was the sleeping apartment of such miners as stayed on the premises, for the majority of the men went home to their families when their work was done.

There were three shifts of men on the Pactolus during the twenty-four hours, and each shift worked eight hours at a time—the first going on at midnight and knocking off at eight in the morning, the second commencing at eight and ending at four in the afternoon, and the third starting at four and lasting until midnight again, when the first shift of men began anew.

Consequently, when M. Vandeloup awoke next morning at six o'clock the first shift were not yet up, and some of the miners who had to go on at eight were sleeping heavily in their beds. The sleeping places were berths, ranging along two sides of the room, and divided into upper and lower compartments like those on shipboard.

Gaston having roused himself naturally wanted to see where he was, so rubbing his eyes and yawning he leaned on his elbow and took a leisurely survey of his position.

He saw a rather large room lighted at regular intervals by three square windows, and as these were uncurtained, the cold, searching light of daybreak was slowly stealing through them into the apartment, and all the dusky objects therein were gradually revealing themselves in the still light. He could hear the heavy, monotonous breathing of the men, and the restless turning and tossing of those who could not sleep.

Gaston yawned once or twice, then feeling disinclined for any more sleep, he softly put on his clothes, so as not to awake Pierre, who slept in the berth below, and descending from his sleeping-place groped his way to the door and went out into the cool fragrant morning.

There was a chill wind blowing from the bush, bringing with it a faint aromatic odour, and on glancing downwards he saw that the grass was wet with dew. The dawn was burning redly in the east, and the vivid crimson of the sky put him in mind of that sunset under which he had landed with his companion on the Queensland coast. Suddenly a broad shaft of yellow light broke into the pale pink of the sky, and with a burst of splendour the sun rose slowly into sight from behind the dark bush, and all the delicate workings of the dawn disappeared in the flood of golden light which poured over the landscape.

Vandeloup looked idly at all this beauty with an unobservant eye, being too much occupied with his thoughts to take notice of anything; and it was only when two magpies near him broke into a joyous duet, in which each strove to emulate the other's mellow notes, that he awoke from his brown study, and began to walk back again to the mine.

"I must let nothing stand in my way to acquire money," he said, musingly; "with it one can rule the world; without it—but how trite and bald these well-worn maxims seem! Why do I repeat them, parrot-like, when I see what I have to do so clearly before me? That woman, for instance—I must begin by making her my friend. Bah! she is that already; I saw it in her eyes, which she can't control as she does her face. Yes, I must make her my friend; my very dear friend—and then—well, to my mind, the world-pivot is a woman. I will spare no one in order to attain my ends—I will make myself my own God, and consider no one but myself, and those who stand in my path must get out of it or run the chance of being crushed. This," with a cynical smile, "is what some would call the devil's philosophy; at all events, it is good enough for me."

He was near the mine by this time, and hearing someone calling to him he looked up, and saw McIntosh walking towards him. There was a stir in the men's quarters now, and he could see the door was open and several figures were moving briskly about, while a number of others were crossing the fields. The regular beat of the machinery still continued, and the smoke was pouring out thick and black from the tall red chimney, while the wheels were spinning round in the poppet-heads as the mine slowly disgorged the men who had been working all night.

McIntosh came slowly along with his hands in his pockets and a puzzled look on his severe face. He could not make up his mind whether to like or dislike this young man, but Madame Midas had seemed so impressed that he had half made up his mind to dislike him out of a spirit of contradiction.

"Weemen are sae easy pleased, puir feckless bodies," he said to himself, "a bonny face is a' they fash their heads aboot, though the same may be already in the grip of auld Nickyben. Weel, weel, if Madam does fancy the lad—an' he's no bad lookin', I'll say that—she may just hae her ain way, and I'll keep my e'e on baith."

He looked grimly at the young man as he came briskly forward with a gay smile.

"Ye're a verra early bird," he said, fondling his frill of white hair, and looking keenly at the tall, slim figure of the Frenchman.

"Case of 'must', my friend," returned Vandeloup, coolly; "it's only rich men can afford to be in bed, not poor devils like me."

"You're no muckle like ither folk," said the suspicious old Scotchman, with a condemnatory sniff.

"Of that I am glad," retorted Vandeloup, with suavity, as he walked beside him to the men's quarters. "What a horrible thing to be the duplicate of half-a-dozen other men. By the way," breaking off into a new subject, "Madame Midas is charming."

"Aye, aye," said Archie, jealously, "we ken all aboot they French-fangled way o' gieing pretty words, and deil a scrap of truth in ony o' them."

Gaston was about to protest that he said no more than he felt, which was indeed the truth, but Archie impatiently hurried him off to breakfast at the office, as he declared himself famishing. They made a hearty meal, and, having had a smoke and a talk, prepared to go below.

First of all, they arrayed themselves in underground garments—not grave clothes, though the name is certainly suggestive of the cemetery—which consisted of canvas trousers, heavy boots, blue blouses of a rough woollen material, and a sou'wester each. Thus accoutred, they went along to the foot of the poppet heads, and Archie having opened a door therein, Vandeloup saw the mouth of the shaft yawning dark and gloomy at his feet. As he stood there, gazing at the black hole which seemed to pierce down into the entrails of the earth, he turned round to take one last look at the sun before descending to the nether world.

"This is quite a new experience to me," he said, as they stepped into the wet iron cage, which had ascended to receive them in answer to Archie's signal, and now commenced to drop down silently and swiftly into the pitchy darkness. "It puts me in mind of Jules Verne's romances."

Archie did not reply, for he was too much occupied in lighting his candle to answer, and, moreover, knew nothing about romances, and cared still less. So they went on sliding down noiselessly into the gloom, while the water, falling from all parts of the shaft, kept splashing constantly on the top of the cage and running in little streams over their shoulders.

"It's like a nightmare," thought the Frenchman, with a nervous shudder, as he saw the wet walls gleaming in the faint light of the candle. "Worthy of Dante's 'Inferno'."

At last they reached the ground, and found themselves in the main chamber, from whence the galleries branched off to east and west.

It was upheld on all sides by heavy wooden supports of bluegum and stringy bark, the scarred surfaces of which made them look like the hieroglyphic pillars in old Egyptian temples. The walls were dripping with damp, and the floor of the chamber, though covered with iron plates, was nearly an inch deep with yellow-looking water, discoloured by the clay of the mine. Two miners in rough canvas clothes were waiting here, and every now and then a trolly laden with wash would roll suddenly out of one of the galleries with a candle fastened in front of it, and would be pushed into the cage and sent up to the puddlers. Round the walls candles fastened to spikes were stuck into the woodwork, and in their yellow glimmer the great drops of water clinging to the roof and sides of the chamber shone like diamonds.

"Aladdin's garden," observed Vandeloup, gaily, as he lighted his candle at that of Archie's and went towards the eastern gallery, "only the jewels are not substantial enough."

Archie showed the Frenchman how to carry his candle in the miner's manner, so that it could not go out, which consisted in holding it low down between the forefinger and third finger, so that the hollow palm of the hand formed a kind of shield; and then Vandeloup, hearing the sound of falling water close to him, asked what it was, whereupon Archie explained it was for ventilating purposes. The water fell the whole height of the mine through a pipe into a bucket, and a few feet above this another pipe was joined at right angles to the first and stretched along the gallery near the roof like a never-ending serpent right to the end of the drive. The air was driven along this by the water, and then, being released from the pipe, returned back through the gallery, so that there was a constant current circulating all through the mine.

As they groped their way slowly along, their feet splashed into pools of yellow clayey water at the sides of the drive, or stumbled over the rough ground and rugged rails laid down for the trollies. All along the gallery, at regular intervals, were posts of stringy bark in a vertical position, while beams of the same were laid horizontally across the top, but so low that Vandeloup had to stoop constantly to prevent himself knocking his head against their irregular projections.

Clinging to these side posts were masses of white fungus, which the miners use to remove discolorations from their hands, and from the roof also it hung like great drifts of snow, agitated with every breath of wind as the keen air, damped and chilled by the underground darkness, rushed past them. Every now and then they would hear a faint rumble in the distance, and Archie would drag his companion to one side while a trolly laden with white, wet-looking wash, and impelled by a runner, would roll past with a roaring and grinding of wheels.

At intervals on each side of the main drive black chasms appeared, which Archie informed his companion were drives put in to test the wash, and as these smaller galleries continued branching off, Vandeloup thought the whole mine resembled nothing so much as a herring-bone.

Being accustomed to the darkness and knowing every inch of the way, the manager moved forward rapidly, and sometimes Vandeloup lagged so far behind that all he could see of his guide was the candle he carried, shining like a pale yellow star in the pitchy darkness. At last McIntosh went into one of the side galleries, and going up an iron ladder fixed to the side of the wall, they came to a second gallery thirty feet above the other, and branching off at right angles.

This was where the wash was to be found, for, as Archie informed Vandeloup, the main drives of a mine were always put down thirty or forty feet below the wash, and then they could work up to the higher levels, the reason of this being that the leads had a downward tendency, and it was necessary for the main drive to be sunk below, as before mentioned, in order to get the proper levels and judge the gutters correctly. At the top of the ladder they found some empty trucks which had delivered their burden into a kind of shoot, through which it fell to the lower level, and there another truck was waiting to take it to the main shaft, from whence it went up to the puddlers.

Archie made Vandeloup get into one of these trucks, and though they were all wet and covered with clay, he was glad to do so, and be smoothly carried along, instead of stumbling over the rails and splashing among the pools of water. Every now and then as they went along there would be a gush of water from the dripping walls, which was taken along in pipes to the main chamber, and from thence pumped out of the mine by a powerful pump, worked by a beam engine, by which means the mine was kept dry.

At last, after they had gone some considerable distance, they saw the dim light of a candle, and heard the dull blows of a pick, then found themselves at the end of the drive, where a miner was working at the wash. The wash wherein the gold is found was exceedingly well defined, and represented a stratified appearance, being sandwiched in between a bed of white pipe-clay and a top layer of brownish earth, interspersed with gravel. Every blow of the pick sent forth showers of sparks in all directions, and as fast as the wash was broken down the runner filled up the trollies with it. After asking the miner about the character of the wash, and testing some himself in a shovel, Archie left the gallery, and going back to the shoot, they descended again to the main drive, and visited several other faces of wash, the journey in each instance being exactly the same in all respects. Each face had a man working at it, sometimes two, and a runner who loaded the trucks, and ran them along to the shoots. In spite of the ventilation, Vandeloup felt as if he was in a Turkish bath, and the heat was in some places very great. At the end of one of the drives McIntosh called Vandeloup, and on going towards him the young man found him seated on a truck with the plan of the mine before him, as he wanted to show him all the ramifications of the workings.

The plan looked more like a map of a city than anything else, with the main drive doing duty as the principal street, and all the little galleries, branching off in endless confusion, looked like the lanes and alleys of a populous town.

"It's like the catacombs in Rome," said Vandeloup to McIntosh, after he had contemplated the plan for some time; "one could easily get lost here."

"He micht," returned McIntosh, cautiously, "if he didna ken a' aboot the lie of the mine—o'er yonder," putting one finger on the plan and pointing with the other to the right of the tunnel; "we found a twenty-ounce nugget yesterday, and ain afore that o' twenty-five, and in the first face we were at twa months ago o'er there," pointing to the left, "there was yin big ain I ca'd the Villiers nugget, which as ye ken is Madame's name."

"Oh, yes, I know that," said Vandeloup, much interested; "do you christen all your nuggets?"

"If they're big enough," replied Archie.

"Then I hope you will find a hundred-ounce lump of gold, and call it the Vandeloup," returned the young man, laughing.

"There's mony a true word spoke in jest, laddie," said Archie, gravely; "when we get to the Deil's Lead we may find ain o' that size."

"What do you mean by leads?" asked Vandeloup, considerably puzzled.

Thereupon Archie opened his mouth, and gave the young man a scientific lecture on mining, the pith of which was as follows:—

"Did ye no ken," said Mr. McIntosh, sagaciously, "in the auld days—I winna say but what it micht be as far back as the Fa' o' Man, may be a wee bit farther—the rains washed a' the gold fra the taps o' the hills, where the quartz reefs were, down tae the valleys below, where the rivers ye ken were flowin'. And as the ages went on, an' nature, under the guidance o' the Almighty, performed her work, the river bed, wiv a' its gold, would be covered o'er with anither formation, and then the river, or anither yin, would flow on a new bed, and the precious metal would be washed fra the hills in the same way as I tauld ye of, and the second river bed would be also covered o'er, and sae the same game went on and is still progressin'. Sae when the first miners came doon tae this land of Ophir the gold they got by scratchin' the tap of the earth was the latest deposit, and when ye gae doon a few hundred feet ye come on the second river—or rather, I should say, the bed o' the former river-and it is there that the gold is tae be found; and these dried-up rivers we ca' leads. Noo, laddie, ye ma ken that at present we are in the bed o' ain o' these auld streams three hun'red feet frae the tap o' the earth, and it's here we get the gold, and as we gae on we follow the wandrin's o' the river and lose sight o' it."

"Yes," said Vandeloup quickly, "but you lost this river you call the Devil's Lead—how was that?"

"Weel," said Mr. McIntosh, deliberately, "rivers are varra like human bein's in the queer twists they take, and the Deil's Lead seems to hae been ain like that. At present we are on the banks o' it, where we noo get these nuggets; but 'tis the bed I want, d'ye ken, the centre, for its there the gold is; losh, man," he went on, excitedly, rising to his feet and rolling up the plan, "ye dinna ken how rich the Deil's Lead is; there's just a fortune in it."

"I suppose these rivers must stop at a certain depth?"

"Ou, ay," returned the old Scotchman, "we gae doon an' doon till we come on what we ma ca' the primary rock, and under that there is nothin'—except," with a touch of religious enthusiasm, "maybe 'tis the bottomless pit, where auld Hornie dwells, as we are tauld in the Screepture; noo let us gae up again, an' I'll show ye the puddlers at wark."

Vandeloup had not the least idea what the puddlers were, but desirous of learning, he followed his guide, who led him into another gallery, which formed a kind of loop, and joined again with the main drive. As Gaston stumbled along, he felt a touch on his shoulder, and on turning, saw it was Pierre, who had been put to work with the other men, and was acting as one of the runners.

"Ah! you are there, my friend," said Vandeloup, coolly, looking at the uncouth figure before him by the feeble glimmer of his candle; "work away, work away; it's not very pleasant, but at all events," in a rapid whisper, "it's better than New Caledonia."

Pierre nodded in a sullen manner, and went back to his work, while Vandeloup hurried on to catch up to McIntosh, who was now far ahead.

"I wish," said this pleasant young man to himself, as he stumbled along, "I wish that the mine would fall in and crush Pierre; he's such a dead weight to be hanging round my neck; besides, he has such a gaol-bird look about him that it's enough to make the police find out where he came from; if they do, good-bye to wealth and respectability."

He found Archie waiting for him at the entrance to the main drive, and they soon arrived at the bottom of the shaft, got into the cage, and at last reached the top of the earth again. Vandeloup drew a long breath of the fresh pure air, but his eyes felt quite painful in the vivid glare of the sun.

"I don't envy the gnomes," he said gaily to Archie as they went on to the puddlers; "they must have been subject to chronic rheumatism."

Mr. McIntosh, not having an acquaintance with fairy lore, said nothing in reply, but took Vandeloup to the puddlers, and showed all the process of getting the gold.

The wash was carried along in the trucks from the top of the shaft to the puddlers, which were large circular vats into which water was constantly gushing. The wash dirt being put into these, there was an iron ring held up by chains, having blunt spikes to it, which was called a harrow. Two of these being attached to beams laid crosswise were dragged round and round among the wash by the constant revolution of the cross-pieces. This soon reduced all the wash dirt to a kind of fine, creamy-looking syrup, with heavy white stones in it, which were removed every now and then by the man in charge of the machine. Descending to the second story of the framework, Vandeloup found himself in a square chamber, the roof of which was the puddler. In this roof was a trap-door, and when the wash dirt had been sufficiently mixed the trap-door was opened, and it was precipitated through on to the floor of the second chamber. A kind of broad trough, running in a slanting direction and called a sluice, was on one side, and into this a quantity of wash was put, and a tap at the top turned on, which caused the water to wash the dirt down the sluice. Another man at the foot, with a pitchfork, kept shifting up the stones which were mixed up with the gravel, and by degrees all the surplus dirt was washed away, leaving only these stones and a kind of fine black sand, in which the gold being heavy, had stayed. This sand was carefully gathered up with a brush and iron trowel into a shallow tin basin, and then an experienced miner carefully manipulated the same with clear water. What with blowing with the breath, and allowing the water to flow gently over it, all the black sand was soon taken away, and the bottom of the tin dish was then covered with dirty yellow grains of gold interspersed with little water-worn nuggets. Archie took the gold and carried it down to the office, where it was first weighed and then put into a little canvas bag, which would be taken to the bank in Ballarat, and there sold at the rate of four pounds an ounce or thereabouts.

"Sae this, ye ken," said Archie, when he had finished all his explanations, "is the way ye get gold."

"My faith," said Vandeloup, carelessly, with a merry laugh, "gold is as hard to get in its natural state as in its artificial."

"An' harder," retorted Archie, "forbye there's nae sic wicked wark aboot it."

"Madame will be rich some day," remarked Vandeloup, as they left the office and walked up towards the house.

"Maybe she will," replied the other, cautiously. "Australia's a gran' place for the siller, ye ken. I'm no verra far wrang but what wi' industry and perseverance ye may mak a wee bit siller yersel', laddie."

"It won't be my fault if I don't,' returned M. Vandeloup, gaily; "and Madame Midas," he added, mentally, "will be an excellent person to assist me in doing so."

VI

KITTY

Gaston Vandeloup having passed all his life in cities found that his existence on the Pactolus claim was likely to be very dreary. Day after day he arose in the morning, did his office work, ate his meals, and after a talk with Madame Midas in the evening went to bed at ten o'clock. Such Arcadian simplicity as this was not likely to suit the highly cultivated tastes he had acquired in his earlier life. As to the episode of New Caledonia M. Vandeloup dismissed it completely from his mind, for this young man never permitted his thoughts to dwell on disagreeable subjects.

His experiences as a convict had been novel but not pleasant, and he looked upon the time which had elapsed since he left France in the convict ship to the day he landed on the coast of Queensland in an open boat as a bad nightmare, and would willingly have tried to treat it as such, only the constant sight of his dumb companion, Pierre Lemaire, reminded him only too vividly of the reality of his trouble. Often and often did he wish that Pierre would break his neck, or that the mine would fall in and crush him to death; but nothing of the sort happened, and Pierre continued to vex his eyes and to follow him about with a dog-like fidelity which arose—not from any love of the young man, but—from the fact that he found himself a stranger in a strange land, and Vandeloup was the only person he knew. With such a millstone round his neck, the young Frenchman often despaired of being able to get on in Australia. Meanwhile he surrendered himself to the situation with a kind of cynical resignation, and looked hopefully forward to the time when a kind Providence would rid him of his unpleasant friend.

The feelings of Madame Midas towards Vandeloup were curious. She had been a very impressionable girl, and her ill-fated union with Villiers had not quite succeeded in deadening all her feelings, though it had doubtless gone a good way towards doing so. Being of an appreciative nature, she liked to hear Vandeloup talk of his brilliant life in Paris, Vienna, London, and other famous cities, which to her were merely names. For such a young man he had certainly seen a great deal of life, and, added to this, his skill as a talker was considerable, so that he frequently held Madame, Selina, and McIntosh spell-bound by his fairy-like descriptions and eloquent conversation. Of course, he only talked of the most general subjects to Mrs. Villiers, and never by any chance let slip that he knew the seamy side of life—a side with which this versatile young gentleman was pretty well acquainted. As a worker, Gaston was decidedly a success. Being quick at figures and easily taught anything, he soon mastered all the details of the business connected with the Pactolus claim, and Madame found that she could leave everything to him with perfect safety, and could rely on all matters of business being well and promptly attended to. But she was too clever a woman to let him manage things himself, or even know how much she trusted him; and Vandeloup knew that whatever he did those calm dark eyes were on him, and that the least slip or neglect on his part would bring Madame Midas to his side with her quiet voice and inflexible will to put him right again.

Consequently the Frenchman was careful not to digress or to take too much upon himself, but did his work promptly and carefully, and soon became quite indispensable to the work of the mine. In addition to this he had made himself very popular with the men, and as the months rolled on was looked upon quite as a fixture in the Pactolus claim.

As for Pierre Lemaire, he did his work well, ate and slept, and kept his eye on his companion in case he should leave him in the lurch; but no one would have guessed that the two men, so different in appearance, were bound together by a guilty secret, or were, morally speaking, both on the same level as convicts from a French prison.

A whole month had elapsed since Madame had engaged M. Vandeloup and his friend, but as yet the Devil's Lead had not been found. Madame, however, was strong in her belief that it would soon be discovered, for her luck—the luck of Madame Midas—was getting quite a proverb in Ballarat.

One bright morning Vandeloup was in the office running up endless columns of figures, and Madame, dressed in her underground garments, was making ready to go below, just having stepped in to see Gaston.

"By the way, M. Vandeloup," she said in English, for it was only in the evenings they spoke French, "I am expecting a young lady this morning, so you can tell her I have gone down the mine, but will be back in an hour if she will wait for me."

"Certainly, Madame," said Vandeloup, looking up with his bright smile; "and the young lady's name?"

"Kitty Marchurst," replied Madame, pausing a moment at the door of the office; "she is the daughter of the Rev. Mark Marchurst, a minister at Ballarat. I think you will like her, M. Vandeloup," she went on, in a conversational tone; "she is a charming girl—only seventeen, and extremely pretty."

"Then I am sure to like her," returned Gaston, gaily; "I never could resist the charm of a pretty woman."

"Mind," said Madame, severely, holding up her finger, "you must not turn my favourite's head with any of your idle compliments; she has been very strictly brought up, and the language of gallantry is Greek to her."

Vandeloup tried to look penitent, and failed utterly.

"Madame," he said, rising from his seat, and gravely bowing, "I will speak of nothing to Mademoiselle Kitty but of the weather and the crops till you return."

Madame laughed pleasantly.

"You are incorrigible, M. Vandeloup," she said, as she turned to go. "However, don't forget what I said, for I trust you."

When Mrs. Villiers had gone, closing the office door after her, Gaston was silent for a few minutes, and then burst out laughing.

"She trusts me," he said, in a mocking tone. "In heaven's name, why? I never did pretend to be a saint, and I'm certainly not going to be one because I'm put on my word of honour. Madame," with an ironical bow in the direction of the closed door, "since you trust me I will not speak of love to this bread-and-butter miss, unless she proves more than ordinarily pretty, in which case," shrugging his shoulders, "I'm afraid I must betray your trust, and follow my own judgment."

He laughed again, and then, going back to his desk, began to add up his figures. At the second column, however, he paused, and commenced to sketch faces on the blotting paper.

"She's the daughter of a minister," he said, musingly. "I can guess, then, what like she is—prim and demure, like a caricature by Cham. In that case she will be safe from me, for I could never bear an ugly woman. By the way, I wonder if ugly women think themselves pretty; their mirrors must lie most obligingly if they do. There was Adele, she was decidedly plain, not to say ugly, and yet so brilliant in her talk. I was sorry she died; yes, even though she was the cause of my exile to New Caledonia. Bah! it is always a woman one has to thank for one's misfortunes—curse them; though why I should I don't know, for they have always been good friends to me. Ah, well, to return to business, Mademoiselle Kitty is coming, and I must behave like a bear in case she should think my intentions are wrong."

He went to work on the figures again, when suddenly he heard a high clear voice singing outside. At first he thought it was a bird, but no bird could execute such trills and shakes, so by the time the voice arrived at the office door M. Vandeloup came to the conclusion that the owner of the voice was a woman, and that the woman was Miss Kitty Marchurst.

He leaned back in his chair and wondered idly if she would knock at the door or enter without ceremony. The latter course was the one adopted by Miss Marchurst, for she threw open the door and stood there blushing and pouting at the embarrassing situation in which she now found herself.

"I thought I would find Mrs. Villiers here," she said, in a low, sweet voice, the peculiar timbre of which sent a thrill through Gaston's young blood, as he arose to his feet. Then she looked up, and catching his dark eyes fixed on her with a good deal of admiration in them, she looked down and commenced drawing figures on the dusty floor with the tip of a very dainty shoe.

"Madame has gone down the mine," said M. Vandeloup, politely, "but she desired me to say that she would be back soon, and that you were to wait here, and I was to entertain you;" then, with a grave bow, he placed the only chair in the office at the disposal of his visitor, and leaned up against the mantelpiece in an attitude of unstudied grace. Miss Marchurst accepted his offer, and depositing her small person in the big cane chair, she took furtive glances at him, while Gaston, whose experience of women was by no means limited, looked at her coolly, in a manner which would have been rude but for the charming smile which quivered upon his lips.

Kitty Marchurst was a veritable fairy in size, and her hands and feet were exquisitely formed, while her figure had all the plumpness and roundness of a girl of seventeen—which age she was, though she really did not look more than fourteen. An innocent child-like face, two limpid blue eyes, a straight little nose, and a charming rose-lipped mouth were Kitty's principal attractions, and her hair was really wonderful, growing all over her head in crisp golden curls. Child-like enough her face looked in repose, but with the smile came the woman— such a smile, a laughing merry expression such as the Greeks gave to

Hebe. Dressed in a rough white dress trimmed with pale blue ribbons, and her golden head surmounted by a sailor hat, with a scarf of the same azure hue tied around it, Kitty looked really charming, and Vandeloup could hardly restrain himself from taking her up in his arms and kissing her, so delightfully fresh and piquant she appeared. Kitty, on her side, had examined Gaston with a woman's quickness of taking in details, and she mentally decided he was the best-looking man she had ever seen, only she wished he would talk. Shyness was not a part of her nature, so after waiting a reasonable time for Vandeloup to commence, she determined to start herself.

"I'm waiting to be entertained," she said, in a hurried voice, raising her eyes; then afraid of her own temerity, she looked down again.

Gaston smiled a little at Kitty's outspoken remark, but remembering Madame's injunction he rather mischievously determined to carry out her desires to the letter.

"It is a very nice day," he said, gravely. Kitty looked up and laughed merrily.

"I don't think that's a very original remark," she said coolly, producing an apple from her pocket. "If that's all you've got to say, I hope Madame won't be long."

Vandeloup laughed again at her petulance, and eyed her critically as she took a bit out of the red side of the apple with her white teeth.

"You like apples?" he asked, very much amused by her candour.

"Pretty well," returned Miss Marchurst, eyeing the fruit in a disparaging manner; "peaches are nicer; are Madame's peaches ripe?" looking anxiously at him.

"I think they are," rejoined Gaston, gravely.

"Then we'll have some for tea," decided Kitty, taking another bite out of her apple.

"I'm going to stay to tea, you know," she went on in a conversational tone. "I always stay to tea when I'm on a visit here, and then Brown—that's our man," in an explanatory manner, "comes and fetches me home."

"Happy Brown!" murmured Vandeloup, who really meant what he said.

Kitty laughed, and blushed.

"I've heard all about you," she said, coolly, nodding to him.

"Nothing to my disadvantage, I hope," anxiously.

"Oh dear, no: rather the other way," returned Miss Marchurst, gaily. "They said you were good-looking—and so you are, very good-looking."

Gaston bowed and laughed, rather amused at the way she spoke, for he was used to being flattered by women, though hardly in the outspoken way of this country maiden.

"She's been strictly brought up," he muttered sarcastically, "I can see that. Eve before the fall in all her innocence."

"I don't like your eyes," said Miss Kitty, suddenly.

"What's the matter with them?" with a quizzical glance.

"They look wicked."

"Ah, then they belie the soul within," returned Vandeloup, seriously. "I assure you, I'm a very good young man."

"Then I'm sure not to like you," said Kitty, gravely shaking her golden head. "Pa's a minister, you know, and nothing but good young men come to our house; they're all so horrid," viciously, "I hate 'em."

Vandeloup laughed so much at this that Kitty rose to her feet and looked offended.

"I don't know what you are laughing at," she said, throwing her half-eaten apple out of the door; "but I don't believe you're a good young man. You look awfully bad," seriously. "Really, I don't think I ever saw anyone look so bad."

"Suppose you undertake my reformation?" suggested Vandeloup, eagerly.

"Oh! I couldn't; it wouldn't be right; but," brightly, "pa will."

"I don't think I'll trouble him," said Gaston, hastily, who by no means relished the idea. "I'm too far gone to be any good."

She was about to reply when Madame Midas entered, and Kitty flew to her with a cry of delight.

"Why, Kitty," said Madame, highly pleased, "I am so glad to see you, my dear; but keep off, or I'll be spoiling your dress."

"Yes, so you will," said Kitty, retreating to a safe distance; "what a long time you have been."

"Have I, dear?" said Madame, taking off her underground dress; "I hope M. Vandeloup has proved a good substitute."

"Madame," answered Vandeloup, gaily, as he assisted Mrs. Villiers to doff her muddy garments, "we have been talking about the crops and the weather."

"Oh, indeed," replied Mrs. Villiers, who saw the flush on Kitty's cheek, and by no means approved of it; "it must have been very entertaining."

"Very!" assented Gaston, going back to his desk.

"Come along, Kitty," said Madame, with a keen glance at her clerk, and taking Kitty's arm within her own, "let us go to the house, and see if we can find any peaches."

"I hope we'll find some big ones," said Kitty, gluttonously, as she danced along by the side of Mrs. Villiers.

"Temptation has been placed in my path in a very attractive form," said Vandeloup to himself, as he went back to those dreary columns of figures, "and I'm afraid that I will not be able to resist."

When he came home to tea he found Kitty was as joyous and full of life as ever, in spite of the long hot afternoon and the restless energy with which she had been running about. Even Madame Midas felt weary and worn out by the heat of the day, and was sitting tranquilly by the window; but Kitty, with bright eyes and restless feet, followed Selina all over the house, under the pretence of helping her, an infliction which that sage spinster bore with patient resignation.

After tea it was too hot to light the lamp, and even Selina let the fire go out, while all the windows and doors were open to let the cool night wind blow in. Vandeloup sat on the verandah with McIntosh smoking cigarettes and listening to Madame, who was playing Mendelssohn's "In a Gondola", that dreamy melody full of the swing and rhythmic movement of the waves. Then to please old Archie she played "Auld Lang Syne"—that tender caressing air which is one of the most pathetic and heart-stirring melodies in the world. Archie leaned forward with bowed head as the sad melody floated on the air, and his thoughts went back to the heather-clad Scottish hills. And what was this Madame was now playing, with its piercing sorrow and sad refrain? Surely "Farewell to Lochaber", that bitter lament of the exile leaving bonny Scotland far behind. Vandeloup, who was not attending to the music, but thinking of Kitty, saw two big tears steal down McIntosh's severe face, and marvelled at such a sign of weakness.

"Sentiment from him?" he muttered, in a cynical tone; "why, I should have as soon expected blood from a stone."

Suddenly the sad air ceased, and after a few chords, Kitty commenced to sing to Madame's accompaniment. Gaston arose to his feet, and leaned up against the door, for she was singing Gounod's charming valse from "Mirella", the bird-like melody of which suited her high clear voice to perfection. Vandeloup was rather astonished at hearing this innocent little maiden execute the difficult valse with such ease, and her shake was as rapid and true as if she had been trained in the best schools of Europe. He did not know that Kitty had naturally a very flexible voice, and that Madame had trained her for nearly a year. When the song was ended Gaston entered the room to express his thanks and astonishment, both of which Kitty received with bursts of laughter.

"You have a fortune in your throat, mademoiselle," he said, with a bow, "and I assure you I have heard all the great singers of to-day from Patti downwards."

"I have only been able to teach her very little," said Madame, looking affectionately at Miss Marchurst, who now stood by the table, blushing at Vandeloup's praises, "but when we find the Devil's Lead I am going to send her home to Italy to study singing."

"For the stage?" asked Vandeloup.

"That is as it may be," replied Madame, enigmatically, "but now, M. Vandeloup, you must sing us something."

"Oh, does he sing?" said Kitty, joyously.

"Yes, and play too," answered Madame, as she vacated her seat at the piano and put her arm round Kitty, "sing us something from the 'Grand Duchess', Monsieur."

He shook his head.

"Too gay for such an hour," he said, running his fingers lightly over the keys; "I will give you something from 'Faust'."

He had a pleasant tenor voice, not very strong, but singularly pure and penetrating, and he sang "Salve Dinora", the exquisite melody of which touched the heart of Madame Midas with a vague longing for love and affection, while in Kitty's breast there was a feeling she had never felt before. Her joyousness departed, her eyes glanced at the singer in a half-frightened manner, and she clung closer to Madame Midas as if she were afraid, as indeed she was.

When Vandeloup finished the song he dashed into a riotous student song which he had heard many a time in midnight Paris, and finally ended with singing Alfred de Musset's merry little chanson, which he thought especially appropriate to Kitty:—

Bonjour, Suzon, ma fleur des bois, Es-tu toujours la plus jolie, Je reviens, tel que tu me vois,

D'un grand votage en Italie.

Altogether Kitty had enjoyed her evening immensely, and was quite sorry when Brown came to take her home. Madame wrapped her up well and put her in the buggy, but was rather startled to see her flushed cheeks, bright eyes, and the sudden glances she stole at Vandeloup, who stood handsome and debonair in the moonlight.

"I'm afraid I've made a mistake," she said to herself as the buggy drove off.

She had, for Kitty had fallen in love with the Frenchman.

And Gaston?

He walked back to the house beside Madame, thinking of Kitty, and humming the gay refrain of the song he had been singing—

"Je passe devant ta maison Ouvre ta porte, Bonjour, Suzon."

Decidedly it was a case of love at first sight on both sides.

VII

Mr. Villiers Pays a Visit

Slivers and his friend Villiers were by no means pleased with the existing state of things. In sending Vandeloup to the Pactolus claim, they had thought to compromise Madame Midas by placing her in the society of a young and handsome man, and counting on one of two things happening—either that Madame would fall in love with the attractive Frenchman, and seek for a divorce in order to marry him—which divorce Villiers would of course resist, unless she bribed him by giving him an interest in the Pactolus—or that Villiers could assume an injured tone and accuse Vandeloup of being his wife's lover, and threaten to divorce her unless she made him her partner in the claim. But they had both reckoned wrongly, for neither of these things happened, as Madame was not in love with Vandeloup, and acted with too much circumspection to give any opportunity for scandal. Consequently, Slivers and Co., not finding matters going to their satisfaction, met one day at the office of the senior partner for the purpose of discussing the affair, and seeing what could be done towards bringing Madame Midas to their way of thinking.

Villiers was lounging in one of the chairs, dressed in a white linen suit, and looked rather respectable, though his inflamed face and watery eyes showed what a drunkard he was. He was sipping a glass of whisky and water and smoking his pipe, while he watched Slivers stumping up and down the office, swinging his cork arm vehemently to and fro as was his custom when excited. Billy sat on the table and eyed his master with a steady stare, or else hopped about among the papers talking to himself.

"You thought you were going to do big things when you sent that jackadandy out to the Pactolus," said Villiers, after a pause.

"At any rate, I did something," snarled Slivers, in a rage, "which is more than you did, you whisky barrel."

"Look here, don't you call names," growled Mr. Villiers, in a sulky tone. "I'm a gentleman, remember that."

"You were a gentleman, you mean," corrected the senior partner, with a malignant glance of his one eye. "What are you now?"

"A stockbroker," retorted the other, taking a sip of whisky.

"And a damned poor one at that," replied the other, sitting on the edge of the table, which position caused his wooden leg to stick straight out, a result which he immediately utilized by pointing it threateningly in the direction of Villiers.

"Look here," said that gentleman, suddenly sitting up in his chair in a defiant manner, "drop these personalities and come to business; what's to be done? Vandeloup is firmly established there, but there's not the slightest chance of my wife falling in love with him."

"Wait," said Slivers, stolidly wagging his wooden leg up and down; "wait, you blind fool, wait."

"Wait for the waggon!" shrieked Billy, behind, and then supplemented his remarks by adding, "Oh, my precious mother!" as he climbed up on Slivers' shoulder.

"You always say wait," growled Villiers, not paying any attention to Billy's interruption; "I tell you we can't wait much longer; they'll drop on the Devil's Lead shortly, and then we'll be up a tree."

"Then, suppose you go out to the Pactolus and see your wife," suggested Slivers.

"No go," returned Villiers, gloomily, "she'd break my head."

"Bah! you ain't afraid of a woman, are you?" snarled Slivers, viciously.

"No, but I am of McIntosh and the rest of them," retorted Villiers. "What can one man do against twenty of these devils. Why, they'd kill me if I went out there; and that infernal wife of mine wouldn't raise her little finger to save me."

"You're a devil!" observed Billy, eyeing Villiers from his perch on Slivers' shoulder. "Oh, Lord! ha! ha! ha!" going into fits of laughter; then drawing himself suddenly up, he exclaimed "Pickles!" and shut up.

"It's no good beating about the bush," said the wooden-legged man, getting down from the table. "You go out near the claim, and see if you can catch her; then give it to her hot."

"What am I to say?" asked Villiers, helplessly.

Slivers looked at him with fiery scorn in his one eye.

"Say!" he shrieked, waving his cork arm, "talk about your darned honour! Say she's dragging your noble name through the mud, and say you'll divorce her if she don't give you half a share in the Pactolus; that will frighten her."

"Pickles!" again exclaimed the parrot.

"Oh, no, it won't," said Villiers; "Brag's a good dog, but he don't bite. I've tried that game on before, and it was no go."

"Then try it your own way," grumbled Slivers, sulkily, going to his seat and pouring himself out some whisky. "I don't care what you do, as long as I get into the Pactolus, and once I'm in the devil himself won't get me out."

Villiers thought a moment, then turned to go.

"I'll try," he said, as he went out of the door, "but it's no go, I tell you, she's stone," and with a dismal nod he slouched away.

"Stone, is she?" cried the old man, pounding furiously on the floor with his wooden leg, "then I'd smash her; I'd crush her; I'd grind her into little bits, damn her," and overcome by his rage, Slivers shook Billy off his shoulder and took a long drink.

Meanwhile Mr. Villiers, dreading lest his courage should give way, went to the nearest hotel and drank pretty freely so that he might bring himself into an abnormal condition of bravery. Thus primed, he went to the railway station, took the train to the Pactolus claim, and on arriving at the end of his journey had one final glass of whisky to steady his nerves.

The last straw, however, breaks the camel's back, and this last drink reduced Mr. Villiers to that mixed state which is known in colonial phrase as half-cocked. He lurched out of the hotel, and went in the direction of the Pactolus claim. His only difficulty was that, as a matter of fact, the solitary mound of white earth which marked the entrance to the mine, suddenly appeared before his eyes in a double condition, and he beheld two Pactolus claims, which curious optical delusion rather confused him, inasmuch as he was undecided to which he should go.

"Itsh the drinksh," he said at length, stopping in the middle of the white dusty road, and looking preternaturally solemn; "it maksh me see double: if I see my wife, I'll see two of her, then"—with a drunken giggle—"I'll be a bigamist."

This idea so tickled him, that he commenced to laugh, and, finding it inconvenient to do so on his legs, he sat down to indulge his humour freely. A laughing jackass perched on the fence at the side of the road heard Mr. Villiers' hilarity, and, being of a convivial turn of mind itself, went off into fits of laughter also. On hearing this echo Mr. Villiers tried to get up, in order to punish the man who mocked him, but, though his intentions were good, his legs were unsteady, and after one or two ineffectual attempts to rise he gave it up as a bad job. Then rolling himself a little to one side of the dusty white road, he went sound asleep, with his head resting on a tuft of green grass. In his white linen suit he was hardly distinguishable in the fine white dust of the road, and though the sun blazed hotly down on him and the mosquitos stung him, yet he slept calmly on, and it was not till nearly four o'clock in the afternoon that he woke up. He was more sober, but still not quite steady, being in that disagreeable temper to which some men are subject when suffering a recovery. Rising to his feet, with a hearty curse, he picked up his hat and put it on; then, thrusting his hands into his pockets, he slouched slowly along, bent upon meeting his wife and picking a quarrel with her.

Unluckily for Madame Midas, she had that day been to Ballarat, and was just returning. She had gone by train, and was now leaving the station and walking home to the Pactolus along the road. Being absorbed in thought, she did not notice the dusty figure in front of her, otherwise she would have been sure to have recognised her husband, and would have given him a wide berth by crossing the fields instead of going by the road. Mr. Villiers, therefore, tramped steadily on towards the Pactolus, and his wife tramped steadily after him, until at last, at the turn of the road where it entered her property, she overtook him.

A shudder of disgust passed through her frame as she raised her eyes and saw him, and she made a sudden gesture as though to fall behind and thus avoid him. It was, however, too late, for Mr. Villiers, hearing footsteps, turned suddenly and saw the woman he had come to see standing in the middle of the road.

Husband and wife stood gazing at one another for a few moments in silence, she looking at him with an expression of intense loathing on her fine face, and he vainly trying to assume a dignified carriage—a task which his late fit of drunkenness rendered difficult.

At last, his wife, drawing her dress together as though his touch would have contaminated her, tried to pass, but on seeing this he sprang forward, before she could change her position, and caught her wrist.

"Not yet!" he hissed through his clenched teeth; "first you must have a word with me."

Madame Midas looked around for aid, but no one was in sight. They were some distance from the Pactolus, and the heat of the afternoon being intense, every one was inside. At last Madame saw some man moving towards them, down the long road which led to the station, and knowing that Vandeloup had been into town, she prayed in her heart that it might be he, and so prepared to parley with her husband till he should come up. Having taken this resolution, she suddenly threw off Villiers' grasp, and turned towards him with a superb gesture of scorn.

"What do you want?" she asked in a low, clear voice, but in a tone of concentrated passion.

"Money!" growled Villiers, insolently planting himself directly in front of her, "and I'm going to have it."

"Money!" she echoed, in a tone of bitter irony; "have you not had enough yet? Have you not squandered every penny I had from my father in your profligacy and evil companions? What more do you want?"

"A share in the Pactolus," he said, sullenly.

His wife laughed scornfully. "A share in the Pactolus!" she echoed, with bitter sarcasm, "A modest request truly. After squandering my fortune, dragging me through the mire, and treating me like a slave, this man expects to be rewarded. Listen to me, Randolph Villiers," she said, fiercely, stepping up to him and seizing his hand, "this land we now stand on is mine—the gold underneath is mine; and if you were to go on your knees to me and beg for a morsel of bread to save you from starving, I would not lift one finger to succour you."

Villiers writhed like a snake under her bitter scorn.

"I understand," he said, in a taunting tone; "you want it for your lover."

"My lover? What do you mean?"

"What I say," he retorted boldly, "all Ballarat knows the position that young Frenchman holds in the Pactolus claim."

Mrs. Villiers felt herself grow faint—the accusation was so horrible. This man, who had embittered her life from the time she married him, was still her evil genius, and was trying to ruin her in the eyes of the world. The man she had seen on the road was now nearly up to them, and with a revulsion of feeling she saw that it was Vandeloup. Recovering herself with an effort, she turned and faced him steadily.

"You lied when you spoke just now," she said in a quiet voice. "I will not lower myself to reply to your accusation; but, as there is a God above us, if you dare to cross my path again, I will kill you."

She looked so terrible when she said this that Villiers involuntarily drew back, but recovering himself in a moment, he sprang forward and caught her arm.

"You devil! I'll make you pay for this," and he twisted her arm till she thought it was broken. "You'll kill me, will you?—you!—you!" he shrieked, still twisting her arm and causing her intense pain, "you viper!"

Suddenly, when Madame was almost fainting with pain, she heard a shout, and knew that Vandeloup had come to the rescue. He had recognised Madame Midas down the road, and saw that her companion was threatening her; so he made all possible speed, and arrived just in time.

Madame turned round to see Vandeloup throw her husband into a ditch by the side of the road, and walk towards her. He was not at all excited, but seemed as cool and calm as if he had just been shaking hands with Mr. Villiers instead of treating him violently.

"You had better go home, Madame," he said, in his usual cool voice, "and leave me to deal with this—gentleman; you are not hurt?"

"Only my arm," replied Mrs. Villiers, in a faint voice; "he nearly broke it. But I can walk home alone."

"If you can, do so," said Vandeloup, with a doubtful look at her. "I will send him away."

"Don't let him hurt you."

"I don't think there's much danger," replied the young man, with a glance at his arms, "I'm stronger than I look."

"Thank you, Monsieur," said Madame Midas, giving him her hand; "you have rendered me a great service, and one I will not forget."

He bent down and kissed her hand, which action was seen by Mr. Villiers as he crawled out of the ditch. When Madame Midas was gone and Vandeloup could see her walking homeward, he turned to look for Mr. Villiers, and found him seated on the edge of the ditch, all covered with mud and streaming with water—presenting a most pitiable appearance. He regarded M. Vandeloup in a most malignant manner, which, however, had no effect on that young gentleman, who produced a cigarette, and having lighted it proceeded to talk.

"I'm sorry I can't offer you one," said Gaston, affably, "but I hardly think you would enjoy it in your present damp condition. If I might be permitted to suggest anything," with a polite smile, "a bath and a change of clothes would be most suitable to you, and you will find both at Ballarat. I also think," said Vandeloup, with an air of one who thinks deeply, "that if you hurry you will catch the next train, which will save you a rather long walk."

Mr. Villiers glared at his tormentor in speechless anger, and tried to look dignified, but, covered as he was with mud, his effort was not successful.

"Do you know who I am?" he said at length, in a blustering manner.

"Under some circumstances," said M. Vandeloup, in a smooth voice, "I should have taken you for a mud bank, but as you both speak and smile I presume you are a man of the lowest type; as you English yourselves say—a blackguard."

"I'll smash you!" growled Villiers, stepping forward.

"I wouldn't try if I were you," retorted Vandeloup, with a disparaging glance. "I am young and strong, almost a total abstainer; you, on the contrary, are old and flabby, with the shaking nerves of an incurable drunkard. No, it would be hardly fair for me to touch you."

"You dare not lay a finger on me," said Villiers, defiantly.

"Quite right," replied Vandeloup, lighting another cigarette, "you're rather too dirty for close companionship. I really think you'd better go; Monsieur Sleeves no doubt expects you."

"And this is the man that I obtained work for," said Mr. Villiers, addressing the air.

"It's a very ungrateful world," said Vandeloup, calmly, with a shrug of his shoulders; "I never expect anything from it; I'm sorry if you do, for you are sure to be disappointed."

Villiers, finding he could make nothing out of the imperturbable coolness of the young Frenchman, turned to go, but as he went, said spitefully—

"You can tell my wife I'll pay her for this."

"Accounts are paid on Saturdays," called out M. Vandeloup, gaily; "if you call I will give you a receipt of the same kind as you had to-day."

Villiers made no response, as he was already out of hearing, and went on his way to the station with mud on his clothes and rage in his heart.

Vandeloup looked after him for a few minutes with a queer smile on his lips, then turned on his heel and walked home, humming a song.

VIII

MADAME MIDAS STRIKES "ILE"

Aesop knew human nature very well when he wrote his fable of the old man and his ass, who tried to please everybody and ended up by pleasing nobody. Bearing this in mind, Madame Midas determined to please herself, and take no one's advice but her own with regard to Vandeloup. She knew if she dismissed him from the mine it would give colour to her husband's vile insinuations, so she thought the wisest plan would be to take no notice of her meeting with him, and let things remain as they were. It turned out to be the best thing she could have done, for though Villiers went about Ballarat accusing her of being the young Frenchman's mistress, everyone was too well aware of existing circumstances to believe what he said. They knew that he had squandered his wife's fortune, and that she had left him in disgust at his profligacy, so they declined to believe his accusations against a woman who had proved herself true steel in withstanding bad fortune. So Mr. Villiers' endeavours to ruin his wife only recoiled on his own head, for the Ballarat folk argued, and rightly, that whatever she did it was not his place to cast the first stone at her, seeing that the unsatisfactory position she was now in was mainly his own work. Villiers, therefore, gained nothing by his attempt to blacken his wife's character except the contempt of everyone, and even the few friends he had gained turned their backs on him until no one would associate with him but Slivers, who did so in order to gain his own ends. The company had quarrelled over the unsuccessful result of Villiers' visit to the Pactolus, and Slivers, as senior partner, assisted by Billy, called Villiers all the names he could lay his tongue to, which abuse Villiers accepted in silence, not even having the spirit to resent it. But though he was outwardly sulky and quiet, yet within he cherished a deep hatred against his wife for the contempt with which he was treated, and inwardly vowed to pay her out on the first feasible opportunity.

It was now nearly six months since Vandeloup had become clerk at the Pactolus, and he was getting tired of it, only watching his opportunity to make a little money and go to Melbourne, where he had not much doubt as to his success. With a certain sum of money to work on, M. Vandeloup thought that with his talents and experience of human nature he would soon be able to make a fortune, particularly as he was quite unfettered by any scruples, and as long as he made money he did not care how he gained it. With such an adaptable nature he could hardly help doing well, but in order to give him the start he required a little capital, so stayed on at the Pactolus and saved every penny he earned in the hope of soon accumulating enough to leave. Another thing that kept him there was his love for Kitty—not a very pure or elevating love certainly, still it was love for all that, and Vandeloup could not tear himself away from the place where she resided.

He had called on Kitty's father, the Rev. Mark Marchurst, who lived at the top of Black Hill, near Ballarat, and did not like him. Mr. Marchurst, a grave, quiet man, who was the pastor of a particular sect, calling themselves very modestly "The Elect", was hardly the kind of individual to attract a brilliant young fellow like Vandeloup, and the wonder was that he ever had such a charming daughter.

Kitty had fallen deeply in love with Vandeloup, so as he told her he loved her in return, she thought that some day they would get married. But nothing was farther from M. Vandeloup's thoughts than marriage, even with Kitty, for he knew how foolish it would be for him to marry before making a position.

"I don't want a wife to drag me back," he said to himself one day when Kitty had hinted at matrimony; "when I am wealthy it will be time enough to think of marriage, but it will be long before I am rich, and can I wait for Bebe all that time? Alas! I do not think so."

The fact was, the young man was very liberal in his ideas, and infinitely preferred a mistress to a wife. He had not any evil designs towards Kitty, but her bright manner and charming face pleased him, and he simply enjoyed the hours as they passed. She idolised him, and Gaston, who was accustomed to be petted and caressed by women, accepted all her affection as his due. Curiously enough, Madame Midas, lynx-eyed as she was, never suspected the true state of affairs. Vandeloup had told Kitty that no one was to know of their love for one another, and though Kitty was dying to tell Madame about it, yet she kept silent at his request, and acted so indifferently towards him when under Mrs. Villiers' eye, that any doubts that lady had about the fascinations of her clerk soon vanished.

As to M. Vandeloup, the situation was an old one for him accustomed as he had been to carry on with guilty wives under the very noses of unsuspecting husbands, and on this occasion he acted admirably. He was very friendly with Kitty in public—evidently looking upon her as a mere child, although he made no difference in his manner. And this innocent intrigue gave a piquant flavour to his otherwise dull life.

Meanwhile, the Devil's Lead was still undiscovered, many people declaring it was a myth, and that such a lead had never existed. Three people, however, had a firm belief in its existence, and were certain it would be found some day—this trio being McIntosh, Madame Midas, and Slivers.

The Pactolus claim was a sort of Naboth's vineyard to Slivers, who, in company with Billy, used to sit in his dingy little office and grind his teeth as he thought of all the wealth lying beneath those green fields. He had once even gone so far as to offer to buy a share in the claim from Madame Midas, but had been promptly refused by that lady—a circumstance which by no means added to his love for her.

Still the Devil's Lead was not found, and people were beginning to disbelieve in its existence, when suddenly indications appeared which showed that it was near at hand. Nuggets, some large, some small, began to be constantly discovered, and every day news was brought into Ballarat about the turning-up of a thirty-ounce or a twenty-ounce nugget in the Pactolus, when, to crown all, the news came and ran like wildfire through the city that a three hundred ounce nugget had been unearthed.

There was great excitement over this, as such a large one had not been found for some time, and when Slivers heard of its discovery he cursed and swore most horribly; for with his long experience of gold mining, he knew that the long-looked for Devil's Lead was near at hand. Billy, becoming excited with his master, began to swear also; and these two companions cursed Madame Midas and all that belonged to her most heartily. If Slivers could only have seen the interior of Madame Midas's dining room, by some trick of necromancy, he would certainly not have been able to do the subject justice in the swearing line.

There were present Madame Midas, Selina, McIntosh, and Vandeloup, and they were all gathered round the table looking at the famous nugget. There it lay in the centre of the table, a virgin mass of gold, all water-worn and polished, hollowed out like a honeycomb, and dotted over with white pebbles like currants in a plum pudding.

"I think I'll send it to Melbourne for exhibition," said Mrs. Villiers, touching the nugget very lightly with her fingers.

"'Deed, mum, and 'tis worth it," replied McIntosh, whose severe face was relaxed in a grimly pleasant manner; "but losh! 'tis naething tae what 'ull come oot o' the Deil's Lead."

"Oh, come, now," said Vandeloup, with a disbelieving smile, "the Devil's Lead won't consist of nuggets like that."

"Maybe no," returned the old Scotchman, dryly; "but every mickle makes a muckle, and ye ken the Lead wull hae mony sma' nuggets, which is mair paying, to my mind, than yin large ain."

"What's the time?" asked Madame, rather irrelevantly, turning to Archie.

Mr. McIntosh drew out the large silver watch, which was part and parcel of himself, and answered gravely that it was two o'clock.

"Then I'll tell you what," said Mrs. Villiers, rising; "I'll take it in with me to Ballarat and show it to Mr. Marchurst."

McIntosh drew down the corners of his mouth, for, as a rigid Presbyterian, he by no means approved of Marchurst's heretical opinions, but of course said nothing as Madame wished it.

"Can I come with you, Madame?" said Vandeloup, eagerly, for he never lost an opportunity of seeing Kitty if he could help it.

"Certainly," replied Madame, graciously; "we will start at once."

Vandeloup was going away to get ready, when McIntosh stopped him.

"That friend o' yours is gangin' awa' t' the toun the day," he said, touching Vandeloup lightly on the shoulder.

"What for?" asked the Frenchman, carelessly.

"'Tis to see the play actors, I'm thinkin'," returned Archie, dryly. "He wants tae stap all nicht i' the toun, so I've let him gae, an' have tauld him to pit up at the Wattle Tree Hotel, the landlord o' which is a freend o' mine."

"Very kind of you, I'm sure," said Vandeloup, with a pleasant smile; "but may I ask what play actors you refer to?"

"I dinna ken anythin' about sic folk," retorted Mr. McIntosh, piously, "the deil's ain bairns, wha wull gang into the pit of Tophet."

"Aren't you rather hard on them, Archie?" said Madame Midas, smiling quietly. "I'm very fond of the theatre myself."

"It's no for me to give ma opeenion about ma betters," replied Archie, ungraciously, as he went out to see after the horse and trap; "but I dinna care aboot sitting in the seat of the scornfu', or walking in the ways of the unrighteous," and with this parting shot at Vandeloup he went away.

That young man shrugged his shoulders, and looked at Madame Midas in such a comical manner that she could not help smiling.

"You must forgive Archie," she said, pausing at the door of her bedroom for a moment. "He has been brought up severely, and it is hard to rid oneself of the traditions of youth."

"Very traditional in this case, I'm afraid," answered Gaston, referring to McIntosh's age.

"If you like," said Madame, in a kindly tone, "you can stay in to-night yourself, and go to the theatre."

"Thank you, Madame," replied Gaston, gravely. "I will avail myself of your kind permission."

"I'm afraid you will find an Australian provincial company rather a change after the Parisian theatres," said Mrs. Villiers, as she vanished into her room.

Vandeloup smiled, and turned to Selina, who was busy about her household work.

"Mademoiselle Selina," he said, gaily, "I am in want of a proverb to answer Madame; if I can't get the best I must be content with what I can get. Now what piece of wisdom applies?"

Selina, flattered at being applied to, thought a moment, then raised her head triumphantly—

"'Half a loaf is better than none,'" she announced, with a sour smile.

"Mademoiselle," said Vandeloup, gravely regarding her as he stood at the door, "your wisdom is only equalled by your charming appearance," and with an ironical bow he went out.

Selina paused a moment in her occupation of polishing spoons, and looked after him, doubtful as to whether he was in jest or earnest. Being unable to decide, she resumed her work with a stifled chuckle, and consoled herself with a proverb.

"To be good is better than to be beautiful," which saying, as everyone knows, is most consoling to plain-looking people.

The great nugget was carefully packed in a stout wooden box by Archie, and placed in the trap by him with such caution that Madame, who was already seated in it, asked him if he was afraid she would be robbed.

"It's always best to be on the richt side, mem," said Archie, handing her the reins; "we dinna ken what may happen."

"Why, no one knows I am taking this to Ballarat to-day," said Madame, drawing on her gloves.

"Don't they?" thought M. Vandeloup, as he took his seat beside her. "She doesn't know that I've told Pierre."

And without a single thought for the woman whose confidence he was betraying, and of whose bread and salt he had partaken, Vandeloup shook the reins, and the horse started down the road in the direction of Ballarat, carrying Madame Midas and her nugget.

"You carry Caesar and his fortunes, M. Vandeloup," she said, with a smile.

"I do better," he answered, gaily, "I carry Madame Midas and her luck."

IX

Love's Young Dream

Mr. Mark Marchurst was a very peculiar man. Brought up in the Presbyterian religion, he had early displayed his peculiarity by differing from the elders of the church he belonged to regarding their doctrine of eternal punishment. They, holding fast to the teachings of Knox and Calvin, looked upon him in horror for daring to have an opinion of his own; and as he refused to repent and have blind belief in the teachings of those grim divines, he was turned out of the bosom of the church. Drifting to the opposite extreme, he became a convert to Catholicism; but, after a trial of that ancient faith, found it would not suit him, so once more took up a neutral position. Therefore, as he did not find either religion perfectly in accordance with his own views, he took the law into his own hands and constructed one which was a queer jumble of Presbyterianism, Catholicism, and Buddhism, of which last religion he was a great admirer. As anyone with strong views and a clever tongue will find followers, Mr. Marchurst soon gathered a number of people around him who professed a blind belief in the extraordinary doctrines he promulgated. Having thus founded a sect he got sufficient money out of them to build a temple—for so he called the barn-like edifice he erected—and christened this new society which he had called into existence "The Elect". About one hundred people were members of his church, and with their subscriptions, and also having a little money of his own, he managed to live in a quiet manner in a cottage on the Black Hill near to his temple. Every Sunday he held forth morning and evening, expounding his views to his sparse congregation, and was looked upon by them as a kind of prophet. As a matter of fact, the man had that peculiar power of fascination which seems to be inseparable from the prophetic character, and it was his intense enthusiasm and eloquent tongue that cast a spell over the simple-minded people who believed in him. But his doctrines were too shallow and unsatisfactory ever to take root, and it could be easily seen that when Marchurst died "The Elect" would die also,—that is, as a sect, for it was not pervaded by that intense religious fervour which is the life and soul of a new doctrine. The fundamental principles of his religion were extremely simple; he saved his friends and damned his enemies, for so he styled those who were not of the same mind as himself. If you were a member of "The Elect", Mr. Marchurst assured you that the Golden Gate was wide open for you, whereas if you belonged to any other denomination you were lost for ever; so according to this liberal belief, the hundred people who formed his congregation would all go straight to Heaven, and all the rest of mankind would go to the devil.

In spite of the selfishness of this theory, which condemned so many souls to perdition, Marchurst was a kindly natured man, and his religion was more of an hallucination than anything else. He was very clever at giving advice, and Madame Midas esteemed him highly on this account. Though Marchurst had often tried to convert her, she refused to believe in the shallow sophistries he set forth, and told him she had her own views on religion, which views she declined to impart to him, though frequently pressed to do so. The zealot regretted this obstinacy, as, according to his creed, she was a lost soul, but he liked her too well personally to quarrel with her on that account, consoling himself with the reflection that sooner or later, she would seek the fold. He was more successful with M. Vandeloup, who, having no religion whatever, allowed Marchurst to think he had converted him, in order to see as much as he could of Kitty. He used to attend the Sunday services regularly, and frequently came in during the week ostensibly to talk to Marchurst about the doctrines of "The Elect", but in reality to see the old man's daughter.

On this bright afternoon, when everything was bathed in sunshine, Mr. Marchurst, instead of being outside and enjoying the beauties of Nature, was mewed up in his dismal little study, with curtains closely drawn to exclude the light, a cup of strong tea, and the Bible open at "The Lamentations of Jeremiah". His room was lined with books, but they had not that friendly look books generally have, but, bound in dingy brown calf, looked as grim and uninviting as their contents, which were mostly sermons and cheerful anticipations of the bottomless pit. It was against Marchurst's principles to gratify his senses by having nice things around him, and his whole house was furnished in the same dismal manner.

So far did he carry this idea of mortifying the flesh through the eyes that he had tried to induce Kitty to wear sad-coloured dresses and poke bonnets; but in this attempt he failed lamentably, as Kitty flatly refused to make a guy of herself, and always wore dresses of the lightest and gayest description.

Marchurst groaned over this display of vanity, but as he could do nothing with the obdurate Kitty, he allowed her to have her own way, and made a virtue of necessity by calling her his "thorn in the flesh".

He was a tall thin man, of a bleached appearance, from staying so much in the dark, and so loosely put together that when he bowed he did not as much bend as tumble down from a height. In fact, he looked so carelessly fixed up that when he sat down he made the onlooker feel quite nervous lest he should subside into a ruin, and scatter his legs, arms, and head promiscuously all over the place. He had a sad, pale, eager-looking face, with dreamy eyes, which always seemed to be looking into the spiritual world. He wore his brown hair long, as he always maintained a man's hair was as much his glory as a woman's was hers, quoting Samson and Absalom in support of this opinion. His arms were long and thin, and when he gesticulated in the pulpit on Sundays flew about like a couple of flails, which gave him a most unhappy resemblance to a windmill. The "Lamentations of Jeremiah" are not the most cheerful of reading, and Mr. Marchurst, imbued with the sadness of the Jewish prophet, drinking strong tea and sitting in a darkened room, was rapidly sinking into a very dismal frame of mind, which an outsider would have termed a fit of the blues. He sat in his straight-backed chair taking notes of such parts of the "Lamentations" as would tend to depress the spirits of the "Elect" on Sunday, and teach them to regard life in a proper and thoroughly miserable manner.

He was roused from his dismal musings by the quick opening of the door of his study, when Kitty, joyous and gay in her white dress, burst like a sunbeam into the room.

"I wish, Katherine," said her father, in a severe voice, "I wish you would not enter so noisily and disturb my meditations."

"You'll have to put your meditations aside for a bit," said Kitty, disrespectfully, crossing to the window and pulling aside the curtains, "for Madame Midas and M. Vandeloup have come to see you."

A flood of golden light streamed into the dusky room, and Marchurst put his hand to his eyes for a moment, as they were dazzled by the sudden glare.

"They've got something to show you, papa," said Kitty, going back to the door: "a big nugget—such a size—as large as your head."

Her father put his hand mechanically to his head to judge of the size, and was about to answer when Madame Midas, calm, cool, and handsome, entered the room, followed by Vandeloup, carrying a wooden box containing the nugget. It was by no means light, and Vandeloup was quite thankful when he placed it on the table.

"I hope I'm not disturbing you, Mr. Marchurst," said Madame, sitting down and casting a glance at the scattered papers, the cup of tea, and the open Bible, "but I couldn't help gratifying my vanity by bringing the new nugget for you to see."

"It's very kind of you, I'm sure," responded Mr. Marchurst, politely, giving way suddenly in the middle as if he had a hinge in his back, which was his idea of a bow. "I hope this," laying his hand on the box, "may be the forerunner of many such."

"Oh, it will," said Vandeloup, cheerfully, "if we can only find the Devil's Lead."

"An unholy name," groaned Marchurst sadly, shaking his head. "Why did you not call it something else?"

"Simply because I didn't name it," replied Madame Midas, bluntly; "but if the lead is rich, the name doesn't matter much."

"Of course not," broke in Kitty, impatiently, being anxious to see the nugget. "Do open the box; I'm dying to see it."

"Katherine! Katherine!" said Marchurst, reprovingly, as Vandeloup opened the box, "how you do exaggerate—ah!" he broke off his exhortation suddenly, for the box was open, and the great mass of gold was glittering in its depths. "Wonderful!"

"What a size!" cried Kitty, clapping her hands as Vandeloup lifted it out and placed it on the table; "how much is it worth?"

"About twelve hundred pounds," said Madame, quietly, though her heart throbbed with pride as she looked at her nugget; "it weighs three hundred ounces."

"Wonderful!" reiterated the old man, passing his thin hand lightly over the rough surface; "verily the Lord hath hidden great treasure in the entrails of the earth, and the Pactolus would seem to be a land of Ophir when it yields such wealth as this."

The nugget was duly admired by everyone, and then Brown and Jane, who formed the household of Marchurst, were called in to look at it. They both expressed such astonishment and wonder, that Marchurst felt himself compelled to admonish them against prizing the treasures of earth above those of heaven. Vandeloup, afraid that they were in for a sermon, beckoned quietly to Kitty, and they both stealthily left the room, while Marchurst, with Brown, Jane, and Madame for an audience, and the nugget for a text, delivered a short discourse.

Kitty put on a great straw hat, underneath which her piquant face blushed and grew pink beneath the fond gaze of her lover as they left the house together and strolled up to the Black Hill.

Black Hill no doubt at one time deserved its name, being then covered with dark trees and representing a black appearance at a distance; but at present, owing to the mines which have been worked there, the whole place is covered with dazzling white clay, or mulloch, which now renders the title singularly inappropriate. On the top of the hill there is a kind of irregular gully or pass, which extends from one side of the hill to the other, and was cut in the early days for mining purposes. Anything more extraordinary can hardly be imagined than this chasm, for the sides, which tower up on either side to the height of some fifty or sixty feet, are all pure white, and at the top break into all sorts of fantastic forms. The white surface of the rocks are all stained with colours which alternate in shades of dark brown, bright red and delicate pink. Great masses of rock have tumbled down on each side, often coming so close together as to almost block up the path. Here and there in the white walls can be seen the dark entrances of disused shafts; and one, at the lowest level of the gully, pierces through the hill and comes out on the other side. There is an old engine-house near the end of the gully, with its red brick chimney standing up gaunt and silent beside it, and the ugly tower of the winding gear adjacent. All the machinery in the engine-house, with the huge wheels and intricate mechanism, is silent now—for many years have elapsed since this old shaft was abandoned by the Black Hill Gold Mining Company.

At the lower end of the pass there is an engine-house in full working order, and a great plateau of slate-coloured mulloch runs out for some yards, and then there is a steep sloping bank formed by the falling earth. In the moonlight this wonderful white gully looks weird and bizarre; and even as Vandeloup and Kitty stood at the top looking down into its dusty depths in the bright sunshine, it looks fantastic and picturesque.

Seated on the highest point of the hill, under the shadow of a great rock, the two lovers had a wonderful view of Ballarat. Here and there they could see the galvanized iron roofs of the houses gleaming like silver in the sunlight from amid the thick foliage of the trees with which the city is studded. Indeed, Ballarat might well be called the City of Trees, for seen from the Black Hill it looks more like a huge park with a sprinkling of houses in it than anything else. The green foliage rolls over it like the waves of the ocean, and the houses rise up like isolated habitations. Now and then a red brick building, or the slender white spire of a church gave a touch of colour to the landscape, and contrasted pleasantly with the bluish-white roofs and green trees. Scattered all through the town were the huge mounds of earth marking the mining-shafts of various colours, from dark brown to pure white, and beside them, with the utmost regularity, were the skeleton towers of the poppet heads, the tall red chimneys, and the squat, low forms of the engine-houses. On the right, high up, could be seen the blue waters of Lake Wendouree flashing like a mirror in the sunlight. The city was completely encircled by the dark forests, which stretched far away, having a reddish tinge over their trees, ending in a sharply defined line against the clear sky; while, on the left arose Mount Warreneip like an undulating mound and, further along, Mount Bunniyong, with the same appearance.

All this wonderful panorama, however, was so familiar to Kitty and her lover that they did not trouble themselves to look much at it; but the girl sat down under the big rock, and Vandeloup flung himself lazily at her feet.

"Bebe," said Vandeloup, who had given her this pet name, "how long is this sort of life going to last?"

Kitty looked down at him with a vague feeling of terror at her heart. She had never known any life but the simple one she was now leading, and could not imagine it coming to an end.

"I'm getting tired of it," said Vandeloup, lying back on the grass, and, putting his hands under his head, stared idly at the blue sky. "Unfortunately, human life is so short nowadays that we cannot afford to waste a moment of it. I am not suited for a lotus-eating existence, and I think I shall go to Melbourne."

"And leave me?" cried Kitty, in dismay, never having contemplated such a thing as likely to happen.

"That depends on yourself, Bebe," said her lover, quickly rolling over and looking steadily at her, with his chin resting on his hands; "will you come with me?"

"As your wife?" murmured Kitty, whose innocent mind never dreamt of any other form of companionship.

Vandeloup turned away his face to conceal the sneering smile that crept over it. His wife, indeed! as if he were going to encumber himself with marriage before he had made a fortune, and even then it was questionable as to whether he would surrender the freedom of bachelorhood for the ties of matrimony.

"Of course," he said, in a reassuring tone, still keeping his face turned away, "we will get married in Melbourne as soon as we arrive."

"Why can't papa marry us," pouted Kitty, in an aggrieved tone.

"My dear child," said the Frenchman, getting on his knees and coming close to her, "in the first place, your father would not consent to the match, as I am poor and unknown, and not by any means the man he would choose for you; and in the second place, being a Catholic,"—here M. Vandeloup looked duly religious—"I must be married by one of my own priests."

"Then why not in Ballarat?" objected Kitty, still unconvinced.

"Because your father would never consent," he whispered, putting his arm round her waist; "we must run away quietly, and when we are married can ask his pardon and," with a sardonic sneer, "his blessing."

A delicious thrill passed through Kitty when she heard this. A real elopement with a handsome lover—just like the heroines in the story books. It was delightfully romantic, and yet there seemed to be something wrong about it. She was like a timid bather, longing to plunge into the water, yet hesitating through a vague fear. With a quick catching of the breath she turned to Vandeloup, and saw him with his burning scintillating eyes fastened on her face.

"Don't look like that," she said, with a touch of virginal fear, pushing him away, "you frighten me."

"Frighten you, Bebe?" he said, in a caressing tone; "my heart's idol, you are cruel to speak like that; you must come with me, for I cannot and will not leave you behind."

"When do you go?" asked Kitty, who was now trembling violently.

"Ah!" M. Vandeloup was puzzled what to say, as he had no very decided plan of action. He had not sufficient money saved to justify him in leaving the Pactolus—still there were always possibilities, and Fortune was fond of playing wild pranks. At the same time there was nothing tangible in view likely to make him rich, so, as these thoughts rapidly passed through his mind, he resolved to temporize.

"I can't tell you, Bebe," he said, in a caressing tone, smoothing her curly hair. "I want you to think over what I have said, and when I do go, perhaps in a month or so, you will be ready to come with me. No," he said, as Kitty was about to answer, "I don't want you to reply now, take time to consider, little one," and with a smile on his lips he bent over and kissed her tenderly.

They sat silently together for some time, each intent on their own thoughts, and then Vandeloup suddenly looked up.

"Will Madame stay to dinner with you, Bebe?" he asked.

Kitty nodded.

"She always does," she answered; "you will come too."

Vandeloup shook his head.

"I am going down to Ballarat to the Wattle Tree Hotel to see my friend Pierre," he said, in a preoccupied manner, "and will have something to eat there. Then I will come up again about eight o'clock, in time to see Madame off."

"Aren't you going back with her?" asked Kitty, in surprise, as they rose to their feet.

"No," he replied, dusting his knees with his hand, "I stay all night in Ballarat, with Madame's kind permission, to see the theatre. Now, good-bye at present, Bebe," kissing her, "I will be back at eight o'clock, so you can excuse me to Madame till then."

He ran gaily down the hill waving his hat, and Kitty stood looking after him with pride in her heart. He was a lover any girl might have been proud of, but Kitty would not have been so satisfied with him had she known what his real thoughts were.

"Marry!" he said to himself, with a laugh, as he walked gaily along; "hardly! When we get to Melbourne, my sweet Bebe, I will find some way to keep you off that idea—and when we grow tired of one another, we can separate without the trouble or expense of a divorce."

And this heartless, cynical man of the world was the keeper into whose hands innocent Kitty was about to commit the whole of her future life.

After all, the fabled Sirens have their equivalent in the male sex, and Homer's description symbolizes a cruel truth.

X

FRIENDS IN COUNCIL

The Wattle Tree Hotel, to which Mr. McIntosh had directed Pierre, was a quiet little public-house in a quiet street. It was far away from the main thoroughfares of the city, and a stranger had to go up any number of quiet streets to get to it, and turn and twist round corners and down narrow lanes until it became a perfect miracle how he ever found the hotel at all.

To a casual spectator it would seem that a tavern so difficult of access would not be very good for business, but Simon Twexby, the landlord, knew better. It had its regular customers, who came there day after day, and sat in the little back parlour and talked and chatted over their drinks. The Wattle Tree was such a quiet haven of rest, and kept such good liquor, that once a man discovered it he always came back again; so Mr. Twexby did a very comfortable trade.

Rumour said he had made a lot of money out of gold-mining, and that he kept the hotel more for amusement than anything else; but, however this might be, the trade of the Wattle Tree brought him in a very decent income, and Mr. Twexby could afford to take things easy—which he certainly did.

Anyone going into the bar could see old Simon—a stolid, fat man, with a sleepy-looking face, always in his shirt sleeves, and wearing a white apron, sitting in a chair at the end, while his daughter, a sharp, red-nosed damsel, who was thirty-five years of age, and confessed to twenty-two, served out the drinks. Mrs. Twexby had long ago departed this life, leaving behind her the sharp, red-nosed damsel to be her father's comfort. As a matter of fact, she was just the opposite, and Simon often wished that his daughter had departed to a better world in company with her mother. Thin, tight-laced, with a shrill voice and an acidulated temper, Miss Twexby was still a spinster, and not even the fact of her being an heiress could tempt any of the Ballarat youth to lead her to the altar. Consequently Miss Twexby's temper was not a golden one, and she ruled the hotel and its inmates—her father included—with a rod of iron.

Mr. Villiers was a frequent customer at the Wattle Tree, and was in the back parlour drinking brandy and water and talking to old Twexby on the day that Pierre arrived. The dumb man came into the bar out of the dusty road, and, leaning over the counter, pushed a letter under Miss Twexby's nose.

"Bills?" queried that damsel, sharply.

Pierre, of course, did not answer, but touched his lips with his hand to indicate he was dumb. Miss Twexby, however, read the action another way.

"You want a drink," she said, with a scornful toss of her head. "Where's your money?"

Pierre pointed out the letter, and although it was directed to her father, Miss Twexby, who managed everything, opened it and found it was from McIntosh, saying that the bearer, Pierre Lemaire, was to have a bed for the night, meals, drinks, and whatever else he required, and that he—McIntosh—would be responsible for the money. He furthermore added that the bearer was dumb.

"Oh, so you're dumb, are you," said Miss Twexby, folding up the letter and looking complacently at Pierre. "I wish there were a few more men the same way; then, perhaps, we'd have less chat."

This being undeniable, the fair Martha—for that was the name of the Twexby heiress—without waiting for any assent, walking into the back parlour, read the letter to her father, and waited instructions, for she always referred to Simon as the head of the house, though as a matter of fact she never did what she was told save when it tallied with her own wishes.

"It will be all right, Martha, I suppose," said Simon sleepily.

Martha asserted with decision that it would be all right, or she would know the reason why; then marching out again to the bar, she drew a pot of beer for Pierre—without asking him what he would have—and ordered him to sit down and be quiet, which last remark was rather unnecessary, considering that the man was dumb. Then she sat down behind her bar and resumed her perusal of a novel called "The Duke's Duchesses, or The Milliner's Mystery," which contained a ducal hero with bigamistic proclivities, and a virtuous milliner whom the aforesaid duke persecuted. All of which was very entertaining and improbable, and gave Miss Twexby much pleasure, judging from the sympathetic sighs she was heaving.

Meanwhile, Villiers having heard the name of Pierre Lemaire, and knowing he was engaged in the Pactolus claim, came round to see him and try to find out all about the nugget. Pierre was sulky at first, and sat drinking his beer sullenly, with his old black hat drawn down so far over his eyes that only his bushy black beard was visible, but Mr. Villiers' suavity, together with the present of half-a-crown, had a marked effect on him. As he was dumb, Mr. Villiers was somewhat perplexed how to carry on a conversation with him, but he ultimately drew forth a piece of paper, and sketched a rough presentation of a nugget thereon, which he showed to Pierre. The Frenchman, however, did not comprehend until Villiers produced a sovereign from his pocket, and pointed first to the gold, and then to the drawing, upon which Pierre nodded his head several times in order to show that he understood. Villiers then drew a picture of the Pactolus claim, and asked Pierre in French if the nugget was still there, as he showed him the sketch. Pierre shook his head, and, taking the pencil in his hand, drew a rough representation of a horse and cart, and put a square box in the latter to show the nugget was on a journey.

"Hullo!" said Villiers to himself, "it's not at her own house, and she's driving somewhere with it, I wonder where to?"

Pierre—who not being able to write, was in the habit of drawing pictures to express his thoughts—nudged his elbow and showed him a sketch of a man in a box waving his arms.

"Auctioneer?" hazarded Mr. Villiers, looking at this keenly. Pierre stared at him blankly; his comprehension of English was none of the best, so he did not know what auctioneer meant. However, he saw that Villiers did not understand, so he rapidly sketched an altar with a priest standing before it blessing the people.

"Oh, a priest, eh?—a minister?" said Villiers, nodding his head to show he understood. "She's taken the nugget to show it to a minister! Wonder who it is?"

This was speedily answered by Pierre, who, throwing down the pencil and paper, dragged him outside on to the road, and pointed to the white top of the Black Hill. Mr. Villiers instantly comprehended.

"Marchurst, by God!" he said in English, smiting his leg with his open hand. "Is Madame there now?" he added in French, turning to Pierre.

The dumb man nodded and slouched slowly back into the hotel. Villiers stood out in the blazing sunshine, thinking.

"She's got the nugget with her in the trap," he said to himself; "and she's taken it to show Marchurst. Well, she's sure to stop there to tea, and won't start for home till about nine o'clock: it will be pretty dark by then. She'll be by herself, and if I—" here he stopped and looked round cautiously, and then, without another word, set off down the street at a run.

The fact was, Mr. Villiers had come to the conclusion that as his wife would not give him money willingly, the best thing to be done would be to take it by force, and accordingly he had made up his mind to rob her of the nugget that night if possible. Of course there was a risk, for he knew his wife was a determined woman; still, while she was driving in the darkness down the hill, if he took her by surprise he would be able to stun her with a blow and get possession of the nugget. Then he could hide it in one of the old shafts of the Black Hill Company until he required it. As to the possibility of his wife knowing him, there would be no chance of that in the darkness, so he could escape any unpleasant inquiries, then take the nugget to Melbourne and get it melted down secretly. He would be able to make nearly twelve hundred pounds out of it, so the game would certainly be worth the candle. Full of this brilliant idea of making a good sum at one stroke, Mr. Villiers went home, had something to eat, and taking with him a good stout stick, the nob of which was loaded with lead, he started for the Black Hill with the intent of watching Marchurst's house until his wife left there, and then following her down the hill and possessing himself of the nugget.

The afternoon wore drowsily along, and the great heat made everybody inclined to sleep. Pierre had demanded by signs to be shown his bedroom, and having been conducted thereto by a crushed-looking waiter, who drifted aimlessly before him, threw himself on the bed and went fast asleep.

Old Simon, in the dimly-lit back parlour, was already snoring, and only Miss Twexby, amid the glitter of the glasses in the bar and the glare of the sunshine through the open door, was wide awake. Customers came in for foaming tankards of beer, and sometimes a little girl, with a jug hidden under her apron, would appear, with a request that it might be filled for "mother", who was ironing. Indeed, the number of women who were ironing that afternoon, and wanted to quench their thirst, was something wonderful; but Miss Twexby seemed to know all about it as she put a frothy head on each jug, and received the silver in exchange. At last, however, even Martha the wide-awake was yielding to the somniferous heat of the day when a young man entered the bar and made her sit up with great alacrity, beaming all over her hard wooden face.

This was none other than M. Vandeloup, who had come down to see Pierre. Dressed in flannels, with a blue scarf tied carelessly round his waist, a blue necktie knotted loosely round his throat under the collar of his shirt, and wearing a straw hat on his fair head, he looked wonderfully cool and handsome, and as he leaned over the counter composedly smoking a cigarette, Miss Twexby thought that the hero of her novel must have stepped bodily out of the book. Gaston stared complacently at her while he pulled at his fair moustache, and thought how horribly plain-looking she was, and what a contrast to his charming Bebe.

"I'll take something cool to drink," he said, with a yawn, "and also a chair, if you have no objection," suiting the action to the word; "whew! how warm it is."

"What would you like to drink, sir?" asked the fair Martha, putting on her brightest smile, which seemed rather out of place on her features; "brandy and soda?"

"Thank you, I'll have a lemon squash if you will kindly make me one," he said, carelessly, and as Martha flew to obey his order, he added, "you might put a little curacoa in it."

"It's very hot, ain't it," observed Miss Twexby, affably, as she cut up the lemon; "par's gone to sleep in the other room," jerking her head in the direction of the parlour, "but Mr. Villiers went out in all the heat, and it ain't no wonder if he gets a sunstroke."

"Oh, was Mr. Villiers here?" asked Gaston, idly, not that he cared much about that gentleman's movements, but merely for something to say.

"Lor, yes, sir," giggled Martha, "he's one of our regulars, sir."

"I can understand that, Mademoiselle," said Vandeloup, bowing as he took the drink from her hand.

Miss Twexby giggled again, and her nose grew a shade redder at the pleasure of being bantered by this handsome young man.

"You're a furriner," she said, shortly; "I knew you were," she went on triumphantly as he nodded, "you talk well enough, but there's something wrong about the way you pronounces your words."

Vandeloup hardly thought Miss Twexby a mistress of Queen's English, but he did not attempt to contradict her.

"I must get you to give me a few lessons," he replied, gallantly, setting down the empty glass; "and what has Mr. Villiers gone out into the heat for?"

"It's more nor I can tell," said Martha, emphatically, nodding her head till the short curls dangling over her ears vibrated as if they were made of wire. "He spoke to the dumb man and drew pictures for him, and then off he goes."

The dumb man! Gaston pricked up his ears at this, and, wondering what Villiers wanted to talk to Pierre about, he determined to find out.

"That dumb man is one of our miners from the Pactolus," he said, lighting another cigarette; "I wish to speak to him—has he gone out also?"

"No, he ain't," returned Miss Twexby, decisively; "he's gone to lie down; d'ye want to see him; I'll send for him—" with her hand on the bell-rope.

"No, thank you," said Vandeloup, stopping her, "I'll go up to his room if you will show me the way."

"Oh, I don't mind," said Martha, preparing to leave the bar, but first ringing the bell so that the crushed-looking waiter might come and attend to possible customers; "he's on the ground floor, and there ain't no stairs to climb—now what are you looking at, sir?" with another gratified giggle, as she caught Vandeloup staring at her.

But he was not looking at her somewhat mature charms, but at a bunch of pale blue flowers, among which were some white blossoms she wore in the front of her dress.

"What are these?" he asked, touching the white blossoms lightly with his finger.

"I do declare it's that nasty hemlock!" said Martha, in surprise, pulling the white flowers out of the bunch; "and I never knew it was there. Pah!" and she threw the blossom down with a gesture of disgust. "How they smell!"

Gaston picked up one of the flowers, and crushed it between his fingers, upon which it gave out a peculiar mousy odour eminently disagreeable. It was hemlock sure enough, and he wondered how such a plant had come into Australia.

"Does it grow in your garden?" he asked Martha.

That damsel intimated it did, and offered to show him the plant, so that he could believe his own eyes.

Vandeloup assented eagerly, and they were soon in the flower garden at the back of the house, which was blazing with vivid colours, in the hot glare of the sunshine.

"There you are," said Miss Twexby, pointing to a corner of the garden near the fence where the plant was growing; "par brought a lot of seeds from home, and that beastly thing got mixed up with them. Par keeps it growing, though, 'cause no one else has got it. It's quite a curiosity."

Vandeloup bent down and examined the plant, with its large, round, smooth, purple-spotted stem—its smooth, shining green leaves, and the tiny white flowers with their disagreeable odour.

"Yes, it is hemlock," he said, half to himself; "I did not know it could be grown here. Some day, Mademoiselle," he said, turning to Miss Twexby and walking back to the house with her, "I will ask you to let me have some of the roots of that plant to make an experiment with."

"As much as you like," said the fair Martha, amiably; "it's a nasty smelling thing. What are you going to make out of it?"

"Nothing particular," returned Vandeloup, with a yawn, as they entered the house and stopped at the door of Pierre's room. "I'm a bit of a chemist, and amuse myself with these things."

"You are clever," observed Martha, admiringly; "but here's that man's room—we didn't give him the best"—apologetically—"as miners are so rough."

"Mademoiselle," said Vandeloup, eagerly, as she turned to go, "I see there are a few blossoms of hemlock left in your flower there," touching it with his finger; "will you give them to me?"

Martha Twexby stared; surely this was the long-expected come at last—she had secured a lover; and such a lover—handsome, young, and gallant,—the very hero of her dreams. She almost fainted in delighted surprise, and unfastening the flowers with trembling fingers, gave them to Gaston. He placed them in a button-hole of his flannel coat, then before she could scream, or even draw back in time, this audacious young man put his arm round her and kissed her virginal lips. Miss Twexby was so taken by surprise, that she could offer no resistance, and by the time she had recovered herself, Gaston had disappeared into Pierre's room and closed the door after him.

"Well," she said to herself, as she returned to the bar, "if that isn't a case of love at first sight, my name ain't Martha Twexby," and she sat down in the bar with her nerves all of a flutter, as she afterwards told a female friend who dropped in sometimes for a friendly cup of tea.

Gaston closed the door after him, and found himself in a moderately large room, with one window looking on to the garden, and having a dressing-table with a mirror in front of it. There were two beds, one on each side, and on the farthest of these Pierre was sleeping heavily, not even Gaston's entrance having roused him. Going over to him,

Vandeloup touched him slightly, and with a spring the dumb man sat up in bed as if he expected to be arrested, and was all on the alert to escape.

"It's only I, my friend," said Gaston, in French, crossing over to the other bed and sitting on it. "Come here; I wish to speak to you."

Pierre rose from his sleeping place, and, stumbling across the room, stood before Gaston with downcast eyes, his shaggy hair all tossed and tumbled by the contact with the pillow. Gaston himself coolly relit his cigarette, which had gone out, threw his straw hat on the bed, and then, curling one leg inside the other, looked long and keenly at Pierre.

"You saw Madame's husband to-day?" he said sharply, still eyeing the slouching figure before him, that seemed so restless under his steady gaze.

Pierre nodded and shuffled his large feet.

"Did he want to know about his wife?"

Another nod.

"I thought so; and about the new nugget also, I presume?"

Still another nod.

"Humph," thoughtfully. "He'd like to get a share of it, I've no doubt."

The dumb man nodded violently; then, crossing over to his own bed, he placed the pillow in the centre of it, and falling on his knees, imitated the action of miners in working at the wash. Then he arose to his feet and pointed to the pillow.

"I see," said M. Vandeloup, who had been watching this pantomime with considerable interest; "that pillow is the nugget of which our friend wants a share."

Pierre assented; then, snatching up the pillow, he ran with it to the end of the room.

"Oh," said Gaston, after a moment's thought, "so he's going to run away with it. A very good idea; but how does he propose to get it?"

Pierre dropped his pillow and pointed in the direction of the Black Hill.

"Does he know it's up there?" asked Vandeloup; "you told him, I suppose?" As Pierre nodded, "Humph! I think I can see what Mr. Villiers intends to do—rob his wife as she goes home tonight."

Pierre nodded in a half doubtful manner.

"You're not quite sure," interrupted M. Vandeloup, "but I am. He won't stop at anything to get money. You stay all night in town?"

The dumb man assented.

"So do I," replied Vandeloup; "it's a happy coincidence, because I see a chance of our getting that nugget." Pierre's dull eyes brightened, and he rubbed his hands together in a pleased manner.

"Sit down," said Vandeloup, in a peremptory tone, pointing to the floor. "I wish to tell you what I think."

Pierre obediently dropped on to the floor, where he squatted like a huge misshapen toad, while Vandeloup, after going to the door to see that it was closed, returned to the bed, sat down again, and, having lighted another cigarette, began to speak. All this precaution was somewhat needless, as he was talking rapidly in French, but then M. Vandeloup knew that walls have ears and possibly might understand foreign languages.

"I need hardly remind you," said Vandeloup, in a pleasant voice, "that when we landed in Australia I told you that there was war between ourselves and society, and that, at any cost, we must try to make money; so far, we have only been able to earn an honest livelihood—a way of getting rich which you must admit is remarkably slow. Here, however, is a chance of making, if not a fortune, at least a good sum of money at one stroke. This M. Villiers is going to rob his wife, and his plan will no doubt be this: he will lie in wait for her, and when she drives slowly down the hill, he will spring on to the trap and perhaps attempt to kill her; at all events, he will seize the box containing the nugget, and try to make off with it. How he intends to manage it I cannot tell you—it must be left to the chapter of accidents; but," in a lower voice, bending forward, "when he does get the nugget we must obtain it from him."

Pierre looked up and drew his hand across his throat.

"Not necessarily," returned Vandeloup, coolly; "I know your adage, 'dead men tell no tales,' but it is a mistake—they do, and to kill him is dangerous. No, if we stun him we can go off with the nugget, and then make our way to Melbourne, where we can get rid of it quietly. As to Madame Midas, if her husband allows her to live—which I think is unlikely—I will make our excuses to her for leaving the mine. Now, I'm going up to M. Marchurst's house, so you can meet me at the top of the hill, at eight o'clock tonight. Madame will probably start at half-past eight or nine, so that will give us plenty of time to see what M. Villiers is going to do."

They both rose to their feet. Then Vandeloup put on his hat, and, going to the glass, arranged his tie in as cool and nonchalant a manner as if he had been merely planning the details for a picnic instead of a possible crime. While admiring himself in the glass he caught sight of the bunch of flowers given to him by Miss Twexby, and, taking them from his coat, he turned round to Pierre, who stood watching him in his usual sullen manner.

"Do you see these?" he asked, touching the white blossoms with the cigarette he held between his fingers.

Pierre intimated that he did.

"From the plant of these, my friend," said Vandeloup, looking at them critically, "I can prepare a vegetable poison as deadly as any of Caesar Borgia's. It is a powerful narcotic, and leaves hardly any trace. Having been a medical student, you know," he went on, conversationally, "I made quite a study of toxicology, and the juice of this plant," touching the white flower, "has done me good service, although it was the cause of my exile to New Caledonia. Well," with a shrug of the shoulders as he put the flowers back in his coat, "it is always something to have in reserve; I did not know that I could get this plant here, my friend. But now that I have I will prepare a little of this poison,—it will always be useful in emergencies."

Pierre looked steadily at the young man, and then slipping his hand behind his back he drew forth from the waistband of his trousers a long, sharp, cruel-looking knife, which for safety had a leather sheath. Drawing this off, the dumb man ran his thumb along the keen edge, and held the knife out towards Vandeloup, who refused it with a cynical smile.

"You don't believe in this, I can see," he said, touching the dainty bunch of flowers as Pierre put the knife in its sheath again and returned it to its hiding-place. "I'm afraid your ideas are still crude—you believe in the good old-fashioned style of blood-letting. Quite a mistake, I assure you; poison is much more artistic and neat in its work, and to my mind involves less risk. You see, my Pierre," he continued, lazily watching the blue wreaths of smoke from his cigarette curl round his head, "crime must improve with civilization; and since the Cain and Abel epoch we have refined the art of murder in a most wonderful manner—decidedly we are becoming more civilized; and now, my friend," in a kind tone, laying his slender white hand on the shoulder of the dumb man, "you must really take a little rest, for I have no doubt but what you will need all your strength tonight should M. Villiers prove obstinate. Of course," with a shrug, "if he does not succeed in getting the nugget, our time will be simply wasted, and then," with a gay smile, touching the flowers, "I will see what I can do in the artistic line."

Pierre lay down again on the bed, and turning his face to the wall fell fast asleep, while M. Vandeloup, humming a merry tune, walked gaily out of the room to the bar, and asked Miss Twexby for another drink.

"Brandy and soda this time, please," he said, lazily lighting another cigarette; "this heat is so enervating, and I'm going to walk up to Black Hill. By the way, Mademoiselle," he went on, as she opened the soda water, "as I see there are two beds in my friend's room I will stay here all night."

"You shall have the best room," said Martha, decisively, as she handed him the brandy and soda.

"You are too kind," replied M. Vandeloup, coolly, as he took the drink from her, "but I prefer to stay with my silent friend. He was one of the sailors in the ship when I was wrecked, as you have no doubt heard, and looks upon me as a sort of fetish."

Miss Twexby knew all about the wreck, and thought it was beautiful that he should condescend to be so friendly with a common sailor. Vandeloup received all her speeches with a polite smile, then set down his empty glass and prepared to leave.

"Mademoiselle," he said, touching the flowers, "you see I still have them—they will remind me of you," and raising his hat he strolled idly out of the hotel, and went off in the direction of the Black Hill.

Miss Twexby ran to the door, and shading her eyes with her hands from the blinding glare of the sun, she watched him lounging along the street, tall, slender, and handsome.

"He's just lovely," she said to herself, as she returned to the bar "but his eyes are so wicked; I don't think he's a good young man."

What would she have said if she had heard the conversation in the bedroom?

XI

Theodore Wopples, Actor

Mr. Villiers walked in a leisurely manner along the lower part of the town, with the intent of going up to his destination through the old mining gully. He took this route for two reasons—first, because the afternoon was hot, and it was easier climbing up that way than going by the ordinary road; and, second, on his journey through the chasm he would be able to mark some place where he could hide the nugget. With his stick under his arm, Mr. Villiers trudged merrily along in a happy humour, as if he was bent on pleasure instead of robbery. And after all, as he said to himself, it could not be called a genuine robbery, as everything belonging to his wife was his by right of the marriage service, and he was only going to have his own again. With this comfortable thought he climbed slowly up the broken tortuous path which led to the Black Hill, and every now and then would pause to rest, and admire the view.

It was now nearly six o'clock, and the sun was sinking amid a blaze of splendour. The whole of the western sky was a sea of shimmering gold, and this, intensified near the horizon to almost blinding brightness, faded off towards the zenith of the sky into a delicate green, and thence melted imperceptibly into a cold blue.

Villiers, however, being of the earth, earthy, could not be troubled looking very long at such a common-place sight as a sunset; the same thing occurred every evening, and he had more important things to do than to waste his time gratifying his artistic eye. Arriving on the plateau of earth just in front of the gully, he was soon entering the narrow gorge, and tramped steadily along in deep thought, with bent head and wrinkled brows. The way being narrow, and Villiers being preoccupied, it was not surprising that as a man was coming down in the opposite direction, also preoccupied, they should run against one another. When this took place it gave Mr. Villiers rather a start, as it suggested a possible witness to the deed he contemplated, a thing for which he was by no means anxious.

"Really, sir," said the stranger, in a rich, rolling voice, and in a dignified tone, "I think you might look where you are going. From what

I saw of you, your eyes were not fixed on the stars, and thus to cause your unwatched feet to stumble; in fact," said the speaker, looking up to the sky, "I see no stars whereon you could fix your gaze."

This somewhat strange mode of remonstrance was delivered in a solemn manner, with appropriate gestures, and tickled Mr. Villiers so much that he leaned up against a great rock abutting on the path, and laughed long and loudly.

"That is right, sir," said the stranger, approvingly; "laughter is to the soul what food is to the body. I think, sir," in a Johnsonian manner, "the thought is a happy one."

Villiers assented with a nod, and examined the speaker attentively. He was a man of medium height, rather portly than otherwise, with a clean-shaved face, clearly-cut features, and two merry grey eyes, which twinkled like stars as they rested on Villiers. His hair was greyish, and inclined to curl, but could not follow its natural inclination owing to the unsparing use of the barber's shears. He wore a coat and trousers of white flannel, but no waistcoat; canvas shoes were on his feet, and a juvenile straw hat was perched on his iron-grey hair, the rim of which encircled his head like a halo of glory. He had small, well-shaped hands, one of which grasped a light cane, and the other a white silk pocket handkerchief, with which he frequently wiped his brow. He seemed very hot, and, leaning on the opposite side of the path against a rock, fanned himself first with his handkerchief and then with his hat, all the time looking at Mr. Villiers with a beaming smile. At last he took a silver-mounted flask from his pocket and offered it to Villiers, with a pleasant bow.

"It's very hot, you know," he said, in his rich voice, as Villiers accepted the flask.

"What, this?" asked Villiers, indicating the flask, as he slowly unscrewed the top.

"No; the day, my boy, the day. Ha! ha! ha!" said the lively stranger, going off into fits of laughter, which vibrated like small thunder amid the high rocks surrounding them. "Good line for a comedy, I think. Ha! ha!—gad, I'll make a note of it," and diving into one of the pockets of his coat, he produced therefrom an old letter, on the back of which he inscribed the witticism with the stump of a pencil.

Meanwhile Villiers, thinking the flask contained brandy, or at least whisky, took a long drink of it, but found to his horror it was merely a weak solution of sherry and water.

"Oh, my poor stomach," he gasped, taking the flask from his lips.

"Colic?" inquired the stranger with a pleasant smile, as he put back the letter and pencil, "hot water fomentations are what you need. Wonderful cure. Will bring you to life again though you were at your last gasp. Ha!" struck with a sudden idea, "'His Last Gasp', good title for a melodrama—mustn't forget that," and out came the letter and the pencil again.

Mr. Villiers explained in a somewhat gruff tone that it was not colic, but that his medical attendant allowed him to drink nothing but whisky.

"To be taken twenty times a day, I presume," observed the stranger, with a wink; "no offence meant, sir," as Villiers showed a disposition to resent this, "merely a repartee. Good for a comedy, I fancy; what do you think?"

"I think," said Mr. Villiers, handing him back the flask, "that you're very eccentric."

"Eccentric?" replied the other, in an airy tone, "not at all, sir. I'm merely a civilized being with the veneer off. I am not hidden under an artificial coat of manner. No, I laugh—ha! ha! I skip, ha! ha!" with a light trip on one foot. "I cry," in a dismal tone. "In fact, I am a man in his natural state—civilized sufficiently, but not over civilized."

"What's your name?" asked Mr. Villiers, wondering whether the portly gentleman was mad.

For reply the stranger dived into another pocket, and, bringing to light a long bill-poster, held it up before Mr. Villiers.

"Read! mark! and inwardly digest!" he said in a muffled tone behind the bill.

This document set forth in red, black, and blue letters, that the celebrated Wopples Family, consisting of twelve star artistes, were now in Ballarat, and would that night appear at the Academy of Music in their new and original farcical comedy, called "The Cruet-Stand". Act I: Pepper! Act II: Mustard! Act III: Vinegar.

"You, then," said Villiers, after he had perused this document, "are Mr. Wopples?"

"Theodore Wopples, at your service," said that gentleman, rolling up the bill, then putting it into his pocket, he produced therefrom a batch of tickets. "One of these," handing a ticket to Villiers, "will admit you to the stalls tonight, where you will see myself and the children in 'The Cruet-Stand'."

"Rather a peculiar title, isn't it?" said Villiers, taking the ticket.

"The play is still more peculiar, sir," replied Mr. Wopples, restoring the bulky packet of tickets to his pocket, "dealing as it does with the adventures of a youth who hides his father's will in a cruet stand, which is afterwards annexed by a comic bailiff."

"But isn't it rather a curious thing to hide a will in a cruet stand?" asked Villiers, smiling at the oddity of the idea.

"Therein, sir, lies the peculiarity of the play," said Mr. Wopples, grandly. "Of course the characters find out in Act I that the will is in the cruet stand; in Act II, while pursuing it, they get mixed up with the bailiff's mother-in-law; and in Act III," finished Mr. Wopples, exultingly, "they run it to earth in a pawnshop. Oh, I assure you it is a most original play."

"Very," assented the other, dryly; "the author must be a man of genius—who wrote it?"

"It's a translation from the German, sir," said Mr. Wopples, taking a drink of sherry and water, "and was originally produced in London as 'The Pickle Bottle', the will being hidden with the family onions. In Melbourne it was the success of the year under the same title. I," with an air of genius, "called it 'The Cruet Stand'."

"Then how did you get a hold of it," asked Villiers.

"My wife, sir," said the actor, rolling out the words in his deep voice. "A wonderful woman, sir; paid a visit to Melbourne, and there, sir, seated at the back of the pit between a coal-heaver and an apple-woman, she copied the whole thing down."

"But isn't that rather mean?"

"Certainly not," retorted Wopples, haughtily; "the opulent Melbourne managers refuse to let me have their new pieces, so I have to take the law into my own hands. I'll get all the latest London successes in the same way. We play 'Ours' under the title of 'The Hero's Return, or the Soldier's Bride': we have done the 'Silver King' as 'The Living Dead', which was an immense success."

Villiers thought that under such a contradictory title it would rather pique the curiosity of the public.

"To-morrow night," pursued Mr. Wopples, "we act 'Called Back', but it is billed as 'The Blind Detective'; thus," said the actor, with virtuous scorn, "do we evade the grasping avarice of the Melbourne managers, who would make us pay fees for them."

"By the way," said Mr. Wopples, breaking off suddenly in a light and airy manner, "as I came down here I saw a lovely girl—a veritable fairy, sir—with golden hair, and a bright smile that haunts me still. I exchanged a few remarks with her regarding the beauty of the day, and thus allegorically referred to the beauty of herself—a charming flight of fancy, I think, sir."

"It must have been Kitty Marchurst," said Villiers, not attending to the latter portion of Mr. Wopples' remarks.

"Ah, indeed," said Mr. Wopples, lightly, "how beautiful is the name of Kitty; it suggests poetry immediately—for instance:

Kitty, ah Kitty, You are so pretty, Charming and witty, That 'twere a pity I sung not this ditty In praise of my Kitty.

On the spur of the moment, sir, I assure you; does it not remind you of Herrick?"

Mr. Villiers bluntly said it did not.

"Ah! perhaps it's more like Shakespeare?" observed the actor, quite unabashed. "You think so?"

Mr. Villiers was doubtful, and displayed such anxiety to get away that Mr. Wopples held out his hand to say goodbye.

"You'll excuse me, I know," said Mr. Wopples, in an apologetic tone, "but the show commences at eight, and it is now half-past six. I trust I shall see you tonight."

"It's very kind of you to give me this ticket," said Villiers, in whom the gentlemanly instinct still survived.

"Not at all; not at all," retorted Mr. Wopples, with a wink. "Business, my boy, business. Always have a good house first night, so must go into the highways and byways for an audience. Ha! Biblical illustration, you see;" and with a gracious wave of his hand he skipped lightly down the path and disappeared from sight.

It was now getting dark; so Mr. Villiers went on his own way, and having selected a mining shaft where he could hide the nugget, he climbed up to the top of the hill, and lying down under the shadow of a rock where he could get a good view of Marchurst's house, he waited patiently till such time as his wife would start for home.

"I'll pay you out for all you've done," he muttered to himself, as he lay curled up in the black shadow like a noisome reptile. "Tit for tat, my lady!—tit for tat!"

XII

Highway Robbery

Dinner at Mr. Marchurst's house was not a particularly exhilarating affair. As a matter of fact, though dignified with the name of dinner, it was nothing more than one of those mixed meals known as high tea. Vandeloup knew this, and, having a strong aversion to the miscellaneous collection of victuals which appeared on Mr. Marchurst's table, he dined at Craig's Hotel, where he had a nice little dinner, and drank a pint bottle of champagne in order to thoroughly enjoy himself. Madame Midas also had a dislike to tea-dinners, but, being a guest, of course had to take what was going; and she, Kitty, and Mr. Marchurst, were the only people present at the festive board. At last Mr. Marchurst finished and delivered a long address of thanks to Heaven for the good food they had enjoyed, which good food, being heavy and badly cooked, was warranted to give them all indigestion and turn their praying to cursing. In fact, what with strong tea, hurried meals, and no exercise, Mr. Marchurst used to pass an awful time with the nightmare, and although he was accustomed to look upon nightmares as visions, they were due more to dyspepsia than inspiration.

After dinner Madame sat and talked with Marchurst, but Kitty went outside into the warm darkness of the summer night, and tried to pierce the gloom to see if her lover was coming. She was rewarded, for M. Vandeloup came up about half-past eight o'clock, having met Pierre as arranged. Pierre had found out Villiers in his hiding-place, and was watching him while Villiers watched the house. Being, therefore, quite easy in his mind that things were going smoothly, Vandeloup came up to the porch where Kitty was eagerly waiting for him, and taking her in his arms kissed her tenderly. Then, after assuring himself that Madame was safe with Marchurst, he put his arm round Kitty's waist, and they walked up and down the path with the warm wind blowing in their faces, and the perfume of the wattle blossoms permeating the drowsy air. And yet while he was walking up and down, talking lover-like nonsense to the pretty girl by his side, Vandeloup knew that Villiers was watching the house far off, with evil eyes, and he also knew that Pierre was watching Villiers with all the insatiable desire of a wild beast for blood. The moon rose, a great shield of silver, and all the ground was strewn with the aerial shadows of the trees. The wind sighed through the branches of the wattles, and made their golden blossoms tremble in the moonlight, while hand in hand the lovers strolled down the path or over the short dry grass. Far away in the distance they heard a woman singing, and the high sweet voice floated softly towards them through the clear air.

Suddenly they heard the noise of a chair being pushed back inside the house, and knew that Madame was getting ready to go. They moved simultaneously towards the door, but in the porch Gaston paused for a moment, and caught Kitty by the arm.

"Bebe," he whispered softly, "when Madame is gone I am going down the hill to Ballarat, so you will walk with me a little way, will you not?"

Of course, Kitty was only too delighted at being asked to do so, and readily consented, then ran quickly into the house, followed by Vandeloup.

"You here?" cried Madame, in surprise, pausing for a moment in the act of putting on her bonnet. "Why are you not at the theatre?"

"I am going, Madame," replied Gaston, calmly, "but I thought I would come up in order to assist you to put the nugget in the trap."

"Oh, Mr. Marchurst would have done that," said Madame, much gratified at Vandeloup's attention. "I'm sorry you should miss your evening's pleasure for that."

"Ah, Madame, I do but exchange a lesser pleasure for a greater one," said the gallant Frenchman, with a pleasant smile; "but are you sure you will not want me to drive you home?"

"Not at all," said Madame, as they all went outside; "I am quite safe."

"Still, with this," said Mr. Marchurst, bringing up the rear, with the nugget now safely placed in its wooden box, "you might be robbed."

"Not I," replied Mrs. Villiers, brightly, as the horse and trap were brought round to the gate by Brown. "No one knows I've got it in the trap, and, besides, no one can catch up with Rory when he once starts."

Marchurst put the nugget under the seat of the trap, but Madame was afraid it might slip out by some chance, so she put the box containing it in front, and then her feet on the box, so that it was absolutely impossible that it could get lost without her knowing. Then saying goodbye to everyone, and telling M. Vandeloup to be out at the Pactolus before noon the next day, she gathered up the reins and drove slowly down the hill, much to the delight of Mr. Villiers, who was getting tired of waiting. Kitty and Vandeloup strolled off in the moonlight, while Marchurst went back to the house.

Villiers arose from his hiding-place, and looked up savagely at the serene moon, which was giving far too much light for his scheme to succeed. Fortunately, however, he saw a great black cloud rapidly advancing which threatened to hide the moon; so he set off down the hill at a run in order to catch his wife at a nasty part of the road some distance down, where she would be compelled to go slowly, and thus give him a chance to spring on the trap and take her by surprise. But quick as he was, Pierre was quicker, and both Vandeloup and Kitty could see the two black figures running rapidly along in the moonlight.

"Who are those?" asked Kitty, with a sudden start. "Are they going after Madame?"

"Little goose," whispered her lover, with a laugh; "if they are they will never catch up to that horse. It's all right, Bebe," with a reassuring smile, seeing that Kitty still looked somewhat alarmed, "they are only some miners out on a drunken frolic."

Thus pacified, Kitty laughed gaily, and they wandered along in the moonlight, talking all the fond and foolish nonsense they could think of.

Meanwhile the great black cloud had completely hidden the moon, and the whole landscape was quite dark. This annoyed Madame, as, depending on the moonlight, the lamps of the trap were not lighted, and she could not see in the darkness how to drive down a very awkward bit of road that she was now on.

It was very steep, and there was a high bank on one side, while on the other there was a fall of about ten feet. She felt annoyed at the darkness, but on looking up saw that the cloud would soon pass, so drove on slowly quite content. Unluckily she did not see the figure on the high bank which ran along stealthily beside her, and while turning a corner, Mr. Villiers—for it was he—dropped suddenly from the bank on to the trap, and caught her by the throat.

"My God!" cried the unfortunate woman, taken by surprise, and, involuntarily tightening the reins, the horse stopped—"who are you?"

Villiers never said a word, but tightened his grasp on her throat and shortened his stick to give her a blow on the head. Fortunately, Madame Midas saw his intention, and managed to wrench herself free, so the blow aimed at her only slightly touched her, otherwise it would have killed her.

As it was, however, she fell forward half stunned, and Villiers, hurriedly dropping his stick, bent down and seized the box which he felt under his feet and intuitively guessed contained the nugget.

With a cry of triumph he hurled it out on to the road, and sprang out after it; but the cry woke his wife from the semi-stupor into which she had fallen.

Her head felt dizzy and heavy from the blow, but still she had her senses about her, and the moon bursting out from behind a cloud, rendered the night as clear as day.

Villiers had picked up the box, and was standing on the edge of the bank, just about to leave. The unhappy woman recognised her husband, and uttered a cry.

"You! you!" she shrieked, wildly, "coward! dastard! Give me back that nugget!" leaning out of the trap in her eagerness.

"I'll see you damned first," retorted Villiers, who, now that he was recognised, was utterly reckless as to the result. "We're quits now, my lady," and he turned to go.

Maddened with anger and disgust, his wife snatched up the stick he had dropped, and struck him on the head as he took a step forward. With a stifled cry he staggered and fell over the embankment, still clutching the box in his arms. Madame let the stick fall, and fell back fainting on the seat of the trap, while the horse, startled by the noise, tore down the road at a mad gallop.

Madame Midas lay in a dead faint for some time, and when she came to herself she was still in the trap, and Rory was calmly trotting along the road home. At the foot of the hill, the horse, knowing every inch of the way, had settled down into his steady trot for the Pactolus, but when Madame grasped the situation, she marvelled to herself how she had escaped being dashed to pieces in that mad gallop down the Black Hill.

Her head felt painful from the effects of the blow she had received, but her one thought was to get home to Archie and Selina, so gathering up the reins she sent Rory along as quickly as she could. When she drove up to the gate Archie and Selina were both out to receive her, and when the former went to lift her off the trap, he gave a cry of horror at seeing her dishevelled appearance and the blood on her face.

"God save us!" he cried, lifting her down; "what's come t' ye, and where's the nugget?" seeing it was not in the trap.

"Lost!" she said, in a stupor, feeling her head swimming, "but there's worse."

"Worse?" echoed Selina and Archie, who were both standing looking terrified at one another.

"Yes," said Mrs. Villiers, in a hollow whisper, leaning forward and grasping Archie's coat, "I've killed my husband," and without another word, she fell fainting to the ground.

At the same time Vandeloup and Pierre walked into the bar at the Wattle Tree Hotel, and each had a glass of brandy, after which Pierre went to his bed, and Vandeloup, humming a gay song, turned on his heel and went to the theatre.

XIII

A Glimpse of Bohemia

A h!" says Thackeray, pathetically, "Prague is a pleasant city, but we all lose our way to it late in life."

The Wopples family were true Bohemians, and had not yet lost their way to the pleasant city. They accepted good and bad fortune with wonderful equanimity, and if their pockets were empty one day, there was always a possibility of their being full the next. When this was the case they generally celebrated the event by a little supper, and as their present season in Ballarat bid fair to be a successful one, Mr. Theodore Wopples determined to have a convivial evening after the performance was over.

That the Wopples family were favourites with the Ballarat folk was amply seen by the crowded house which assembled to see "The Cruet Stand". The audience were very impatient for the curtain to rise, as they did not appreciate the overture, which consisted of airs from "La Mascotte", adapted for the violin and piano by Mr. Handel Wopples, who was the musical genius of the family, and sat in the conductor's seat, playing the violin and conducting the orchestra of one, which on this occasion was Miss Jemima Wopples, who presided at the piano. The Wopples family consisted of twelve star artistes, beginning with Mr. Theodore Wopples, aged fifty, and ending with Master Sheridan Wopples, aged ten, who did the servants' characters, delivered letters, formed the background in tableaux, and made himself generally useful. As the cast of the comedy was only eight, two of the family acted as the orchestra, and the remaining two took money at the door. When their duties in this respect were over for the night, they went into the pit to lead the applause.

At last the orchestra finished, and the curtain drew up, displaying an ancient house belonging to a decayed family. The young Squire, present head of the decayed family (Mr. Cibber Wopples), is fighting with his dishonest steward (admirably acted by Mr. Dogbery Wopples), whose daughter he wants to marry. The dishonest steward, during Act I, without any apparent reason, is struck with remorse, and making his will in favour of the Squire, departs to America, but afterwards appears in the last act as someone else. Leaving his will on the drawing-room table, as he naturally would, it is seized by an Eton boy (Master Sheridan Wopples), who hides it, for some unexplained reason, in the cruet-stand, being the last piece of family plate remaining to the decayed family. This is seized by a comic bailiff (Mr. Theodore Wopples), who takes it to his home; and the decayed family, finding out about the will, start to chase the bailiff and recover the stolen property from him. This brought the play on to Act II, which consisted mainly of situations arising out of the indiscriminate use of doors and windows for entrances and exits. The bailiff's mother-in-law (Mrs. Wopples) appears in this act, and, being in want of a new dress, takes the cruet stand to her "uncle" and pawns it; so Act II ends with a general onslaught of the decayed family on Mrs. Wopples.

Then the orchestra played the "Wopples' Waltz", dedicated to Mr. Theodore Wopples by Mr. Handel Wopples, and during the performance of this Mr. Villiers walked into the theatre. He was a little pale, as was only natural after such an adventure as he had been engaged in, but otherwise seemed all right. He walked up to the first row of the stalls, and took his seat beside a young man of about twenty-five, who was evidently much amused at the performance.

"Hullo, Villiers!" said this young gentleman, turning round to the new arrival, "what d'ye think of the play?"

"Only just got in," returned Mr. Villiers, sulkily, looking at his programme. "Any good?" in a more amiable tone.

"Well, not bad," returned the other, pulling up his collar; "I've seen it in Melbourne, you know—the original, I mean; this is a very second-hand affair."

Mr. Villiers nodded, and became absorbed in his programme; so, seeing he was disinclined for more conversation, the young gentleman turned his attention to the "Wopples Waltz", which was now being played fast and furiously by the indefatigable orchestra of two.

Bartholomew Jarper—generally called Barty by his friends—was a bank clerk, and had come up to Ballarat on a visit. He was well known in Melbourne society, and looked upon himself quite as a leader of fashion. He went everywhere, danced divinely—so the ladies said—sang two or three little songs, and played the same accompaniment to each of them, was seen constantly at the theatres, plunged a little at the races, and was altogether an extremely gay dog. It is, then, little to be wondered at that, satiated as he was with Melbourne gaiety, he should be vastly critical of the humble efforts of the Wopples family to please him. He had met Villiers at his hotel, when both of them being inebriated they swore eternal friendship. Mr. Villiers, however, was very sulky on this particular night, for his head still pained him, so Barty stared round the house in a supercilious manner, and sucked the nob of his cane for refreshment between the acts.

Just as the orchestra were making their final plunge into the finale of the "Wopples' Waltz", M. Vandeloup, cool and calm as usual, strolled into the theatre, and, seeing a vacant seat beside Villiers, walked over and took it.

"Good evening, my friend," he said, touching Villiers on the shoulder. "Enjoying the play, eh?"

Villiers angrily pushed away the Frenchman's hand and glared vindictively at him.

"Ah, you still bear malice for that little episode of the ditch," said Vandeloup with a gay laugh. "Come, now, this is a mistake; let us be friends."

"Go to the devil!" growled Villiers, crossly.

"All right, my friend," said M. Vandeloup, serenely crossing his legs. "We'll all end up by paying a visit to that gentleman, but while we are on earth we may as well be pleasant. Seen your wife lately?"

This apparently careless inquiry caused Mr. Villiers to jump suddenly out of his seat, much to the astonishment of Barty, who did not know for what reason he was standing up.

"Ah! you want to look at the house, I suppose," remarked M. Vandeloup, lazily; "the building is extremely ugly, but there are some redeeming features in it. I refer, of course, to the number of pretty girls," and Gaston turned round and looked steadily at a red-haired damsel behind him, who blushed and giggled, thinking he was referring to her.

Villiers resumed his seat with a sigh, and seeing that it was quite useless to quarrel with Vandeloup, owing to that young man's coolness, resolved to make the best of a bad job, and held out his hand with a view to reconciliation.

"It's no use fighting with you," he said, with an uneasy laugh, as the other took his hand, "you are so deuced amiable."

"I am," replied Gaston, calmly examining his programme; "I practise all the Christian virtues."

Here Barty, on whom the Frenchman's appearance and conversation had produced an impression, requested Villiers, in a stage whisper, to introduce him—which was done. Vandeloup looked the young man coolly up and down, and eventually decided that Mr. Barty Jarper was a "cad", for whatever his morals might be, the Frenchman was a thorough gentleman. However, as he was always diplomatic, he did not give utterance to his idea, but taking a seat next to Barty's, he talked glibly to him until the orchestra finished with a few final bangs, and the curtain drew up on Act III.

The scene was the interior of a pawnshop, where the pawnbroker, a gentleman of Hebraic descent (Mr. Buckstone Wopples), sells the cruet to the dishonest steward, who has come back from America disguised as a sailor. The decayed family all rush in to buy the cruet stand, but on finding it gone, overwhelm the pawnbroker with reproaches, so that to quiet them he hides them all over the shop, on the chance that the dishonest steward will come back. The dishonest steward does so, and having found the will tears it up on the stage, upon which he is assaulted by the decayed family, who rush out from all parts. Ultimately, he reveals himself and hands back the cruet stand and the estates to the decayed family, after which a general marrying all round took place, which proceeding was very gratifying to the boys in the gallery, who gave their opinions very freely, and the curtain fell amid thunders of applause. Altogether "The Cruet Stand" was a success, and would have a steady run of three nights at least, so Mr. Wopples said—and as a manager of long standing, he was thoroughly well up in the subject.

Villiers, Vandeloup, and Barty went out and had a drink, and as none of them felt inclined to go to bed, Villiers told them he knew Mr. Theodore Wopples, and proposed that they should go behind the scenes and see him. This was unanimously carried, and after some difficulty with the door-keeper—a crusty old man with a red face and white hair, that stood straight up in a tuft, and made him look like an infuriated cockatoo—they obtained access to the mysterious regions of the stage, and there found Master Sheridan Wopples practising a breakdown while waiting for the rest of the family to get ready. This charming youth, who was small, dried-up and wonderfully sharp, volunteered to guide them to his father's dressing-room, and on knocking at the door Mr. Wopples' voice boomed out "Come in," in such an unexpected manner that it made them all jump.

On entering the room they found Mr. Wopples, dressed in a light tweed suit, and just putting on his coat. It was a small room, with a flaring gas-jet, under which there was a dressing-table littered over with grease, paints, powder, vaseline and wigs, and upon it stood a small looking-glass. A great basket-box with the lid wide open stood at the end of the room, with a lot of clothes piled up on it, and numerous other garments were hung up upon the walls. A washstand, with a basin full of soapy water, stood under a curtainless window, and there was only one chair to be seen, which Mr. Wopples politely offered to his visitor. Mr. Villiers, however, told him he had brought two gentlemen to introduce to him, at which Mr. Wopples was delighted; and on the introduction taking place, assured both Vandeloup and Barty that it was one of the proudest moments of his life—a stock phrase he always used when introduced to visitors. He was soon ready, and preceded the party out of the room, when he stopped, struck with a sudden idea.

"I have left the gas burning in my dressing-room," he said, in his rolling voice, "and, if you will permit me, gentlemen, I will go back and turn it off."

This was rather difficult to manage, inasmuch as the stairs were narrow, and three people being between Mr. Wopples and his dressing-room, he could not squeeze past.

Finally the difficulty was settled by Villiers, who was last, and who went back and turned out the gas.

When he came down he found Mr. Wopples waiting for him.

"I thank you, sir," he said, grandly, "and will feel honoured if you will give me the pleasure of your company at a modest supper consisting principally of cold beef and pickles."

Of course, they all expressed themselves delighted, and as the entire Wopples family had already gone to their hotel, Mr. Wopples with his three guests went out of the theatre and wended their way towards the same place, only dropping into two or three bars on the way to have drinks at Barty's expense.

They soon arrived at the hotel, and having entered, Mr. Wopples pushed open the door of a room from whence the sound of laughter proceeded, and introduced the three strangers to his family. The whole ten, together with Mrs. Wopples, were present, and were seated around a large table plentifully laden with cold beef and pickles, salads, bottles of beer, and other things too numerous to mention. Mr. Wopples presented them first to his wife, a faded, washed-out looking lady, with a perpetual simper on her face, and clad in a lavender muslin gown with ribbons of the same description, she looked wonderfully light and airy. In fact she had a sketchy appearance as if she required to be touched up here and there, to make her appear solid, which was of great service to her in her theatrical career, as it enabled her to paint on the background of herself any character she wished to represent.

"This," said Mr. Wopples in his deep voice, holding his wife's hand as if he were afraid she would float upward thro' the ceiling like a bubble—a not unlikely thing seeing how remarkably ethereal she looked; "this is my flutterer."

Why he called her his flutterer no one ever knew, unless it was because her ribbons were incessantly fluttering; but, had he called her his shadow, the name would have been more appropriate.

Mrs. Wopples fluttered down to the ground in a bow, and then fluttered up again.

"Gentlemen," she said, in a thin, clear voice, "you are welcome. Did you enjoy the performance?"

"Madame," returned Vandeloup, with a smile, "need you ask that?"

A shadowy smile floated over Mrs. Wopples' indistinct features, and then her husband introduced the rest of the family in a bunch.

"Gentlemen," he said, waving his hand to the expectant ten, who stood in a line of five male and five female, "the celebrated Wopples family."

The ten all simultaneously bowed at this as if they were worked by machinery, and then everyone sat down to supper, Mr. Theodore Wopples taking the head of the table. All the family seemed to admire him immensely, and kept their eyes fastened on his face with affectionate regard.

"Pa," whispered Miss Siddons Wopples to Villiers, who sat next to her, "is a most wonderful man. Observe his facial expression."

Villiers observed it, and admitted also in a whisper that it was truly marvellous.

Cold beef formed the staple viand on the table, and everyone did full justice to it, as also to beer and porter, of which Mr. Wopples was very generous.

"I prefer to give my friends good beer instead of bad champagne," he said, pompously. "Ha! ha! the antithesis, I think, is good."

The Wopples family unanimously agreed that it was excellent, and Mr. Handel Wopples observed to Barty that his father often made jokes worthy of Tom Hood, to which Barty agreed hastily, as he did not know who Tom Hood was, and besides was flirting in a mild manner with Miss Fanny Wopples, a pretty girl, who did the burlesque business.

"And are all these big boys and girls yours, Madame?" asked Vandeloup, who was rather astonished at the number of the family, and thought some of them might have been hired for theatrical purposes. Mrs. Wopples nodded affirmatively with a gratified flutter, and her husband endorsed it.

"There are four dead," he said, in a solemn voice. "Rest their souls."

All the ten faces round the board reflected the gloom on the parental countenance, and for a few moments no one spoke.

"This," said Mr. Wopples, looking round with a smile, at which all the other faces lighted up, "this is not calculated to make our supper enjoyable, children. I may tell you that, in consequence of the great success of 'The Cruet Stand', we play it again to-morrow night."

"Ah!" said Mr. Buckstone Wopples, with his mouth full, "I knew it would knock 'em; that business of yours, father, with the writ is simply wonderful."

All the family chorused "Yes," and Mr. Wopples admitted, with a modest smile, that it was wonderful.

"Practise," said Mr. Wopples, waving a fork with a piece of cold beef at the end of it, "makes perfect. My dear Vandeloup, if you will permit me to call you so, my son Buckstone is truly a wonderful critic."

Vandeloup smiled at this, and came to the conclusion that the Wopples family was a mutual admiration society. However, as it was now nearly twelve o'clock, he rose to take his leave.

"Oh, you're not going yet," said Mr. Wopples, upon which all the family echoed, "Surely, not yet," in a most hospitable manner.

"I must," said Vandeloup, with a smile. "I know Madame will excuse me," with a bow to Mrs. Wopples, who thereupon fluttered nervously; "but I have to be up very early in the morning."

"In that case," said Mr. Wopples, rising, "I will not detain you; early to bed and early to rise, you know; not that I believe in it much myself, but I understand it is practised with good results by some people."

Vandeloup shook hands with Mr. and Mrs. Wopples, but feeling unequal to taking leave of the ten star artistes in the same way, he bowed in a comprehensive manner, whereupon the whole ten arose from their chairs and bowed unanimously in return.

"Good night, Messrs Villiers and Jarper," said Vandeloup, going out of the door, "I will see you to-morrow."

"And we also, I hope," said Mr. Wopples, ungrammatically. "Come and see 'The Cruet Stand' again. I'll put your name on the free list."

M. Vandeloup thanked the actor warmly for this kind offer, and took himself off; as he passed along the street he heard a burst of laughter from the Wopples family, no doubt caused by some witticism of the head of the clan.

He walked slowly home to the hotel, smoking a cigarette, and thinking deeply. When he arrived at the "Wattle Tree" he saw a light still burning in the bar, and, on knocking at the door, was admitted by Miss Twexby, who had been making up accounts, and whose virgin head was adorned with curl-papers.

"My!" said this damsel, when she saw him, "you are a nice young man coming home at this hour—twelve o'clock. See?" and, as a proof of her assertion, she pointed to the clock.

"Were you waiting up for me, dear?" asked Vandeloup, audaciously.

"Not I," retorted Miss Twexby, tossing her curl-papers; "I've been attending to par's business; but, oh, gracious!" with a sudden recollection of her head-gear, "you've seen me in undress."

"And you look more charming than ever," finished Vandeloup, as he took his bedroom candle from her. "I will see you in the morning. My friend still asleep, I suppose?"

"I'm sure I don't know. I haven't seen him all the evening," replied Miss Twexby, tossing her head, "now, go away. You're a naughty, wicked, deceitful thing. I declare I'm quite afraid of you."

"There's no need, I assure you," replied Vandeloup, in a slightly sarcastic voice, as he surveyed the plain-looking woman before him; "you are quite safe from me."

He left the bar, whistling an air, while the fair Martha returned to her accounts, and wondered indignantly whether his last remark was a compliment or otherwise.

The conclusion she came to was that it was otherwise, and she retired to bed in a very wrathful frame of mind.

XIV

A Mysterious Disappearance

Madame Midas, as may be easily guessed, did not pass a very pleasant night after the encounter with Villiers. Her head was very painful with the blow he had given her, and added to this she was certain she had killed him.

Though she hated the man who had ruined her life, and who had tried to rob her, still she did not care about becoming his murderess, and the thought was madness to her. Not that she was afraid of punishment, for she had only acted in self-defence, and Villiers, not she, was the aggressor.

Meanwhile she waited to hear if the body had been found, for ill news travels fast; and as everyone knew Villiers was her husband, she was satisfied that when the corpse was found she would be the first to be told about it.

But the day wore on, and no news came, so she asked Archie to go into Ballarat and see if the discovery had been made.

"'Deed, mem," said Archie, in a consoling tone, "I'm thinkin' there's na word at all. Maybe ye only stapped his pranks for a wee bit, and he's a' richt."

Madame shook her head.

"I gave him such a terrible blow," she said, mournfully, "and he fell like a stone over the embankment."

"He didna leave go the nugget, onyhow, ye ken," said Archie, dryly; "so he couldna hae been verra far gone, but I'll gang intil the toun and see what I can hear."

There was no need for this, however, for just as McIntosh got to the door, Vandeloup, cool and complacent, sauntered in, but stopped short at the sight of Mrs. Villiers sitting in the arm-chair looking so ill.

"My dear Madame," he cried in dismay, going over to her, "what is the matter with you?"

"Matter enow," growled McIntosh, with his hand on the door handle; "that deil o' a' husband o' her's has robbed her o' the nugget."

"Yes, and I killed him," said Madame between her clenched teeth.

"The deuce you did," said Vandeloup, in surprise, taking a seat, "then he was the liveliest dead man I ever saw."

"What do you mean?" asked Madame, leaning forward, with both hands gripping the arms of her chair; "is—is he alive?"

"Of course he is," began Vandeloup; "I—" but here he was stopped by a cry from Selina, for her mistress had fallen back in her chair in a dead faint.

Hastily waving for the men to go away, she applied remedies, and Madame soon revived. Vandeloup had gone outside with McIntosh, and was asking him about the robbery, and then told him in return about Villiers' movements on that night. Selina called them in again, as Madame wanted to hear all about her husband, and Vandeloup was just entering when he turned to McIntosh.

"Oh, by the way," he said, in a vexed tone, "Pierre will not be at work today."

"What for no?" asked McIntosh, sharply.

"He's drunk," replied Vandeloup, curtly, "and he's likely to keep the game up for a week."

"We'll see about that," said Mr. McIntosh, wrathfully; "I tauld yon gowk o' a Twexby to give the mon food and drink, but I didna tell him to mack the deil fu'."

"It wasn't the landlord's fault," said Vandeloup; "I gave Pierre money—if I had known what he wanted it for I wouldn't have done it—but it's too late now."

McIntosh was about to answer sharply as to the folly of giving the man money, when Madame's voice was heard calling them impatiently, and they both had to go in at once.

Mrs. Villiers was ghastly pale, but there was a look of determination about her which showed that she was anxious to hear all. Pointing to a seat near herself she said to Vandeloup—

"Tell me everything that happened from the time I left you last night."

"My faith," replied Vandeloup, carelessly taking the seat, "there isn't much to tell—I said goodbye to Monsieur Marchurst and Mademoiselle Kitty and went down to Ballarat."

"How was it you did not pass me on the way?" asked Madame, quickly fixing her piercing eyes on him. "I drove slowly."

He bore her scrutiny without blenching or even changing colour.

"Easily enough," he said, calmly, "I went the other direction instead of the usual way, as it was the shortest route to the place I was stopping at."

"The 'Wattle Tree', ye ken, Madame," interposed McIntosh.

"I had something to eat there," pursued Vandeloup, "and then went to the theatre. Your husband came in towards the end of the performance and sat next to me."

"Was he all right?" asked Mrs. Villiers, eagerly.

Vandeloup shrugged his shoulders.

"I didn't pay much attention to him," he said, coolly; "he seemed to enjoy the play, and afterwards, when we went to supper with the actors, he certainly ate very heartily for a dead man. I don't think you need trouble yourself, Madame; your husband is quite well."

"What time did you leave him?" she asked, after a pause.

"About twenty minutes to twelve, I think," replied Vandeloup, "at least, I reached the 'Wattle Tree' at about twelve o'clock, and I think it did take twenty minutes to walk there. Monsieur Villiers stopped behind with the theatre people to enjoy himself."

Enjoying himself, and she, thinking him dead, was crying over his miserable end; it was infamous! Was this man a monster who could thus commit a crime one moment and go to an amusement the next? It seemed like it, and Mrs. Villiers felt intense disgust towards her husband as she sat with tightly clenched hands and dry eyes listening to Vandeloup's recital.

"Weel," said Mr. McIntosh at length, rubbing his scanty hair, "the deil looks after his ain, as we read in Screepture, and this child of Belial is flourishing like a green bay tree by mony waters; but we ma' cut it doon an' lay an axe at the root thereof."

"And how do you propose to chop him down?" asked Vandeloup, flippantly.

"Pit him intil the Tolbooth for rinnin' awa' wi' the nugget," retorted Mr. McIntosh, vindictively.

"A very sensible suggestion," said Gaston, approvingly, smoothing his moustache. "What do you say, Madame?"

She shook her head.

"Let him keep his ill-gotten gains," she said, resignedly. "Now that he has obtained what he wanted, perhaps he'll leave me alone; I will do nothing."

"Dae naethin'!" echoed Archie, in great wrath. "Will ye let that freend o' Belzibub rin awa' wid a three hun'red ounces of gold an' dae naethin'? Na, na, ye mauna dae it, I tell ye. Oh, aye, ye may sit there, mem, and glower awa' like a boggle, but ye aren'a gangin' to make yoursel' a martyr for yon. Keep the nugget? I'll see him damned first."

This was the first time that Archie had ever dared to cross Mrs. Villiers' wishes, and she stared in amazement at the unwonted spectacle. This time, however, McIntosh found an unexpected ally in Vandeloup, who urged that Villiers should be prosecuted.

"He is not only guilty of robbery, Madame," said the young Frenchman, "but also of an attempt to murder you, and while he is allowed to go free, your life is not safe."

Selina also contributed her mite of wisdom in the form of a proverb:—

"A stitch in time saves nine," intimating thereby that Mr. Villiers should be locked up and never let out again, in case he tried the same game on with the next big nugget found.

Madame thought for a few moments, and, seeing that they were all unanimous, she agreed to the proposal that Villiers should be prosecuted, with the stipulation, however, that he should be first written to and asked to give up the nugget. If he did, and promised to leave the district, no further steps would be taken; but if he declined to do so, his wife would prosecute him with the uttermost rigour of the law. Then Madame dismissed them, as she was anxious to get a little sleep, and Vandeloup went to the office to write the letter, accompanied by McIntosh, who wanted to assist in its composition.

Meanwhile there was another individual in Ballarat who was much interested in Villiers, and this kind-hearted gentleman was none other than Slivers. Villiers was accustomed to come and sit in his office every morning, and talk to him about things in general, and the Pactolus claim in particular. On this morning, however, he did not arrive, and Slivers was much annoyed thereat. He determined to give Villiers a piece of his mind when he did see him. He went about his business at "The Corner", bought some shares, sold others, and swindled as many people as he was able, then came back to his office and waited in all the afternoon for his friend, who, however, did not come.

Slivers was just going out to seek him when the door of his office was violently flung open, and a tall, raw-boned female entered in a very excited manner. Dressed in a dusty black gown, with a crape bonnet placed askew on her rough hair, this lady banged on Slivers' table a huge umbrella and demanded where Villiers was.

"I don't know," snapped Slivers, viciously; "how the devil should I?"

"Don't swear at me, you wooden-legged little monster," cried the virago, with another bang of the umbrella, which raised such a cloud of dust that it nearly made Slivers sneeze his head off. "He ain't been home all night, and you've been leading him into bad habits, you cork-armed libertine."

"Hasn't been home all night, eh?" said Slivers, sitting up quickly, while Billy, who had been considerably alarmed at the gaunt female, retired to the fireplace, and tried to conceal himself up the chimney. "May I ask who you are?"

"You may," said the angry lady, folding her arms and holding the umbrella in such an awkward manner that she nearly poked Slivers' remaining eye out.

"Well, who are you?" snapped Slivers, crossly, after waiting a reasonable time for an answer and getting none.

"I'm his landlady," retorted the other, with a defiant snort. "Matilda Cheedle is my name, and I don't care who knows it."

"It's not a pretty name," snarled Slivers, prodding the ground with his wooden leg, as he always did when angry. "Neither are you. What do you mean by banging into my office like an insane giraffe?"—this in allusion to Mrs. Cheedle's height.

"Oh, go on! go on!" said that lady defiantly; "I've heard it all before; I'm used to it; but here I sit until you tell me where my lodger is;" and suiting the action to the word, Mrs. Cheedle sat down in a chair with such a bang that Billy gave a screech of alarm and said, "Pickles!"

"Pickles, you little bag of bones!" cried Mrs. Cheedle, who thought that the word had proceeded from Slivers, "don't you call me 'Pickles'—but I'm used to it. I'm a lonely woman since Cheedle went to the cemetery, and I'm always being insulted. Oh, my nerves are shattered under such treatment"—this last because she saw the whisky bottle on the table, and thought she might get some.

Slivers took the hint, and filling a glass with whisky and water passed it to her, and Mrs. Cheedle, with many protestations that she never touched spirits, drank it to the last drop.

"Was Villiers always in the habit of coming home?" he asked.

"Always," replied Mrs. Cheedle; "he's bin with me eighteen months and never stopped out one night; if he had," grimly, "I'd have known the reason of his rampagin'."

"Strange," said Slivers, thoughtfully, fixing Mrs. Cheedle with his one eye; "when did you see him last?"

"About three o'clock yesterday," said Mrs. Cheedle, looking sadly at a hole in one of her cotton gloves; "his conduct was most extraordinary;

he came home at that unusual hour, changed his linen clothes for a dark suit, and, after he had eaten something, put on another hat, and walked off with a stick under his arm."

"And you've never seen him since?"

"Not a blessed sight of him," replied Mrs. Cheedle; "you don't think any harm's come to him, sir? Not as I care much for him—the drunken wretch—but still he's a lodger and owes me rent, so I don't know but what he might be off to Melbourne without paying, and leaving his boxes full of bricks behind."

"I'll have a look round, and if I see him I'll send him home," said Slivers, rising to intimate the interview was at end.

"Very well, mind you do," said the widow, rising and putting the empty glass on the table, "send him home at once and I'll speak to him. And perhaps," with a bashful glance, "you wouldn't mind seeing me up the street a short way, as I'm alone and unprotected."

"Stuff!" retorted Slivers, ungraciously, "there's plenty of light, and you are big enough to look after yourself."

At this Mrs. Cheedle snorted loudly like a war-horse, and flounced out of the office in a rage, after informing Slivers in a loud voice that he was a selfish, cork-eyed little viper, from which confusion of words it will easily be seen that the whisky had taken effect on the good lady.

When she had gone Slivers locked up his office, and sallied forth to find the missing Villiers, but though he went all over town to that gentleman's favourite haunts, mostly bars, yet he could see nothing of him; and on making inquiries heard that he had not been seen in Ballarat all day. This was so contrary to Villiers' general habits that Slivers became suspicious, and as he walked home thinking over the subject he came to the conclusion there was something up.

"If," said Slivers, pausing on the pavement and addressing a street lamp, "he doesn't turn up to-morrow I'll have a look for him again. If that don't do I'll tell the police, and I shouldn't wonder," went on Slivers, musingly, "I shouldn't wonder if they called on Madame Midas."

XV

Slivers in Search of Evidence

S livers was puzzled over Villiers' disappearance, so he determined to go in search of evidence against Madame Midas, though for what reason he wanted evidence against her no one but himself—and perhaps Billy—knew. But then Slivers always was an enigma regarding his reasons for doing things, and even the Sphinx would have found him a difficult riddle to solve.

The reasons he had for turning detective were simply these: It soon became known that Madame Midas had been robbed by her husband of the famous nugget, and great was the indignation of everyone against Mr. Villiers. That gentleman would have fared very badly if he had made his appearance, but for some reason or another he did not venture forth. In fact, he had completely disappeared, and where he was no one knew. The last person who saw him was Barty Jarper, who left him at the corner of Lydiard and Sturt Streets, when Mr. Villiers had announced his intention of going home. Mrs. Cheedle, however, asserted positively that she had never set eyes on him since the time she stated to Slivers, and as it was now nearly two weeks since he had disappeared things were beginning to look serious. The generally received explanation was that he had bolted with the nugget, but as he could hardly dispose of such a large mass of gold without suspicion, and as the police both in Ballarat and Melbourne had made inquiries, which proved futile, this theory began to lose ground.

It was at this period that Slivers asserted himself—coming forward, he hinted in an ambiguous sort of way that Villiers had met with foul play, and that some people had their reasons for wishing to get rid of him. This was clearly an insinuation against Madame Midas, but everyone refused to believe such an impossible story, so Slivers determined to make good his words, and went in search of evidence.

The Wopples Family having left Ballarat, Slivers was unable to see Mr. Theodore Wopples, who had been in Villiers' company on the night of his disappearance.

Mr. Barty Jarper, however, had not yet departed, so Slivers waylaid him, and asked him in a casual way to drop into his office and have a drink, with a view of finding out from him all the events of that night.

Barty was on his way to a lawn tennis party, and was arrayed in a flannel suit of many colours, with his small, white face nearly hidden under a large straw hat. Being of a social turn of mind, he did not refuse Slivers' invitation, but walked into the dusty office and assisted himself liberally to the whisky.

"Here's fun, old cock!" he said, in a free and easy manner, raising his glass to his lips; "may your shadow never be less."

Slivers hoped devoutly that his shadow never would be less, as that would involve the loss of several other limbs, which he could ill spare; so he honoured Mr. Jarper's toast with a rasping little laugh, and prepared to talk.

"It's very kind of you to come and talk to an old chap like me," said Slivers, in as amiable a tone as he could command, which was not much. "You're such a gay young fellow!"

Mr. Jarper acknowledged modestly that he was gay, but that he owed certain duties to society, and had to be mildly social.

"And so handsome!" croaked Slivers, winking with his one eye at Billy, who sat on the table. "Oh, he's all there, ain't he, Billy?"

Billy, however, did not agree to this, and merely observed "Pickles," in a disbelieving manner.

Mr. Jarper felt rather overcome by this praise, and blushed in a modest way, but felt that he could not return the compliment with any degree of truth, as Slivers was not handsome, neither was he all there.

He, however, decided that Slivers was an unusually discerning person, and worthy to talk to, so prepared to make himself agreeable.

Slivers, who had thus gained the goodwill of the young man by flattery, plunged into the subject of Villiers' disappearance.

"I wonder what's become of Villiers," he said, artfully pushing the whisky bottle toward Barty.

"I'm sure I don't know," said Barty in a languid, used-up sort of voice, pouring himself out some more whisky, "I haven't seen him since last Monday week."

"Where did you leave him on that night?" asked Slivers.

"At the corner of Sturt and Lydiard Streets."

"Early in the morning, I suppose?"

"Yes—pretty early—about two o'clock, I think."

"And you never saw him after that?"

"Not a sight of him," replied Barty; "but, I say, why all this thusness?"

"I'll tell you after you have answered my questions," retorted Slivers, rudely, "but I'm not asking out of curiosity—its business."

Barty thought that Slivers was very peculiar, but determined to humour him, and to take his leave as early as possible.

"Well, go on," he said, drinking his whisky, "I'll answer."

"Who else was with you and Villiers on that night?" asked Slivers in a magisterial kind of manner.

"A French fellow called Vandeloup."

"Vandeloup!" echoed Slivers in surprise; "oh, indeed! what the devil was he doing?"

"Enjoying himself," replied Barty, coolly; "he came into the theatre and Villiers introduced him to me; then Mr. Wopples asked us all to supper."

"You went, of course?"

"Rather, old chap; what do you take us for?"—this from Barty, with a knowing wink.

"What time did Vandeloup leave?" asked Slivers, not paying any attention to Barty's pantomime.

"About twenty minutes to twelve."

"Oh! I suppose that was because he had to drive out to the Pactolus?"

"Not such a fool, dear boy; he stayed all night in town."

"Oh!" exclaimed Slivers, in an excited manner, drumming on the table with his fingers, "where did he stay?"

"At the Wattle Tree Hotel."

Slivers mentally made a note of this, and determined to go there and find out at what time Vandeloup had come home on the night in question, for this suspicious old man had now got it into his head that Vandeloup was in some way responsible for Villiers' disappearance.

"Where did Villiers say he was going when he left you?" he asked.

"Straight home."

"Humph! Well, he didn't go home at all."

"Didn't he?" echoed Barty, in some astonishment. "Then what's become of him? Men don't disappear in this mysterious way without some reason."

"Ah, but there is a reason," replied Slivers, bending across the table and clawing at the papers thereon with the lean fingers of his one hand.

"Why! what do you think is the reason?" faltered Barty, letting his eye-glass drop out of his eye, and edging his chair further away from this terrible old man.

"Murder!" hissed the other through his thin lips. "He's been murdered!"

"Lord!" exclaimed Barty, jumping up from his chair in alarm; "you're going too far, old chap."

"I'm going further," retorted Slivers, rising from his chair and stumping up and down the room; "I'm going to find out who did it, and then I'll grind her to powder; I'll twist her neck off, curse her."

"Is it a woman?" asked Barty, who now began to think of making a retreat, for Slivers, with his one eye blazing, and his cork arm swinging rapidly to and fro, was not a pleasant object to contemplate.

This unguarded remark recalled Slivers to himself.

"That's what I want to find out," he replied, sulkily, going back to his chair. "Have some more whisky?"

"No, thanks," answered Barty, going to the door, "I'm late as it is for my engagement; ta, ta, old chap, I hope you'll drop on the he or she you're looking for; but you're quite wrong, Villiers has bolted with the nugget, and that's a fact, sir," and with an airy wave of his hand Barty went out, leaving Slivers in anything but a pleasant temper.

"Bah! you peacock," cried this wicked old man, banging his wooden leg against the table, "you eye-glass idiot—you brainless puppy—I'm wrong, am I? we'll see about that, you rag-shop." This last in allusion to Barty's picturesque garb. "I've found out all I want from you, and I'll track her down, and put her in gaol, and hang her—hang her till she's as dead as a door nail."

Having given vent to this pleasant sentiment, Slivers put on his hat, and, taking his stick, walked out of his office, but not before Billy saw his intention and had climbed up to his accustomed place on the old man's shoulder. So Slivers stumped along the street, with the cockatoo on his shoulder, looking like a depraved Robinson Crusoe, and took his way to the Wattle Tree Hotel.

"If," argued Slivers to himself, as he pegged bravely along, "if Villiers wanted to get rid of the nugget he'd have come to me, for he knew I'd keep quiet and tell no tales. Well, he didn't come to me, and there's no one else he could go to. They've been looking for him all over the shop, and they can't find him; he can't be hiding or he'd have let me know; there's only one explanation—he's been murdered—but not for the gold—oh, dear no—for nobody knew he had it. Who wanted him out of the way?—his wife. Would she stick at anything?—I'm damned if she would. So it's her work. The only question is did she do it personally or by deputy. I say deputy, 'cause she'd be too squeamish to do it herself.

Who would she select as deputy?—Vandeloup! Why?—'cause he'd like to marry her for her money. Yes, I'm sure it's him. Things look black against him: he stayed in town all night, a thing he never did before—leaves the supper at a quarter to twelve, so as to avoid suspicion; waits till Villiers comes out at two in the morning and kills him. Aha! my handsome jackadandy," cried Slivers, viciously, suddenly stopping and shaking his stick at an imaginary Vandeloup; "I've got you under my thumb, and I'll crush the life out of you—and of her also, if I can;" and with this amiable resolution Slivers resumed his way.

Slivers' argument was plausible, but there were plenty of flaws in it, which, however, he did not stop to consider, so carried away was he by his anger against Madame Midas. He stumped along doggedly, revolving the whole affair in his mind, and by the time he arrived at the Wattle Tree Hotel he had firmly persuaded himself that Villiers was dead, and that Vandeloup had committed the crime at the instigation of Mrs. Villiers.

He found Miss Twexby seated in the bar, with a decidedly cross face, which argued ill for anyone who held converse with her that day; but as Slivers was quite as crabbed as she was, and, moreover, feared neither God nor man—much less a woman—he tackled her at once.

"Where's your father?" he asked, abruptly, leaning on his stick and looking intently at the fair Martha's vinegary countenance.

"Asleep!" snapped that damsel, jerking her head in the direction of the parlour; "what do you want?"—very disdainfully.

"A little civility in the first place," retorted Slivers, rudely, sitting down on a bench that ran along the wall, and thereby causing his wooden leg to stick straight out, which, being perceived by Billy, he descended from the old man's shoulder and turned the leg into a perch, where he sat and swore at Martha.

"You wicked old wretch," said Miss Twexby, viciously—her nose getting redder with suppressed excitement—"go along with you, and take that irreligious parrot with you, or I'll wake my par."

"He won't thank you for doing so," replied Slivers, coolly; "I've called to see him about some new shares just on the market, and if you don't treat me with more respect I'll go, and he'll be out of a good thing."

Now, Miss Twexby knew that Slivers was in the habit of doing business with her parent, and, moreover was a power in the share market, so she did not deem it diplomatic to go too far, and bottling up her wrath for a future occasion, when no loss would be involved, she graciously asked Slivers what he'd be pleased to have.

"Whisky," said Slivers, curtly, leaning his chin on his stick, and following her movements with his one eye. "I say!"

"Well?" asked Miss Twexby, coming from behind the bar with a glass and a bottle of whisky, "what do you say?"

"How's that good-looking Frenchman?" asked Slivers, pouring himself out some liquor, and winking at her in a rakish manner with his one eye.

"How should I know?" snapped Martha, angrily, "he comes here to see that friend of his, and then clears out without as much as a good day; a nice sort of friend, indeed," wrathfully, "stopping here nearly two weeks and drunk all the time; he'll be having delirious trimmings before he's done."

"Who wills?" said Slivers, taking a sip of his whisky and water.

"Why, that other Frenchman!" retorted Martha, going to her place behind the bar, "Peter something; a low, black wretch, all beard, with no tongue, and a thirst like a lime-kiln."

"Oh, the dumb man."

Miss Twexby nodded.

"That's him," she said, triumphantly, "he's been here for the last two weeks."

"Drunk, I think you said," remarked Slivers, politely.

Martha laughed scornfully, and took out some sewing.

"I should just think so," she retorted, tossing her head, "he does nothing but drink all day, and run after people with that knife."

"Very dangerous," observed Slivers, gravely shaking his head; "why don't you get rid of him?"

"So we are," said Miss Twexby, biting off a bit of cotton, as if she wished it were Pierre's head; "he is going down to Melbourne the day after to-morrow."

Slivers got weary of hearing about Pierre, and plunged right off into the object of his visit.

"That Vandeloup," he began.

"Well?" said Miss Twexby, letting the work fall on her lap.

"What time did he come home the night he stopped here?"

"Twelve o'clock."

"Get along with you," said Slivers, in disgust, "you mean three o'clock."

"No, I don't," retorted Martha, indignantly; "you'll be telling me I don't know the time next."

"Did he go out again?

"No, he went to bed."

This quite upset Slivers' idea—as if Vandeloup had gone to bed at twelve, he certainly could not have murdered Villiers nearly a mile away at two o'clock in the morning. Slivers was puzzled, and then the light broke on him—perhaps it was the dumb man.

"Did the other stay here all night also?"

Miss Twexby nodded. "Both in the same room," she answered.

"What time did the dumb chap come in?"

"Half-past nine."

Here was another facer for Slivers—as it could not have been Pierre.

"Did he go to bed?"

"Straight."

"And did not leave the house again?"

"Of course not," retorted Miss Twexby, impatiently; "do you think I'm a fool—no one goes either in or out of this house without my knowing it. The dumb devil went to bed at half-past nine, and Mr. Vandeloup at half-past twelve, and they neither of them came out of their rooms till next morning."

"How do you know Vandeloup was in at twelve?" asked Slivers, still unconvinced.

"Drat the man, what's he worryin' about?" rejoined Miss Twexby, snappishly; "I let him in myself."

This clearly closed the subject, and Slivers arose to his feet in great disgust, upsetting Billy on to the floor.

"Devil!" shrieked Billy, as he dropped. "Oh, my precious mother. Devil—devil—devil—you're a liar—you're a liar—Bendigo and Ballarat—Ballarat and Bendigo—Pickles!"

Having thus run through a portion of his vocabulary, he subsided into silence, and let Slivers pick him up in order to go home.

"A nice pair you are," muttered Martha, grimly, looking at them. "I wish I had the thrashing of you. Won't you stay and see par?" she called out as Slivers departed.

"I'll come to-morrow," answered Slivers, angrily, for he felt very much out of temper; then, in a lower voice, he observed to himself, "I'd like to put that jade in a teacup and crush her."

He stumped home in silence, thinking all the time; and it was only when he arrived back in his office that he gave utterance to his thoughts.

"It couldn't have been either of the Frenchmen," he said, lighting his pipe. "She must have done it herself."

XVI

McIntosh Speaks His Mind

It was some time before Mrs. Villiers recovered from the shock caused by her encounter with her husband. The blow he had struck her on the side of the head turned out to be more serious than was at first anticipated, and Selina deemed it advisable that a doctor should be called in. So Archie went into Ballarat, and returned to the Pactolus with Dr. Gollipeck, an eccentric medical practitioner, whose peculiarities were the talk of the city.

Dr. Gollipeck was tall and lank, with an unfinished look about him, as if Nature in some sudden freak had seized an incomplete skeleton from a museum and hastily covered it with parchment. He dressed in rusty black, wore dingy cotton gloves, carried a large white umbrella, and surveyed the world through the medium of a pair of huge spectacles. His clothes were constantly coming undone, as he scorned the use of buttons, and preferred pins, which were always scratching his hands. He spoke very little, and was engaged in composing an erudite work on "The Art of Poisoning, from Borgia to Brinvilliers".

Selina was not at all impressed with his appearance, and mentally decided that a good wash and a few buttons would improve him wonderfully. Dr. Gollipeck, however, soon verified the adage that appearances are deceptive—as Selina afterwards remarked to Archie—by bringing Madame Midas back to health in a wonderfully short space of time. She was now convalescent, and, seated in the arm-chair by the window, looked dreamily at the landscape. She was thinking of her husband, and in what manner he would annoy her next; but she half thought—and the wish was father to the half thought—that having got the nugget he would now leave her alone.

She knew that he had not been in Ballarat since that fatal night when he had attacked her, but imagined that he was merely hiding till such time as the storm should blow over and he could enjoy his ill-gotten gains in safety. The letter asking him to give up the nugget and ordering him to leave the district under threat of prosecution had been sent to his lodgings, but was still lying there unopened. The letters accumulated into quite a little pile as weeks rolled on, yet Mr. Villiers, if he was alive, made no sign, and if he was dead, no traces had been found of his body. McIntosh and Slivers had both seen the police about the affair, one in order to recover the nugget, the other actuated by bitter enmity against Madame Midas. To Slivers' hints, that perhaps Villiers' wife knew more than she chose to tell, the police turned a deaf ear, as they assured Slivers that they had made inquiries, and on the authority of Selina and McIntosh could safely say that Madame Midas had been home that night at half-past nine o'clock, whereas Villiers was still alive in Ballarat—as could be proved by the evidence of Mr. Jarper—at two o'clock in the morning. So, foiled on every side in his endeavours to implicate Mrs. Villiers in her husband's disappearance, Slivers retired to his office, and, assisted by his ungodly cockatoo, passed many hours in swearing at his bad luck and in cursing the absent Villiers.

As to M. Vandeloup, he was indefatigable in his efforts to find Villiers, for, as he very truly said, he could never repay Madame Midas sufficiently for her kindness to him, and he wanted to do all in his power to punish her cruel husband. But in spite of all this seeking, the whereabouts of Mr. Randolph Villiers remained undiscovered, and at last, in despair, everyone gave up looking. Villiers had disappeared entirely, and had taken the nugget with him, so where he was and what he was doing remained a mystery.

One result of Madame's illness was that M. Vandeloup had met Dr. Gollipeck, and the two, though apparently dissimilar in both character and appearance, had been attracted to one another by a liking which they had in common. This was the study of toxicology, a science at which the eccentric old man had spent a lifetime. He found in Vandeloup a congenial spirit, for the young Frenchman had a wonderful liking for the uncanny subject; but there was a difference in the aims of both men, Gollipeck being drawn to the study of poisons from a pure love of the subject, whereas Vandeloup wanted to find out the secrets of toxicology for his own ends, which were anything but disinterested.

Wearied of the dull routine of the office work, Vandeloup was taking a walk in the meadows which surrounded the Pactolus, when he saw Dr. Gollipeck shuffling along the dusty white road from the railway station.

"Good day, Monsieur le Medecin," said Vandeloup, gaily, as he came up to the old man; "are you going to see our mutual friend?"

Gollipeck, ever sparing of words, nodded in reply, and trudged on in silence, but the Frenchmen, being used to the eccentricities of his companion, was in nowise offended at his silence, but went on talking in an animated manner.

"Ah, my dear friend," he said, pushing his straw hat back on his fair head; "how goes on the great work?"

"Capitally," returned the doctor, with a complacent smile; "just finished 'Catherine de Medici'—wonderful woman, sir—quite a mistress of the art of poisoning."

"Humph," returned Vandeloup, thoughtfully, lighting a cigarette, "I do not agree with you there; it was her so-called astrologer, Ruggieri, who prepared all her potions. Catherine certainly had the power, but Ruggieri possessed the science—a very fair division of labour for getting rid of people, I must say—but what have you got there?" nodding towards a large book which Gollipeck carried under his arm.

"For you," answered the other, taking the book slowly from under his arm, and thereby causing another button to fly off, "quite new,—work on toxicology."

"Thank you," said Vandeloup, taking the heavy volume and looking at the title; "French, I see! I'm sure it will be pleasant reading."

The title of the book was "Les Empoisonneurs d'Aujourd'hui, par Mм. Prevol et Lebrun", and it had only been published the previous year; so as he turned over the leaves carelessly, M. Vandeloup caught sight of a name which he knew. He smiled a little, and closing the book put it under his arm, while he turned smilingly towards his companion, whom he found looking keenly at him.

"I shall enjoy this book immensely," he said, touching the volume. Dr. Gollipeck nodded and chuckled in a hoarse rattling kind of way.

"So I should think," he answered, with another sharp look, "you are a very clever young man, my friend."

Vandeloup acknowledged the compliment with a bow, and wondered mentally what this old man meant. Gaston, however, was never without an answer, so he turned to Gollipeck again with a nonchalant smile on his handsome lips.

"So kind of you to think well of me," he said, coolly flicking the ash off the end of his cigarette with his little finger; "but why do you pay me such a compliment?"

Gollipeck answered the question by asking another.

"Why are you so fond of toxicology?" he said, abruptly, shuffling his feet in the long dry grass in which they were now walking in order to rub the dust off his ungainly, ill-blacked shoes.

Vandeloup shrugged his shoulders.

"To pass the time," he said, carelessly, "that is all; even office work, exciting as it is, becomes wearisome, so I must take up some subject to amuse myself."

"Curious taste for a young man," remarked the doctor, dryly.

"Nature," said M. Vandeloup, "does not form men all on the same pattern, and my taste for toxicology has at least the charm of novelty."

Gollipeck looked at the young man again in a sharp manner.

"I hope you'll enjoy the book," he said, abruptly, and vanished into the house.

When he was gone, the mocking smile so habitual to Vandeloup's countenance faded away, and his face assumed a thoughtful expression. He opened the book, and turned over the leaves rapidly, but without finding what he was in search of. With an uneasy laugh he shut the volume with a snap, and put it under his arm again.

"He's an enigma," he thought, referring to the doctor; "but he can't suspect anything. The case may be in this book, but I doubt if even this man with the barbarous name can connect Gaston Vandeloup, of Ballarat, with Octave Braulard, of Paris."

His face reassumed its usual gay look, and throwing away the half-smoked cigarette, he walked into the house and found Madame Midas seated in her arm-chair near the window looking pale and ill, while Archie was walking up and down in an excited manner, and talking volubly in broad Scotch. As to Dr. Gollipeck, that eccentric individual was standing in front of the fire, looking even more dilapidated than usual, and drying his red bandanna handkerchief in an abstract manner. Selina was in another room getting a drink for Madame, and as Vandeloup entered she came back with it.

"Good day, Madame," said the Frenchman, advancing to the table, and putting his hat and the book down on it. "How are you today?"

"Better, much better, thank you," said Madame, with a faint smile; "the doctor assures me I shall be quite well in a week."

"With perfect rest and quiet, of course," interposed Gollipeck, sitting down and spreading his handkerchief over his knees.

"Which Madame does not seem likely to get," observed Vandeloup, dryly, with a glance at McIntosh, who was still pacing up and down the room with an expression of wrath on his severe face.

"Ou, ay," said that gentleman, stopping in front of Vandeloup, with a fine expression of scorn. "I ken weel 'tis me ye are glowerin' at—div ye no' ken what's the matter wi' me?"

"Not being in your confidence," replied Gaston, smoothly, taking a seat, "I can hardly say that I do."

"It's just that Peter o' yours," said Archie, with a snort; "a puir weecked unbaptised child o' Satan."

"Archie!" interposed Madame, with some severity.

"Your pardon's begged, mem," said Archie, sourly turning to her; "but as for that Peter body, the Lord keep me tongue fra' swearin', an' my hand from itching to gie him ain on the lug, when I think o' him."

"What's he been doing?" asked Vandeloup, coolly. "I am quite prepared to hear anything about him in his present state."

"It's just this," burst forth Archie, wrathfully. "I went intil the toun to the hotel, to tell the body he must come back tae the mine, and I find him no in a fit state for a Christian to speak to."

"Therefore," interposed Vandeloup, in his even voice, without lifting his eyes, "it was a pity you did speak to him."

"I gang t' the room," went on Archie excitedly, without paying any attention to Vandeloup's remark, "an' the deil flew on me wi' a dirk, and wud hae split my weasand, but I hed the sense to bang the door to, and turn the key in the lock. D'y ca' that conduct for a ceevilized body?"

"The fact is, M. Vandeloup," said Madame, quietly, "Archie is so annoyed at this conduct that he does not want Lemaire to come back to work."

"Ma certie, I should just think so," cried McIntosh, rubbing his head with his handkerchief. "Fancy an imp of Beelzebub like yon in the bowels o' the earth. Losh! but it macks my bluid rin cauld when I think o' the bluidthirsty pagan."

To Vandeloup, this information was not unpleasant. He was anxious to get rid of Pierre, who was such an incubus, and now saw that he could send him away without appearing to wish to get rid of him. But as he was a diplomatic young man he did not allow his satisfaction to appear on his face.

"Aren't you rather hard on him?" he said, coolly, leaning back in his chair; "he is simply drunk, and will be all right soon."

"I tell ye I'll no have him back," said Archie, firmly; "he's ain o' they foreign bodies full of revolutions an' confusion o' tongues, and I'd no feel safe i' the mine if I kenned that deil was doon below wi' his dirk."

"I really think he ought to go," said Madame, looking rather anxiously at Vandeloup, "unless, M. Vandeloup, you do not want to part with him."

"Oh, I don't want him," said Vandeloup, hastily; "as I told you, he was only one of the sailors on board the ship I was wrecked in, and he followed me up here because I was the only friend he had, but now he has got money—or, at least, his wages must come to a good amount."

"Forty pounds," interposed Archie.

"So I think the best thing he can do is to go to Melbourne, and see if he can get back to France."

"And you, M. Vandeloup?" asked Dr. Gollipeck, who had been listening to the young Frenchman's remarks with great interest; "do you not wish to go to France?"

Vandeloup rose coolly from his chair, and, picking up his book and hat, turned to the doctor.

"My dear Monsieur," he said, leaning up against the wall in a graceful manner, "I left France to see the world, so until I have seen it I don't think it would be worthwhile to return."

"Never go back when you have once put your hand to the plough," observed Selina, opportunely, upon which Vandeloup bowed to her.

"Mademoiselle," he said, quietly, with a charming smile, "has put the matter into the shell of a nut; Australia is my plough, and I do not take my hand away until I have finished with it."

"But that deil o' a Peter," said Archie, impatiently.

"If you will permit me, Madame," said Vandeloup, "I will write out a cheque for the amount of money due to him, and you will sign it. I will go into Ballarat to-morrow, and get him away to Melbourne. I propose to buy him a box and some clothes, as he certainly is not capable of getting them himself."

"You have a kind heart, M. Vandeloup," said Madame, as she assented with a nod.

A stifled laugh came from the Doctor, but as he was such an extremely eccentric individual no one minded him.

"Come, Monsieur," said Vandeloup, going to the door, "let us be off to the office and see how much is due to my friend," and with a bow to Madame, he went out.

"A braw sort o' freend," muttered Archie, as he followed.

"Quite good enough for him," retorted Dr. Gollipeck, who overheard him.

Archie looked at him approvingly, nodded his head, and went out after the Frenchman, but Madame, being a woman and curious, asked the doctor what he meant.

His reply was peculiar.

"Our friend," he said, putting his handkerchief in his pocket and seizing his greasy old hat, "our friend believes in the greatest number."

"And what is the greatest number?" asked Madame, innocently.

"Number one," retorted the Doctor, and took his leave abruptly, leaving two buttons and several pins on the floor as traces of his visit.

XVII

THE BEST OF FRIENDS MUST PART

U nion is strength, and if Dr. Gollipeck had only met Slivers and revealed his true opinion of Vandeloup to him, no doubt that clever young man would have found himself somewhat embarrassed, as a great deal of a man's past history can be found out by the simple plan of putting two and two together. Fortunately, however, for Gaston, these two gentlemen never met, and Gollipeck came to the conclusion that he could see nothing to blame in Vandeloup's conduct, though he certainly mistrusted him, and determined mentally to keep an eye on his movements. What led him to be suspicious was the curious resemblance the appearance of this young man had to that of a criminal described in the "Les Empoisonneurs d'Aujourd'hui" as having been transported to New Caledonia for the crime of poisoning his mistress. Everything, however, was vague and uncertain; so Dr. Gollipeck, when he arrived home, came to the above-named conclusion that he would watch Vandeloup, and then, dismissing him from his mind, went to work on his favourite subject.

Meanwhile, M. Vandeloup slept the sleep of the just, and next morning, after making his inquiries after the health of Madame Midas—a thing he never neglected to do—he went into Ballarat in search of Pierre. On arriving at the Wattle Tree Hotel he was received by Miss Twexby in dignified silence, for that astute damsel was beginning to regard the fascinating Frenchman as a young man who talked a great deal and meant nothing.

He was audacious enough to win her virgin heart and then break it, so Miss Twexby thought the wisest thing would be to keep him at a distance. So Vandeloup's bright smiles and merry jokes failed to call forth any response from the fair Martha, who sat silently in the bar, looking like a crabbed sphinx.

"Is my friend Pierre in?" asked Vandeloup, leaning across the counter, and looking lovingly at Miss Twexby.

That lady intimated coldly that he was in, and had been for the last two weeks; also that she was sick of him, and she'd thank M. Vandeloup to clear him out—all of which amused Vandeloup mightily, though he still continued to smile coolly on the sour-faced damsel before him.

"Would you mind going and telling him I want to see him?" he asked, lounging to the door.

"Me!" shrieked Martha, in a shrill voice, shooting up from behind the counter like an infuriated jack-in-the-box. "No, I shan't. Why, the last time I saw him he nearly cut me like a ham sandwich with that knife of his. I am not," pursued Miss Twexby, furiously, "a loaf of bread to be cut, neither am I a pin-cushion to have things stuck into me; so if you want to be a corpse, you'd better go up yourself."

"I hardly think he'll touch me," replied Vandeloup, coolly, going towards the door which led to Pierre's bedroom. "You've had a lot of trouble with him, I'm afraid; but he's going down to Melbourne tonight, so it will be all right."

"And the bill?" queried Miss Twexby, anxiously.

"I will pay it," said Vandeloup, at which she was going to say he was very generous, but suppressed the compliment when he added, "out of his own money."

Gaston, however, failed to persuade Pierre to accompany him round to buy an outfit. For the dumb man lay on his bed, and obstinately refused to move out of the room. He, however, acquiesced sullenly when his friend told him he was going to Melbourne, so Vandeloup left the room, having first secured Pierre's knife, and locked the door after him. He gave the knife to Miss Twexby, with injunctions to her to keep it safe, then sallied forth to buy his shipwrecked friend a box and some clothes.

He spent about ten pounds in buying an outfit for the dumb man, hired a cab to call at the "Wattle Tree" Hotel at seven o'clock to take the box and its owner to the station. And then feeling he had done his duty and deserved some recompense, he had a nice little luncheon and a small bottle of wine for which he paid out of Pierre's money. When he finished he bought a choice cigar, had a glass of Chartreuse, and after resting in the commercial room for a time he went out for a walk, intending to call on Slivers and Dr. Gollipeck, and in fact do anything to kill time until it would be necessary for him to go to Pierre and take him to the railway station.

He walked slowly up Sturt Street, and as the afternoon was so warm, thought he would go up to Lake Wendouree, which is at the top of the town, and see if it was any cooler by the water. The day was oppressively hot, but not with the bright, cheery warmth of a summer's day, for the sun was hidden behind great masses of angry-looking clouds, and it seemed as if a thunderstorm would soon break over the city. Even Vandeloup, full of life and animation as he was, felt weighed down by the heaviness of the atmosphere, and feeling quite exhausted when he arrived at the lake, he was glad enough to sit down on one of the seats for a rest.

The lake under the black sky was a dull leaden hue, and as there was no wind the water was perfectly still. Even the trees all round it were motionless, as there came no breeze to stir their leaves, and the only sounds that could be heard were the dull croaking of the frogs amid the water grasses, and the shrill cries of children playing on the green turf. Every now and then a steamer would skim across the surface of the water in an airy manner, looking more like a child's clockwork toy than anything else, and Vandeloup, when he saw one of these arrive at the little pier, almost expected to see a man put in a huge key to the paddle wheels and wind it up again.

On one of the seats Vandeloup espied a little figure in white, and seeing that it was Kitty, he strolled up to her in a leisurely manner. She was looking at the ground when he came up, and was prodding holes in the spongy turf with her umbrella, but glanced up carelessly as he came near. Then she sprang up with a cry of joy, and throwing her arms around his neck, she kissed him twice.

"I haven't seen you for ages," said Kitty, putting her arm in his as they sat down. "I just came up here for a week, and did not think I'd see you."

"The meeting was quite accidental, I know," replied Gaston, leaning back lazily; "but none the less pleasant on that account."

"Oh, no," said Kitty, gravely shaking her head; "unexpected meetings are always pleasanter than those arranged, for there's never any disappointment about them."

"Oh, that's your experience, is it?" answered her lover, with an amused smile, pulling out his cigarette case. "Well, suppose you reward me for my accidental presence here, and light a cigarette for me."

Kitty was of course delighted, and took the case while M. Vandeloup leaned back in the seat, his hands behind his head, and stared reflectively at the leaden-coloured sky. Kitty took out a cigarette from the case, placed it between her pretty lips, and having obtained a match from one of her lover's pockets, proceeded to light it, which was not done without a great deal of choking and pretty confusion. At length she managed it, and bending over Gaston, placed it in his mouth, and gave him a kiss at the same time.

"If pa knew I did this, he'd expire with horror," she said, sagely nodding her head.

"Wouldn't be much loss if he did," replied Vandeloup, lazily, glancing at her pretty face from under his eyelashes; "your father has a great many faults, dear."

"Oh, 'The Elect' think him perfect," said Kitty, wisely.

"From their point of view, perhaps he is," returned Gaston, with a faint sneer; "but he's not a man given to exuberant mirth."

"Well, he is rather dismal," assented Kitty, doubtfully.

"Wouldn't you like to leave him and lead a jollier life?" asked Vandeloup, artfully, "in Melbourne, for instance."

Kitty looked at him half afraid.

"I—I don't know," she faltered, looking down.

"But I do, Bebe," whispered Gaston, putting his arm round her waist; "you would like to come with me."

"Why? Are you going?" cried Kitty, in dismay.

Vandeloup nodded.

"I think I spoke about this before," he said, idly brushing some cigarette ash off his waistcoat.

"Yes," returned Kitty, "but I thought you did not mean it."

"I never say anything I do not mean," answered Vandeloup, with the ready lie on his lips in a moment; "and I have got letters from France with money, so I am going to leave the Pactolus."

"And me?" said Kitty, tearfully.

"That depends upon yourself, Bebe," he said rapidly, pressing her burning cheek against his own; "your father would never consent to my marriage, and I can't take you away from Ballarat without suspicions, so—"

"Yes?" said Kitty, eagerly, looking at him.

"You must run away," he whispered, with a caressing smile.

"Alone?"

"For a time, yes," he answered, throwing away his cigarette; "listen— next week you must meet me here, and I will give you money to keep you in Melbourne for some time; then you must leave Ballarat at once and wait for me at the Buttercup Hotel in Gertrude Street, Carlton; you understand?"

"Yes," faltered Kitty, nervously; "I—I understand."

"And you will come?" he asked anxiously, looking keenly at her, and pressing the little hand he held in his own. Just as she was going to answer, as if warning her of the fatal step she was about to take, a low roll of thunder broke on their ears, and Kitty shrank back appalled from her lover's embrace.

"No! no! no!" she almost shrieked, hysterically, trying to tear herself away from his arms, "I cannot; God is speaking."

"Bah!" sneered Vandeloup, with an evil look on his handsome face, "he speaks too indistinctly for us to guess what he means; what are you afraid of? I will join you in Melbourne in two or three weeks, and then we will be married."

"But my father," she whispered, clasping her hot hands convulsively.

"Well, what of him?" asked Vandeloup, coolly; "he is so wrapped up in his religion that he will not miss you; he will never find out where you are in Melbourne, and by the time he does you will be my wife. Come," he said, ardently, whispering the temptation in her ear, as if he was afraid of being heard, "you must consent; say yes, Bebe; say yes."

She felt his hot breath on her cheek, and felt rather than saw the scintillations of his wonderful eyes, which sent a thrill through her; so, utterly exhausted and worn out by the overpowering nervous force possessed by this man, she surrendered.

"Yes," she whispered, clinging to him with dry lips and a beating heart; "I will come!" Then her overstrained nature gave way, and with a burst of tears she threw herself on his breast.

Gaston let her sob quietly for some time, satisfied with having gained his end, and knowing that she would soon recover. At last Kitty grew calmer, and drying her eyes, she rose to her feet wan and haggard, as if she was worn out for the want of sleep, and not by any manner of means looking like a girl who was in love. This appearance was caused by the revolt of her religious training against doing what she knew was wrong. In her breast a natural instinct had been fighting against an artificial one; and as Nature is always stronger than precept, Nature had conquered.

"My dear Bebe," said Vandeloup, rising also, and kissing her white cheek, "you must go home now, and get a little sleep; it will do you good."

"But you?" asked Kitty, in a low voice, as they walked slowly along.

"Oh, I," said M. Vandeloup, airily; "I am going to the Wattle Tree Hotel to see my friend Pierre off to Melbourne."

Then he exerted himself to amuse Kitty as they walked down to town, and succeeded so well that by the time they reached Lydiard Street, where Kitty left him to go up to Black Hill, she was laughing as merrily as possible. They parted at the railway crossing, and Kitty went gaily up the white dusty road, while M. Vandeloup strolled leisurely along the street on his way to the Wattle Tree Hotel.

When he arrived he found that Pierre's box had come, and was placed outside his door, as no one had been brave enough to venture inside, although Miss Twexby assured them he was unarmed—showing the knife as a proof.

Gaston, however, dragged the box into the room, and having made Pierre dress himself in his new clothes, he packed all the rest in a box, corded it, and put a ticket on it with his name and destination, then gave the dumb man the balance of his wages. It was now about six o'clock, so Vandeloup went down to dinner; then putting Pierre and his box into the cab, stepped in himself and drove off.

The promise of rain in the afternoon was now fulfilled, and it was pouring in torrents. The gutters were rivers, and every now and then through the driving rain came the bluish dart of a lightning flash.

"Bah!" said Vandeloup, with a shiver, as they got out on the station platform, "what a devil of a night."

He made the cab wait for him, and, having got Pierre's ticket, put him in a second-class carriage and saw that his box was safely placed in the luggage-van. The station was crowded with people going and others coming to say goodbye; the rain was beating on the high-arched tin roof, and the engine at the end of the long train was fretting and fuming like a living thing impatient to be gone.

"You are now on your own responsibility, my friend," said Vandeloup to Pierre, as he stood at the window of the carriage; "for we must part, though long together have we been. Perhaps I will see you in Melbourne; if I do you will find I have not forgotten the past," and, with a significant look at the dumb man, Vandeloup lounged slowly away.

The whistle blew shrilly, the last goodbyes were spoken, the guard shouted "All aboard for Melbourne," and shut all the doors, then, with another shriek and puff of white steam, the train, like a long, lithe serpent, glided into the rain and darkness with its human freight.

"At last I have rid myself of this dead weight," said Vandeloup, as he drove along the wet streets to Craig's Hotel, where he intended to stay for the night, "and can now shape my own fortune. Pierre is gone, Bebe will follow, and now I must look after myself."

XVIII

M. Vandeloup is Unjustly Suspected

It never rains but it pours' is an excellent proverb, and a very true one, for it is remarkable how events of a similar nature follow closely on one another's heels when the first that happened has set the ball a-rolling. Madame Midas believed to a certain extent in this, and she half expected that when Pierre went he would be followed by M. Vandeloup, but she certainly did not think that the disappearance of her husband would be followed by that of Kitty Marchurst. Yet such was the case, for Mr. Marchurst, not seeing Kitty at family prayers, had sent in the servant to seek for her, and the scared domestic had returned with a startled face and a letter for her master. Marchurst read the tear-blotted little note, in which Kitty said she was going down to Melbourne to appear on the stage. Crushing it up in his hand, he went on with family prayers in his usual manner, and after dismissing his servants for the night, he went up to his daughter's room, and found that she had left nearly everything behind, only taking a few needful things with her. Seeing her portrait on the wall he took it down and placed it in his pocket. Then, searching through her room, he found some ribbons and lace, a yellow-backed novel, which he handled with the utmost loathing, and a pair of gloves. Regarding these things as the instruments of Satan, by which his daughter had been led to destruction, he carried them downstairs to his dismal study and piled them in the empty fireplace. Placing his daughter's portrait on top he put a light to the little pile of frivolities, and saw them slowly burn away. The novel curled and cracked in the scorching flame, but the filmy lace vanished like cobwebs, and the gloves crackled and shrank into mere wisps of black leather. And over all, through the flames, her face, bright and charming, looked out with laughing lips and merry eyes—so like her mother's, and yet so unlike in its piquant grace—until that too fell into the hollow heart of the flames, and burned slowly away into a small pile of white ashes.

Marchurst, leaving the dead ashes cold and grey in the dark fireplace, went to his writing table, and falling on his knees he passed the rest of the night in prayer.

Meanwhile, the man who was the primary cause of all this trouble was working in the office of the Pactolus claim with a light heart and cool head. Gaston had really managed to get Kitty away in a very clever manner, inasmuch as he never appeared publicly to be concerned in it, but directed the whole business secretly. He had given Kitty sufficient money to keep her for some months in Melbourne, as he was in doubt when he could leave the Pactolus without being suspected of being concerned in her disappearance. He also told her what day to leave, and all that day stayed at the mine working at his accounts, and afterwards spent the evening very pleasantly with Madame Midas. Next day McIntosh went into Ballarat on business, and on returning from the city, where he had heard all about it—rumour, of course, magnifying the whole affair greatly—he saw Vandeloup come out of the office, and drew up in the trap beside the young man.

"Aha, Monsieur," said Vandeloup, gaily, rolling a cigarette in his slender fingers, and shooting a keen glance at Archie; "you have had a pleasant day."

"Maybe yes, maybe no," returned McIntosh, cautiously, fumbling in the bag; "there's naething muckle in the toun, but—deil tack the bag," he continued, tetchily shaking it. "I've gotten a letter or so fra' France."

"For me?" cried Vandeloup, eagerly, holding out his hands.

"An' for who else would it be?" grumbled Archie, giving the letter to him—a thin, foreign looking envelope with the Parisian post mark on it; "did ye think it was for that black-avised freend o' yours?"

"Hardly!" returned Vandeloup, glancing at the letter with satisfaction, and putting it in his pocket. "Pierre couldn't write himself, and I doubt very much if he had any friends who could—not that I knew his friends," he said, hastily catching sight of McIntosh's severe face bent inquiringly on him, "but like always draws to like."

Archie's only answer to this was a grunt.

"Are ye no gangin' tae read yon?" he asked sourly.

"Not at present," replied Vandeloup, blowing a thin wreath of blue smoke, "by-and-bye will do. Scandal and oysters should both be fresh to be enjoyable, but letters—ah, bah," with a shrug, "they can wait. Come, tell me the news; anything going on?"

"Weel," said McIntosh, with great gusto, deliberately flicking a fly off the horse's back with a whip, "she's ta'en the bit intil her mouth and gane wrang, as I said she would."

"To what special 'she' are you alluding to?" asked Vandeloup, lazily smoothing his moustache; "so many of them go wrong, you see, one likes to be particular. The lady's name is—?"

"Katherine Marchurst, no less," burst forth Archie, in triumph; "she's rin awa' to be a play-actor."

"What? that child?" said Vandeloup, with an admirable expression of surprise; "nonsense! It cannot be true."

"D'ye think I would tell a lee?" said Archie, wrathfully, glowering down on the tall figure pacing leisurely along. "God forbid that my lips should fa' tae sic iniquity. It's true, I tell ye; the lass has rin awa' an' left her faither—a godly mon, tho' I'm no of his way of thinkin—to curse the day he had sic a bairn born until him. Ah, 'tis sorrow and dule she hath brought tae his roof tree, an' sorrow and dule wull be her portion at the hands o' strangers," and with this scriptural ending Mr. McIntosh sharply whipped up Rory, and went on towards the stable, leaving Vandeloup standing in the road.

"I don't think he suspects, at all events," thought that young man, complacently. "As to Madame Midas—pouf! I can settle her suspicions easily; a little virtuous indignation is most effective as a blind;" and M. Vandeloup, with a gay laugh, strolled on towards the house in the gathering twilight.

Suddenly he recollected the letter, which had escaped his thoughts, in his desire to see how McIntosh would take the disappearance of Kitty, so as there was still light to see, he leaned up against a fence, and, having lighted another cigarette, read it through carefully. It appeared to afford him considerable satisfaction, and he smiled as he put it in his pocket again.

"It seems pretty well forgotten, this trouble about Adele," he said, musingly, as he resumed his saunter; "I might be able to go back again in a few years, if not to Paris at least to Europe—one can be very happy in Monaco or Vienna, and run no risk of being found out; and, after all," he muttered, thoughtfully, fingering his moustache, "why not to Paris? The Republic has lasted too long already. Sooner or later there will be a change of Government, and then I can go back a free man, with a fortune of Australian gold. Emperor, King, or President, it's all the same to me, as long as I am left alone."

He walked on slowly, thinking deeply all the time, and when he arrived at the door of Mrs. Villiers' house, this clever young man, with his accustomed promptitude and decision, had settled what he was going to do.

"Up to a certain point, of course," he said aloud, following his thoughts, "after that, chance must decide."

Madame Midas was very much grieved at the news of Kitty's Escapade, particularly as she could not see what motive she had for running away, and, moreover, trembled to think of the temptations the innocent girl would be exposed to in the metropolis. After tea, when Archie had gone outside to smoke his pipe, and Selina was busy in the kitchen washing the dishes, she spoke to Vandeloup on the subject. The young Frenchman was seated at the piano in the darkness, striking a few random chords, while Madame was by the fire in the arm-chair. It was quite dark, with only the rosy glow of the fire shining through the room. Mrs. Villiers felt uneasy; was it likely that Vandeloup could have any connection with Kitty's disappearance? Impossible! he had given her his word of honour, and yet—it was very strange. Mrs. Villiers was not, by any means, a timid woman, so she determined to ask Gaston right out, and get a decided answer from him, so as to set her mind at rest.

"M. Vandeloup," she said, in her clear voice, "will you kindly come here a moment?

"Certainly, Madame," said Gaston, rising with alacrity from the piano, and coming to the fireside; "is there anything I can do?"

"You have heard of Miss Marchurst's disappearance?" she asked, looking up at him.

Vandeloup leaned his elbow on the mantelpiece, and looked down into the fire, so that the full blaze of it could strike his face. He knew Madame Midas prided herself on being a reader of character, and knowing he could command his features admirably, he thought it would be politic to let her see his face, and satisfy herself as to his innocence.

"Yes, Madame," he answered, in his calm, even tones, looking down inquiringly at the statuesque face of the woman addressing him; "Monsieur," nodding towards the door, "told me, but I did not think it true."

"I'm afraid it is," sighed Madame, shaking her head. "She is going on the stage, and her father will never forgive her."

"Surely, Madame—" began Vandeloup, eagerly.

"No," she replied, decisively, "he is not a hard man, but his way of looking at things through his peculiar religious ideas has warped his judgment—he will make no attempt to save her, and God knows what she will come to."

"There are good women on the stage," said Vandeloup, at a loss for a reply.

"Certainly," returned Madame, calmly, "there are black and white sheep in every flock, but Kitty is so young and inexperienced, that she may become the prey of the first handsome scoundrel she meets."

Madame had intuitively guessed the whole situation, and Vandeloup could not help admiring her cleverness. Still his face remained the same, and his voice was as steady as ever as he answered—

"It is much to be regretted; but still we must hope for the best."

Was he guilty? Madame could not make up her mind, so determined to speak boldly.

"Do you remember that day I introduced her to you?"

Vandeloup bowed.

"And you gave me your word of honour you would not try to turn her head," pursued Madame, looking at him; "have you kept your word?"

"Madame," said Vandeloup, gravely, "I give you my word of honour that I have always treated Mlle Kitty as a child and your friend. I did not know that she had gone until I was told, and whatever happens to her, I can safely say that it was not Gaston Vandeloup's fault."

An admirable actor this man, not a feature of his face moved, not a single deviation from the calmness of his speech—not a quickening of the pulse, nor the rush of betraying blood to his fair face—no! Madame withdrew her eyes quite satisfied, M. Vandeloup was the soul of honour and was innocent of Kitty's disgrace.

"Thank God!" she said, reverently, as she looked away, for she would have been bitterly disappointed to have found her kindness to this man repaid by base treachery towards her friend; "I cannot tell you how relieved I feel."

M. Vandeloup withdrew his face into the darkness, and smiled in a devilish manner to himself. How these women believed—was there any lie too big for the sex to swallow? Evidently not—at least, so he thought. But now that Kitty was disposed of, he had to attend to his own private affairs, and put his hand in his pocket for the letter.

"I wanted to speak to you on business, Madame," he said, taking out the letter; "the long-expected has come at last."

"You have heard from Paris?" asked Madame, in an eager voice.

"I have," answered the Frenchman, calmly; "I have now the letter in my hand, and as soon as Mlle Selina brings in the lights I will show it to you."

At this moment, as if in answer to his request, Selina appeared with the lamp, which she had lighted in the kitchen and now brought in to place on the table. When she did so, and had retired again, Vandeloup placed his letter in Madame's hand, and asked her to read it.

"Oh, no, Monsieur," said Mrs. Villiers, offering it back, "I do not wish to read your private correspondence."

Vandeloup had calculated on this, for, as a matter of fact, there was a good deal of private matter in the letter, particularly referring to his trip to New Caledonia, which he would not have allowed her to see. But he knew it would inspire her with confidence in him if he placed it wholly in her hands, and resolved to boldly venture to do so. The result was as he guessed; so, with a smile, he took it back again.

"There is nothing private in it, Madame," he said, opening the letter; "I wanted you to see that I had not misrepresented myself—it is from my family lawyer, and he has sent me out a remittance of money, also some letters of introduction to my consul in Melbourne and others; in fact," said M. Vandeloup, with a charming smile, putting the letter in his pocket, "it places me in my rightful position, and I shall assume it as soon as I have your permission."

"But why my permission ?" asked Madame, with a faint smile, already regretting bitterly that she was going to lose her pleasant companion.

"Madame," said Vandeloup, impressively, bending forward, "in the words of the Bible—when I was hungry you gave me food; when I was naked you gave me raiment. You took me on, Madame, an unknown waif, without money, friends, or a character; you believed in me when no one else did; you have been my guardian angel: and do you think that I can forget your goodness to me for the last six months? No! Madame," rising, "I have a heart, and while I live that heart will ever remember you with gratitude and love;" and bending forward he took her hand and kissed it gallantly.

"You think too much of what I have done," said Madame, who was, nevertheless, pleased at this display of emotion, albeit, according to her English ideas, it seemed to savour too much of the footlights. "I only did to you what I would do to all men. I am glad, in this instance, to find my confidence has not been misplaced; when do you think of leaving us?"

"In about two or three weeks," answered Vandeloup, carelessly, "but not till you find another clerk; besides, Madame, do not think you have lost sight of me for ever; I will go down to Melbourne, settle all my affairs, and come up and see you again."

"So you say," replied Mrs. Villiers, sceptically smiling.

"Well," replied M. Vandeloup, with a shrug, "we will see—at all events, gratitude is such a rare virtue that there is decided novelty in possessing it."

"M. Vandeloup," said Madame, suddenly, after they had been chatting for a few moments, "one thing you must do for me in Melbourne."

"I will do anything you wish," said Vandeloup, gravely.

"Then," said Madame, earnestly, rising and looking him in the face, "you must find Kitty, and send her back to me."

"Madame," said Vandeloup, solemnly, "it will be the purpose of my life to restore her to your arms."

XIX

The Devil's Lead

There was great dismay at the Pactolus Mine when it became known that Vandeloup was going to leave. During his short stay he had made himself extremely popular with the men, as he always had a bright smile and a kind word for everyone, so they all felt like losing a personal friend. The only two who were unfeignedly glad at Vandeloup's departure were Selina and McIntosh, for these two faithful hearts had seen with dismay the influence the Frenchman was gradually gaining over Madame Midas. As long as Villiers lived they felt safe, but now that he had so mysteriously disappeared, and was to all appearances dead, they dreaded lest their mistress, in a moment of infatuation, should marry her clerk. They need not, however, have been afraid, for much as Mrs. Villiers liked the young Frenchman, such an idea had never entered her head, and she was far too clever a woman ever to tempt matrimony a second time, seeing how dearly it had cost her.

Madame Midas had made great efforts to find Kitty, but without success; and, in spite of all inquiries and advertisements in the papers, nothing could be discovered regarding the missing girl.

At last the time drew near for Vandeloup's departure, when all the sensation of Kitty's escapade and Villiers' disappearance was swallowed up in a new event, which filled Ballarat with wonder. It began in a whisper, and grew into such a roar of astonishment that not only Ballarat, but all Victoria, knew that the far-famed Devil's Lead had been discovered in the Pactolus claim. Yes, after years of weary waiting, after money had been swallowed up in apparently useless work, after sceptics had sneered and friends laughed, Madame Midas obtained her reward. The Devil's Lead was discovered, and she was now a millionaire.

For some time past McIntosh had not been satisfied with the character of the ground in which he had been working, so abandoning the shaft he was then in, he had opened up another gallery to the west, at right angles from the place where the famous nugget had been found. The wash was poor at first, but McIntosh persevered, having an instinct that he was on the right track. A few weeks' work proved that he was right, for the wash soon became richer; and as they went farther on towards the west, following the gutter, there was no doubt that the long-lost Devil's Lead had been struck. The regular return had formerly been five ounces to the machine, but now the washing up invariably gave twenty ounces, and small nuggets of water-worn gold were continually found in the three machines. The main drive following the lead still continued dipping westward, and McIntosh now commenced blocking and putting in side galleries, expecting when this was done he would thoroughly prove the Devil's Lead, for he was quite satisfied he was on it. Even now the yield was three hundred and sixty ounces a week, and after deducting working expenses, this gave Madame Midas a weekly income of one thousand one hundred pounds, so she now began to see what a wealthy woman she was likely to be. Everyone unfeigningly rejoiced at her good fortune, and said that she deserved it. Many thought that now she was so rich Villiers would come back again, but he did not put in an appearance, and it was generally concluded he had left the colony.

Vandeloup congratulated Madame Midas on her luck when he was going away, and privately determined that he would not lose sight of her, as, being a wealthy woman, and having a liking for him, she would be of great use. He took his farewell gracefully, and went away, carrying the good wishes of all the miners; but McIntosh and Selina, still holding to their former opinion, were secretly pleased at his departure. Madame Midas made him a present of a hundred pounds, and, though he refused it, saying that he had money from France, she asked him as a personal favour to take it; so M. Vandeloup, always gallant to ladies, could not refuse. He went in to Ballarat, and put up at the Wattle Tree Hotel, intending to start for the metropolis next morning; but on his way, in order to prepare Kitty for his coming, sent a telegram for her, telling her the train he would arrive by, in order that she might be at the station to meet him.

After his dinner he suddenly recollected that he still had the volume which Dr. Gollipeck had lent him, so, calling a cab, he drove to the residence of that eccentric individual to return it.

When the servant announced M. Vandeloup, she pushed him in and suddenly closed the door after her, as though she was afraid of some of the doctor's ideas getting away.

"Good evening, doctor," said Vandeloup, laying the book down on the table at which Gollipeck was seated; "I've come to return you this and say good-bye."

"Aha, going away?" asked Gollipeck, leaning back in his chair, and looked sharply at the young man through his spectacles, "right—see the world—you're clever—won't go far wrong—no!"

"It doesn't matter much if I do," replied Vandeloup, shrugging his shoulders, and taking a chair, "nobody will bother much about me."

"Eh!" queried the doctor, sharply, sitting up. "Paris—friends— relations."

"My only relation is an aunt with a large family; she's got quite enough to do looking after them, without bothering about me," retorted M. Vandeloup; "as to friends—I haven't got one."

"Oh!" from Gollipeck, with a cynical smile, "I see; let us say— acquaintances."

"Won't make any difference," replied Vandeloup, airily; "I turned my acquaintances into friends long ago, and then borrowed money off them; result: my social circle is nil. Friends," went on M. Vandeloup, reflectively, "are excellent as friends, but damnable as bankers."

Gollipeck chuckled, and rubbed his hands, for this cynicism pleased him. Suddenly his eye caught the book which the young man had returned.

"You read this?" he said, laying his hand on it; "good, eh?"

"Very good, indeed," returned M. Vandeloup, smoothly; "so kind of you to have lent it to me—all those cases quoted were known to me."

"The case of Adele Blondet, for instance, eh?" asked the old man sharply.

"Yes, I was present at the trial," replied Vandeloup, quietly; "the prisoner Octave Braulard was convicted, condemned to death, reprieved, and sent to New Caledonia."

"Where he now is," said Gollipeck, quickly, looking at him.

"I presume so," replied Vandeloup, lazily. "After the trial I never bothered my head about him."

"He poisoned his mistress, Adele Blondet," said the doctor.

"Yes," answered Vandeloup, leaning forward and looking at Gollipeck, "he found she was in love with an Englishman, and poisoned her—you will find it all in the book."

"It does not mention the Englishman," said the doctor, thoughtfully tapping the table with his hand.

"Nevertheless he was implicated in it, but went away from Paris the day Braulard was arrested," answered Vandeloup. "The police tried to find him, but could not; if they had, it might have made some difference to the prisoner."

"And the name of this Englishman?"

"Let me see," said Vandeloup, looking up reflectively; "I almost forget it—Kestroke or Kestrike, some name like that. He must have been a very clever man to have escaped the French police."

"Ah, hum!" said the doctor, rubbing his nose, "very interesting indeed; strange case!"

"Very," assented M. Vandeloup, as he arose to go, "I must say good-bye now, doctor; but I am coming up to Ballarat on a visit shortly."

"Ah, hum! of course," replied Gollipeck, also rising, "and we can have another talk over this book."

"That or any book you like," said Vandeloup, with a glance of surprise; "but I don't see why you are so much taken up with that volume; it is not a work of genius."

"Well, no," answered Gollipeck, looking at him; "still, it contains some excellent cases of modern poisoning."

"So I saw when I read it," returned Vandeloup, indifferently. "Good-bye," holding out his hand, "or rather I should say au revoir."

"Wine?" queried the Doctor, hospitably.

Vandeloup shook his head, and walked out of the room with a gay smile, humming a tune. He strolled slowly down Lydiard Street, turning over in his mind what the doctor had said to him.

"He is suspicious," muttered the young man to himself, thoughtfully, "although he has nothing to go on in connecting me with the case. Should I use the poison here I must be careful, for that man will be my worst enemy."

He felt a hand on his shoulder, and turning round saw Barty Jarper before him. That fashionable young man was in evening dress, and represented such an extent of shirt front and white waistcoat,—not to mention a tall collar, on the top of which his little head was perched like a cocoanut on a stick,—that he was positively resplendent.

"Where are you going to?" asked the gorgeous Barty, smoothing his incipient moustache.

"Well, I really don't know," answered Vandeloup, lighting a cigarette. "I am leaving for Melbourne to-morrow morning, but to-night I have nothing to do. You, I see, are engaged," with a glance at the evening dress.

"Yes," returned Barty, in a bored voice; "musical party on,—they want me to sing."

Vandeloup had heard Barty's vocal performance, and could not forbear a smile as he thought of the young man's three songs with the same accompaniment to each. Suppressing, however, his inclination to laugh, he asked Barty to have a drink, which invitation was promptly accepted, and they walked in search of a hotel. On the way, they passed Slivers' house, and here Vandeloup paused.

"This was the first house I entered here," he said to Barty, "and I must go in and say good-bye to my one-armed friend with the cockatoo."

Mr. Jarper, however, drew back.

"I don't like him," he said bluntly, "he's an old devil."

"Oh, it's always as well to accustom oneself to the society of devils," retorted Vandeloup, coolly, "we may have to live with them constantly some day."

Barty laughed at this, and putting his arm in that of Vandeloup's, they went in.

Slivers' door stood ajar in its usual hospitable manner, but all within was dark.

"He must be out," said Barty, as they stood in the dark passage.

"No," replied Vandeloup, feeling for a match, "someone is talking in the office."

"It's that parrot," said Barty, with a laugh, as they heard Billy rapidly running over his vocabulary; "let's go in."

He pushed open the door, and was about to step into the room, when catching sight of something on the floor, he recoiled with a cry, and caught Vandeloup by the arm.

"What's the matter?" asked the Frenchman, hastily.

"He's dead," returned Barty, with a sort of gasp; "see, he's lying on the floor dead!"

And so he was! The oldest inhabitant of Ballarat had joined the great majority, and, as it was afterwards discovered, his death was caused by the breaking of a blood-vessel. The cause of it was not clear, but the fact was, that hearing of the discovery of the Devil's Lead, and knowing that it was lost to him for ever, Slivers had fallen into such a fit of rage, that he burst a blood-vessel and died in his office with no one by him.

The light of the street lamp shone through the dusty windows into the dark room, and in the centre of the yellow splash lay the dead man, with his one eye wide open, staring at the ceiling, while perched on his wooden leg, which was sticking straight out, sat the parrot, swearing. It was a most repulsive sight, and Barty, with a shudder of disgust, tried to drag his companion away, but M. Vandeloup refused to go, and searched his pockets for a match to see more clearly what the body was like.

"Pickles," cried Billy, from his perch on the dead man's wooden leg; "oh, my precious mother,—devil take him."

"My faith," said M. Vandeloup, striking a match, "the devil has taken him," and leaving Barty shivering and trembling at the door, he advanced into the room and stood looking at the body. Billy at his approach hopped off the leg and waddled up to the dead man's shoulder, where he sat cursing volubly, and every now and then going into shrieks of demoniacal laughter. Barty closed his ears to the devilish mirth, and saw M. Vandeloup standing over the corpse, with the faint light of the match flickering in his hand.

"Do you know what this is?" he asked, turning to Barty.

The other looked at him inquiringly.

"It is the comedy of death," said the Frenchman, throwing down the match and going to the door.

They both went out to seek assistance, and left the dark room with the dead man lying in the pool of yellow light, and the parrot perched on the body, muttering to itself. It was a strange mingling of the horrible and grotesque, and the whole scene was hit off in the phrase applied to it by Vandeloup. It was, indeed, "The Comedy of Death"!

PART II

I

Tempus Fugit

A whole year had elapsed since the arrival of Vandeloup in Melbourne, and during that time many things had happened. Unfortunately, in spite of his knowledge of human nature, and the fact that he started with a good sum of money, Gaston had not made his fortune. This was due to the fact that he was indisposed to work when his banking account was at all decent; so he had lived like a prince on his capital, and trusted to his luck furnishing him with more when it was done.

Kitty had joined him in Melbourne as arranged, and Gaston had established her in a place in Richmond. It was not a regular boarding-house, but the lady who owned it, Mrs. Pulchop by name, was in the habit of letting apartments on reasonable terms; so Vandeloup had taken up his abode there with Kitty, who passed as his wife.

But though he paid her all the deference and respect due to a wife, and though she wore a marriage ring, yet, as a matter of fact, they were not married. Kitty had implored her lover to have the ceremony performed as soon as he joined her; but as the idea was not to M. Vandeloup's taste, he had put her off, laughingly at first, then afterwards, when he began to weary of her, he said he could not marry her for at least a year. The reason he assigned for this was the convenient one of family affairs; but, in reality, he foresaw he would get tired of her in that time, and did not want to tie himself so that he could not leave her when he wished. At first, the girl had rebelled against this delay, for she was strongly biased by her religious training, and looked with horror on the state of wickedness in which she was living. But Gaston laughed at her scruples, and as time went on, her finer feelings became blunted, and she accepted the position to which she was reduced in an apathetic manner.

Sometimes she had wild thoughts of running away, but she still loved him too well to do so; and besides, there was no one to whom she could go, as she well knew her father would refuse to receive her. The anomalous position which she occupied, however, had an effect on her spirits, and from being a bright and happy girl, she became irritable and fretful. She refused to go out anywhere, and when she went into town, either avoided the principal streets, or wore a heavy veil, so afraid was she of being recognised by anyone from Ballarat and questioned as to how she lived. All this was very disagreeable to M. Vandeloup, who had a horror of being bored, and not finding Kitty's society pleasant enough, he gradually ceased to care for her, and was now only watching for an opportunity to get rid of her without any trouble. He was a member of the Bachelor's Club, a society of young men which had a bad reputation in Melbourne, and finding Kitty was so lachrymose, he took a room at the Club, and began to stay away four or five days at a time. So Kitty was left to herself, and grew sad and tearful, as she reflected on the consequence of her fatal passion for this man. Mrs. Pulchop was vastly indignant at Vandeloup neglecting his wife, for, of course, she never thought she was anything else to the young man, and did all in her power to cheer the girl up, which, however, was not much, as Mrs. Pulchop herself was decidedly of a funereal disposition.

Meanwhile, Gaston was leading a very gay life in Melbourne. His good looks and clever tongue had made him a lot of friends, and he was very popular both in drawing-room and club. The men voted him a jolly sort of fellow and a regular swagger man, while the ladies said that he was heavenly; for, true to his former tactics, Vandeloup always made particular friends of women, selecting, of course, those whom he thought would be likely to be of use to him. Being such a favourite entailed going out a great deal, and as no one can pose as a man of fashion without money, M. Vandeloup soon found that his capital was rapidly melting away. He then went in for gambling, and the members of The Bachelors, being nearly all rich young men, Gaston's dexterity at ecarte and baccarat was very useful to him, and considerably augmented his income.

Still, card-playing is a somewhat precarious source from which to derive an income, so Vandeloup soon found himself pretty hard up, and was at his wit's end how to raise money. His gay life cost him a good deal, and Kitty, of course, was a source of expense, although, poor girl, she never went anywhere; but there was a secret drain on his purse of which no one ever dreamed. This was none other than Pierre Lemaire, who, having spent all the money he got at the Pactolus, came and worried Vandeloup for more. That astute young man would willingly have refused him, but, unfortunately, Pierre knew too much of his past life for him to do so, therefore he had to submit to the dumb man's extortions with the best grace he could. So what with Kitty's changed manner, Pierre wanting money, and his own lack of coin, M. Vandeloup was in anything but an enviable position, and began to think it was time his luck—if he ever had any—should step in. He thought of running up to Ballarat and seeing Madame Midas, whom he knew would lend him some money, but he had a certain idea in his head with regard to that lady, so wished to retain her good opinion, and determined not to apply to her until all other plans for obtaining money failed. Meanwhile, he went everywhere, was universally admired and petted, and no one who saw him in society with his bright smile and nonchalant manner, would have imagined what crafty schemes there were in that handsome head.

Madame Midas was still up at Ballarat and occupying the same cottage, although she was now so wealthy she could have inhabited a palace, had she been so minded. But prosperity had not spoiled Mrs. Villiers. She still managed her own affairs, and did a great deal of good with her money,—expending large sums for charitable purposes, because she really wished to do good, and not, like so many rich people, for the purpose of advertising herself.

The Pactolus was now a perfect fortune, and Madame Midas being the sole owner, her wealth was thought to be enormous, as every month a fresh deluge of gold rolled into her coffers from the inexhaustible Devil's Lead. McIntosh, of course, still managed the mine, and took great pride in his success, especially after so many people had scoffed at it.

Various other mines had started in the vicinity, and had been floated on the Melbourne market, where they kept rising and falling in unison with the monthly yield of the Pactolus. The Devil's Lead was rather unequal, as sometimes the ground would be rich, while another time it would turn out comparatively poor. People said it was patchy, and some day would run out altogether, but it did not show any signs of exhaustion, and even if it had, Madame Midas was now so wealthy that it mattered comparatively little. When the monthly yield was small, the mines round about would fall in the share market to a few shillings, but if it was large, they would rush up again to as many pounds, so that the brokers managed to do pretty well out of the fluctuations of the stock.

One thing astonished Madame Midas very much, and that was the continuous absence of her husband. She did not believe he was dead, and fully expected to see him turn up some time; but as the months passed on, and he did not appear, she became uneasy. The idea of his lurking round was a constant nightmare to her, and at last she placed the matter in the hands of the police, with instructions to try to ascertain what became of him.

The police did everything in their power to discover Villiers' whereabouts, but without success. Unfortunately, Slivers, who might have helped them, being so well acquainted with the missing man's habits, was dead; and, after trying for about three months to find some traces of Villiers, the police gave up the search in despair. Madame Midas, therefore, came to the conclusion that he was either dead or had left the colony, and though half doubtful, yet hoped that she had now seen the last of him.

She had invested her money largely in land, and thus being above the reach of poverty for the rest of her life, she determined to take up her abode in Melbourne for a few months, prior to going to England on a visit. With this resolution, she gave up her cottage to Archie, who was to live in it, and still manage the mine, and made preparations to come down to Melbourne with Selina Sprotts.

Vandeloup heard of this resolution, and secretly rejoiced at it, for he thought that seeing she liked him so much, now that her husband was to all appearances dead, she might marry him, and it was to this end he had kept up his acquaintance with her. He never thought of the girl he had betrayed, pining away in a dull lodging. No, M. Vandeloup, untroubled by the voice of conscience, serenely waited the coming of Madame Midas, and determined, if he could possibly arrange it, to marry her. He was the spider, and Madame Midas the fly; but as the spider knew the fly he had to inveigle into his web was a very crafty one, he determined to act with great caution; so, having ascertained when Madame Midas would be in Melbourne, he awaited her arrival before doing anything, and trusted in some way to get rid of Kitty before she came. It was a difficult game, for M. Vandeloup knew that should Kitty find out his intention she would at once go to Mrs. Villiers, and then Madame would discover his baseness in ruining the girl. M. Vandeloup, however, surveyed the whole situation calmly, and was not ill-pleased at the position of affairs. Life was beginning to bore him in Melbourne, and he wanted to be amused. Here was a comedy worthy of Moliere—a jealous woman, a rich lady, and a handsome man.

"My faith," said M. Vandeloup, smiling to himself as he thought of the situation, "it's a capital comedy, certainly; but I must take care it doesn't end as a tragedy."

II

DISENCHANTMENT

It is said that "creaking doors hang the longest," and Mrs. Pulchop, of Carthage Cottage, Richmond, was an excellent illustration of the truth of this saying. Thin, pale, with light bleached-looking hair, and eyebrows and eyelashes to match, she looked so shadowy and unsubstantial, than an impression was conveyed to the onlooker that a breath might blow her away. She was often heard to declare, when anything extra-ordinary happened, that one might "knock her down with a feather", which, as a matter of fact, was by no means a stretch of fancy, provided the feather was a strong one and Mrs. Pulchop was taken unawares. She was continually alluding to her "constitootion", as if she had an interest in politics, but in reality she was referring to her state of health, which was invariably bad. According to her own showing, there was not a single disease under the sun with which she had not been afflicted, and she could have written a whole book on the subject of medicine, and put herself in, in every instance, as an illustrative case.

Mr. Pulchop had long since departed this life, being considerably assisted in his exit from this wicked world by the quantity of patent medicines his wife compelled him to take to cure him, which unfortunately, however, had the opposite effect.

Mrs. Pulchop said he had been a handsome man, but according to the portrait she had of him he resembled a bull-dog more than anything else in nature. The young Pulchops, of which there were two, both of the female sex, took after their father in appearance and their mother in temperament, and from the time they could talk and crawl knew as much about drops, poultices, bandages, and draughts as many a hospital nurse of mature age.

One day Vandeloup sent a telegram to Kitty saying he would be home to dinner, and as he always required something extra in the way of cooking, Kitty went to interview Mrs. Pulchop on the subject. She found that lady wrapped up in a heavy shawl, turning herself into a tea-kettle by drinking hot water, the idea being, as she assured Kitty, to rouse up her liver. Miss Topsy Pulchop was tying a bandage round her face, as she felt a toothache coming on, while Miss Anna Pulchop was unfortunately quite well, and her occupation being gone, was seated disconsolately at the window trying to imagine she felt pains in her back.

"Ah!" groaned Mrs. Pulchop, in a squeaky voice, sipping her hot water; "you don't know, my dear, what it is to be aworrited by your liver—tortures and inquisitions ain't in it, my love."

Kitty said she was very sorry, and asked her if nothing would relieve her sufferings, but Mrs. Pulchop shook her head triumphantly.

"My sweet young thing," said the patient, with great gusto, "I've tried everything under the sun to make it right, but they ain't no good; it's always expanding and a contracting of itself unbeknown to me, and throwing the bile into the stomach, which ain't its proper place."

"It does sound rather nasty," assented Kitty; "and Topsy seems to be ill, too."

"Toothache," growled Topsy, who had a deep, bass voice, and being modelled on the canine lines of her late lamented father, the growl suited her admirably. "I had two out last week, and now this one's started."

"Try a roasted fig, Topsy dear," suggested her mother, who, now, having finished her hot water, looked longingly at the kettle for more.

"Toothache," growled Topsy, in reply, "not gumboil;" the remedy suggested by Mrs. Pulchop being for the latter of these ills.

"You are quite well, at any rate," said Kitty to Anna, cheerfully.

Anna, however, declined to be considered in good health. "I fancy my back is going to ache," she said, darkly placing her hand in the small of it. "I'll have to put a linseed poultice on it tonight, to draw the cold out."

Then she groaned dismally, and her mother and sister, hearing the familiar sound, also groaned, so there was quite a chorus, and Kitty felt inclined to groan also, out of sympathy.

"M. Vandeloup is coming to dinner tonight," she said, timidly, to Mrs. Pulchop.

"And a wonder it is, my sweet angel," said that lady, indignantly, rising and glancing at the pretty girl, now so pale and sad-looking, "it's once in a blue moon as he comes 'ome, a—leaving you to mope at home like a broken-hearted kitten in a coal box. Ah, if he only had a liver, that would teach him manners."

Groans of assent from the Misses Pulchops, who both had livers and were always fighting with them.

"And what, my neglected cherub," asked Mrs. Pulchop, going to a looking-glass which always hung in the kitchen, for the three to examine their tongues in, "what shall I give you for dinner?"

Kitty suggested a fowl, macaroni cheese, and fruit for dessert, which bill of fare had such an effect on the family that they all groaned in unison.

"Macaroni cheese," growled Topsy, speaking from the very depth of the cork soles she wore to keep her feet dry; "there's nothing more bilious. I couldn't look at it."

"Ah," observed Mrs. Pulchop, "you're only a weak gal, and men is that obstinate they'd swaller bricks like ostriges sooner nor give in as it hurt 'em. You shall 'ave a nice dinner, Mrs. Vanloops, tho' I can't deny but what it ull be bilious."

Thus warned, Kitty retired into her own room and made herself nice for Gaston to look on when he came.

Poor thing, it was so rarely now that he came home to dinner, that a visit from him was regarded by her in the light of a treat. She dressed herself in a pretty white dress and tied a blue sash round her waist, so that she might look the same to him as when he first saw her. But her face was now worn and white, and as she looked at her pallor in the glass she wished she had some rouge to bring a touch of colour to her cheeks. She tried to smile in her own merry way at the wan reflection she beheld, but the effort was a failure, and she burst into tears.

At six o'clock everything was ready for dinner, and having seen that all was in good order, Kitty walked outside to watch for Gaston.

There was a faint, warm, light outside, and the sky was of a pale opaline tint, while the breeze blowing across the garden brought the perfume of the flowers to her, putting Kitty in mind of Mrs. Villiers' garden at Ballarat. Oh, those innocent days! would they never come again? Alas! she knew that they would not—the subtle feeling of youth had left her for ever; and this girl, leaning up against the house with her golden head resting on her arm, knew that the change had come over her which turns all from youth to age.

Suddenly she heard the rattle of wheels, and rousing herself from her reverie, she saw a hansom cab at the gate, and M. Vandeloup standing on the pavement paying the driver. She also heard her lover tell the cabman to call for him at eight o'clock, and her heart sank within her as she thought that he would be gone again in two hours. The cab drove off, and she stood cold and silent on the verandah waiting for Gaston, who sauntered slowly up the walk with one hand in the pocket of his trousers. He was in evening dress, and the night being warm he did not wear an overcoat, so looked tall and slim in his dark clothes as he came up the path swinging his cane gaily to and fro.

"Well, Bebe," he said, brightly, as he bent down and kissed her, "here I am, you see; I hope you've got a nice dinner for me?"

"Oh, yes," answered Kitty, trying to smile, and walking before him into the house; "I told Mrs. Pulchop, and she has made special preparations."

"How is that walking hospital?" asked Vandeloup, carelessly taking off his hat; "I suppose she is ill as usual."

"So she says," replied Kitty, with a laugh, as he put his arm in hers and walked into the room; "she is always ill."

"Why, Bebe, how charming you look tonight," said Vandeloup, holding her at arm's length; "quite like your old self."

And indeed she looked very pretty, for the excitement of seeing him had brightened her eyes and flushed her cheeks, and standing in the warm light of the lamp, with her golden hair floating round her head, she looked like a lovely picture.

"You are not going away very soon?" she whispered to Gaston, coming close to him, and putting her hand on his shoulder; "I see so little of you now."

"My dear child, I can't help it," he said, carelessly removing her hand and walking over to the dinner table; "I have an engagement in town tonight."

"Ah, you no longer care for me," said Kitty, with a stifled sob.

Vandeloup shrugged his shoulders.

"If you are going to make a scene," he said, coldly, "please postpone it. I don't want my appetite taken away; would you kindly see if the dinner is ready?"

Kitty dried her eyes and rang the bell, upon which Mrs. Pulchop glided into the room, still wrapped in her heavy shawl.

"It ain't quite ready yet, sir," she said, in answer to Gaston's question; "Topsy 'aving been bad with the toothache, which you can't expect people to cook dinners as is ill!"

"Why don't you send her to the hospital?" said Vandeloup, with a yawn, looking at his watch.

"Never," retorted Mrs. Pulchop, in a decisively shrill voice; "their medicines ain't pure, and they leaves you at the mercy of doctors to be practised on like a pianer. Topsy may go to the cemetery like her poor dear father, but never to an inquisition of a hospital;" and with this Mrs. Pulchop faded out of the room, for her peculiar mode of egress could hardly be called walking out.

At last dinner made its appearance, and Kitty recovering her spirits, they had a very pleasant meal together, and then Gaston sat over his coffee with a cigarette, talking to Kitty.

He never was without a cigarette in his mouth, and his fingers were all stained a yellowish brown by the nicotine. Kitty lay back in a big arm-chair listening to his idle talk and admiring him as he sat at the dinner table.

"Can't you stay tonight?" she said, looking imploringly at him.

Vandeloup shook his head gently.

"I have an engagement, as I told you before," he said, lazily; "besides, evenings at home are so dreary."

"I will be here," said Kitty, reproachfully.

"That will, of course, make a difference," answered Gaston, with a faint sneer; "but you know," shrugging his shoulders, "I do not cultivate the domestic virtues."

"What will you do when we are married?" said Kitty, with an uneasy laugh.

"Enough for the day is the evil thereof," replied M. Vandeloup, with a gay smile.

"What do you mean?" asked the girl, with a sudden start.

Vandeloup arose from his seat, and lighting another cigarette he lounged over to the fireplace, and leaned against the mantelpiece with his hands in his pockets.

"I mean that when we are married it will be time enough to talk about such things," he answered, looking at her through his eyelashes.

"Then we will talk about them very shortly," said Kitty, with an angry laugh, as her hands clenched the arms of the chair tightly; "for the year is nearly up, and you promised to marry me at the end of it."

"How many things do we intend to do that are never carried out?" said Gaston, gently. "Do you mean that you will break your promise?" she asked, with a scared face.

Vandeloup removed the cigarette from his mouth, and, leaning one elbow on the mantelpiece, looked at her with a smile.

"My dear," he said, quietly, "things are not going well with me at present, and I want money badly."

"Well?" asked Kitty in a whisper, her heart beating loudly.

"You are not rich," said her lover, "so why should we two paupers get married, only to plunge ourselves into misery?"

"Then you refuse to marry me?" she said, rising to her feet.

He bowed his head gently.

"At present, yes," he answered, and replaced the cigarette between his lips.

Kitty stood for a moment as if turned to stone, and then throwing up her hands with a gesture of despair, fell back into the chair, and burst into a flood of tears. Vandeloup shrugged his shoulders in a resigned sort of manner, and glanced at his watch to see when it would be time for him to go. Meanwhile he smoked quietly on, and Kitty, after sobbing for some time, dried her eyes, and sat up in the chair again.

"How long is this going to last?" she asked, in a hard voice.

"Till I get rich!"

"That may be a long time?"

"It may."

"Perhaps never?"

"Perhaps!"

"And then I will never be your wife?"

"Unfortunately, no."

"You coward!" burst forth Kitty, rising from her seat, and crossing over to him; "you made me leave my home with your false promises, and now you refuse to make me the only reparation that is in your power."

"Circumstances are against any virtuous intentions I may entertain," retorted Vandeloup, coolly.

Kitty looked at him for a moment, then ran over to a desk near the window, and took from thence a small bottle of white glass with two red bands round it. She let the lid of the desk fall with a bang, then crossed to Vandeloup, holding the bottle up before him.

"Do you know what this is?" she asked, in a harsh voice.

"The poison I made in Ballarat," he answered, coolly, blowing a wreath of smoke; "how did you get hold of it?"

"I found it in your private desk," she said, coldly.

"That was wrong, my dear," he answered, gently, "you should never betray confidences—I left the desk in your charge, and it should have been sacred to you."

"Out of your own mouth are you condemned," said the girl, quickly;

"you have betrayed my confidence and ruined me, so if you do not fix a day for our marriage, I swear I will drink this and die at your feet."

"How melodramatic you are, Bebe," said Vandeloup, coolly; "you put me in mind of Croisette in 'Le Sphinx'."

"You don't believe I will do it."

"No! I do not."

"Then see." She took the stopper out of the bottle and held it to her lips. Vandeloup did not stir, but, still smoking, stood looking at her with a smile. His utter callousness was too much for her, and replacing the stopper again, she slipped the bottle into her pocket and let her hands fall idly by her side.

"I thought you would not do it," replied Gaston, smoothly, looking at his watch; "you must really excuse me, I hear the cab wheels outside."

Kitty, however, placed herself in front of him as he moved towards the door.

"Listen to me," she said, in a harsh voice, with white face and flaming eyes; "to-night I leave this house for ever."

He bowed his head.

"As it pleases you," he replied, simply.

"My God!" she cried, "have you no love for me now?"

"No," he answered, coldly and brutally, "I am tired of you."

She fell on her knees and clutched his hand.

"Dear Gaston! dear Gaston!" she cried, covering it with kisses, "think how young I am, how my life is ruined, and by you. I gave up everything for your sake—home, father, and friends—you will not cast me off like this after all I have sacrificed for you? Oh, for God's sake, speak—speak!"

"My dear," said Vandeloup, gravely, looking down at the kneeling figure with the streaming eyes and clenched hands, "as long as you choose to stay here I will be your friend—I cannot afford to marry you, but while you are with me our lives will be as they have been; good-bye at present," touching her forehead coldly with his lips, "I will call to-morrow afternoon to see how you are, and I trust this will be the last of such scenes."

He drew his hand away from hers, and she sat on the floor dull and silent, with her eyes fixed on the ground and an aching in her heart. Vandeloup went into the hall, put on his hat, then lighting another cigarette and taking his stick, walked gaily out of the house, humming an air from "La Belle Helene". The cab was waiting for him at the door, and telling the man to drive to the Bachelors' Club, he entered the cab and rattled away down the street without a thought for the broken-hearted woman he left behind.

Kitty sat on the floor with her folded hands lying carelessly on her lap and her eyes staring idly at the carpet. This, then, was the end of all her hopes and joys—she was cast aside carelessly by this man now that he wearied of her. Love's young dream had been sweet indeed; but, ah! how bitter was the awakening. Her castles in the air had all melted into clouds, and here in the very flower of her youth she felt that her life was ruined, and she was as one wandering in a sterile waste, with a black and starless sky overhead. She clasped her hands with a sensation of pain, and a rose at her breast fell down withered and dead. She took it up with listless fingers, and with the quiver of her hand the leaves fell off and were scattered over her white dress in a pink shower. It was an allegory of her life, she thought. Once it had been as fresh and full of fragrance as this dead rose; then it had withered, and now she saw all her hopes and beliefs falling off one by one like the faded petals. Ah, there is no despair like that of youth; and Kitty, sitting on the floor with hot dry eyes and a pain in her heart, felt that the sun of her life had set for ever.

So STILL THE NIGHT WAS. No moon as yet, but an innumerable blaze of stars set like diamonds in the dark blue sky. A smoky yellowish haze hung over the city, but down in the garden amid the flowers all was cool and fragrant. The house was quite dark, and a tall mulberry tree on one side of it was black against the clear sky. Suddenly the door opened, and a figure came out and closed the door softly after it. Down the path it came, and standing in the middle of the garden, raised a white tear-stained face to the dark sky. A dog barked in the distance, and then a fresh cold breeze came sweeping through the trees and stirring the still perfumes of the flowers. The figure threw its hands out towards the house with a gesture of despair, then gliding down the path it went out of the gate and stole quietly down the lonely street.

III

M. Vandeloup Hears Something to his Advantage

As he drove rapidly into town Gaston's thoughts were anything but pleasant. Not that he was thinking about Kitty, for he regarded the scene he had with her as merely an outburst of hysterical passion, and did not dream she would take any serious step. He forgot all about her when he left the house, and, lying back in the cab smoking one of his everlasting cigarettes, pondered about his position. The fact was he was very hard up for money, and did not know where to turn for more. His luck at cards was so great that even the Bachelors, used as they were to losing large sums, began to murmur among themselves that M. Vandeloup was too clever, and as that young gentleman by no means desired to lose his popularity he stopped playing cards altogether, and so effectually silenced everyone. So this mode of making money was gone, and until Madame Midas arrived in town Vandeloup did not see how he was going to keep on living in his former style. But as he never denied himself anything while he had the money, he ordered the cabman to drive to Paton's, the florist in Swanston Street, and there purchased a dainty bunch of flowers for his button hole. From thence he drove to his club, and there found a number of young fellows, including Mr. Barty Jarper, all going to the Princess Theatre to see "The Mikado". Barty rushed forward when Vandeloup appeared and noisily insisted he should come with them. The men had been dining, and were exhilarated with wine, so Vandeloup, not caring to appear at the theatre with such a noisy lot, excused himself. Barty and his friends, therefore, went off by themselves, and left Vandeloup alone. He picked up the evening paper and glanced over it with a yawn, when a name caught his eye which he had frequently noticed before.

"I say," he said to a tall, fair young fellow who had just entered, "who is this Meddlechip the paper is full of?"

"Don't you know?" said the other, in surprise; "he's one of our richest men, and very generous with his money."

"Oh, I see! buys popularity," replied Vandeloup, coolly; "how is it I've never met him?"

"He's been to China or Chile—or—something commencing with a C," returned the young man, vaguely; "he only came back to Melbourne last week; you are sure to meet him sooner or later."

"Thanks, I'm not very anxious," replied Vandeloup, with a yawn; "money in my eyes does not compensate for being bored; where are you going to-night?"

"'Mikado'," answered the other, whose name was Bellthorp; "Jarper asked me to go up there; he's got a box."

"How does he manage to pay for all these things?" asked Vandeloup, rising; "he's only in a bank, and does not get much money."

"My dear fellow," said Bellthorp, putting his arm in that of Vandeloup's, "wherever he gets it, he always has it, so as long as he pays his way it's none of our business; come and have a drink."

Vandeloup assented with a laugh, and they went to the bar.

"I've got a cab at the door," he said to Bellthorp, after they had finished their drinks, and were going downstairs; "come with me, and I'll go up to the Princess also; Jarper asked me and I refused, but men as well as women are entitled to change their minds."

They got into the cab and drove up Collins Street to the Princess Theatre. After dismissing the cab, they went up stairs and found the first act was just over, and the bar was filled with a crowd of gentlemen, among whom Barty and his friends were conspicuous. On the one side the doors opened on to the wide stone balcony, where a number of ladies were seated, and on the other balcony a lot of men were smoking. Leaving Bellthorp with Jarper, Vandeloup ordered a brandy and soda and went out on the balcony to smoke.

The bell rang to indicate the curtain was going to rise on the second act, and the bar and balconies gradually emptied themselves into the theatre. M. Vandeloup, however, still sat smoking, and occasionally drinking his brandy and soda, while he thought over his difficulties, and wondered how he could get out of them. It was a wonderfully hot night, and not even the dark blue of the moonless sky, studded with stars, could give any sensation of coolness. Round the balcony were several windows belonging to the dressing-rooms of the theatre, and the lights within shone through the vivid red of the blinds with which they were covered. The door leading into the bar was wide open, and within everything seemed hot, even under the cool, white glare of the electric lights, which shone in large oval-shaped globes hanging from the brass supports in clusters like those grapes known as ladies' fingers. In front stretched the high balustrade of the balcony, and as Vandeloup leaned back in his chair he could see the white blaze of the electric lights rising above this, and then the luminous darkness of the summer's night. Beyond a cluster of trees, with a path, lit by gas lamps, going through it, the lights of which shone like dull yellow stars. On the right arose the great block of Parliament-buildings, with the confused mass of the scaffolding, standing up black and dense against the sky. A pleasant murmur arose from the crowded pavement below, and through the incessant rattle of cabs and sharp, clear cries of the street boys, Gaston could hear the shrill tones of a violin playing the dreamy melody of the "One Summer's Night in Munich" valse, about which all Melbourne was then raving.

He was so occupied with his own thoughts that he did not notice two gentlemen who came in from the bar, and taking seats a little distant from him, ordered drinks from the waiter who came to attend to them. They were both in evening dress, and had apparently left the opera in order to talk business, for they kept conversing eagerly, and their voices striking on Vandeloup's ear he glanced round at them and then relapsed into his former inattentive position. Now, however, though apparently absorbed in his own thoughts, he was listening to every word they said, for he had caught the name of The Magpie Reef, a quartz mine, which had lately been floated on the market, the shares of which had run up to a pound, and then, as bad reports were circulated about it, dropped suddenly to four shillings. Vandeloup recognised one as Barraclough, a well-known stockbroker, but the other was a dark, wiry-looking man of medium height, whom he had never seen before.

"I tell you it's a good thing," said Barraclough, vehemently laying his hand on the table; "Tollerby is the manager, and knows everything about it."

"Gad, he ought to," retorted the other with a laugh, "if he's the manager; but I don't believe in it, dear boy, I never did; it started with a big splash, and was going to be a second Long Tunnel according to the prospectus; now the shares are only four shillings—pshaw!"

"Yes, but you forget the shares ran up to a pound," replied Barraclough, quickly; "and now they are so cheap we can snap them up all over the market, and then—"

"Well?" asked the other, with interest.

"They will run up, old fellow—see?" and the Broker rubbed his hands gleefully.

"How are you going to get up a 'Boom' on them?" asked the wiry man, sceptically; "the public won't buy blindly, they must see something."

"And so they shall," said Barraclough, eagerly; "Tollerby is sending down some of the stone."

"From the Magpie Reef?" asked the other, suspiciously.

"Of course," retorted the Broker, indignantly; "you did not think it was salted, did you? There is gold in the reef, but it is patchy. See," pulling out a pocket-book, "I got this telegram from Tollerby at four o'clock to-day;" he took a telegram from the pocket-book and handed it to his companion.

"Struck it rich—evidently pocket—thirty ounces to machine," read the other slowly; "gad! that looks well, why don't you put it in the papers?"

"Because I don't hold enough shares," replied the other, impatiently; "don't you understand? To-morrow I go on 'Change and buy up all the shares at four shillings I can lay my hands on, then at the end of the week the samples of stone—very rich—come down. I publish this telegram from the manager, and the 'Boom' starts."

"How high do you think the shares will go?" asked the wiry man, thoughtfully.

Barraclough shrugged his shoulders, and replaced the telegram in his pocket-book.

"Two or three pounds, perhaps more," he replied, rising. "At all events, it's a good thing, and if you go in with me, we'll clear a good few thousand out of it."

"Come and see me to-morrow morning," said the wiry man, also rising. "I think I'll stand in."

Barraclough rubbed his hands gleefully, and then slipping his arm in that of his companion they left the balcony and went back to the theatre.

Vandeloup felt every nerve in his body tingling. Here was a chance to make money. If he only had a few hundreds he could buy up all the Magpie shares he could get and reap the benefit of the rise. Five hundred pounds! If he could obtain that sum he could buy two thousand five hundred shares, and if they went to three pounds, he could clear nearly eight thousand. What an idea! It was ripe fruit tumbling off the tree without the trouble of plucking it. But five hundred pounds! He had not as many pence, and he did not know where to get it. If he could only borrow it from someone—but then he could offer no security. A sense of his own helplessness came on him as he saw this golden tide flowing past his door, and yet was unable to take advantage of it. Five hundred pounds! The sum kept buzzing in his head like a swarm of bees, and he threw himself down again in his chair to try and think where he could get it.

A noise disturbed him, and he saw that the opera was over, and a crowd of gentlemen were thronging into the bar. Jarper was among them, and he thought he would speak to him on the subject. Yes, Barty was a clever little fellow, and seemed always able to get money. Perhaps he would be able to assist him. He stepped out of the balcony into the light and touched Barty on the shoulder as he stood amid his friends.

"Hullo! it's you!" cried Barty, turning round. "Where have you been, old chap?"

"Out on the balcony," answered Vandeloup, curtly.

"Come and have supper with us," said Barty, hospitably. "We are going to have some at Leslie's."

"Yes, do come," urged Bellthorp, putting his arm in that of Vandeloup's; "we'll have no end of fun."

Vandeloup was just going to accept, as he thought on the way he could speak privately to Barty about this scheme he had, when he saw a stout gentleman at the end of the room taking a cup of coffee at the counter, and talking to another gentleman who was very tall and thin. The figure of the stout gentleman seemed familiar to Vandeloup, and at this moment he turned slowly round and looked down the room. Gaston gave a start when he saw his face, and then smiled in a gratified manner to himself.

"Who is that gentleman with the coffee?" he asked Barty.

"Those stout and lean kine," said Barty, airily, "puts one in mind of Pharaoh's dream, doesn't it?"

"Yes, yes!" retorted Gaston, impatiently; "but who are they?"

"The long one is Fell, the railway contractor," said Barty, glancing with some surprise at Vandeloup, "and the other is old Meddlechip, the millionaire."

"Meddlechip," echoed Vandeloup, as if to himself; "my faith!"

"Yes," broke in Bellthorp, quickly; "the one we were speaking of at the club—do you know him?"

"I fancy I do," said Vandeloup, with a strange smile. "You must excuse me to your supper to-night."

"No, we won't," said Barty, firmly; "you must come."

"Then I'll look in later," said Vandeloup, who had not the slightest intention of going. "Will that do?"

"I suppose it will have to," said Bellthorp, in an injured tone; "but why can't you come now?"

"I've got to see about some business," said Vandeloup.

"What, at this hour of the night?" cried Jarper, in a voice of disgust.

Vandeloup nodded, and lit a cigarette.

"Well, mind you come in later," said Barty, and then he and his friends left the bar, after making Vandeloup promise faithfully he would come.

Gaston sauntered slowly up to the coffee bar, and asked for a cup in his usual musical voice, but when the stout gentleman heard him speak he turned pale and looked up. The thin one had gone off to talk to someone else, so when Vandeloup got his coffee he turned slowly round and looked straight at Meddlechip seated in the chair.

"Good evening, M. Kestrike," he said, quietly.

Meddlechip, whose face was usually red and florid-looking, turned ghastly pale, and sprang to his feet.

"Octave Braulard!" he gasped, placing his coffee cup on the counter.

"At your service," said Vandeloup, looking rapidly round to see that no one overheard the name, "but here I am Gaston Vandeloup."

Meddlechip passed his handkerchief over his face and moistened his dry lips with his tongue.

"How did you get here?" he asked, in a strangled voice.

"It's a long story," said M. Vandeloup, putting his coffee cup down and wiping his lips with his handkerchief; "suppose we go and have supper somewhere, and I'll tell you all about it."

"I don't want any supper," said Meddlechip, sullenly, his face having regained its normal colour. "Possibly not, but I do," replied Vandeloup, sweetly, taking his arm; "come, let us go."

Meddlechip did not resist, but walked passively out of the bar with Vandeloup, much to the astonishment of the thin gentleman, who called out to him but without getting any answer.

Meddlechip went to the cloak room and put on his coat and hat. Then he followed Vandeloup down the stairs and paused at the door while the Frenchman hailed a hansom. When it drove up, however, he stopped short at the edge of the pavement.

"I won't go," he said, determinedly.

Vandeloup looked at him with a peculiar gleam in his dark eyes, and bowed.

"Let me persuade you, Monsieur," he said, blandly, holding the door of the cab open.

Meddlechip glanced at him, and then, with a sigh of resignation, entered the cab, followed by Vandeloup.

"Where to, sir?" asked the cabman, through the trap.

"To Leslie's Supper Rooms," replied the Frenchman, and the cab drove off.

IV

The Case of Adele Blondet

Leslie's Supper Rooms in Bourke Street East were very well known—that is, among a certain class. Religious people and steady businessmen knew nothing about such a place except by reputation, and looked upon it, with horror, as a haunt of vice and dissipation.

Though Leslie's, in common with other places had to close at a certain hour, yet when the shutters were up, the door closed, and the lights extinguished in the front of the house, there was plenty of life and bustle going on at the back, where there were charmingly furnished little rooms for supper parties. Barty Jarper had engaged one of these apartments, and with about a dozen young men was having a good time of it when Vandeloup and Meddlechip drove up. After dismissing the cab and looking up and down the street to see that no policeman was in sight, Vandeloup knocked at the door in a peculiar manner, and it was immediately opened in a stealthy kind of way. Gaston gave his name, whereupon they were allowed to enter, and the door was closed after them in the same quiet manner, all of which was very distasteful to Mr. Meddlechip, who, being a public man and a prominent citizen, felt that he was breaking the laws he had assisted to make. He looked round in some disgust at the crowds of waiters, and at the glimpses he caught every now and then of gentlemen in evening dress, and what annoyed him more than anything else—ladies in bright array. Oh! a dissipated place was Leslie's, and even in the daytime had a rakish-looking appearance as if it had been up all night and knew a thing or two. Mr. Meddlechip would have retreated from this den of iniquity if he could, but as he wanted to have a thorough explanation with Vandeloup, he meekly followed the Frenchman through a well-lighted passage, with statues on either side holding lamps, to a little room beautifully furnished, wherein a supper table was laid out. Here the waiter who conducted them took their hats and Meddlechip's coat and hung them up, then waited respectfully for M. Vandeloup to give his orders. A portly looking waiter he was, with a white waistcoat, a white shirt, which bulged out in a most obtrusive manner, and a large white cravat, which was tied round an equally large white collar. When he walked he rolled along like a white-crested wave, and with his napkin under his arm, the heel of one foot in the hollow of the other, and his large red face, surmounted by a few straggling tufts of black hair, he was truly wonderful to behold.

This magnificent creature, who answered to the name of Gurchy, received Vandeloup's orders with a majestic bend of his head, then rolling up to Mr. Meddlechip, he presented the bill of fare to that gentleman, who, however, refused it.

"I don't want any supper," he said, curtly.

Gurchy, though a waiter, was human, and looked astonished, while Vandeloup remonstrated in a suave manner.

"But, my dear sir," he said, leaning back in his chair, "you must have something to eat. I assure you," with a significant smile, "you will need it."

Meddlechip's lips twitched a little as the Frenchman spoke, then, with an uneasy laugh, he ordered something, and drew his chair up to the table.

"And, waiter," said Vandeloup, softly, as Gurchy was rolling out of the door, "bring some wine, will you? Pommery, I think, is best," he added, turning to Meddlechip.

"What you like," returned that gentleman, impatiently, "I don't care."

"That's a great mistake," replied Gaston, coolly; "bad wine plays the deuce with one's digestion—two bottles of Pommery, waiter."

Gurchy nodded, that is to say his head disappeared for a moment in the foam of his collar, then re-appeared again as he slowly rolled out of the door and vanished.

"Now, then, sir," said Meddlechip, sharply, rising from his seat and closing the door, "what did you bring me here for?"

M. Vandeloup raised his eyebrows in surprise.

"How energetic you are, my dear Kestrike," he said, smoothly, lying down on the sofa, and contemplating his shoes with great satisfaction; "just the same noisy, jolly fellow as of yore."

"Damn you!" said the other, fiercely, at which Gaston laughed.

"You had better leave that to God," he answered, mockingly; "he understands more about it than you do."

"Oh, I know you of old," said Meddlechip, walking up and down excitedly; "I know you of old, with your sneers and your coolness, but it won't do here," stopping opposite the sofa, and glaring down at Vandeloup; "it won't do here!"

"So you've said twice," replied M. Vandeloup, with a yawn. "How do you want me to conduct myself? Do tell me; I am always open to improvement."

"You must leave Australia," said Meddlechip, sharply, and breathing hard.

"If I refuse?" asked M. Vandeloup, lazily, smiling to himself.

"I will denounce you as a convict escaped from New Caledonia!" hissed the other, putting his hands in his pockets, and bending forward.

"Indeed," said Gaston, with a charming smile, "I don't think you will go so far as that, my friend."

"I swear," said Meddlechip, loudly, raising his hand, "I swear—"

"Oh, fie!" observed M. Vandeloup, in a shocked tone; "an old man like you should not swear; it's very wrong, I assure you; besides," with a disparaging glance, "you are not suited to melodrama."

Meddlechip evidently saw it was no good trying to fight against the consummate coolness of this young man, so with a great effort resolved to adapt himself to the exigencies of the case, and fight his adversary with his own weapons.

"Well," he said at length, resuming his seat at the table, and trying to speak calmly, though his flushed face and quivering lips showed what an effort it cost him; "let us have supper first, and we can talk afterwards."

"Ah, that's much better," remarked M. Vandeloup, sitting up to the table, and unrolling his napkin. "I assure you, my dear fellow, if you treat me well, I'm a very easy person to deal with."

The eyes of the two men met for a moment across the table, and Vandeloup's had such a meaning look in them, that Meddlechip dropped his own with a shiver.

The door opened, and the billowy waiter rolled up to the table, and having left a deposit of plates and food thereon, subsided once more out of the door, then rolled in again with the champagne. He drew the cork of one of the bottles, filled the glasses on the table, and then after giving a glance round to see that all was in order, suddenly found that it was ebb-tide, and rolled slowly out of the door, which he closed after him.

Meddlechip ate his supper in silence, but drank a good deal of champagne to keep his courage up for the coming ordeal, which he knew he must go through. Vandeloup, on the other hand, ate and drank very little, as he talked gaily all the time about theatres, racing, boating, in fact of everything except the thing the other man wanted to hear.

"I never mix up business with pleasure, my dear fellow," said Gaston, amiably, guessing his companion's thoughts; "when we have finished supper and are enjoying our cigars, I will tell you a little story."

"I don't want to hear it," retorted the other, harshly, having an intuitive idea what the story would be about.

"Possibly not," replied M. Vandeloup, smoothly; "nevertheless it is my wish that you should hear it."

Meddlechip looked as if he were inclined to resent this plain speaking, but after a pause evidently thought better of it, and went on tranquilly eating his supper.

When they had finished Gaston rang the bell, and when the billow rolled in, ordered a fresh bottle of wine and some choice cigars of a brand well known at Leslie's. Gurchy's head disappeared in foam again, and did not emerge therefrom till he was out of the door.

"Try one of these," said M. Vandeloup, affably, to Meddlechip, when the billow had rolled in with the cigars and wine, "it's an excellent brand."

"I don't care about smoking," answered Meddlechip.

"To please me," urged M. Vandeloup, persuasively; whereupon Meddlechip took one, and having lighted it puffed away evidently under protest, while the billow opened the new bottle of wine, freshened up the glasses, and then rolled majestically out of the door, like a tidal wave.

"Now then for the story," said M. Vandeloup, leaning back luxuriously on the sofa, and blowing a cloud of smoke.

"I don't want to hear it," retorted the other, quickly; "name your terms and let us end the matter."

"Pardon me," said M. Vandeloup, with a smile, "but I refuse to accept any terms till I have given you thoroughly to understand what I mean; so you must hear this little tale of Adele Blondet."

"For God's sake, no!" cried the other, hoarsely, rising to his feet; "I tell you I am haunted by it; by day and by night, sleeping or waking, I see her face ever before me like an accusing angel."

"Curious," murmured M. Vandeloup, "especially as she was not by any means an angel."

"I thought it was done with," said Meddlechip, twisting his fingers together, while the large drops of perspiration stood on his forehead, "but here you come like a spectre from the past and revive all the old horrors."

"If you call Adele a horror," retorted Vandeloup, coolly, "I am certainly going to revive her, so you had best sit down and hear me to the end, for you certainly will not turn me from my purpose."

Meddlechip sank back into his chair with a groan, while his relentless enemy curled himself up on the sofa in a more comfortable position and began to talk.

"We will begin the story," said M. Vandeloup, in a conversational tone, with an airy wave of his delicate white hand, "in the good old-fashioned style of our fairy tales. Once upon a time—let us say three years ago—there lived in Paris a young man called Octave Braulard, who was well born and comfortably off. He had a fancy to be a doctor, and was studying for the medical profession when he became entangled with a woman. Mademoiselle Adele Blondet was a charmingly ugly actress, who was at that time the rage of Paris. She attracted all the men, not by her looks, but by her tongue. Octave Braulard," went on M. Vandeloup, complacently looking at himself, "was handsome, and she fell in love with him. She became his mistress, and caused a nine days' wonder in Paris by remaining constant to him for six months. Then there came to Paris an English gentleman from Australia—name, Kestrike; position, independent; income, enormous. He had left Madame his wife in London, and came to our wicked Paris to amuse himself. He saw Adele Blondet, and was introduced to her by Braulard; result, Kestrike betrayed his friend Braulard by stealing from him his mistress. Why was this? Was Kestrike handsome? No. Was he fascinating? No. Was he rich? Yes. Therein lay the secret; Adele loved the purse, not the man. Braulard," said Gaston, rising from the sofa quickly and walking across the room, "felt his honour wounded. He remonstrated with Adele, no use; he offered to fight a duel with the perfidious Kestrike, no use; the thief was a coward."

"No," cried Meddlechip, rising, "no coward."

"I say, yes!" said Vandeloup, crossing to him, and forcing him back in his chair; "he betrayed his friend and refused to give him the satisfaction of a gentleman. What did Braulard do? Rest quiet? No. Revenge his honour? Yes! One night," pursued Gaston, in a low concentrated voice, grasping Meddlechip's wrist firmly, and looking at him with fiery eyes, "Braulard prepared a poison, a narcotic which was quick in its action, fatal in its results. He goes to the house of Adele Blondet at half-past twelve o'clock—the hour now," he said, rapidly swinging round and pointing to the clock on the mantelpiece, which had just struck the half-hour; "he found them at supper," releasing Meddlechip's wrist and crossing to the sofa; "he sat opposite Kestrike, as he does now," leaning forward and glaring at Meddlechip, who shrank back in his chair. "Adele, at the head of the table, laughs and smiles; she looks at her old lover and sees murder in his face; she is ill and retires to her room. Kestrike follows her to see what is the matter. Braulard is left alone; he produces a bottle and pours its contents into a cup of coffee, waiting for Adele. Kestrike returns, saying Adele is ill; she wants a drink. He takes her the poisoned cup of coffee; she drinks it and falls"—with a long breath—"asleep. Kestrike returns to the room, asks Braulard to leave the house. Braulard refuses. Kestrike is afraid, and would leave himself; he rises from the table; so does Braulard;"—here Gaston rose and crossed to Meddlechip, who was also on his feet—"he goes to Kestrike, seizes his wrist, thus—drags him to the bedroom, and there on the bed lies Adele Blondet—dead—killed by the poison of one lover given her by the other—and the murderers look at one another—thus."

Meddlechip wrenched his hand from Vandeloup's iron grip and fell back ghastly white in his chair, with a strangled cry, while the Frenchman stood over him with eyes gleaming with hatred.

"Kestrike," pursued Vandeloup, rapidly, "is little known in Paris—his name is an assumed one—he leaves France before the police can discover how he has poisoned Adele Blondet, and crosses to England—meets Madame, his wife, and returns to Australia, where he is called—Meddlechip."

The man in the chair threw up his hands as if to keep the other off, and uttered a stifled cry.

"He then goes to China," went on Gaston, bending nearer to the shrinking figure, "and returns after twelve months, where he meets Octave Braulard in the theatre—yes, the two murderers meet in Melbourne! How came Braulard here? Was it chance? No. Was it design? No. Was it Fate? Yes."

He hissed the words in Meddlechip's ear, and the wretched man shrank away from him again.

"Braulard," pursued Vandeloup, in a calmer tone, "also left the house of Adele Blondet. She is found dead; one of her lovers cannot be found; the other, Braulard, is accused of the crime; he defies the police to prove it; she has been poisoned. Bah! there is no trace. Braulard will be free. Stop! who is this man called Prevol, who appears? He is a fellow student of Braulard's, and knows the poison. Braulard is lost! Prevol examines the body, proves that poison has been given—by whom? Braulard, and none other. He is sentenced to death; but he is so handsome that Paris urges pardon. No; it is not according to the law. Still, spare his life? Yes. His life is spared. The galleys at Toulon? No. New Caledonia? Yes. He is sent there. But is Braulard a coward? No. Does he rest as a convict? No. He makes friends with another convict; they steal a boat, and fly from the island; they drift, and drift, for days and days; the sun rises, the sun sets—still they drift; their food is giving out, the water in the barrel is low—God! are they to die of thirst and famine? No. The sky is red—like blood—the sun is sinking; land is in the distance—they are saved!" falling on his knees; "they are saved, thank God!"

Meddlechip, who had recovered himself, wiped his face with his handkerchief, and sneered with his white lips at the theatrical way Gaston was behaving in. Vandeloup saw this, and, springing to his feet, crossed to the millionaire.

"Braulard," he continued, quickly, "lands on the coast of Queensland; he comes to Sydney—no work; to Melbourne—no work; he goes to Ball'rat—work there at a gold-mine. Braulard takes the name of Vandeloup and makes money; he comes to Melbourne, lives there a year, he is in want of money, he is in despair; at the theatre he overhears a plan which will give him money, but he needs capital—despair again, he will never get it. Aha! Fate once more intervenes—he sees M. Kestrike, now Meddlechip, he will ask him for the money, and the question is, will he get it? So the story is at an end." He ended with his usual smile, all his excitement having passed away, and lounging over to the supper-table lit a cigarette and sat down on the sofa.

Meddlechip sat silently looking at the disordered supper-table and thinking deeply. The dishes were scattered about the white cloth, and some vividly red cherries had fallen down from the fruit dish in the centre, some salt was spilt near his elbow, the napkins, twisted into thin wisps, were lying among the dirty dishes, and the champagne glasses, half filled with the straw-coloured wine, were standing near the empty bottles. Meddlechip thought for a few moments, and then looked up suddenly in a cool, collected, business-like manner.

"As I understand you," he said, in a steady voice, "the case stands thus: you know a portion, or rather, I should say, an episode of my life, I would gladly forget. I did not commit the murder."

"No, but you gave her the poison."

"Innocently I did, I confess."

"Bah! who will believe that?" retorted M. Vandeloup, with a shrug; "but never mind this at present; let me hear what you intend to do."

"You know a secret," said Meddlechip, nervously, "which is dangerous to me; you want to sell it; well, I will be the buyer—name your price."

"Five hundred pounds," said Vandeloup, quietly.

"Is that all?" asked the other, with a start of surprise; "I was prepared for five thousand."

"I am not exorbitant in my demands," answered Vandeloup, smoothly; "and as I told you, I have a scheme on hand by which I may make a lot of money-five hundred pounds is sufficient to do what I want. If the scheme succeeds, I will be rich enough to do without any more money from you."

"Yes; but if it fails?" said Meddlechip, doubtfully.

"If it fails, I will be obliged to draw on you again," returned Gaston, candidly; "you can't say, however, that I am behaving badly to you."

"No," answered Meddlechip, looking at him. "I must say you are easier to deal with than I anticipated. Well, if I give you my cheque for five hundred—"

"Say six hundred," observed Vandeloup, rising and going to a small table in the corner of the room on which were pens and ink. "I want an extra hundred."

"Six hundred then be it," answered Meddlechip, quietly, rising and going to his overcoat, from whence he took his cheque book. "For this amount you will be silent."

M. Vandeloup bowed gracefully.

"On my word of honour," he replied, gaily; "but, of course," with a sudden glance at Meddlechip, "you will treat me as a friend—ask me to your house, and introduce me to Madame, your wife."

"I don't see the necessity," returned Meddlechip, angrily, going over to the small table and sitting down.

"Pardon me, I do" answered the Frenchman, with a dangerous gleam in his eyes.

"Well, well, I agree," said Meddlechip, testily, taking up a pen and opening his cheque book. "You, of course, can dictate your own terms."

"I understand that perfectly," replied Vandeloup, delicately, lighting a cigarette, "and have done so. You can't say they are hard, as I said before."

Meddlechip did not answer, but wrote out a cheque for six hundred pounds, and then handed it to Vandeloup, who received it with a bow and slipped it into his waistcoat pocket.

"With this," he said, touching his pocket, "I hope to make nearly ten thousand in a fortnight."

Meddlechip stared at him.

"I hope you will," he answered, gruffly, "all the better for my purse if you do."

"That, of course, goes without saying," replied Vandeloup, lazily. "Have some more wine?" touching the bell.

"No more, thank you," said Meddlechip, putting on his overcoat. "It's time I was off."

"By the way," said M. Vandeloup, coolly, "I have not any change in my pocket; you might settle for the supper."

Meddlechip burst out laughing.

"Confound your impudence," he said, quickly, "I thought you asked me to supper."

"Oh, yes," replied Vandeloup, taking his hat and stick, "but I intended you to pay for it."

"You were pretty certain of your game, then?"

"I always am," answered Vandeloup, as the door opened, and Gurchy rolled slowly into the room.

Meddlechip paid the bill without making further objections, and then they both left Leslie's with the same precautions as had attended their entry. They walked slowly down Bourke Street, and parted at the corner, Meddlechip going to Toorak, while Vandeloup got into a cab and told the man to drive to Richmond, then lit a cigarette and gave himself up to reflection as he drove along.

"I've done a good stroke of business tonight," he said, smiling, as he felt the cheque in his pocket, "and I'll venture the whole lot on this Magpie reef. If it succeeds I will be rich; if it does not—well, there is always Meddlechip as my banker." Then his thoughts went back to Kitty, for the reason of his going home so late was that he wanted to find out in what frame of mind she was.

"She'll never leave me," he said, with a laugh, as the cab drew up in front of Mrs. Pulchop's house; "if she does, so much the better for me."

He dismissed his cab, and let himself in with the latch key; then hanging up his hat in the hall he went straight to the bedroom and lit the gas. He then crossed to the bed, expecting to find Kitty sound asleep, but to his surprise the bed was untouched, and she was not there.

"Ah!" he said, quietly, "so she has gone, after all. Poor little girl, I wonder where she is. I must really look after her to-morrow; at present," he said, pulling off his coat, with a yawn, "I think I'll go to bed."

He went to bed, and laying his head on the pillow was soon fast asleep, without even a thought for the girl he had ruined.

V

The Key of the Street

When Kitty left Mrs. Pulchop's residence she had no very definite idea as to what she was going to do with herself. Her sole thought was to get as far away from her former life as possible—to disappear in the crowd and never to be heard of again. Poor little soul, she never for a moment dreamed that it was a case of out of the frying pan into the fire, and that the world at large might prove more cruel to her than Vandeloup in particular. She had been cut to the heart by his harsh cold words, but notwithstanding he had spoken so bitterly she still loved him, and would have stayed beside him, but her jealous pride forbade her to do so. She who had been queen of his heart and the idol of his life could not bear to receive cold looks and careless words, and to be looked upon as an encumbrance and a trouble. So she thought if she left him altogether and never saw him again he would, perhaps, be sorry for her and cherish her memory tenderly for evermore. If she had only known Gaston's true nature she would not thus have buoyed herself up with false hopes of his sorrow, but as she believed in him as implicitly as a woman in love with a man always does, in a spirit of self-abnegation she cut herself off from him, thinking it would be to his advantage if not to her own.

She went into town and wandered about listlessly, not knowing where to go, till nearly twelve o'clock, and the streets were gradually emptying themselves of their crowds. The coffee stalls were at all the corners, with hungry-looking people of both sexes crowded round them, and here and there in door steps could be seen some outcasts resting in huddled heaps, while the policemen every now and then would come up and make them move on.

Kitty was footsore and heart-weary, and felt inclined to cry, but was nevertheless resolved not to go back to her home in Richmond. She dragged herself along the lonely street, and round the corner came on a coffee stall with no one at it except one small boy whose head just reached up to the counter. Such a ragged boy as he was, with a broad comical-looking face—a shaggy head of red hair and a hat without any brim to it—his legs were bandy and his feet were encased in a pair of men's boots several sizes too large for him. He had a bundle of newspapers under one arm and his other hand was in his pocket rattling some coppers together while he bargained with the coffee-stall keeper over a pie. The coffee stall had the name of Spilsby inscribed on it, so it is fair to suppose that the man therein was Spilsby himself. He had a long grey beard and a meek face, looking so like an old wether himself it appeared almost the act of a cannibal on his part to eat a mutton pie. A large placard at the back of the stall set forth the fact that "Spilsby's Specials" were sold there for the sum of one penny, and it was over "Spilsby's Specials" the ragged boy was arguing.

"I tell you I ain't agoin' to eat fat," he said, in a hoarse voice, as if his throat was stuffed up with one of his own newspapers. "I want a special, I don't want a hordinary."

"This are a special, I tells you," retorted Spilsby, ungrammatically, pushing a smoking pie towards the boy; "what a young wiper you are, Grattles, a-comin' and spoilin' my livin' by cussin' my wictuals."

"Look 'ere," retorted Grattles, standing on the tips of his large boots to look more imposing, "my stumick's a bit orf when it comes to fat, and I wants the vally of my penny; give us a muttony one, with lots of gravy."

"'Ere y'are, then," said Spilsby, quite out of temper with his fastidious customer; "'ere's a pie as is all made of ram as 'adn't got more fat on it than you 'ave."

Grattles examined the article classed under this promising description with a critical air, and then laid down his penny and took the pie.

"It's a special, ain't it?" he asked, suspiciously smelling it.

"It's the specialest I've got, any'ow," answered Spilsby, testily, putting the penny in his pocket; "you'd eat a 'ole sheep if you could get it for a penny, you greedy young devil, you."

Here Kitty, who was feeling faint and ill with so much walking, came forward and asked for a cup of coffee.

"Certainly, dear," said Spilsby, with a leer, pouring out the coffee; "I'm allays good to a pretty gal."

"It's more nor your coffee is," growled Grattles, who had finished his special and was now licking his fingers, "it's all grounds and 'ot water."

"Go away, you wicious thing," retorted Spilsby, mildly, giving Kitty her coffee and change out of the money she handed him, "or I'll set the perlice on yer."

"Oh, my eye!" shrieked Grattles, executing a grimace after the fashion of a favourite comedian; "he ain't a tart, oh, no—'es a pie, 'e are, a special, a muttony special; 'e don't kill no kittings and call 'em sheep, oh, no; 'e don't buy chicory and calls it coffee, blest if 'e does; 'e's a corker, 'e are, and 'is name ain't the same as 'is father's."

"What d'ye mean," asked Spilsby, fiercely—that is, as fiercely as his meek appearance would let him; "what do you know of my parents, you bandy-legged little devil? who's your—progenitor, I'd like to know?"

"A dook, in course," said Grattles loftily; "but we don't, in consequence of 'er Nibs bein' mixed up with the old man's mother, reweal the family skeletons to low piemen," then, with a fresh grimace, he darted along the street as quickly as his bandy legs could carry him.

Spilsby took no notice of this, but, seeing some people coming round the corner, commenced to sing out his praises of the specials.

"'Ere yer are—all 'ot an' steamin'," he cried, in a kind of loud bleat, which added still more to his sheep-like appearance: "Spilsby's Specials—oh, lovely—ain't they nice; my eye, fine muttin pies; who ses Spilsby's; 'ave one, miss?" to Kitty.

"Thank you, no," replied Kitty, with a faint smile as she put down her empty cup; "I'm going now."

Spilsby was struck by the educated manner in which she spoke and by the air of refinement about her.

"Go home, my dear," he said, kindly, leaning forward; "this ain't no time for a young gal like you to be out."

"I've got no home," said Kitty, bitterly, "but if you could direct me—"

"Here, you," cried a shrill female voice, as a woman dressed in a flaunting blue gown rushed up to the stall, "give us a pie quick; I'm starvin', I've got no time to wait."

"No, nor manners either," said Spilsby, with a remonstrating bleat, pushing a pie towards her; "who are you, a-shovin' your betters, Portwine Annie?"

"My betters," scoffed the lady in blue, looking Kitty up and down with a disdainful smile on her painted face; "where are they, I'd like to know?"

"'Ere, 'old your tongue," bleated Spilsby, angrily, "or I'll tell the perlice at the corner."

"And much I care," retorted the shrill-voiced female, "seeing he's a particular friend of mine."

"For God's sake tell me where I can find a place to stop in," whispered Kitty to the coffee-stall keeper.

"Come with me, dear," said Portwine Annie, eagerly, having overheard what was said, but Kitty shrank back, and then gathering her cloak around her ran down the street.

"What do you do that for, you jade?" said Spilsby, in a vexed tone; "don't you see the girl's a lady."

"Of course she is," retorted the other, finishing her pie; "we're all ladies; look at our dresses, ain't they fine enough? Look at our houses, aren't they swell enough?"

"Yes, and yer morals, ain't they bad enough?" said Spilsby, washing up the dirty plate.

"They're quite as good as many ladies in society, at all events," replied Portwine Annie, with a toss of her head as she walked off.

"Oh, it's a wicked world," bleated Spilsby, in a soft voice, looking after the retreating figure. "I'm sorry for that poor gal—I am indeed— but this ain't business," and once more raising his voice he cried up his wares, "Oh, lovely; ain't they muttony? Spilsby's specials, all 'ot; one penny."

Meanwhile Kitty was walking quickly down Elizabeth Street, and turning round the corner ran right up against a woman.

"Hullo!" said the woman, catching her wrist, "where are you off to?"

"Let me go," cried Kitty, in a panting voice.

The woman was tall and handsome, but her face had a kindly expression on it, and she seemed touched with the terrified tone of the girl.

"My poor child," she said, half contemptuously, releasing her, "I won't hurt you. Go if you like. What are you doing out at this time of the night?"

"Nothing," faltered Kitty, with quivering lips, lifting her face up to the pale moon. The other saw it in the full light and marked how pure and innocent it was.

"Go home, dear," she said, in a soft tone, touching the girl kindly on the shoulder, "it's not fit for you to be out at this hour. You are not one of us."

"My God! no," cried Kitty, shrinking away from her.

The other smiled bitterly.

"Ah! you draw away from me now," she said, with a sneer; "but what are you, so pure and virtuous, doing on the streets at this hour? Go home in time, child, or you will become like me."

"I have no home," said Kitty, turning to go.

"No home!" echoed the other, in a softer tone; "poor child! I cannot take you with me—God help me; but here is some money," forcing a shilling into the girl's hand, "go to Mrs. Rawlins at Victoria Parade, Fitzroy—anyone will tell you where it is—and she will take you in."

"What kind of a place is it?" said Kitty.

"A home for fallen women, dear," answered the other, kindly.

"I'm not a fallen woman!" cried the girl, wildly, "I have left my home, but I will go back to it—anything better than this horrible life on the streets."

"Yes, dear," said the woman, softly, "go home; go home, for God's sake, and if you have a father and mother to shield you from harm, thank heaven for that. Let me kiss you once," she added, bending forward, "it is so long since I felt a good woman's kiss on my lips. Good-bye."

"Good-bye," sobbed Kitty, raising her face, and the other bent down and kissed the child-like face, then with a stifled cry, fled away through the moonlit night.

Kitty turned away slowly and walked up the street. She knew there was a cab starting opposite the Town Hall which went to Richmond, and determined to go home. After all, hard though her life might be in the future, it would be better than this cruel harshness of the streets.

At the top of the block, just as she was about to cross Swanston Street, a party of young men in evening dress came round the corner singing, and evidently were much exhilarated with wine. These were none other than Mr. Jarper and his friends, who, having imbibed a good deal more than was good for them, were now ripe for any mischief. Bellthorp and Jarper, both quite intoxicated, were walking arm-in-arm, each trying to keep the other up, so that their walking mostly consisted of wild lurches forward, and required a good deal of balancing.

"Hullo!" cried Bellthorp solemnly—he was always solemn when intoxicated—"girl—pretty—eh!"

"Go 'way," said Barty, staggering back against the wall, "we're Christian young men."

Kitty tried to get away from this inebriated crew, but they all closed round her, and she wrung her hands in despair. "If you are gentlemen you will let me go," she cried, trying to push past.

"Give us kiss first," said a handsome young fellow, with his hat very much on one side, putting his arm round her waist, "pay toll, dear."

She felt his hot breath on her cheek and shrieked out wildly, trying to push him away with all her force. The young man, however, paid no attention to her cries, but was about to kiss her when he was taken by the back of the neck and thrown into the gutter.

"Gentlemen!" said a rich rolling voice, which proceeded from a portly man who had just appeared on the scene. "I am astonished," with the emphasis on the first person singular, as if he were a man of great note.

"Old boy," translated Bellthorp to the others, "is 'tonished."

"You have," said the stranger, with an airy wave of his hand, "the appearance of gentlemen, but, alas! you are but whited sepulchres, fair to look upon, but full of dead men's bones within."

"Jarper," said Bellthorp, solemnly, taking Barty's arm, "you're a tombstone with skeleton inside—come along—old boy is right—set of cads 'suiting an unprotected gal—good night, sir."

The others picked up their companion out of the gutter, and the whole lot rolled merrily down the street.

"And this," said the gentleman, lifting up his face to the sky in mute appeal to heaven, "this is the generation which is to carry on Australia. Oh, Father Adam, what a dissipated family you have got—ah!—good for a comedy, I think."

"Oh!" cried Kitty, recognising a familiar remark, "it's Mr. Wopples."

"The same," said the airy Theodore, laying his hand on his heart, "and you, my dear—why, bless me," looking closely at her, "it is the pretty girl I met in Ballarat—dear, dear—surely you have not come to this."

"No, no," said Kitty, quickly, laying her hand on his arm, "I will tell you all about it, Mr. Wopples; but you must be a friend to me, for I sadly need one."

"I will be your friend," said the actor, emphatically, taking her arm and walking slowly down the street; "tell me how I find you thus."

"You won't tell anyone if I do?" said Kitty, imploringly.

"On the honour of a gentleman," answered Wopples, with grave dignity.

Kitty told him how she had left Ballarat, but suppressed the name of her lover, as she did not want any blame to fall on him. But all the rest she told freely, and when Mr. Wopples heard how on that night she had left the man who had ruined her, he swore a mighty oath.

"Oh, vile human nature," he said, in a sonorous tone, "to thus betray a confiding infant! Where," he continued, looking inquiringly at the serene sky, "where are the thunderbolts of Heaven that they fall not on such?"

No thunderbolt making its appearance to answer the question, Mr.

Wopples told Kitty he would take her home to the family, and as they were just starting out on tour again, she could come with them.

"But will Mrs. Wopples receive me?" asked Kitty, timidly.

"My dear," said the actor, gravely, "my wife is a good woman, and a mother herself, so she can feel for a poor child like you, who has been betrayed through sheer innocence."

"You do not despise me?" said Kitty, in a low voice.

"My dear," answered Wopples, quietly, "am I so pure myself that I can judge others? Who am I," with an oratorical wave of the hand, "that I should cast the first stone?—ahem!—from Holy Writ. In future I will be your father; Mrs. Wopples, your mother, and you will have ten brothers and sisters—all star artistes."

"How kind you are," sobbed Kitty, clinging trustfully to him as they went along.

"I only do unto others as I would be done by," said Mr. Wopples, solemnly. "That sentiment," continued the actor, taking off his hat, "was uttered by One who, tho' we may believe or disbelieve in His divinity as a God, will always remain the sublimest type of perfect manhood the world has ever seen."

Kitty did not answer, and they walked quickly along; and surely this one good deed more than compensated for the rest of the actor's failings.

VI

On Change

Young Australia has a wonderful love for the excitement of gambling—take him away from the betting ring and he goes straight to the share market to dabble in gold and silver shares. The Great Humbug Gold Mining Company is floated on the Melbourne market—a perfect fortune in itself, which influential men are floating in a kind of semi-philanthropic manner to benefit mankind at large, and themselves in particular. Report by competent geologists; rich specimens of the reef exhibited to the confiding public; company of fifty thousand shares at a pound each; two shillings on application; two shillings on allotment; the balance in calls which influential men solemnly assure confiding public will never be needed. Young Australia sees a chance of making thousands in a week; buys one thousand shares at four shillings—only two hundred pounds; shares will rise and Young Australia hopefully looks forward to pocketing two or three thousand by his modest venture of two hundred; company floated, shares rising slowly. Young Australia will not sell at a profit, still dazzled by his chimerical thousands. Calls must be made to put up machinery; shares have a downward tendency. Never mind, there will only be one or two calls, so stick to shares as parents of possible thousands. Machinery erected; now crushing; two or three ounces to ton a certainty. Shares have an upward tendency; washing up takes place—two pennyweights to ton. Despair! Shares run down to nothing, and Young Australia sees his thousands disappear like snow in the sun. The Great Humbug Reef proves itself worthy of its name, and the company collapses amid the groans of confiding public and secret joy of influential men, who have sold at the top price.

Vandeloup knew all about this sort of thing, for he had seen it occur over and over again in Ballarat and Melbourne. So many came to the web and never got out alive, yet fresh flies were always to be found. Vandeloup was of a speculative nature himself, and had he been possessed of any surplus cash would, no doubt, have risked it in the jugglery of the share market, but as he had none to spare he stood back and amused himself with looking at the "spider and the fly" business which was constantly going on. Sometimes, indeed, the fly got the better of spider number one, but was unable to keep away from the web, and was sure to fall into the web of spider number two.

M. Vandeloup, therefore, considered the whole affair as too risky to be gone into without unlimited cash; but now he had a chance of making money, he determined to try his hand at the business. True, he knew that he was in for a swindle, but then he was behind the scenes, and would benefit by the knowledge he had gained. If the question at issue had really been that of getting gold out of the reef and paying dividends with the profits, Gaston would have snapped his fingers scornfully, and held aloof; but this was simply a running up of shares by means of a rich reef being struck. He intended to buy at the present market value, which was four shillings, and sell as soon as he could make a good profit—say, at one pound—so there was not much chance of him losing his money. The shares would probably drop again when the pocket of gold was worked out, but then that would be none of his affair, as he would by that time have sold out and made his pile. M. Vandeloup was a fly who was going straight into the webs of stockbroking spiders, but then he knew as much about this particular web as the spiders themselves.

Full of his scheme to make money, Vandeloup started for town to see a broker—first, however, having settled with Mrs. Pulchop over Kitty's disappearance. He had found a letter from Kitty in the bedroom, in which she had bidden him good-bye for ever, but this he did not show to Mrs. Pulchop, merely stating to that worthy lady that his "wife" had left him.

"And it ain't to be wondered at, the outraged angel," she said to Gaston, as he stood at the door, faultlessly dressed, ready to go into town; "the way you treated her were shameful."

Gaston shrugged his shoulders, lit a cigarette, and smiled at Mrs. Pulchop.

"My dear lady," he said, blandly, "pray attend to your medicine bottles and leave my domestic affairs alone; you certainly understand the one, but I doubt your ability to come to any conclusion regarding the other."

"Fine words don't butter no parsnips," retorted Mrs. Pulchop, viciously; "and if Pulchop weren't an Apoller, he had a kind heart."

"Spare me these domestic stories, please," said Vandeloup, coldly, "they do not interest me in the least; since my 'wife'," with a sneer, "has gone, I will leave your hospitable roof. I will send for all my property either today or to-morrow, and if you make out your account in the meantime, my messenger will pay it. Good day!" and without another word Vandeloup walked slowly off down the path, leaving Mrs. Pulchop speechless with indignation.

He went into town first, to the City of Melbourne Bank, and cashed Meddlechip's cheque for six hundred pounds, then, calling a hansom, he drove along to the Hibernian Bank, where he had an account, and paid it into his credit, reserving ten pounds for his immediate use. Then he reentered his hansom, and went along to the office of a stockbroker, called Polglaze, who was a member of "The Bachelors", and in whose hands Vandeloup intended to place his business.

Polglaze was a short, stout man, scrupulously neatly dressed, with iron grey hair standing straight up, and a habit of dropping out his words one at a time, so that the listener had to construct quite a little history between each, in order to arrive at their meaning, and the connection they had with one another.

"Morning!" said Polglaze, letting the salutation fly out of his mouth rapidly, and then closing it again in case any other word might be waiting ready to pop out unknown to him.

Vandeloup sat down and stated his business briefly.

"I want you to buy me some Magpie Reef shares," he said, leaning on the table.

"Many?" dropped out of Polglaze's mouth, and then it shut again with a snap. "Depends on the price," replied Vandeloup, with a shrug; "I see in the papers they are four shillings."

Mr. Polglaze took up his share book, and rapidly turned over the leaves—found what he wanted, and nodded.

"Oh!" said Vandeloup, making a rapid mental calculation, "then buy me two thousand five hundred. That will be about five hundred pounds' worth."

Mr. Polglaze nodded; then whistled.

"Your commission, I presume," said Vandeloup, making another calculation, "will be threepence?"

"Sixpence," interrupted the stockbroker.

"Oh, I thought it was threepence," answered Vandeloup, quietly; "however, that does not make any difference to me. Your commission at that rate will be twelve pounds ten shillings?"

Polglaze nodded again, and sat looking at Vandeloup like a stony mercantile sphinx.

"If you will, then, buy me these shares," said Vandeloup, rising, and taking up his gloves and hat, "when am I to come along and see you?"

"Four," said Polglaze.

"Today?" inquired Vandeloup.

A nod from the stockbroker.

"Very well," said Vandeloup, quietly, "I'll give you a cheque for the amount, then. There's nothing more to be said, I believe?" and he walked over to the door.

"Say!" from Polglaze.

"Yes," replied Gaston, indolently, swinging his stick to and fro.

"New?" inquired the stockbroker.

"You mean to this sort of thing?" said Vandeloup, looking at him, and receiving a nod in token of acquiescence, added, "entirely."

"Risky," dropped from the Polglaze mouth. "I never knew a gold mine that wasn't," retorted Vandeloup, dryly.

"Bad," in an assertive tone, from Polglaze.

"This particular mine, I suppose you mean?" said Gaston, with a yawn, "very likely it is. However, I'm willing to take the risk. Good day! See you at four," and with a careless nod, M. Vandeloup lounged out of the office.

He walked along Collins Street, met a few friends, and kept a look-out for Kitty. He, however, did not see her, but there was a surprise in store for him, for turning round into Swanston Street, he came across Archie McIntosh. Yes, there he was, with his grim, severe Scotch face, with the white frill round it, and Gaston smiled as he saw the old man, dressed in rigid broadcloth, casting disproving looks on the pretty girls walking along.

"A set o' hizzies," growled the amiable Archie to himself, "prancin' alang wi' their gew-gaws an' fine claes, like war horses—the daughters o' Zion that walk wi' mincin' steps an' tinklin' ornaments."

"How do you do?" said Vandeloup, touching the broadcloth shoulder; upon which McIntosh turned.

"Lord save us!" he exclaimed, grimly, "it's yon French body. An' hoo's a' wi' ye, laddie? Eh, but ye're brawly dressed, my young man," with a disproving look; "I'm hopin' they duds are paid for."

"Of course they are," replied Vandeloup, gaily, "do you think I stole them?"

"Weel, I'll no gae sa far as that," remarked Archie, cautiously; "maybe ye have dwelt by the side o' mony waters, an' flourished. If he ken the Screepture ye'll see God helps those wha help themselves."

"That means you do all the work and give God the credit," retorted Gaston, with a sneer; "I know all about that."

"Ah, ye'll gang tae the pit o' Tophet when ye dee," said Mr. McIntosh, who had heard this remark with horror; "an' ye'll no be sae ready wi' your tongue there, I'm thinkin'; but ye are not speerin aboot Mistress Villiers."

"Why, is she in town?" asked Vandeloup, eagerly.

"Ay, and Seliny wi' her," answered Archie, fondling his frill; "she's varra rich noo, as ye've nae doot heard. Ay, ay," he went on, "she's gotten a braw hoose doon at St Kilda, and she's going to set up a carriage, ye ken. She tauld me," pursued Mr. McIntosh, sourly, looking at Vandeloup, "if I saw ye I was to be sure to tell ye to come an' see her."

"Present my compliments to Madame," said Vandeloup, quickly, "and I will wait on her as soon as possible."

"Losh save us, laddie," said McIntosh, irritably, "you're as fu' o' fine wards as a play-actor. Have ye seen onything doon in this pit o' Tophet o' the bairn that rin away?"

"Oh, Miss Marchurst!" said Vandeloup, smoothly, ready with a lie at once. "No, I'm sorry to say I've never set eyes on her."

"The mistress is joost daft aboot her," observed McIntosh, querulously; "and she's ganging tae look all thro' the toun tae find the puir wee thing."

"I hope she will!" said M. Vandeloup, who devoutly hoped she wouldn't. "Will you come and have a glass of wine, Mr. McIntosh?"

"Til hae a wee drappy o' whusky if ye've got it gude," said McIntosh, cautiously, "but I dinna care for they wines that sour on a body's stomach."

McIntosh having thus graciously assented, Vandeloup took him up to the Club, and introduced him all round as the manager of the famous Pactolus. All the young men were wonderfully taken up with Archie and his plain speaking, and had Mr. McIntosh desired he could have drunk oceans of his favourite beverage. However, being a Scotchman and cautious, he took very little, and left Vandeloup to go down to Madame Midas at St Kilda, and bearing a message from the Frenchman that he would call there the next day.

Archie having departed, Vandeloup got through the rest of the day as he best could. He met Mr. Wopples in the street, who told him how he had found Kitty, quite unaware that the young man before him was the villain who had betrayed the girl. Vandeloup was delighted to think that Kitty had not mentioned his name, and quite approved of Mr. Wopples' intention to take the girl on tour. Having thus arranged for Kitty's future, Gaston went along to his broker, and found that the astute Polglaze had got him his shares.

"Going up," said Polglaze, as he handed the scrip to Vandeloup and got a cheque in exchange.

"Oh, indeed!" said Vandeloup, with a smile. "I suppose my two friends have begun their little game already," he thought, as he slipped the scrip into his breast pocket.

"Information?" asked Polglaze, as Vandeloup was going.

"Oh! you'd like to know where I got it," said M. Vandeloup, amiably. "Very sorry I can't tell you; but you see, my dear sir, I am not a woman, and can keep a secret."

Vandeloup walked out, and Polglaze looked after him with a puzzled look, then summed up his opinion in one word, sharp, incisive, and to the point—

"Clever!" said Polglaze, and put the cheque in his safe.

Vandeloup strolled along the street thinking.

"Bebe is out of my way," he thought, with a smile; "I have a small fortune in my pocket, and," he continued, thoughtfully, "Madame Midas is in Melbourne. I think now," said M. Vandeloup, with another smile, "that I have conquered the blind goddess."

VII

THE OPULENCE OF MADAME MIDAS

A wealthy man does not know the meaning of the word friendship. He is not competent to judge, for his wealth precludes him giving a proper opinion. Smug-faced philanthropists can preach comfortable doctrines in pleasant rooms with well-spread tables and good clothing; they can talk about human nature being unjustly accused, and of the kindly impulses and good thoughts in everyone's breasts. Pshaw! anyone can preach thus from an altitude of a few thousands a year, but let these same self-complacent kind-hearted gentlemen descend in the social scale—let them look twice at a penny before spending it—let them face persistent landladies, exorbitant landlords, or the bitter poverty of the streets, and they will not talk so glibly of human nature and its inherent kindness. No; human nature is a sort of fetish which is credited with a great many amiable qualities it never possesses, and though there are exceptions to the general rule, Balzac's aphorism on mankind that "Nature works by self-interest," still holds good today.

Madame Midas, however, had experienced poverty and the coldness of friends, so was completely disillusionised as to the disinterested motives of the people who now came flocking around her. She was very wealthy, and determined to stop in Melbourne for a year, and then go home to Europe, so to this end she took a house at St Kilda, which had been formerly occupied by Mark Frettlby, the millionaire, who had been mixed up in the famous hansom cab murder nearly eighteen months before. His daughter, Mrs. Fitzgerald, was in Ireland with her husband, and had given instructions to her agents to let the house furnished as it stood, but such a large rent was demanded, that no one felt inclined to give it till Mrs. Villiers appeared on the scene. The house suited her, as she did not want to furnish one of her own, seeing she was only going to stop a year, so she saw Thinton and Tarbet, who had the letting of the place, and took it for a year. The windows were flung open, the furniture brushed and renovated, and the solitary charwoman who had been ruler in the lonely rooms so long, was dismissed, and her place taken by a whole retinue of servants. Madame Midas intended to live in style, so went to work over the setting up of her establishment in such an extravagant manner that Archie remonstrated. She took his interference in a good humoured way, but still arranged things as she intended; and when her house was ready, waited for her friends to call on her, and prepared to amuse herself with the comedy of human life. She had not long to wait, for a perfect deluge of affectionate people rolled down upon her. Many remembered her—oh, quite well—when she was the beautiful Miss Curtis; and then her husband—that dreadful Villiers—they hoped he was dead—squandering her fortune as he had done—they had always been sorry for her, and now she was rich—that lovely Pactolus—indeed, she deserved it all—she would marry, of course—oh, but indeed, she must. And so the comedy went on, and all the actors flirted, and ogled, and nodded, and bowed, till Madame Midas was quite sick of the falseness and frivolity of the whole thing. She knew these people, with their simpering and smiling, would visit her and eat her dinners and drink her wines, and then go away and abuse her thoroughly. But then Madame Midas never expected anything else, so she received them with smiles, saw through all their little ways, and when she had amused herself sufficiently with their antics, she let them go.

Vandeloup called on Madame Midas the day after she arrived, and Mrs. Villiers was delighted to see him. Having an object in view, of course Gaston made himself as charming as possible, and assisted Madame to arrange her house, told her about the people who called on her, and made cynical remarks about them, all of which amused Madame Midas mightily. She grew weary of the inane gabble and narrow understandings of people, and it was quite a relief for her to turn to Vandeloup, with his keen tongue and clever brains. Gaston was not a charitable talker—few really clever talkers are—but he saw through everyone with the uttermost ease and summed them up in a sharp incisive way, which had at least the merit of being clever. Madame Midas liked to hear him talk, and seeing what humbugs the people who surrounded her were, and how well she knew their motives in courting her for her wealth, it is not to be wondered at that she should have been amused at having all their little weaknesses laid bare and classified by such a master of satire as Vandeloup. So they sat and watched the comedy and the unconscious actors playing their parts, and felt that the air was filled with heavy sensuous perfume, and the lights were garish, and that there was wanting entirely that keen cool atmosphere which Mallock calls "the ozone of respectability".

Vandeloup had prospered in his little venture in the mining market, for, true to the prediction of Mr. Barraclough—who, by the way, was very much astonished at the sudden demand for shares by Polglaze, and vainly pumped that reticent individual to find out what he was up to—the Magpie Reef shares ran up rapidly. A telegram was published from the manager stating a rich reef had been struck. Specimens of the very richest kind were displayed in Melbourne, and the confiding public suddenly woke to the fact that a golden tide was flowing past their doors. They rushed the share market, and in two weeks the Magpie Reef shares ran from four shillings to as many pounds. Vandeloup intended to sell at one pound, but when he saw the rapid rise and heard everyone talking about this Reef, which was to be a second Long Tunnel, he held his shares till they touched four pounds, then, quite satisfied with his profit, he sold out at once and pocketed nearly ten thousand pounds, so that he was provided for the rest of his life. The shares ran up still higher, to four pounds ten shillings, then dropped to three, in consequence of certain rumours that the pocket of gold was worked out. Then another rich lead was struck, and they ran up again to five pounds, and afterwards sank to two pounds, which gradually became their regular price in the market. That Barraclough and his friend did well was sufficiently proved by the former taking a trip to Europe, while his friend bought a station and set up as a squatter. They, however, never knew how cleverly M. Vandeloup had turned their conversation to his advantage, and that young gentleman, now that he had made a decent sum, determined to touch gold mining no more, and, unlike many people, he kept his word.

Now that he was a man of means, Vandeloup half decided to go to America, as a larger field for a gentleman of his brilliant qualities, but the arrival of Madame Midas in Melbourne made him alter his mind. Her husband was no doubt dead, so Gaston thought that as soon as she had settled down he would begin to pay his court to her, and without doubt would be accepted, for this confident young man never for a moment dreamed of failure. Meanwhile he sent all Kitty's wardrobe after her as she went with the Wopples family, and the poor girl, taking this as a mark of renewed affection, wrote him a very tearful little note, which M. Vandeloup threw into the fire. Then he looked about and ultimately got a very handsome suite of rooms in Clarendon Street, East Melbourne. He furnished these richly, and having invested his money in good securities, prepared to enjoy himself.

Kitty, meanwhile, had become a great favourite with the Wopples family, and they made a wonderful pet of her. Of course, being in Rome, she did as the Romans did, and went on the stage as Miss Kathleen Wopples, being endowed with the family name for dramatic reasons. The family were now on tour among the small towns of Victoria, and seemed to be well-known, as each member got a reception when he or she appeared on the stage. Mr. Theodore Wopples used to send his agent ahead to engage the theatre—or more often a hall—bill the town, and publish sensational little notices in the local papers. Then when the family arrived Mr. Wopples, who was really a gentleman and well-educated, called on all the principal people of the town and so impressed them with the high class character of the entertainment that he never failed to secure their patronage. He also had a number of artful little schemes which he called "wheezes", the most successful of these being a lecture on "The Religious Teaching of Shakespeare", which he invariably delivered on a Sunday afternoon in the theatre of any town he happened to be in, and not infrequently when requested occupied the pulpit and preached capital sermons. By these means Mr. Wopples kept up the reputation of the family, and the upper classes of all the towns invariably supported the show, while the lower classes came as a matter of course. Mr. Wopples, however, was equally as clever in providing a bill of fare as in inducing the public to come to the theatre, and the adaptability of the family was really wonderful. One night they would play farcical comedy; then Hamlet, reduced to four acts by Mr. Wopples, would follow on the second night; the next night burlesque would reign supreme; and when the curtain arose on the fourth night Mr. Wopples and the star artistes would be acting melodrama, and throw one another off bridges and do strong starvation business with ragged clothes amid paper snowstorms.

Kitty turned out to be a perfect treasure, as her pretty face and charming voice soon made her a favourite, and when in burlesque she played Princess to Fanny Wopples' Prince, there was sure to be a crowded house and lots of applause. Kitty's voice was clear and sweet as a lark's, and her execution something wonderful, so Mr. Wopples christened her the Australian Nightingale, and caused her to be so advertised in the papers. Moreover, her dainty appearance, and a certain dash and abandon she had with her, carried the audience irresistibly away, and had Fanny Wopples not been a really good girl, she would have been jealous of the success achieved by the new-comer. She, however, taught Kitty to dance breakdowns, and at Warrnambool they had a benefit, when "Faust, M.D." was produced, and Fanny sang her great success, "I've just had a row with mamma", and Kitty sang the jewel song from "Faust" in a manner worthy of Neilson, as the local critic—who had never heard Neilson—said the next day. Altogether, Kitty fully repaid the good action of Mr. Wopples by making his tour a wonderful success, and the family returned to Melbourne in high glee with full pockets.

"Next year," said Mr. Wopples, at a supper which they had to celebrate the success of their tour, "we'll have a theatre in Melbourne, and I'll make it the favourite house of the city, see if I don't."

It seemed, therefore, as though Kitty had found her vocation, and would develop into an operatic star, but fate intervened, and Miss Marchurst retired from the stage, which she had adorned so much. This was due to Madame Midas, who, driving down Collins Street one day, saw Kitty at the corner walking with Fanny Wopples. She immediately stopped her carriage, and alighting therefrom, went straight up to the girl, who, turning and seeing her for the first time, grew deadly pale.

"Kitty, my dear," said Madame, gravely, "I have been looking for you vainly for a year—but I have found you at last."

Kitty's breast was full of conflicting emotions; she thought that Madame knew all about her intimacy with Vandeloup, and that she would speak severely to her. Mrs. Villiers' next words, however, reassured her.

"You left Ballarat to go on the stage, did you not?" she said kindly, looking at the girl; "why did you not come to me?—you knew I was always your friend."

"Yes, Madame," said Kitty, putting out her hand and averting her head, "I would have come to you, but I thought you would stop me from going."

"My dear child," replied Madame, "I thought you knew me better than that; what theatre are you at?"

"She's with us," said Miss Fanny, who had been staring at this grave, handsomely-dressed lady who had alighted from such a swell carriage; "we are the Wopples Family."

"Ah!" said Mrs. Villiers, thinking, "I remember, you were up at Ballarat last year. Well, Kitty, will you and your friend drive down to St Kilda with me, and I'll show you my new house?"

Kitty would have refused, for she was afraid Madame Midas would perhaps send her back to her father, but the appealing looks of Fanny Wopples, who had never ridden in a carriage in her life, and was dying to do so, decided her to accept. So they stepped into the carriage, and Mrs. Villiers told the coachman to drive home.

As they drove along, Mrs. Villiers delicately refrained from asking Kitty any questions about her flight, seeing that a stranger was present, but determined to find out all about it when she got her alone down at St Kilda.

Kitty, on her part, was thinking how to baffle Madame's inquiries. She knew she would be questioned closely by her, and resolved not to tell more than she could help, as she, curiously enough—considering how he had treated her—wished to shield Vandeloup. But she still cherished a tender feeling for the man she loved, and had Vandeloup asked her to go back and live with him, would, no doubt, have consented. The fact was, the girl's nature was becoming slightly demoralised, and the Kitty who sat looking at Madame Midas now—though her face was as pretty, and her eyes as pure as ever—was not the same innocent Kitty that had visited the Pactolus, for she had eaten of the Tree of Knowledge, and was already cultured in worldly wisdom. Madame, of course, believed that Kitty had gone from Ballarat straight on to the stage, and never thought for a moment that for a whole year she had been Vandeloup's mistress, so when Kitty found this out—as she very soon did—she took the cue at once, and asserted positively to Madame that she had been on the stage for eighteen months.

"But how is it," asked Madame, who believed her fully, "that I could not find you?"

"Because I was up the country all the time," replied Kitty, quickly, "and of course did not act under my real name."

"You would not like to go back to your father, I suppose," suggested Madame.

Kitty made a gesture of dissent.

"No," she answered, determinedly; "I was tired of my father and his religion; I'm on the stage now, and I mean to stick to it."

"Kitty! Kitty!" said Madame, sadly, "you little know the temptations—"

"Oh! yes, I do," interrupted Kitty, impatiently; "I've been nearly two years on the stage, and I have not seen any great wickedness—besides, I'm always with Mrs. Wopples."

"Then you still mean to be an actress?" asked Madame.

"Yes," replied Kitty, in a firm voice; "if I went back to my father, I'd go mad leading that dull life."

"But why not stay with me, my dear?" said Mrs. Villiers, looking at her; "I am a lonely woman, as you know, and if you come to me, I will treat you as a daughter."

"Ah! how good you are," cried the girl in a revulsion of feeling, falling on her friend's neck; "but indeed I cannot leave the stage—I'm too fond of it."

Madame sighed, and gave up the argument for a time, then showed the two girls all over the house, and after they had dinner with her, she sent them back to town in her carriage, with strict injunctions to Kitty to come down next day and bring Mr. Wopples with her. When the two girls reached the hotel where the family was staying, Fanny gave her father a glowing account of the opulence of Madame Midas, and Mr. Wopples was greatly interested in the whole affair. He was grave, however, when Kitty spoke to him privately of what Madame had said to her, and asked her if she would not like to accept Mrs. Villiers' offer. Kitty, however, said she would remain on the stage, and as Wopples was to see Madame Midas next day, made him promise he would say nothing about having found her on the streets, or of her living with a lover. Wopples, who thoroughly understood the girl's desire to hide her shame from her friends, agreed to this, so Kitty went to bed confident that she had saved Vandeloup's name from being dragged into the affair.

Wopples saw Madame next day, and a long talk ensued, which ended in Kitty agreeing to stay six months with Mrs. Villiers, and then, if she still wished to continue on the stage, she was to go to Mr. Wopples. On the other hand, in consideration of Wopples losing the services of Kitty, Madame promised that next year she would give him sufficient money to start a theatre in Melbourne. So both parted mutually satisfied. Kitty made presents to all the family, who were very sorry to part with her, and then took up her abode with Mrs. Villiers, as a kind of adopted daughter, and was quite prepared to play her part in the comedy of fashion.

So Madame Midas had been near the truth, yet never discovered it, and sent a letter to Vandeloup asking him to come to dinner and meet an old friend, little thinking how old and intimate a friend Kitty was to the young man.

It was, as Mr. Wopples would have said, a highly dramatic situation, but, alas, that the confiding nature of Madame Midas should thus have been betrayed, not only by Vandeloup, but by Kitty herself—the very girl whom, out of womanly compassion, she took to her breast.

And yet the world talks about the inherent goodness of human nature.

VIII

M. Vandeloup is Surprised

O wing to the quiet life Kitty had led since she came to Melbourne, and the fact that her appearance on the stage had taken place in the country, she felt quite safe when making her appearance in Melbourne society that no one would recognise her or know anything of her past life. It was unlikely she would meet with any of the Pulchop family again, and she knew Mr. Wopples would hold his tongue regarding his first meeting with her, so the only one who could reveal anything about her would be Vandeloup, and he would certainly be silent for his own sake, as she knew he valued the friendship of Madame Midas too much to lose it. Nevertheless she awaited his coming in considerable trepidation, as she was still in love with him, and was nervous as to what reception she would meet with. Perhaps now that she occupied a position as Mrs. Villiers' adopted daughter he would marry her, but, at all events, when she met him she would know exactly how he felt towards her by his demeanour.

Vandeloup, on the other hand, was quite unaware of the surprise in store for him, and thought that the old friend he was to meet would be some Ballarat acquaintance of his own and Madame's. In his wildest flight of fancy he never thought it would be Kitty, else his cool nonchalance would for once have been upset at the thought of the two women he was interested in being under the same roof. However, where ignorance is bliss—well M. Vandeloup, after dressing himself carefully in evening dress, put on his hat and coat, and, the evening being a pleasant one, thought he would stroll through the Fitzroy Gardens down to the station.

It was pleasant in the gardens under the golden light of the sunset, and the green arcades of trees looked delightfully cool after the glare of the dusty streets. Vandeloup, strolling along idly, felt a touch on his shoulder and wheeled round suddenly, for with his past life ever before him he always had a haunting dread of being recaptured.

The man, however, who had thus drawn his attention was none other than Pierre Lemaire, who stood in the centre of the broad asphalt path, dirty, ragged and disreputable-looking. He had not altered much since he left Ballarat, save that he looked more dilapidated-looking, but stood there in his usual sullen manner, with his hat drawn down over his eyes. Some stray wisps of grass showed that he had been camping out all the hot day on the green turf under the shadow of the trees, and it was easy to see from his appearance what a vagrant he was. Vandeloup was annoyed at the meeting and cast a rapid look around to see if he was observed. The few people, however, passing were too intent on their own business to give more than a passing glance at the dusty tramp and the young man in evening dress talking to him, so Vandeloup was reassured.

"Well, my friend," he said, sharply, to the dumb man, "what do you want?"

Pierre put his hand in his pocket.

"Oh, of course," replied M. Vandeloup, mockingly, "money, money, always money; do you think I'm a bank, always to be drawn on like this?"

The dumb man made no sign that he had heard, but stood sullenly rocking himself to and fro an'd chewing a wisp of the grass he had picked off his coat.

"Here," said the young man, taking out a sovereign and giving it to Pierre; "take this just now and don't bother me, or upon my word," with a disdainful look, "I shall positively have to hand you over to the law."

Pierre glanced up suddenly, and Vandeloup caught the gleam of his eyes under the shadow of the hat.

"Oh! you think it will be dangerous for me," he said, in a gay tone; "not at all, I assure you. I am a gentleman, and rich; you are a pauper, and disreputable. Who will believe your word against mine? My faith! your assurance is quite refreshing. Now, go away, and don't trouble me again, or," with a sudden keen glance, "I will do as I say."

He nodded coolly to the dumb man, and strode gaily along under the shade of the heavily foliaged oaks, while Pierre looked at the sovereign, slipped it into his pocket, and slouched off in the opposite direction without even a glance at his patron.

At the top of the street Vandeloup stepped into a cab, and telling the man to drive to the St Kilda Station, in Elizabeth Street, went off into a brown study. Pierre annoyed him seriously, as he never seemed to get rid of him, and the dumb man kept turning up every now and then like the mummy at the Egyptian feast to remind him of unpleasant things.

"Confound him!" muttered Vandeloup, angrily, as he alighted at the station and paid the cabman, "he's more trouble than Bebe was; she did take the hint and go, but this man, my faith!" shrugging his shoulders, "he's the devil himself for sticking."

All the way down to St Kilda his reflections were of the same unpleasant nature, and he cast about in his own mind how he could get rid of this pertinacious friend. He could not turn him off openly, as Pierre might take offence, and as he knew more of M. Vandeloup's private life than that young gentleman cared about, it would not do to run the risk of an exposure.

"There's only one thing to be done," said Gaston, quietly, as he walked down to Mrs. Villiers' house; "I will try my luck at marrying Madame Midas; if she consents, we can go away to Europe as man and wife; if she does not I will go to America, and, in either case, Pierre will lose trace of me."

With this comfortable reflection he went into the house and was shown into the drawing room by the servant. There were no lights in the room, as it was not sufficiently dark for them, and Vandeloup smiled as he saw a fire in the grate.

"My faith!" he said to himself, "Madame is as chilly as ever."

The servant had retired, and he was all by himself in this large room, with the subdued twilight all through it, and the flicker of the flames on the ceiling. He went to the fire more from habit than anything else, and suddenly came on a big armchair, drawn up close to the side, in which a woman was sitting.

"Ah! the sleeping beauty," said Vandeloup, carelessly; "in these cases the proper thing to do in order to wake the lady is to kiss her."

He was, without doubt, an extremely audacious young man, and though he did not know who the young lady was, would certainly have put his design into execution, had not the white figure suddenly rose and confronted him. The light from the fire was fair on her face, and with a sudden start Vandeloup saw before him the girl he had ruined and deserted.

"Bebe?" he gasped, recoiling a step.

"Yes!" said Kitty, in an agitated tone, "your mistress and your victim."

"Bah!" said Gaston, coolly, having recovered from the first shock of surprise. "That style suits Sarah Bernhardt, not you, my dear. The first act of this comedy is excellent, but it is necessary the characters should know one another in order to finish the play."

"Ah!" said Kitty, with a bitter smile, "do I not know you too well, as the man who promised me marriage and then broke his word? You forgot all your vows to me."

"My dear child," replied Gaston leisurely, leaning up against the mantelpiece, "if you had read Balzac you would discover that he says, 'Life would be intolerable without a certain amount of forgetting.' I must say," smiling, "I agree with the novelist."

Kitty looked at him as he stood there cool and complacent, and threw herself back into the chair angrily.

"Just the same," she muttered restlessly, "just the same."

"Of course," replied Vandeloup, raising his eyebrows in surprise. "You have only been away from me six weeks, and it takes longer than that to alter any one. By the way," he went on smoothly, "how have you been all this time? I have no doubt your tour has been as adventurous as that of Gil Bias."

"No, it has not," replied Kitty, clenching her hands. "You never cared what became of me, and had not Mr. Wopples met me in the street on that fearful night, God knows where I would have been now."

"I can tell you," said Gaston, coolly, taking a seat. "With me. You would have soon got tired of the poverty of the streets, and come back to your cage."

"My cage, indeed!" she echoed, bitterly, tapping the ground with her foot. "Yes, a cage, though it was a gilded one."

"How Biblical you are getting," said the young man, ironically; "but kindly stop speaking in parables, and tell me what position we are to occupy to each other. As formerly?"

"My God, no!" she flashed out suddenly.

"So much the better," he answered, bowing. "We will obliterate the last year from our memories, and I will meet you to-night for the first time since you left Ballarat. Of course," he went on, rather anxiously, "you have told Madame nothing?"

"Only what suited me," replied the girl, coldly, stung by the coldness and utter heartlessness of this man.

"Oh!" with a smile. "Did it include my name?"

"No," curtly.

"Ah!" with a long indrawn breath, "you are more sensible than I gave you credit for."

Kitty rose to her feet and crossed rapidly over to where he sat calm and smiling.

"Gaston Vandeloup!" she hissed in his ear, while her face was quite distorted by the violence of her passion, "when I met you I was an innocent girl—you ruined me, and then cast me off as soon as you grew weary of your toy. I thought you loved me, and," with a stifled sob, "God help me, I love you still."

"Yes, my Bebe," he said, in a caressing tone, taking her hand.

"No! no," she cried, wrenching them away, while an angry spot of colour glowed on her cheek, "I loved you as you were—not as you are now—we are done with sentiment, M. Vandeloup," she said, sneering, "and now our relations to one another will be purely business ones."

He bowed and smiled.

"So glad you understand the position," he said, blandly; "I see the age of miracles is not yet past when a woman can talk sense."

"You won't disturb me with your sneers," retorted the girl, glaring fiercely at him out of the gathering gloom in the room; "I am not the innocent girl I once was."

"It is needless to tell me that," he said, coarsely.

She drew herself up at the extreme insult.

"Have a care, Gaston," she muttered, hurriedly, "I know more about your past life than you think."

He rose from his seat and approached his face, now white as her own, to hers.

"What do you know?" he asked, in a low, passionate voice.

"Enough to be dangerous to you," she retorted, defiantly.

They both looked at one another steadily, but the white face of the woman did not blench before the scintillations of his eyes.

"What you know I don't know," he said, steadily; "but whatever it is, keep it to yourself, or—," catching her wrist.

"Or what?" she asked, boldly.

He threw her away from him with a laugh, and the sombre fire died out of his eyes.

"Bah!" he said, gaily, "our comedy is turning into a tragedy; I am as foolish as you; I think," significantly, "we understand one another."

"Yes, I think we do," she answered, calmly, the colour coming back to her cheek. "Neither of us are to refer to the past, and we both go on our different roads unhindered."

"Mademoiselle Marchurst," said Vandeloup, ceremoniously, "I am delighted to meet you after a year's absence—come," with a gay laugh, "let us begin the comedy thus, for here," he added quickly, as the door opened, "here comes the spectators."

"Well, young people," said Madame's voice, as she came slowly into the room, "you are all in the dark; ring the bell for lights, M. Vandeloup."

"Certainly, Madame," he answered, touching the electric button, "Miss Marchurst and myself were renewing our former friendship."

"How do you think she is looking?" asked Madame, as the servant came in and lit the gas.

"Charming," replied Vandeloup, looking at the dainty little figure in white standing under the blaze of the chandelier; "she is more beautiful than ever."

Kitty made a saucy little curtsey, and burst into a musical laugh.

"He is just the same, Madame," she said merrily to the tall, grave woman in black velvet, who stood looking at her affectionately, "full of compliments, and not meaning one; but when is dinner to be ready?" pathetically, "I'm dying of starvation."

"I hope you have peaches, Madame," said Vandeloup, gaily; "the first time I met Mademoiselle she was longing for peaches."

"I am unchanged in that respect," retorted Kitty, brightly; "I adore peaches still."

"I am just waiting for Mr. Calton," said Madame Midas, looking at her watch; "he ought to be here by now."

"Is that the lawyer, Madame?" asked Vandeloup.

"Yes," she replied, quietly, "he is a most delightful man."

"So I have heard," answered Vandeloup, nonchalantly, "and he had something to do with a former owner of this house, I think."

"Oh, don't talk of that," said Mrs. Villiers, nervously; "the first time I took the house, I heard all about the Hansom Cab murder."

"Why, Madame, you are not nervous," said Kitty, gaily.

"No, my dear," replied the elder, quietly, "but I must confess that for some reason or another I have been a little upset since coming here; I don't like being alone."

"You shall never be that," said Kitty, fondly nestling to her.

"Thank you, puss," said Madame, tapping her cheek; "but I am nervous," she said, rapidly; "at night especially. Sometimes I have to get Selina to come into my room and stay all night."

"Madame Midas nervous," thought Vandeloup to himself; "then I can guess the reason; she is afraid of her husband coming back to her."

Just at this moment the servant announced Mr. Calton, and he entered, with his sharp, incisive face, looking clever and keen.

"I must apologise for being late, Mrs. Villiers," he said, shaking hands with his hostess; "but business, you know, the pleasure of business."

"Now," said Madame, quickly, "I hope you have come to the business of pleasure."

"Very epigrammatic, my dear lady," said Calton, in his high, clear voice; "pray introduce me."

Madame did so, and they all went to dinner, Madame with Calton and Kitty following with Vandeloup.

"This," observed Calton, when they were all seated at the dinner table, "is the perfection of dining; for we are four, and the guests, according to an epicure, should never be less than the Graces nor greater than the Muses."

And a very merry little dinner it was. All four were clever talkers, and Vandeloup and Calton being pitted against one another, excelled themselves; witty remarks, satirical sayings, and well-told stories were constantly coming from their lips, and they told their stories as their own and did not father them on Sydney Smith.

"If Sydney Smith was alive," said Calton, in reference to this, "he would be astonished at the number of stories he did not tell."

"Yes," chimed in Vandeloup, gaily, "and astounded at their brilliancy."

"After all," said Madame, smiling, "he's a sheet-anchor for some people; for the best original story may fail, a dull one ascribed to Sydney Smith must produce a laugh."

"Why?" asked Kitty, in some wonder.

"Because," explained Calton, gravely, "society goes mainly by tradition, and our grandmothers having laughed at Sydney Smith's jokes, they must necessarily be amusing. Depend upon it, jokes can be sanctified by time quite as much as creeds."

"They are more amusing, at all events," said Madame, satirically. "Creeds generally cause quarrels."

Vandeloup shrugged his shoulders.

"And quarrels generally cause stories," he said, smiling; "it is the law of compensation."

They then went to the drawing-room and Kitty and Vandeloup both sang, and treated one another in a delightfully polite way. Madame Midas and Calton were both clever, but how much cleverer were the two young people at the piano.

"Are you going to Meddlechip's ball?" said Calton to Madame.

"Oh, yes," she answered, nodding her head, "I and Miss Marchurst are both going."

"Who is Mr. Meddlechip?" asked Kitty, swinging round on the piano-stool.

"He is the most charitable man in Melbourne," said Gaston, with a faint sneer.

"Great is Diana of the Ephesians," said Calton, mockingly. "Because Mr. Meddlechip suffers from too much money, and has to get rid of it to prevent himself being crushed like Tarpeia by the Sabine shields, he is called charitable."

"He does good, though, doesn't he?" asked Madame.

"See advertisement," scoffed Calton. "Oh, yes! he will give thousands of pounds for any public object, but private charity is a waste of money in his eyes."

"You are very hard on him," said Madame Midas, with a laugh.

"Ah! Mr. Calton believes as I do," cried Vandeloup, "that it's no good having friends unless you're privileged to abuse them."

"It's one you take full advantage of, then," observed Kitty, saucily.

"I always take what I can get," he returned, mockingly; whereon she shivered, and Calton saw it.

"Ah!" said that astute reader of character to himself, "there's something between those two. 'Gad! I'll cross-examine my French friend."

They said good-night to the ladies, and walked to the St Kilda station, from thence took the train to town, and Calton put into force his cross-examination. He might as well have tried his artful questions on a rock as on Vandeloup, for that clever young gentleman saw through the barrister at once, and baffled him at every turn with his epigrammatic answers and consummate coolness.

"I confess," said Calton, when they said good-night to one another, "I confess you puzzle me."

"Language," observed M. Vandeloup, with a smile, "was given to us to conceal our thoughts. Good night!"

And they parted.

"The comedy is over for the night," thought Gaston as he walked along, "and it was so true to nature that the spectators never thought it was art."

He was wrong, for Calton did.

IX

A Professional Philanthropist

We have professional diners-out, professional beauties, professional Christians, then why not professional philanthropists? This brilliant century of ours has nothing to do with the word charity, as it savours too much of stealthy benevolence, so it has substituted in its place the long word philanthropy, which is much more genteel and comprehensive. Charity, the meekest of the Christian graces, has been long since dethroned, and her place is taken by the blatant braggard Philanthropy, who does his good deeds in a most ostentatious manner, and loudly invites the world to see his generosity, and praise him for it. Charity, modestly hooded, went into the houses of the poor, and tendered her gifts with smiles. Philanthropy now builds almshouses and hospitals, and rails at poverty if it has too much pride to occupy them. And what indeed, has poverty to do with pride?—it's far too sumptuous and expensive an article, and can only be possessed by the rich, who can afford to wear it because it is paid for. Mr. Meddlechip was rich, so he bought a large stock of pride, and wore it everywhere. It was not personal pride—he was not good-looking; it was not family pride—he never had a grandfather; nor was it pecuniary pride—he had too much money for that. But it was a mean, sneaking, insinuating pride that wrapped him round like a cloak, and pretended to be very humble, and only holding its money in trust for the poor. The poor ye have always with you—did not Mr. Meddlechip know it? Ask the old men and women in the almshouses, and they would answer yes; but ask the squalid inhabitants of the slums, and they would probably say, "Meddlechip, 'o's 'e?" Not that the great Ebenezer Meddlechip was unknown—oh, dear, no—he was a representative colonial; he sat in Parliament, and frequently spoke at those enlarged vestry meetings about the prosperity of the country. He laid foundation stones. He took the chair at public meetings. In fact, he had his finger in every public pie likely to bring him into notoriety; but not in private pies, oh, dear, no; he never did good by stealth and blush to find it fame. Any blushes he might have had would have been angry ones at his good deed not being known.

He had come in the early days of the colony, and made a lot of money, being a shrewd man, and one who took advantage of every tide in the affairs of men. He was honest, that is honest as our present elastic acceptation of the word goes—and when he had accumulated a fortune he set to work to buy a few things. He bought a grand house at Toorak, then he bought a wife to do the honours of the grand house, and when his domestic affairs were quite settled, he bought popularity, which is about the cheapest thing anyone can buy. When the Society for the Supplying of Aborigines with White Waistcoats was started he headed the list with one thousand pounds—bravo, Meddlechip! The Secretary of the Band of Hard-up Matrons asked him for fifty pounds, and got five hundred—generous Meddlechip! And at the meeting of the Society for the Suppression of Vice among Married Men he gave two thousand pounds, and made a speech on the occasion, which made all the married men present tremble lest their sins should find them out—noble Meddlechip! He would give thousands away in public charity, have it well advertised in the newspapers, and then wonder, with humility, how the information got there; and he would give a poor woman in charge for asking for a penny, on the ground that she was a vagrant. Here, indeed, was a man for Victoria to be proud of; put up a statue to him in the centre of the city; let all the school children study a list of his noble actions as lessons; let the public at large grovel before him, and lick the dust of his benevolent shoes, for he is a professional philanthropist.

Mrs. Meddlechip, large, florid, and loud-voiced, was equally as well known as her husband, but in a different way. He posed as benevolence, she was the type of all that's fashionable—that is, she knew everyone; gave large parties, went out to balls, theatres, and lawn tennis, and dressed in the very latest style, whether it suited her or not. She had been born and brought up in the colonies, but when her husband went to London as a representative colonial she went also, and stayed there a whole year, after which she came out to her native land and ran everything down in the most merciless manner. They did not do this in England—oh! dear no! nothing so common—the people in Melbourne had such dreadfully vulgar manners; but then, of course, they are not English; there was no aristocracy; even the dogs and horses were different; they had not the stamp of centuries of birth and breeding on them. In fact, to hear Mrs. Meddlechip talk one would think that England was a perfect aristocratic paradise, and Victoria a vulgar—

other place. She totally ignored the marvellously rapid growth of the country, and that the men and women in it were actually the men and women who had built it up year by year, so that even now it was taking its place among the nations of the earth. But Mrs. Meddlechip was far too ladylike and fashionable for troubling about such things—oh dear, no—she left all these dry facts to Ebenezer, who could speak about them in his own pompous, blatant style at public meetings.

This lady was one of those modern inventions known as a frisky matron, and said and did all manner of dreadful things, which people winked at because—she was Mrs. Meddlechip, and eccentric. She had a young man always dangling after her at theatres and dances—sometimes one, sometimes another, but there was one who was a fixture. This was Barty Jarper, who acted as her poodle dog, and fetched and carried for her in the most amiable manner. When any new poodle dog came on the scene Barty would meekly resign his position, and retire into the background until such time as he was whistled back again to go through his antics. Barty attended her everywhere, made up her programmes, wrote out her invitations, danced with whosoever he was told, and was rewarded for all these services by being given the crumbs from the rich man's table. Mr. Jarper had a meek little way with Mrs. Meddlechip, as if he was constantly apologising for having dared to have come into the world without her permission, but to other people he was rude enough, and in his own mean little soul looked upon himself quite as a man of fashion. How he managed to go about as he did was a standing puzzle to his friends, as he got only a small salary at the Hibernian Bank; yet he was to be seen at balls, theatres, tennis parties; constantly driving about in hansoms; in fact, lived as if he had an independent income. The general opinion was that he was supplied with money by Mrs. Meddlechip, while others said he gambled; and, indeed, Barty was rather clever at throwing sixes, and frequently at the Bachelors' Club won a sufficient sum to give him a new suit of clothes or pay his club subscription for the year. He was one of those bubbles which dance on the surface of society, yet are sure to vanish some day, and if God tempered the wind to any particular shorn lamb, that shorn lamb was Barty Jarper.

The Meddlechips were giving a ball, therefore the mansion at Toorak was brilliantly illuminated and crowded with fashionable people. The ball-room was at the side of the house, and from it French windows opened on to a wide verandah, which was enclosed with drapery and hung with many-coloured Chinese lanterns. Beyond this the smooth green lawns stretched away to a thick fringe of trees, which grew beside the fence and screened the Meddlechip residence from the curious gaze of vulgar eyes.

Kitty came under the guardianship of Mrs. Riller, a young matron with dark hair, an imperious manner, and a young man always at her heels. Mrs. Villiers intended to have come, but at the last moment was seized with one of her nervous fits, so decided to stop at home with Selina for company. Kitty, therefore, accompanied Mrs. Riller to the ball, but the guardianship of that lady was more nominal than anything else, as she went off with Mr. Bellthorp after introducing Kitty to Mrs. Meddlechip, and flirted and danced with him the whole evening. Kitty, however, did not in the least mind being left to her own devices, for being an extremely pretty girl she soon had plenty of young men round her anxious to be introduced. She filled her programme rapidly and kept two valses for Vandeloup, as she knew he was going to be present, but he as yet had not made his appearance.

He arrived about a quarter past ten o'clock, and was strolling leisurely up to the house, when he saw Pierre, standing amid a number of idlers at the gate. The dumb man stepped forward, and Vandeloup paused with a smile on his handsome lips, though he was angry enough at the meeting.

"Money again, I suppose?" he said to Pierre, in a low voice, in French; "don't trouble me now, but come to my rooms to-morrow."

The dumb man nodded, and Vandeloup walked leisurely up the path. Then Pierre followed him right up to the steps which led to the house, saw him enter the brilliantly-lighted hall, and then hid himself in the shrubs which grew on the edge of the lawn. There, in close hiding, he could hear the sound of music and voices, and could see the door of the fernery wide open, and caught glimpses of dainty dresses and bare shoulders within.

Vandeloup, quite ignorant that his friend was watching the house, put on his gloves leisurely, and walked in search of his hostess.

Mrs. Meddlechip glanced approvingly at Vandeloup as he came up, for he was extremely good-looking, and good-looking men were Mrs. Meddlechip's pet weakness. Barty was in attendance on his liege lady, and when he saw how she admired Vandeloup, he foresaw he would be off duty for some time. It would be Vandeloup promoted vice Jarper resigned, but Barty very well knew that Gaston was not a man to conduct himself like a poodle dog, so came to the conclusion he would be retained for use and M. Vandeloup for ornament. Meanwhile, he left Mrs. Meddlechip to cultivate the acquaintance of the young Frenchman, and went off with a red-haired girl to the supper-room. Red-haired girl, who was remarkably ugly and self-complacent, had been a wallflower all the evening, but thought none the less of herself on that account. She assured Barty she was not hungry, but when she finished supper Mr. Jarper was very glad, for the supper's sake, she had no appetite.

"She's the hungriest girl I ever met in my life," he said to Bellthorp afterwards; "ate up everything I gave her, and drank so much lemonade, I thought she'd go up like a balloon."

When Barty had satisfied the red-haired girl's appetite—no easy matter—he left her to play wallflower and make spiteful remarks on the girls who were dancing, and took out another damsel, who smiled and smiled, and trod on his toes when he danced, till he wished her in Jericho. He asked if she was hungry, but, unlike the other girl, she was not; he said she must be tired, but oh, dear no, she was quite fresh; so she danced the whole waltz through and bumped Barty against everyone in the room; then said his step did not suit hers, which exasperated him so much—for Barty flattered himself on his waltzing—that he left her just as she was getting up a flirtation, and went to have a glass of champagne to soothe his feelings. Released from Mrs. Meddlechip, Gaston went in search of Kitty, and found her flirting with Felix Rolleston, who was amusing her with his gay chatter.

"This is a deuced good-looking chappie," said Mr. Rolleston, fixing his eyeglass in his eye and looking critically at Gaston as he approached them; "M. Vandeloup, isn't it?"

Kitty said it was.

"Oh! yes," went on Felix, brightly, "saw him about town—don't know him personally; awfully like a fellow I once knew called Fitzgerald—Brian Fitzgerald—married now and got a family; funny thing, married Miss Frettlby, who used to live in your house."

"Oh! that hansom cab murder," said Kitty, looking at him, "I've heard all about that."

"Egad! I should think you had," observed Mr. Rolleston, with a grin, "it was a nine days' wonder; but here's your friend, introduce me, pray," as Vandeloup came up.

Kitty did so, and Felix improved the occasion.

"Knew you by sight," he said, shaking hands with Gaston, "but it's a case of we never speak as we pass by, and all that sort of thing—come and look me up," hospitably, "South Yarra."

"Delighted," said Gaston, smoothly, taking Kitty's programme and putting his name down for the two vacant waltzes.

"Reciprocal, I assure you," said the lively Felix. "Oh, by Jove! excuse me, Miss Marchurst—there's a polka—got to dance with a girl—you'll see me in a minute—she's a maypole—I'm not, ha! ha! You'll say it's the long and the short of it—ta-ta at present."

He hopped off gaily, and they soon saw him steering the maypole round the room, or rather, the maypole steered Felix, for her idea of the dance was to let Felix skip gaily round her; then she lifted him up and put him down a few feet further on, when he again skipped, and so the performance went on, to the intense amusement of Kitty and Gaston.

"My faith!" said Vandeloup, satirically, dropping into a seat beside Kitty, "she is a maypole, and he's a merry peasant dancing round it. By the way, Bebe, why isn't Madame here to-night?"

"She's not well," replied Kitty, unfurling her fan; "I don't know what's come over her, she's so nervous."

"Oh! indeed," said Vandeloup, politely; "Hum!—still afraid of her husband turning up," he said to himself, as Kitty was carried away for a valse by Mr. Bellthorp; "how slow all this is?" he went on, yawning, and rising from his seat; "I shan't stay long, or that old woman will be seizing me again. Poor Kestrike, surely his sin has been punished enough in having such a wife," and M. Vandeloup strolled away to speak to Mrs. Riller, who, being bereft of Bellthorp, was making signals to him with her fan.

Barty Jarper had been hard at work all night on the poodle-dog system, and had danced with girls who could not dance, and talked with girls that could not talk, so, as a reward for his work, he promised himself a dance with Kitty. At the beginning of the evening he had secured a dance from her, and now, all his duties for the evening being over, he went to get it. Bellthorp had long since returned to Mrs. Riller and flirtation, and Kitty had been dancing with a tall young man, with unsteady legs and an eye-glass that would not stick in his eye. She did not particularly care about Mr. Jarper, with his effeminate little ways, but was quite glad when he came to carry her off from the unsteady legs and the eye-glass. The dance was the Lancers; but Kitty declared she would not dance it as she felt weary, so made Mr. Jarper take her to supper. Barty was delighted, as he was hungry himself, so they secured a pleasant little nook, and Barty foraged for provisions.

"You know all about this house," said Kitty, when she saw how successful the young man was in getting nice things.

"Oh, yes," murmured Barty, quite delighted, "I know most of the houses in Melbourne—I know yours."

"Mrs. Villiers'?" asked Kitty.

Barty nodded.

"Used to go down there a lot when Mr. Frettlby lived there," he said, sipping his wine. "I know every room in it."

"You'd be invaluable as a burglar," said Kitty, a little contemptuously, as she looked at his slim figure.

"I dare say," replied Barty, who took the compliment in good faith. "Some night I'll climb up to your room and give you a fright."

"Shows how much you know," retorted Miss Marchurst. "My room is next to Madame's on the ground floor."

"I know," said Barty, sagely, nodding his head. "It used to be a boudoir—nice little room. By the way, where is Mrs. Villiers to-night?"

"She's not well," replied Kitty, yawning behind her fan, for she was weary of Barty and his small talk. "She's very worried."

"Over money matters, I suppose?"

Kitty laughed and shook her head.

"Hardly," she answered.

"I dare say," replied Barty, "she's awfully rich. You know, I'm in the bank where her account is, and I know all about her. Rich! oh, she is rich! Lucky thing for that French fellow if he marries her."

"Marries her?" echoed Kitty, her face growing pale. "M. Vandeloup?"

"Yes," replied Barty, pleased at having made a sensation. "Her first husband has vanished, you know, and all the fellows are laying bets about Van marrying the grass widow."

"What nonsense!" said Kitty, in an agitated voice. "M. Vandeloup is her friend—nothing more."

Barty grinned.

"I've seen so much of that 'friendship, and nothing more', business," he said, significantly, whereupon Kitty rose to her feet.

"I'm tired," she said, coldly. "Kindly take me to Mrs. Riller."

"I've put my foot into it," thought Jarper, as he led her away. "I believe she's spoons on Van herself."

Mrs. Riller was not very pleased to see Kitty, as Mr. Bellthorp was telling her some amusing scandals about her dearest friends, and, of course, had to stop when Kitty came up.

"Not dancing, dear?" she asked, with a sympathetic smile, glancing angrily at Bellthorp, who seemed more struck with Kitty than he had any right to be, considering he was her property.

"No," replied Kitty, "I'm a little tired."

"Miss Marchurst," observed Bellthorp, leaning towards her, "I'm sure I've seen you before."

Kitty felt a chill running through her veins as she remembered where their last meeting had been. The extremity of the danger gave her courage.

"I dare say," she replied, coldly turning her back on the young man, "I'm not invisible."

Mrs. Riller looked with all her eyes, for she wanted to know all about this pretty girl who dropped so unexpectedly into Melbourne society, so she determined to question Bellthorp when she got him alone. To this end she finessed.

"Oh! there's that lovely valse," she said, as the band struck up "One summer's night in Munich". "If you are not engaged, Mr. Bellthorp, we must have a turn."

"Delighted," replied Bellthorp, languidly offering his arm, but thinking meanwhile, "confound these women, how they do work a man."

"You, I suppose," said Mrs. Riller to Kitty, "are going to play wallflower."

"Hardly," observed a cool voice behind them; "Miss Marchurst dances this with me—you see, Mrs. Riller," as that lady turned and saw Vandeloup, "she has not your capability at playing wallflower," with a significant glance at Bellthorp.

Mrs. Riller understood the look, which seemed to pierce into the very depths of her frivolous little soul, and flushed angrily as she moved away with Mr. Bellthorp and mentally determined to be even with Vandeloup on the first occasion.

Gaston, quite conscious of the storm he had raised, smiled serenely, and then offered his arm to Kitty, which she refused, as she was determined to find out from his own lips the truth of Jarper's statement regarding Madame Midas.

"I don't want to dance," she said curtly, pointing to the seat beside her as an invitation for him to sit down.

"Pardon me," observed Vandeloup, blandly, "I do; we can talk afterwards if you like."

Their eyes met, and then Kitty arose and took his arm, with a charming pout. It was no good fighting against the quiet, masterful manner of this man, so she allowed him to put his arm round her waist and swing her slowly into the centre of the room. "One summer's night in Munich" was a favourite valse, and everyone who could dance, and a good many who could not, were up on the floor. Every now and then, through the steady beat of the music, came the light laugh of a woman or the deeper tones of a man's voice; and the glare of the lights, the flashing jewels on the bare necks and arms of women, the soft frou-frou of their dresses, as their partners swung them steadily round, and the subtle perfume of flowers gave an indescribable sensuous flavour to the whole scene. And the valse—who does not know it? with its sad refrain, which comes in every now and then throughout, even in the most brilliant passages. The whole story of a man's faith and a woman's treachery is contained therein.

"One summer's night in Munich," sighed the heavy bass instruments, sadly and reproachfully, "I thought your heart was true!" Listen to the melancholy notes of the prelude which recall the whole scene—do you not remember? The stars are shining, the night wind is blowing, and we are on the terrace looking down on the glittering lights of the city. Hark! that joyous sparkling strain, full of riant laughter, recalls the sad students who wandered past, and then from amid the airy ripple of notes comes the sweet, mellow strain of the 'cello, which tells of love eternal amid the summer roses; how the tender melody sweeps on full of the perfume and mystic meanings of that night. Hark! is that the nightingale in the trees, or only the silvery notes of a violin, which comes stealing through the steady throb and swing of the heavier stringed instruments? Ah! why does the rhythm stop? A few chords breaking up the dream, the sound of a bugle calling you away, and the valse goes into the farewell motif with its tender longing and passionate anguish. Good-bye! you will be true? Your heart is mine, good-bye, sweetheart! Stop! that discord of angry notes—she is false to her soldier lover! The stars are pale, the nightingale is silent, the rose leaves fall, and the sad refrain comes stealing through the room again with its bitter reproach, "One summer's night in Munich I knew your heart was false."

Kitty danced for a little time, but was too much agitated to enjoy the valse, in spite of the admirable partner M. Vandeloup made. She was determined to find out the truth, so stopped abruptly, and insisted on Vandeloup taking her to the conservatory.

"What for?" he asked, as they threaded their way through the crowded room. "Is it important?"

"Very," she replied, looking straight at him; "it is essential to our comedy."

M. Vandeloup shrugged his shoulders.

"My faith!" he murmured, as they entered the fernery; "this comedy is becoming monotonous."

X

In the Fernery

The fernery was a huge glass building on one side of the ballroom, filled with Australian and New Zealand ferns, and having a large fountain in the centre sending up a sparkling jet of water, which fell into the shallow stone basin filled with water lilies and their pure white flowers. At the end was a mimic representation of a mountain torrent, with real water tumbling down real rocks, and here and there in the crannies and crevices grew delicate little ferns, while overhead towered the great fronds of the tree ferns. The roof was a dense mass of greenery, and wire baskets filled with sinuous creepers hung down, with their contents straggling over. Electric lights in green globes were skilfully hidden all round, and a faint aquamarine twilight permeated the whole place, and made it look like a mermaid's grotto in the depths of the sea. Here and there were delightful nooks, with well-cushioned seats, many of which were occupied by pretty girls and their attendant cavaliers. On one side of the fernery a wide door opened on to a low terrace, from whence steps went down to the lawn, and beyond was the dark fringe of trees wherein Pierre was concealed.

Kitty and Vandeloup found a very comfortable nook just opposite the door, and they could see the white gleam of the terrace in the luminous starlight. Every now and then a couple would pass, black silhouettes against the clear sky, and around they could hear the murmur of voices and the musical tinkling of the fountain, while the melancholy music of the valse, with its haunting refrain, sounded through the pale green twilight. Barty Jarper was talking near them, in his mild little way, to a tall young lady in a bilious-looking green dress, and further off Mr. Bellthorp was laughing with Mrs. Riller behind the friendly shelter of her fan.

"Well," said Vandeloup, amiably, as he sank into a seat beside Kitty, "what is this great matter you wish to speak about?"

"Madame Midas," retorted Kitty, looking straight at him.

"Such a delightful subject," murmured Gaston, closing his eyes, as he guessed what was coming; "go on, I'm all attention."

"You are going to marry her," said Miss Marchurst, bending towards him and closing her fan with a snap.

Vandeloup smiled faintly.

"You don't say so?" he murmured, opening his eyes and looking at her lazily; "who told you this news—for news it is to me, I assure you?"

"Then it's not true?" added Kitty, eagerly, with a kind of gasp.

"I'm sure I don't know," he replied, indolently fingering his moustache; "I haven't asked her yet."

"You are not going to do so?" she said, rapidly, with a flush on her face.

"Why not?" in surprise; "do you object?"

"Object? my God!" she exclaimed, in a low fierce tone; "have you forgotten what we are to one another?"

"Friends, I understand," he said, looking at his hands, admiringly.

"And something more," she added, bitterly; "lovers!"

"Don't talk so loud, my dear," replied Vandeloup, coolly; "it doesn't do to let everyone know your private business."

"It's private now," she said, in a voice of passion, "but it will soon be public enough."

"Indeed! which paper do you advertise in?"

"Listen to me, Gaston," she said, taking no notice of his sneer; "you will never marry Madame Midas; sooner than that, I will reveal all and kill myself."

"You forget," he said, gently; "it is comedy, not tragedy, we play."

"That is as I choose," she retorted; "see!" and with a sudden gesture she put her hand into the bosom of her dress and took out the bottle of poison with the red bands. "I have it still."

"So I perceive," he answered, smiling. "Do you always carry it about with you, like a modern Lucrezia Borgia?"

"Yes," she answered quietly; "it never leaves me, you see," with a sneer. "As you said yourself, it's always well to be prepared for emergencies."

"So it appears," observed Vandeloup, with a yawn, sitting up. "I wouldn't use that poison if I were you; it is risky."

"Oh, no, it's not," answered Kitty; "it is fatal in its results, and leaves no trace behind."

"There you are wrong," replied Gaston, coolly; "it does leave traces behind, but makes it appear as if apoplexy was the cause of death. Give me the bottle?" peremptorily.

"No!" she answered, defiantly, clenching it in her hand.

"I say yes," he said, in an angry whisper; "that poison is my secret, and I'm not going to have you play fast and loose with it; give it up," and he placed his hand on her wrist.

"You hurt my wrist," she said.

"I'll break your wrist, my darling," he said, quietly, "if you don't give me that bottle."

Kitty wrenched her hand away, and rose to her feet.

"Sooner than that, I'll throw it away," she said, and before he could stop her, she flung the bottle out on to the lawn, where it fell down near the trees.

"Bah! I will find it," he said, springing to his feet, but Kitty was too quick for him.

"M. Vandeloup," she said aloud, so that everyone could hear; "kindly take me back to the ball-room, will you, to finish our valse."

Vandeloup would have refused, but she had his arm, and as everyone was looking at him, he could not refuse without being guilty of marked discourtesy. Kitty had beaten him with his own weapons, so, with a half-admiring glance at her, he took her back to the ball-room, where the waltz was just ending.

"At all events," he said in her ear, as they went smoothly gliding round the room, "you won't be able to do any mischief with it now to yourself or to anyone else."

"Won't I?" she retorted quickly; "I have some more at home."

"The deuce!" he exclaimed.

"Yes," she replied, triumphantly; "the bottle I got that belonged to you, I put half its contents into another. So you see I can still do mischief, and," in a fierce whisper, "I will, if you don't give up this idea of marrying Madame Midas."

"I thought you knew me better than that," he said, in a tone of concentrated passion. "I will not."

"Then I'll poison her," she retorted.

"What, the woman who has been so kind to you?"

"Yes, I'd rather see her dead than married to a devil like you."

"How amiable you are, Bebe," he said, with a laugh, as the music stopped.

"I am what you have made me," she replied, bitterly, and they walked into the drawing-room.

After this Vandeloup clearly saw that it was a case of diamond cut diamond, for Kitty was becoming as clever with her tongue as he was. After all, though she was his pupil, and was getting as hardened and cynical as possible, he did not think it fair she should use his own weapons against himself. He did not believe she would try and poison Madame Midas, even though she was certain of not being detected, for he thought she was too tender-hearted. But, alas! he had taught her excellently well, and Kitty was rapidly arriving at the conclusion he had long since come to, that number one was the greatest number. Besides, her love for Vandeloup, though not so ardent as it had been, was too intense for her to let any other woman get a hold of him. Altogether, M. Vandeloup was in an extremely unpleasant position, and one of his own making.

Having given Kitty over to the tender care of Mrs. Rolleston, Vandeloup hurried outside to look for the missing bottle. He had guessed the position it fell in, and, striking a match, went to look over the smooth close-shorn turf. But though he was a long time, and looked carefully, the bottle was gone.

"The devil!" said Vandeloup, startled by this discovery. "Who could have picked it up?"

He went back into the conservatory, and, sitting down in his old place, commenced to review the position.

It was most annoying about the poison, there was no doubt of that. He only hoped that whoever picked it up would know nothing about its dangerous qualities. After all, he could be certain about that, as no one but himself knew what the poison was and how it could be used. The person who picked up the bottle would probably throw it away again as useless; and then, again, perhaps when Kitty threw the bottle away the stopper came out, and the contents would be lost. And then Kitty still had more left, but—bah!—she would not use it on Madame Midas. That was the vague threat of a jealous woman to frighten him. The real danger he was in lay in the fact that she might tell Madame Midas the relations between them, and then there would be no chance of his marrying at all. If he could only stop Kitty's mouth in some way—persuasion was thrown away on her. If he could with safety get rid of her he would. Ah! that was an idea. He had some of this poison— if he could only manage to give it to her, and thus remove her from his path. There would be no risk of discovery, as the poison left no traces behind, and if it came to the worst, it would appear she had committed suicide, for poison similar to what she had used would be found in her possession. It was a pity to kill her, so young and pretty, and yet his safety demanded it; for if she told Madame Midas all, it might lead to further inquiries, and M. Vandeloup well knew his past life would not bear looking into. Another thing, she had threatened him about some secret she held—he did not know what it was, and yet almost guessed; if that was the secret she must be got rid of, for it would imperil not only his liberty, but his life. Well, if he had to get rid of her, the sooner he did so the better, for even on the next day she might tell all—he would have to give her the poison that night—but how? that was the difficulty. He could not do it at this ball, as it would be too apparent if she died—no—it would have to be administered secretly when she went home. But then she would go to Madame Midas' room to see how she was, and then would retire to her own room. He knew where that was—just off Mrs. Villiers' room; there were French windows in both rooms—two in Mrs. Villiers', and one in Kitty's. That was the plan—they would be left open as the night was hot. Suppose he went down to St Kilda, and got into the garden, he knew every inch of the way; then he could slip into the open window, and if it was not open, he could use a diamond ring to cut the glass. He had a diamond ring he never wore, so if Kitty was discovered to be poisoned, and the glass cut, they would never suspect him, as he did not wear rings at all, and the evidence of the cut window would show a diamond must have been used. Well, suppose he got inside, Kitty would be asleep, and he could put the poison into the water carafe, or he could put it in a glass of water and leave it standing; the risk would be, would she drink it or not—he would have to run that risk; if he failed this time, he would not the next. But, then, suppose she awoke and screamed—pshaw! when she saw it was he Kitty would not dare to make a scene, and he could easily make some excuse for his presence there. It was a wild scheme, but then he was in such a dangerous position that he had to try everything.

When M. Vandeloup had come to this conclusion he arose, and, going to the supper room, drank a glass of brandy; for even he, cool as he was, felt a little nervous over the crime he was about to commit. He thought he would give Kitty one last chance, so when she was already cloaked, waiting with Mrs. Riller for the carriage, he drew her aside.

"You did not mean what you said tonight," he whispered, looking searchingly at her.

"Yes, I did," she replied, defiantly; "if you push me to extremities, you must take the consequences."

"It will be the worse for you," he said, threateningly, as the carriage drove up.

"I'm not afraid of you," she retorted, shrugging her shoulders, a trick she had learned from him; "you have ruined my life, but I'm not going to let you ruin Madame's. I'd sooner see her dead than in your arms."

"Remember, I have warned you," he said, gravely, handing her to the carriage. "Good night!"

"Good night!" she answered, mockingly; "and to-morrow," in a low voice, "you will be astonished."

"And to-morrow," he said to himself, as the carriage drove off, "you will be dead."

XI

THE VISION OF MISS KITTY MARCHURST

Everyone knows the story of Damocles, and how uncomfortable he felt with the sword suspended by a hair over his head. No one could enjoy their dinner under such circumstances, and it is much to be thankful for that hosts of the present day do not indulge in these practical jokes. But though history does not repeat itself exactly regarding the suspended sword, yet there are cases when a sense of impending misfortune has the same effect on the spirits. This was the case of Madame Midas. She was not by any means of a nervous temperature, yet ever since the disappearance of her husband she was a prey to a secret dread, which, reacting on her nerves, rendered her miserable. Had Mr. Villiers only appeared, she would have known how to deal with him, and done so promptly, but it was his absence that made her afraid. Was he dead? If so, why was his body not found; if he was not dead, why did he not reappear on the scene. Allowing, for the sake of argument, that he had stolen the nugget and left the colony in order to enjoy the fruits of his villainy—well, the nugget weighed about three hundred ounces—and that if he disposed of it, as he must have done, it would give him a sum of money a little over one thousand pounds. True, his possession of such a large mass of gold would awake suspicions in the mind of anyone he went to; but then, there were people who were always ready to do shady things, provided they were well paid. So whomsoever he went to would levy blackmail on him on threat of informing the police and having him arrested. Therefore, the most feasible thing would be that he had got about half of the value of the nugget, which would be about six hundred pounds. Say that he did so, a whole year had elapsed, and Madame Midas knew her husband well enough to know that six hundred pounds would soon slip through his fingers, so at the present time he must once more be penniless. If he was, why did he not come back to her and demand more money now she was rich? Even had he gone to a distant place, he would always have kept enough money to pay his way back to Victoria, so that he could wring money out of her. It was this unpleasant feeling of being watched that haunted her and made her uneasy. The constant strain began to tell on her; she became ill and haggard-looking, and her eyes were always glancing around in the anxious manner common to hunted animals. She felt as though she were advancing on a masked battery, and at any moment a shot might strike her from the most unexpected quarter. She tried to laugh off the feeling and blamed herself severely for the morbid state of mind into which she was falling; but it was no use, for by day and night the sense of impending misfortune hung over her like the sword of Damocles, ready to fall at any moment. If her husband would only appear, she would settle an income on him, on condition he ceased to trouble her, but at present she was fighting in the dark with an unknown enemy. She became afraid of being left alone, and even when seated quietly with Selina, would suddenly start and look apprehensively towards the door, as if she heard his footstep. Imagination, when uncontrolled, can keep the mind on a mental rack, to which that of the Inquisition was a bed of roses.

Selina was grieved at this state of things, and tried to argue and comfort her mistress with the most amiable proverbs, but she was quite unable to administer to a mind diseased, and Mrs. Villiers' life became a perfect hell upon earth.

"Are my troubles never going to end?" she said to Selina on the night of the Meddlechip ball, as she paced restlessly up and down her room; "this man has embittered the whole of my life, and now he is stabbing me in the dark."

"Let the dead past bury its dead," quoted Selina, who was arranging the room for the night.

"Pshaw!" retorted Madame, impatiently, walking to the French window at the end of the room and opening it; "how do you know he is dead? Come here, Selina," she went on, beckoning to the old woman, and pointing outside to the garden bathed in moonlight; "I have always a dread lest he may be watching the house. Even now he may be concealed yonder"—pointing down the garden.

Selina looked out, but could see nothing. There was a smooth lawn, burnt and yellow with the heat, which stretched for about fifty feet, and ended in a low quickset hedge at the foot of a red brick wall which ran down that side of the property. The top of this wall was set with broken bottles, and beyond was the street, where they could hear people passing along. The moonlight rendered all this as light as day, and, as Selina pointed out to her mistress, there was no place where a man could conceal himself. But this did not satisfy Madame; she left the window half open, so that the cool night wind could blow in, and drew together the red velvet curtains which hung there.

"You've left the window open," remarked Selina, looking at her mistress, "and if you are nervous it will not make you feel safe."

Madame Midas glanced at the window.

"It's so hot," she said, plaintively, "I will get no sleep. Can't you manage to fix it up, so that I can leave it open?"

"I'll try," answered Selina, and she undressed her mistress and put her to bed, then proceeded to fix up a kind of burglar trap. The bed was a four-poster, with heavy crimson curtains, and the top was pushed against the wall, near the window. The curtains of the window and those of the bed prevented any draught blowing in; and directly in front of the window, Selina set a small wood table, so that anyone who tried to enter would throw it over, and thus put the sleeper on the alert. On this she put a night-light, a book, in case Madame should wake up and want to read—a thing she very often did—and a glass of homemade lemonade, for a night drink. Then she locked the other window and drew the curtains, and, after going into Kitty's room, which opened off the larger one, and fixing up the one window there in the same way, she prepared to retire, but Madame stopped her.

"You must stay all night with me, Selina," she said, irritably. "I can't be left alone."

"But, Miss Kitty," objected Selina, "she'll expect to be waited for coming home from the ball."

"Well, she comes in here to go to her own room," said Madame, impatiently; "you can leave the door unlocked."

"Well," observed Miss Sprotts, grimly, beginning to undress herself, "for a nervous woman, you leave a great many windows and doors open."

"I'm not afraid as long as you are with me," said Madame, yawning; "it's by myself I get nervous."

Miss Sprotts sniffed, and observed that "Prevention is better than cure," then went to bed, and both she and Madame were soon fast asleep. Selina slept on the outside of the bed, and Madame, having a sense of security from being with someone, slumbered calmly; so the night wore drowsily on, and nothing could be heard but the steady ticking of the clock and the heavy breathing of the two women.

A sleepy servant admitted Kitty when she came home from the ball, and had said goodbye to Mrs. Riller and Bellthorp. Then Mrs. Riller, whose husband had gone home three hours before, drove away with Bellthorp, and Kitty went into Madame's room, while the sleepy servant, thankful that his vigil for the night was over, went to bed. Kitty found Madame's door ajar, and went in softly, fearful lest she might wake her. She did not know that Selina was in the room, and as she heard the steady breathing of the sleepers, she concluded that Madame was asleep, and resolved to go quietly into her own room without disturbing the sleeper. So eerie the room looked with the faint night-light burning on the table beside the bed, and all the shadows, not marked and distinct as in a strong glare, were faintly confused. Just near the door was a long chevral glass, and Kitty caught sight of herself in it, wan and spectral-looking, in her white dress, and, as she let the heavy blue cloak fall from her shoulders, a perfect shower of apple blossoms were shaken on to the floor. Her hair had come undone from its sleek, smooth plaits, and now hung like a veil of gold on her shoulders. She looked closely at herself in the glass, and her face looked worn and haggard in the dim light. A pungent acrid odour permeated the room, and the heavy velvet curtains moved with subdued rustlings as the wind stole in through the window. On a table near her was a portrait of Vandeloup, which he had given Madame two days before, and though she could not see the face she knew it was his. Stretching out her hand she took the photograph from its stand, and sank into a low chair which stood at the end of the room some distance from the bed. So noiseless were her movements that the two sleepers never awoke, and the girl sat in the chair with the portrait in her hand dreaming of the man whom it represented. She knew his handsome face was smiling up at her out of the glimmering gloom, and clenched her hands in anger as she thought how he had treated her. She let the portrait fall on her lap, and leaning back in the chair, with all her golden hair showering down loosely over her shoulders, gave herself up to reflection.

He was going to marry Madame Midas—the man who had ruined her life; he would hold another woman in his arms and tell her all the false tales he had told her. He would look into her eyes with his own, and she would be unable to see the treachery and guile hidden in their depths. She could not stand it. False friend, false lover, he had been, but to see him married to another—no! it was too much. And yet what could she do? A woman in love believes no ill of the man she adores, and if she was to tell Madame Midas all she would not be believed. Ah! it was useless to fight against fate, it was too strong for her, so she would have to suffer in silence, and see them happy. That story of Hans

Andersen's, which she had read, about the little mermaid who danced, and felt that swords were wounding her feet while the prince smiled on his bride—yes, that was her case. She would have to stand by in silence and see him caressing another woman, while every caress would stab her like a sword. Was there no way of stopping it? Ah! what is that? The poison—no! no! anything but that. Madame had been kind to her, and she could not repay her trust with treachery. No, she was not weak enough for that. And yet suppose Madame died? no one could tell she had been poisoned, and then she could marry Vandeloup. Madame was sleeping in yonder bed, and on the table there was a glass with some liquid in it. She would only have to go to her room, fetch the poison, and put it in there—then retire to bed. Madame would surely drink during the night, and then—yes, there was only one way—the poison!

How still the house was: not a sound but the ticking of the clock in the hall and the rushing scamper of a rat or mouse. The dawn reddens faintly in the east and the chill morning breeze comes up from the south, salt with the odours of the ocean. Ah! what is that? a scream—a woman's voice—then another, and the bell rings furiously. The frightened servants collect from all parts of the house, in all shapes of dress and undress. The bell sounds from the bedroom of Mrs. Villiers, and having ascertained this they all rush in. What a sight meets their eyes. Kitty Marchurst, still in her ball dress, clinging convulsively to the chair; Madame Midas, pale but calm, ringing the bell; and on the bed, with one arm hanging over, lies Selina Sprotts—dead! The table near the bed was overturned on the floor, and the glass and the night-lamp both lie smashed to pieces on the carpet.

"Send for a doctor at once," cried Madame, letting go the bell-rope and crossing to the window; "Selina has had a fit of some sort."

Startled servant goes out to stables and wakes up the grooms, one of whom is soon on horseback riding for dear life to Dr. Chinston. Clatter—clatter along in the keen morning air; a few workmen on their way to work gaze in surprise at this furious rider. Luckily, the doctor lives in St Kilda, and being awoke out of his sleep, dresses himself quickly, and taking the groom's horse, rides back to Mrs. Villiers' house. He dismounts, enters the house, then the bedroom. Kitty, pale and wan, is seated in the chair; the window curtains are drawn, and the cold light of day pours into the room, while Madame Midas is kneeling beside the corpse, with all the servants around her. Dr. Chinston lifts the arm; it falls limply down. The face is ghastly white, the eyes staring; there is a streak of foam on the tightly clenched mouth. The doctor puts his hand on the heart—not a throb; he closes the staring eyes reverently, and turns to the kneeling woman and the frightened servants.

"She is dead," he says, briefly, and orders them to leave the room.

"When did this occur, Mrs. Villiers?" he asked, when the room had been cleared and only himself, Madame, and Kitty remained.

"I can't tell you," replied Madame, weeping; "she was all right last night when we went to bed, and she stayed all night with me because I was nervous. I slept soundly, when I was awakened by a cry and saw Kitty standing beside the bed and Selina in convulsions; then she became quite still and lay like that till you came. What is the cause?"

"Apoplexy," replied the doctor, doubtfully; "at least, judging from the symptoms; but perhaps Miss Marchurst can tell us when the attack came on?"

He turned to Kitty, who was shivering in the chair and looked so pale that Madame Midas went over to her to see what was the matter. The girl, however, shrank away with a cry as the elder woman approached, and rising to her feet moved unsteadily towards the doctor.

"You say she," pointing to the body, "died of apoplexy?"

"Yes," he answered, curtly, "all the symptoms of apoplexy are there."

"You are wrong!" gasped Kitty, laying her hand on his arm, "it is poison!"

"Poison!" echoed Madame and the Doctor in surprise.

"Listen," said Kitty, quickly, pulling herself together by a great effort. "I came home from the ball between two and three, I entered the room to go to my own," pointing to the other door; "I did not know Selina was with Madame."

"No," said Madame, quietly, "that is true, I only asked her to stop at the last moment."

"I was going quietly to bed," resumed Kitty, hurriedly, "in order not to waken Madame, when I saw the portrait of M. Vandeloup on the table; I took it up to look at it."

"How could you see without a light?" asked Dr. Chinston, sharply, looking at her.

"There was a night light burning," replied Kitty, pointing to the fragments on the floor; "and I could only guess it was M. Vandeloup's portrait; but at all events," she said, quickly, "I sat down in the chair over there and fell asleep."

"You see, doctor, she had been to a ball and was tired," interposed Madame Midas; "but go on, Kitty, I want to know why you say Selina was poisoned."

"I don't know how long I was asleep," said Kitty, wetting her dry lips with her tongue, "but I was awoke by a noise at the window there," pointing towards the window, upon which both her listeners turned towards it, "and looking, I saw a hand coming out from behind the curtain with a bottle in it; it held the bottle over the glass on the table, and after pouring the contents in, then withdrew."

"And why did you not cry out for assistance?" asked the doctor, quickly.

"I couldn't," she replied, "I was so afraid that I fainted. I recovered my senses, Selina had drank the poison, and when I got up on my feet and went to the bed she was in convulsions; I woke Madame, and that's all."

"A strange story," said Chinston, musingly, "where is the glass?"

"It's broken, doctor," replied Madame Midas; "in getting out of bed I knocked the table down, and both the night lamp and glass smashed."

"No one could have been concealed behind the curtain of the window?" said the doctor to Madame Midas.

"No," she replied, "but the window was open all night; so if it is as Kitty says, the man who gave the poison must have put his hand through the open window."

Dr. Chinston went to the window and looked out; there were no marks of feet on the flower bed, where it was so soft that anyone standing on it would have left a footmark behind.

"Strange," said the doctor, "it's a peculiar story," looking at Kitty keenly.

"But a true one," she replied boldly, the colour coming back to her face; "I say she was poisoned."

"By whom?" asked Madame Midas, the memory of her husband coming back to her.

"I can't tell you," answered Kitty, "I only saw the hand."

"At all events," said Chinston, slowly, "the poisoner did not know that your nurse was with you, so the poison was meant for Mrs. Villiers."

"For me?" she echoed, ghastly pale; "I knew it,—my husband is alive, and this is his work."

XII

A Startling Discovery

Ill news travels fast, and before noon the death of Selina Sprotts was known all over Melbourne. The ubiquitous reporter, of course, appeared on the scene, and the evening papers gave its own version of the affair, and a hint at foul play. There was no grounds for this statement, as Dr. Chinston told Kitty and Madame Midas to say nothing about the poison, and it was generally understood that the deceased had died from apoplexy. A rumour, however, which originated none knew how, crept about among everyone that poison was the cause of death, and this, being added to by some and embellished in all its little details by others, there was soon a complete story made up about the affair. At the Bachelor's Club it was being warmly spoken about when Vandeloup came in about eight o'clock in the evening; and when he appeared he was immediately overwhelmed with inquiries. He looked cool and calm as usual, and stood smiling quietly on the excited group before him.

"You know Mrs. Villiers," said Bellthorp, in an assertive tone, "so you must know all about the affair." "I don't see that," returned Gaston, pulling at his moustache, "knowing anyone does not include a knowledge of all that goes on in the house. I assure you, beyond what there is in the papers, I am as ignorant as you are."

"They say this woman—Sprotts or Potts, or something—died from poison," said Barty Jarper, who had been all round the place collecting information.

"Apoplexy, the doctor says," said Bellthorp, lighting a cigarette; "she was in the same room with Mrs. Villiers and was found dead in the morning."

"Miss Marchurst was also in the room," put in Barty, eagerly.

"Oh, indeed!" said Vandeloup, smoothly, turning to him; "do you think she had anything to do with it?"

"Of course not," said Rolleston, who had just entered, "she had no reason to kill the woman."

Vandeloup smiled.

"So logical you are," he murmured, "you want a reason for everything."

"Naturally," retorted Felix, fixing in his eyeglass, "there is no effect without a cause."

"It couldn't have been Miss Marchurst," said Bellthorp, "they say that the poison was poured out of a bottle held by a hand which came through the window—it's quite true," defiantly looking at the disbelieving faces round him; "one of Mrs. Villiers' servants heard it in the house and told Mrs. Riller's maid."

"From whence," said Vandeloup, politely, "it was transmitted to you—precisely."

Bellthorp reddened slightly, and turned away as he saw the other smiling, for his relations with Mrs. Riller were well known.

"That hand business is all bosh," observed Felix Rolleston, authoritatively; "it's in a play called 'The Hidden Hand'."

"Perhaps the person who poisoned Miss Sprotts, got the idea from it?" suggested Jarper.

"Pshaw, my dear fellow," said Vandeloup, languidly; "people don't go to melodrama for ideas. Everyone has got their own version of this story; the best thing to do is to await the result of the inquest."

"Is there to be an inquest?" cried all.

"So I've heard," replied the Frenchman, coolly; "sounds as if there was something wrong, doesn't it?"

"It's a curious poisoning case," observed Bellthorp.

"Ah, but it isn't proved that there is any poisoning about it," said Vandeloup, looking keenly at him; "you jump to conclusions."

"There is no smoke without fire," replied Rolleston, sagely. "I expect we'll all be rather astonished when the inquest is held," and so the discussion closed.

The inquest was appointed to take place next day, and Calton had been asked by Madame Midas to be present on her behalf. Kilsip, a detective officer, was also present, and, curled up like a cat in the corner, was listening to every word of the evidence.

The first witness called was Madame Midas, who deposed that the deceased, Selina Jane Sprotts, was her servant. She had gone to bed in excellent health, and next morning she had found her dead.

The Coroner asked a few questions relative to the case.

Q. Miss Marchurst awoke you, I believe?
A. Yes.
Q. And her room is off yours?
A. Yes.
Q. Had she to go through your room to reach her own?

A. She had. There was no other way of getting there.

Q. One of the windows of your room was open?

A. It was—all night.

Miss Kitty Marchurst was then called, and being sworn, gave her story of the hand coming through the window. This caused a great sensation in Court, and Calton looked puzzled, while Kilsip, scenting a mystery, rubbed his lean hands together softly.

Q. You live with Mrs. Villiers, I believe, Miss Marchurst?

A. I do.

Q. And you knew the deceased intimately?

A. I had known her all my life.

Q. Had she anyone who would wish to injure her?

A. Not that I knew of. She was a favourite with everyone.

Q. What time did you come home from the ball you were at?

A. About half-past two, I think. I went straight to Mrs. Villiers' room.

Q. With the intention of going through it to reach your own?

A. Yes.

Q. You say you fell asleep looking at a portrait. How long did you sleep?

A. I don't know. I was awakened by a noise at the window, and saw the hand appear.

Q. Was it a man's hand or a woman's?

A. I don't know. It was too indistinct for me to see clearly; and I was so afraid, I fainted.

Q. You saw it pour something from a bottle into the glass on the table?

A. Yes; but I did not see it withdraw. I fainted right off.

Q. When you recovered your senses, the deceased had drank the contents of the glass?

A. Yes. She must have felt thirsty and drank it, not knowing it was poisoned. Q. How do you know it was poisoned?

A. I only suppose so. I don't think anyone would come to a window and pour anything into a glass without some evil purpose.

The Coroner then asked why the glass with what remained of the contents had not been put in evidence, but was informed that the glass was broken.

When Kitty had ended her evidence and was stepping down, she caught the eye of Vandeloup, who was looking at her keenly. She met his gaze defiantly, and he smiled meaningly at her. At this moment, however, Kilsip bent forward and whispered something to the Coroner, whereupon Kitty was recalled.

Q. You were an actress, Miss Marchurst?
A. Yes. I was on tour with Mr. Theodore Wopples for some time.
Q. Do you know a drama called "The Hidden Hand"?
A. Yes—I have played in it once or twice.
Q. Is there not a strong resemblance between your story of this crime and the drama?
A. Yes, it is very much the same.

Kilsip then gave his evidence, and deposed that he had examined the ground between the window, where the hand was alleged to have appeared, and the garden wall. There were no footmarks on the flower-bed under the window, which was the only place where footmarks would show, as the lawn itself was hard and dry. He also examined the wall, but could find no evidence that anyone had climbed over it, as it was defended by broken bottles, and the bushes at its foot were not crushed or disturbed in any way.

Dr. Chinston was then called, and deposed that he had made a post-mortem examination of the body of the deceased. The body was that of a woman of apparently fifty or fifty-five years of age, and of medium height; the body was well nourished. There were no ulcers or other signs of disease, and no marks of violence on the body. The brain was congested and soft, and there was an abnormal amount of fluid in the spaces known as the ventricles of the brain; the lungs were gorged with dark fluid blood; the heart appeared healthy, its left side was contracted and empty, but the right was dilated and filled with dark fluid blood; the stomach was somewhat congested, and contained a little partially digested food; the intestines here and there were congested, and throughout the body the blood was dark and fluid.

Q. What then, in your opinion, was the cause of death?
A. In my opinion death resulted from serous effusion on the brain, commonly known as serous apoplexy.

Q. Then you found no appearances in the stomach, or elsewhere, which would lead you to believe poison had been taken?

A. No, none.

Q. From the post-mortem examination could you say the death of the deceased was not due to some narcotic poison?

A. No: the post-mortem appearances of the body are quite consistent with those of poisoning by certain poisons, but there is no reason to suppose that any poison has been administered in this case, as I, of course, go by what I see; and the presence of poisons, especially vegetable poisons, can only be detected by chemical analysis.

Q. Did you analyse the contents of the stomach chemically?

A. No; it was not my duty to do so; I handed over the stomach to the police, seeing that there is suspicion of poison, and thence it will go to the Government analyst.

Q. It is stated that the deceased had convulsions before she died—is this not a symptom of narcotic poisoning?

A. In some cases, yes, but not commonly; aconite, for instance, always produces convulsions in animals, seldom in man.

Q. How do you account for the congested condition of the lungs?

A. I believe the serous effusion caused death by suspended respiration.

Q. Was there any odour perceptible?

A. No, none whatsoever.

The inquest was then adjourned till next day, and there was great excitement over the affair. If Kitty Marchurst's statement was true, the deceased must have died from the administration of poison; but, on the other hand, Dr. Chinston asserted positively that there was no trace of poison, and that the deceased had clearly died from apoplexy. Public opinion was very much divided, some asserting that Kitty's story was true, while others said she had got the idea from "The Hidden Hand", and only told it in order to make herself notorious. There were plenty of letters written to the papers on the subject, each offering a new solution of the difficulty, but the fact remained the same, that Kitty said the deceased had been poisoned; the doctor that she had died of apoplexy. Calton was considerably puzzled over the matter. Of course, there was no doubt that the man who committed the murder had intended to poison Madame Midas, but the fact that Selina stayed all night with her, had resulted in the wrong person being killed. Madame Midas told Calton the whole story of her life, and asserted positively that if the poison was meant for her, Villiers must have administered it. This was all very well, but the question then arose, was Villiers alive? The police were once more set to work, and once more their search resulted in nothing. Altogether the whole affair was wrapped in mystery, as it could not even be told if a murder had been committed, or if the deceased had died from natural causes. The only chance of finding out the truth would be to have the stomach analysed, and the cause of death ascertained; once that was done, and the matter could be gone on with, or dropped, according to the report of the analyst. If he said it was apoplexy, Kitty's story would necessarily have to be discredited as an invention; but if, on the other hand, the traces of poison were found, search would have to be made for the murderer. Matters were at a deadlock, and everyone waited impatiently for the report of the analyst. Suddenly, however, a new interest was given to the case by the assertion that a Ballarat doctor, called Gollipeck, who was a noted toxicologist, had come down to Melbourne to assist at the analysis of the stomach, and knew something which would throw light on the mysterious death.

Vandeloup saw the paragraph which gave this information, and it disturbed him very much.

"Curse that book of Prevol's," he said to himself, as he threw down the paper: "it will put them on the right track, and then—well," observed M. Vandeloup, sententiously, "they say danger sharpens a man's wits; it's lucky for me if it does."

XIII

Diamond Cut Diamond

M. Vandeloup's rooms in Clarendon Street, East Melbourne, were very luxuriously and artistically furnished, in perfect accordance with the taste of their owner, but as the satiated despot is depicted by the moralists as miserable amid all his splendour, so M. Gaston Vandeloup, though not exactly miserable, was very ill at ease. The inquest had been adjourned until the Government analyst, assisted by Dr. Gollipeck, had examined the stomach, and according to a paragraph in the evening paper, some strange statements, implicating various people, would be made next day. It was this that made Vandeloup so uneasy, for he knew that Dr. Gollipeck would trace a resemblance between the death of Selina Sprotts in Melbourne and Adele Blondet in Paris, and then the question would arise how the poison used in the one case came to be used in the other. If that question arose it would be all over with him, for he would not dare to face any examination, and as discretion is the better part of valour, M. Vandeloup decided to leave the country. With his usual foresight he had guessed that Dr. Gollipeck would be mixed up in the affair, so had drawn his money out of all securities in which it was invested, sent most of it to America to a New York bank, reserving only a certain sum for travelling purposes. He was going to leave Melbourne next morning by the express train for Sydney, and there would catch the steamer to San Francisco via New Zealand and Honolulu. Once in America and he would be quite safe, and as he now had plenty of money he could enjoy himself there. He had given up the idea of marrying Madame Midas, as he dare not run the risk of remaining in Australia, but then there were plenty of heiresses in the States he could marry if he chose, so to give her up was a small matter. Another thing, he would be rid of Pierre Lemaire, for once let him put the ocean between him and the dumb man he would take care they never met again. Altogether, M. Vandeloup had taken all precautions to secure his own safety with his usual promptitude and coolness, but notwithstanding that another twelve hours would see him on his way to Sydney en route for the States, he felt slightly uneasy, for as he often said, "There are always possibilities."

It was about eight o'clock at night, and Gaston was busy in his rooms packing up to go away next morning. He had disposed of his apartments to Bellthorp, as that young gentleman had lately come in for some money and was dissatisfied with the paternal roof, where he was kept too strictly tied up.

Vandeloup, seated in his shirt sleeves in the midst of a chaos of articles of clothing, portmanteaux, and boxes, was, with the experience of an accomplished traveller, rapidly putting these all away in the most expeditious and neatest manner. He wanted to get finished before ten o'clock, so that he could go down to his club and show himself, in order to obviate any suspicion as to his going away. He did not intend to send out any P.P.C. cards, as he was a modest young man and wanted to slip unostentatiously out of the country; besides, there was nothing like precaution, as the least intimation of his approaching departure would certainly put Dr. Gollipeck on the alert and cause trouble. The gas was lighted, there was a bright glare through all the room, and everything was in confusion, with M. Vandeloup seated in the centre, like Marius amid the ruins of Carthage. While thus engaged there came a ring at the outer door, and shortly afterwards Gaston's landlady entered his room with a card.

"A gentleman wants to see you, sir," she said, holding out the card.

"I'm not at home," replied Vandeloup, coolly, removing the cigarette he was smoking from his mouth; "I can't see anyone tonight."

"He says you'd like to see him, sir," answered the woman, standing at the door.

"The deuce he does," muttered Vandeloup, uneasily; "I wonder what this pertinacious gentleman's name is? and he glanced at the card, whereon was written "Dr. Gollipeck".

Vandeloup felt a chill running through him as he rose to his feet. The battle was about to begin, and he knew he would need all his wit and skill to get himself out safely. Dr. Gollipeck had thrown down the gauntlet, and he would have to pick it up. Well, it was best to know the worst at once, so he told the landlady he would see Gollipeck downstairs. He did not want him to come up there, as he would see all the evidences of his intention to leave the country.

"I'll see him downstairs," he said, sharply, to the landlady; "ask the gentleman to wait."

The landlady, however, was pushed roughly to one side, and Dr. Gollipeck, rusty and dingy-looking as ever, entered the room.

"No need, my dear friend," he said in his grating voice, blinking at the young man through his spectacles, "we can talk here."

Vandeloup signed to the landlady to leave the room, which she did, closing the door after her, and then, pulling himself together with a great effort, he advanced smilingly on the doctor.

"Ah, my dear Monsieur," he said, in his musical voice, holding out both hands, "how pleased I am to see you."

Dr. Gollipeck gurgled pleasantly in his throat at this and laughed, that is, something apparently went wrong in his inside and a rasping noise came out of his mouth.

"You clever young man," he said, affectionately, to Gaston, as he unwound a long crimson woollen scarf from his throat, and thereby caused a button to fly off his waistcoat with the exertion. Dr. Gollipeck, however, being used to these little eccentricities of his toilet, pinned the waistcoat together, and then, sitting down, spread his red bandanna handkerchief over his knees, and stared steadily at Vandeloup, who had put on a loose velvet smoking coat, and, with a cigarette in his mouth, was leaning against the mantelpiece. It was raining outside, and the pleasant patter of the raindrops was quite audible in the stillness of the room, while every now and then a gust of wind would make the windows rattle, and shake the heavy green curtains. The two men eyed one another keenly, for they both knew they had an unpleasant quarter of an hour before them, and were like two clever fencers—both watching their opportunity to begin the combat. Gollipeck, with his greasy coat, all rucked up behind his neck, and his frayed shirt cuffs coming down on his ungainly hands, sat sternly silent, so Vandeloup, after contemplating him for a few moments, had to begin the battle.

"My room is untidy, is it not?" he said, nodding his head carelessly at the chaos of furniture. "I'm going away for a few days."

"A few days; ha, ha!" observed Gollipeck, something again going wrong with his inside. "Your destination is—"

"Sydney," replied Gaston, promptly.

"And then?" queried the doctor.

Gaston shrugged his shoulders.

"Depends upon circumstances," he answered, lazily.

"That's a mistake," retorted Gollipeck, leaning forward; "it depends upon me."

Vandeloup smiled.

"In that case, circumstances, as represented by you, will permit me to choose my own destinations."

"Depends entirely upon your being guided by circumstances, as represented by me," retorted the Doctor, grimly.

"Pshaw!" said the Frenchman, coolly, "let us have done with allegory, and come to common sense. What do you want?"

"I want Octave Braulard," said Gollipeck, rising to his feet.

Vandeloup quite expected this, and was too clever to waste time in denying his identity.

"He stands before you," he answered, curtly, "what then?"

"You acknowledge, then, that you are Octave Braulard, transported to New Caledonia for the murder of Adele Blondet?" said the Doctor tapping the table with one hand.

"To you—yes," answered Vandeloup, crossing to the door and locking it; "to others—no."

"Why do you lock the door?" asked Gollipeck, gruffly.

"I don't want my private affairs all over Melbourne," retorted Gaston, smoothly, returning to his position in front of the fireplace; "are you afraid?"

Something again went wrong with Dr. Gollipeck's inside, and he grated out a hard ironical laugh.

"Do I look afraid?" he asked, spreading out his hands.

Vandeloup stooped down to the portmanteau lying open at his feet, and picked up a revolver, which he pointed straight at Gollipeck.

"You make an excellent target," he observed, quickly, putting his finger on the trigger.

Dr. Gollipeck sat down, and arranged his handkerchief once more over his knees.

"Very likely," he answered, coolly, "but a target you won't practise on."

"Why not?" asked Vandeloup, still keeping his finger on the trigger.

"Because the pistol-shot would alarm the house," said Gollipeck, serenely, "and if I was found dead, you would be arrested for my murder. If I was only wounded I could tell a few facts about M. Octave Braulard that would have an unpleasant influence on the life of M. Gaston Vandeloup."

Vandeloup laid the pistol down on the mantelpiece with a laugh, lit a cigarette, and, sitting down in a chair opposite Gollipeck, began to talk.

"You are a brave man," he said, coolly blowing a wreath of smoke, "I admire brave men."

"You are a clever man," retorted the doctor; "I admire clever men."

"Very good," said Vandeloup, crossing one leg over the other. "As we now understand one another, I await your explanation of this visit."

Dr. Gollipeck, with admirable composure, placed his hands on his knees, and acceded to the request of M. Vandeloup.

"I saw in the Ballarat and Melbourne newspapers," he said, quietly, "that Selina Sprotts, the servant of Mrs. Villiers, was dead. The papers said foul play was suspected, and according to the evidence of Kitty Marchurst, whom, by the way, I remember very well, the deceased had been poisoned. An examination was made of the body, but no traces of poison were found. Knowing you were acquainted with Madame Midas, and recognising this case as a peculiar one—seeing that poison was asserted to have been given, and yet no appearances could be found—I came down to Melbourne, saw the doctor who had analysed the body, and heard what he had to say on the subject. The symptoms were described as apoplexy, similar to those of a woman who died in Paris called Adele Blondet, and whose case was reported in a book by Messrs Prevol and Lebrun. Becoming suspicious, I assisted at a chemical analysis of the body, and found that the woman Sprotts had been poisoned by an extract of hemlock, the same poison used in the case of Adele Blondet. The man who poisoned Adele Blondet was sent to New Caledonia, escaped from there, and came to Australia, and prepared this poison at Ballarat; and why I called here tonight was to know the reason M. Octave Braulard, better known as Gaston Vandeloup, poisoned Selina Sprotts in mistake for Madame Midas."

If Doctor Gollipeck had thought to upset Vandeloup by this recital, he was never more mistaken in his life, for that young gentleman heard him coolly to the end, and taking the cigarette out of his mouth, smiled quietly.

"In the first place," he said, smoothly, "I acknowledge the truth of all your story except the latter part, and I must compliment you on the admirable way you have guessed the identity of Braulard with Vandeloup, as you have no proof to show that they are the same. But with regard to the death of Mademoiselle Sprotts, she died as you have said; but I, though the maker of the poison, did not administer it."

"Who did, then?" asked Gollipeck, who was quite prepared for this denial.

Vandeloup smoothed his moustache, and looked at the doctor with a keen glance.

"Kitty Marchurst," he said, coolly.

The rain was beating wildly against the windows and someone in the room below was playing the eternal waltz, "One summer's night in Munich", while Vandeloup, leaning back in his chair, stared at Dr. Gollipeck, who looked at him disbelievingly.

"It's not true," he said, harshly; "what reason had she to poison the woman Sprotts?"

"None at all," replied Vandeloup, blandly; "but she had to poison Mrs. Villiers."

"Go on," said Gollipeck, gruffly; "I've no doubt you will make up an admirable story."

"So kind of you to compliment me," observed Vandeloup, lightly; "but in this instance I happen to tell the truth—Kitty Marchurst was my mistress."

"It was you that ruined her, then?" cried Gollipeck, pushing back his chair.

Vandeloup shrugged his shoulders.

"If you put it that way—yes," he answered, simply; "but she fell into my mouth like ripe fruit. Surely," with a sneer, "at your age you don't believe in virtue?"

"Yes, I do," retorted Gollipeck, fiercely.

"More fool you!" replied Gaston, with a libertine look on his handsome face. "Balzac never said a truer word than that 'a woman's virtue is man's greatest invention.' Well, we won't discuss morality now. She came with me to Melbourne and lived as my mistress; then she wanted to marry me, and I refused. She had a bottle of the poison which I had made, and threatened to take it and kill herself. I prevented her, and then she left me, went on the stage, and afterwards meeting Madame Midas, went to live with her, and we renewed our acquaintance. On the night of this—well, murder, if you like to call it so—we were at a ball together. Mademoiselle Marchurst heard that I was going to marry Madame Midas. She asked me if it was true. I did not deny it; and she said she would sooner poison Mrs. Villiers than see her married to me. She went home, and not knowing the dead woman was in bed with Madame Midas, poisoned the drink, and the consequences you know. As to this story of the hand, bah! it is a stage play, that is all!"

Dr. Gollipeck rose and walked to and fro in the little clear space left among the disorder.

"What a devil you are!" he said, looking at Vandeloup admiringly.

"What, because I did not poison this woman?" he said, in a mocking tone. "Bah! you are less moral than I thought you were."

The doctor did not take any notice of this sneer, but, putting his hands in his pockets, faced round to the young man.

"I give my evidence to-morrow," he said quietly, looking keenly at the young man, "and I prove conclusively the woman was poisoned. To do this, I must refer to the case of Adele Blondet, and then that implicates you."

"Pardon me," observed Vandeloup, coolly, removing some ash from his velvet coat, "it implicates Octave Braulard, who is at present," with a sharp look at Gollipeck, "in New Caledonia."

"If that is the case," asked the doctor, gruffly, "who are you?"

"I am the friend of Braulard," said Vandeloup, in a measured tone. "Myself, Braulard, and Prevol—one of the writers of the book you refer to—were medical students together, and we all three emphatically knew about this poison extracted from hemlock."

He spoke so quietly that Gollipeck looked at him in a puzzled manner, not understanding his meaning.

"You mean Braulard and Prevol were medical students?" he said, doubtfully.

"Exactly," assented M. Vandeloup, with an airy wave of his hand. "Gaston Vandeloup is a fictitious third person I have called into existence for my own safety—you understand. As Gaston Vandeloup, a friend of Braulard, I knew all about this poison, and manufactured it in Ballarat for a mere experiment, and as Gaston Vandeloup I give evidence against the woman who was my mistress on the ground of poisoning Selina Sprotts with hemlock."

"You are not shielding yourself behind this girl?" asked the doctor, coming close to him.

"How could I?" replied Vandeloup, slipping his hand into his pocket. "I could not have gone down to St Kilda, climbed over a wall with glass bottles on top, and committed the crime, as Kitty Marchurst says it was done. If I had done this there would be some trace—no, I assure you Mademoiselle Marchurst, and none other, is the guilty woman. She was in the room—Madame Midas asleep in bed. What was easier for her than to pour the poison into the glass, which stood ready to receive it? Mind you, I don't say she did it deliberately—impulse—hallucination— madness—what you like—but she did it."

"By God!" cried Gollipeck, warmly, "you'd argue a rope round the girl's neck even before she has had a trial. I believe you did it yourself."

"If I did," retorted Vandeloup, coolly, "when I am in the witness-box I run the risk of being found out. Be it so. I take my chance of that; but I ask you to keep silent as to Gaston Vandeloup being Octave Braulard."

"Why should I?" said the doctor, harshly.

"For many admirable reasons," replied Vandeloup, smoothly. "In the first place, as Braulard's friend, I can prove the case against Mademoiselle Marchurst quite as well as if I appeared as Braulard himself. In the next place, you have no evidence to prove I am identical with the murderer of Adele Blondet; and, lastly, suppose you did prove it, what satisfaction would it be to you to send me back to a French prison? I have suffered enough for my crime, and now I am rich and respectable, why should you drag me back to the depths again? Read 'Les Miserables' of our great Hugo before you answer, my friend."

"Read the book long ago," retorted Gollipeck, gruffly, more moved by the argument than he cared to show; "I will keep silent about this if you leave the colony at once."

"I agree," said Vandeloup, pointing to the floor; "you see I had already decided to travel before you entered. Any other stipulation?"

"None," retorted the doctor, putting on his scarf again; "with Octave Braulard I have nothing to do: I want to find out who killed Selina Sprotts, and if you did, I won't spare you."

"First, catch your hare," replied Vandeloup, smoothly, going to the door and unlocking it; "I am ready to stand the test of a trial, and surely that ought to content you. As it is, I'll stay in Melbourne long enough to give you the satisfaction of hanging this woman for the murder, and then I will go to America."

Dr. Gollipeck was disgusted at the smooth brutality of this man, and moved hastily to the door.

"Will you not have a glass of wine?" asked Vandeloup, stopping him.

"Wine with you?" said the doctor, harshly, looking him up and down; "no, it would choke me," and he hurried away.

"I wish it would," observed M. Vandeloup, pleasantly, as he reentered the room, "whew! this devil of a doctor—what a dangerous fool, but I have got the better of him, and at all events," he said, lighting another cigarette, "I have saved Vandeloup from suffering for the crime of Braulard."

XIV

CIRCUMSTANTIAL EVIDENCE

There was no doubt the Sprotts' poisoning case was the sensation of the day in Melbourne. The papers were full of it, and some even went so far as to give a plan of the house, with dotted lines thereon, to show how the crime was committed. All this was extremely amusing, for, as a matter of fact, the evidence as yet had not shown any reasonable ground for supposing foul play had taken place. One paper, indeed, said that far too much was assumed in the case, and that the report of the Government analyst should be waited for before such emphatic opinions were given by the press regarding the mode of death. But it was no use trying to reason with the public, they had got it into their sage heads that a crime had been committed, and demanded evidence; so as the press had no real evidence to give, they made it up, and the public, in private conversations, amplified the evidence until they constructed a complete criminal case.

"Pshaw!" said Rolleston, when he read these sensational reports, "in spite of the quidnuncs the mountain will only produce a mouse after all."

But he was wrong, for now rumours were started that the Government analyst and Dr. Gollipeck had found poison in the stomach, and that, moreover, the real criminal would be soon discovered. Public opinion was much divided as to who the criminal was—some, having heard the story of Madame's marriage, said it was her husband; others insisted Kitty Marchurst was the culprit, and was trying to shield herself behind this wild story of the hand coming from behind the curtains; while others were in favour of suicide. At all events, on the morning when the inquest was resumed, and the evidence was to be given of the analysis of the stomach, the Court was crowded, and a dead silence pervaded the place when the Government analyst stood up to give his evidence. Madame Midas was present, with Kitty seated beside her, the latter looking pale and ill; and Kilsip, with a gratified smile on his face which seemed as though he had got a clue to the whole mystery, was seated next to Calton. Vandeloup, faultlessly dressed, and as cool and calm as possible, was also in Court; and Dr. Gollipeck, as he awaited his turn to give evidence, could not help admiring the marvellous nerve and courage of the young man.

The Government analyst being called, was sworn in the usual way, and deposed that the stomach of the deceased had been sent to him to be analysed. He had used the usual tests, and found the presence of the alkaloid of hemlock, known under the name of conia. In his opinion the death of the deceased was caused by the administration of an extract of hemlock. (Sensation in the Court.)

Q. Then in your opinion the deceased has been poisoned?
A. Yes, I have not the least doubt on the subject, I detected the conia very soon after the tests were applied.

There was great excitement when this evidence was concluded, as it gave quite a new interest to the case. The question as to the cause of death was now set at rest—the deceased had been murdered, so the burning anxiety of every one was to know who had committed the crime. All sorts of opinions were given, but the murmur of voices ceased when Dr. Gollipeck stood up to give his evidence.

He deposed that he was a medical practitioner, practising at Ballarat; he had seen the report of the case in the papers, and had come down to Melbourne as he thought he could throw a certain light on the affair—for instance, where the poison was procured. (Sensation.) About three years ago a crime had been committed in Paris, which caused a great sensation at the time. The case being a peculiar one, was reported in a medical work, by Messieurs Prevol and Lebrun, which he had obtained from France some two years back. The facts of the case were shortly these: An actress called Adele Blondet died from the effects of poison, administered to her by Octave Braulard, who was her lover; the deceased had also another lover, called Kestrike, who was supposed to be implicated in the crime, but he had escaped; the woman in this case had been poisoned by an extract of hemlock, the same poison used as in the case of Selina Sprotts, and it was the similarity of the symptoms that made him suspicious of the sudden death. Braulard was sent out to New Caledonia for the murder. While in Paris he had been a medical student with two other gentlemen, one of whom was Monsieur Prevol, who had reported the case, and the other was at present in Court, and was called M. Gaston Vandeloup. (Sensation in Court, everyone's eye being fixed on Vandeloup, who was calm and unmoved.) M. Vandeloup had manufactured the poison used in this case, but with regard to how it was administered to the deceased, he would leave that evidence to M. Vandeloup himself.

When Gollipeck left the witness-box there was a dead silence, as everyone was too much excited at his strange story to make any comment thereon. Madame Midas looked with some astonishment on Vandeloup as his name was called out, and he moved gracefully to the witness-box, while Kitty's face grew paler even than it was before. She did not know what Vandeloup was going to say, but a great dread seized her, and with dry lips and clenched hands she sat staring at him as if paralysed. Kilsip stole a look at her and then rubbed his hands together, while Calton sat absolutely still, scribbling figures on his notepaper.

M. Gaston Vandeloup, being sworn, deposed: He was a native of France, of Flemish descent, as could be seen from his name; he had known Braulard intimately; he also knew Prevol; he had been eighteen months in Australia, and for some time had been clerk to Mrs. Villiers at Ballarat; he was fond of chemistry—yes; and had made several experiments with poisons while up at Ballarat with Dr. Gollipeck, who was a great toxicologist; he had seen the hemlock in the garden of an hotel-keeper at Ballarat, called Twexby, and had made an extract therefrom; he only did it by way of experiment, and had put the bottle containing the poison in his desk, forgetting all about it; the next time he saw that bottle was in the possession of Miss Kitty Marchurst (sensation in Court); she had threatened to poison herself; he again saw the bottle in her possession on the night of the murder; this was at the house of M. Meddlechip. A report had been circulated that he (the witness) was going to marry Mrs. Villiers, and Miss Marchurst asked him if it was true; he had denied it, and Miss Marchurst had said that sooner than he (the witness) should marry Mrs. Villiers she would poison her; the next morning he heard that Selina Sprotts was dead.

Kitty Marchurst heard all this evidence in dumb horror. She now knew that after ruining her life this man wanted her to die a felon's death. She arose to her feet and stretched out her hands in protest against him, but before she could speak a word the place seemed to whirl round her, and she fell down in a dead faint. This event caused great excitement in court, and many began to assert positively that she must be guilty, else why did she faint. Kitty was taken out of Court, and the examination was proceeded with, while Madame Midas sat pale and horror-struck at the revelations which were now being made.

The Coroner now proceeded to cross-examine Vandeloup.

Q. You say you put the bottle containing this poison into your desk; how did Miss Marchurst obtain it?

A. Because she lived with me for some time, and had access to my private papers.

Q. Was she your wife?

A. No, my mistress (sensation in Court).

Q. Why did she leave you?

A. We had a difference of opinion about the question of marriage, so she left me.

Q. She wanted you to make reparation; in other words, to marry her?

A. Yes.

Q. And you refused?

A. Yes.

Q. It was on this occasion she produced the poison first?

A. Yes. She told me she had taken it from my desk, and would poison herself if I did not marry her; she changed her mind, however, and went away.

Q. Did you know what became of her?

A. Yes; I heard she went on the stage with M. Wopples.

Q. Did she take the poison with her?

A. Yes.

Q. How do you know she took the poison with her?

A. Because next time I saw her it was still in her possession.

Q. That was at Mr. Meddlechip's ball?

A. Yes.

Q. On the night of the commission of the crime?

A. Yes.

Q. What made her take it to the ball?

A. Rather a difficult question to answer. She heard rumours that I was to marry Mrs. Villiers, and even though I denied it declined to believe me; she then produced the poison, and said she would take it.

Q. Where did this conversation take place?

A. In the conservatory.

Q. What did you do when she threatened to take the poison?

A. I tried to take it from her.

Q. Did you succeed?

A. No; she threw it out of the door.

Q. Then when she left Mr. Meddlechip's house to come home she had no poison with her?

A. I don't think so.

Q. Did she pick the bottle up again after she threw it out?

A. No, because I went back to the ball-room with her; then I came out myself to look for the bottle, but it was gone.

Q. You have never seen it since.

A. No, it must have been picked up by someone who was ignorant of its contents.

Q. By your own showing, M. Vandeloup, Miss Marchurst had no poison with her when she left Mr. Meddlechip's house. How, then, could she commit this crime?

A. She told me she still had some poison left; that she divided the contents of the bottle she had taken from my desk, and that she still had enough left at home to poison Mrs. Villiers.

Q. Did she say she would poison Mrs. Villiers?

A. Yes, sooner than see her married to me. (Sensation.)

Q. Do you believe she went away from you with the deliberate intention of committing the crime.

A. I do.

M. Vandeloup then left the box amid great excitement, and Kilsip was again examined. He deposed that he had searched Miss Marchurst's room, and found half a bottle of extract of hemlock. The contents of the bottle had been analysed, and were found identical with the conia discovered in the stomach of the deceased.

Q. You say the bottle was half empty?

A. Rather more than that: three-quarters empty.

Q. Miss Marchurst told M. Vandeloup she had poured half the contents of one bottle into the other. Would not this account for the bottle being three-quarters empty?

A. Possibly; but if the first bottle was full, it is probable she would halve the poison exactly; so if it had been untouched, it ought to be half full.

Q. Then you think some of the contents of this bottle were used?

A. That is my opinion.

Vandeloup was recalled, and deposed that the bottle Kitty took from his desk was quite full; and moreover, when the other bottle which had been found in her room, was shown to him, he declared that it was as nearly as possible the same size as the missing bottle. So the inference drawn from this was that the bottle produced being three-quarters empty, some of the poison had been used.

The question now arose that as the guilt of Miss Marchurst seemed so certain, how was it that Selina Sprotts was poisoned instead of her mistress; but this was settled by Madame Midas, who being recalled, deposed that Kitty did not know Selina slept with her on that night, and the curtains being drawn, could not possibly tell two people were in the bed.

This was all the evidence obtainable, and the coroner now proceeded to sum up.

The case, he said, was a most remarkable one, and it would be necessary for the jury to consider very gravely all the evidence laid before them in order to arrive at a proper conclusion before giving their verdict. In the first place, it had been clearly proved by the Government analyst that the deceased had died from effects of conia, which was, as they had been told, the alkaloid of hemlock, a well-known hedge plant which grows abundantly in most parts of Great Britain. According to the evidence of Dr. Chinston, the deceased had died from serous apoplexy, and from all the post-mortem appearances this was the case. But they must remember that it was almost impossible to detect certain vegetable poisons, such as aconite and atropia, without minute chemical analysis. They would remember a case which startled London some years ago, in which the poisoner had poisoned his brother-in-law by means of aconite, and it taxed all the ingenuity and cleverness of experts to find the traces of poison in the stomach of the deceased. In this case, however, thanks to Dr. Gollipeck, who had seen the similarity of the symptoms between the post-mortem appearance of the stomach of Adele Blondet and the present case, the usual tests for conia were applied, and as they had been told by the Government analyst, the result was conia was found. So they could be quite certain that the deceased had died of poison—that poison being conia. The next thing for them to consider was how the poison was administered. According to the evidence of Miss Marchurst, some unknown person had been standing outside the window and poured the poison into the glass on the table. Mrs. Villiers had stated that the window was open all night, and from the position of the table near it—nothing would be easier than for anyone to introduce the poison into the glass as asserted by Miss Marchurst. On the other hand, the evidence of the detective Kilsip went to show that no marks were visible as to anyone having been at the window; and another thing which rendered Miss Marchurst's story doubtful was the resemblance it had to a drama in which she had frequently acted, called "The Hidden Hand". In the last act of that drama poison was administered to one of the characters in precisely the same manner, and though of course such a thing might happen in real life, still in this case it was a highly suspicious circumstance that a woman like Miss Marchurst, who had frequently acted in the drama, should see the same thing actually occur off the stage. Rejecting, then, as improbable the story of the hidden hand, seeing that the evidence was strongly against it, the next thing was to look into Miss Marchurst's past life and see if she had any motive for committing the crime. Before doing so, however, he would point out to them that Miss Marchurst was the only person in the room when the crime was committed. The window in her own room and one of the windows in Mrs. Villiers' room were both locked, and the open window had a table in front of it, so that anyone entering would very probably knock it over, and thus awaken the sleepers. On the other hand, no one could have entered in at the door, because they would not have had time to escape before the crime was discovered. So it was clearly shown that Miss Marchurst must have been alone in the room when the crime was committed. Now to look into her past life—it was certainly not a very creditable one. M. Vandeloup had sworn that she had been his mistress for over a year, and had taken the poison manufactured by himself out of his private desk. Regarding M. Vandeloup's motives in preparing such a poison he could say nothing. Of course, he probably did it by way of experiment to find out if this colonial grown hemlock possessed the same poisonous qualities as it did in the old world. It was a careless thing of him, however, to leave it in his desk, where it could be obtained, for all such dangerous matters should be kept under lock and key. To go back, however, to Miss Marchurst. It had been proved by M. Vandeloup that she was his mistress, and that they quarrelled. She produced this poison, and said she would kill herself. M. Vandeloup persuaded her to abandon the idea, and she subsequently left him, taking the poison with her. She then went on the stage, and subsequently left it in order to live with Mrs. Villiers as her companion. All this time she still had the poison, and in order to prevent her losing it she put half of it into another bottle. Now this looked very suspicious, as, if she had not intended to use it she certainly would never have taken such trouble over preserving it. She meets M. Vandeloup at a ball, and, hearing that he is going to marry Mrs. Villiers, she loses her head completely, and threatens to poison herself. M. Vandeloup tries to wrench the poison from her, whereupon she flings it into the garden. This bottle has disappeared, and the presumption is that it was picked up. But if the jury had any idea that the poison was administered from the lost bottle, they might as well dismiss it from their minds, as it was absurd to suppose such an improbable thing could happen. In the first place no one but M. Vandeloup and Miss Marchurst knew what the contents were, and in the second place what motive could anyone who picked it up have in poisoning Mrs. Villiers, and why should they adopt such an extraordinary way of doing it, as Miss Marchurst asserted they did? On the other hand, Miss Marchurst tells M. Vandeloup that she still has some poison left, and that she will kill Mrs. Villiers sooner than see her married to him. She declares to M. Vandeloup that she will kill her, and leaves the house to go home with, apparently, all the intention of doing so. She comes home filled with all the furious rage of a jealous woman, and enters Mrs. Villiers' room, and here the jury will recall the evidence of Mrs. Villiers, who said Miss Marchurst did not know that the deceased was sleeping with her. So when Miss Marchurst entered the room, she naturally thought that Mrs. Villiers was by herself, and would, as a matter of course, refrain from drawing the curtains and looking into the bed, in case she should awaken her proposed victim. There was a glass with drink on the table; she was alone with Mrs. Villiers, her heart filled with jealous rage against a woman she thinks is her rival. Her own room is a few steps away—what, then, was easier for her than to go to her own room, obtain the poison, and put it into the glass? The jury will remember in the evidence of Mr. Kilsip, the bottle was three-quarters empty, which argued some of it had been used. All the evidence against Miss Marchurst was purely circumstantial, for if she committed the crime, no human eye beheld her doing so. But the presumption of her having done so, in order to get rid of a successful rival, was very strong, and the weight of evidence was dead against her. The jury would, therefore, deliver their verdict in accordance with the facts laid before them.

The jury retired, and the court was very much excited. Everyone was quite certain that Kitty was guilty, but there was a strong feeling against

M. Vandeloup as having been in some measure the cause, though indirectly, of the crime. But that young gentleman, in accordance with his usual foresight, had left the court and gone straight home, as he had no wish to face a crowd of sullen faces, and perhaps worse. Madame Midas sat still in the court awaiting the return of the jury, with the calm face of a marble sphinx. But, though she suffered, no appearances of suffering were seen on her serene face. She never had believed in human nature, and now the girl whom she had rescued from comparative poverty and placed in opulence had wanted to kill her. M. Vandeloup, whom she admired and trusted, what black infamy he was guilty of—he had sworn most solemnly he never harmed Kitty, and yet he was the man who had ruined her. Madame Midas felt that the worst had come—Vandeloup false, Kitty a murderess, her husband vanished, and Selina dead. All the world was falling into ruins around her, and she remained alone amid the ruins with her enormous fortune, like a golden statue in a deserted temple. With clasped hands, aching heart, but impassive face, she sat waiting for the end.

The jury returned in about half an hour, and there was a dead silence as the foreman stood up to deliver the verdict.

The jury found as follows:—

That the deceased, Selina Jane Sprotts, died on the 21st day of November, from the effects of poison, namely, conia, feloniously administered by one Katherine Marchurst, and the jury, on their oaths, say that the said Katherine Marchurst feloniously, wilfully, and maliciously did murder the said deceased.

That evening Kitty was arrested and lodged in the Melbourne Gaol, to await her trial on a charge of wilful murder.

XV

Kismet

Of two evils it is always best to choose the least, and as M. Vandeloup had to choose between the loss of his popularity or his liberty, he chose to lose the former instead of the latter. After all, as he argued to himself, Australia at large is a small portion of the world, and in America no one would know anything about his little escapade in connection with Kitty. He knew that he was in Gollipeck's power, and that unless he acceded to that gentleman's demand as to giving evidence he would be denounced to the authorities as an escaped convict from New Caledonia, and would be sent back there. Of course, his evidence could not but prove detrimental to himself, seeing how badly he had behaved to Kitty, but still as going through the ordeal meant liberty, he did so, and the result was as he had foreseen. Men, as a rule, are not very squeamish, and view each other's failings, especially towards women, with a lenient eye, but Vandeloup had gone too far, and the Bachelors' Club unanimously characterised his conduct as "damned shady", so a letter was sent requesting M. Vandeloup to take his name off the books of the club. He immediately resigned, and wrote a polite letter to the secretary, which brought uneasy blushes to the cheek of that gentleman by its stinging remarks about his and his fellow clubmen's morality. He showed it to several of the members, but as they all had their little redeeming vices, they determined to take no notice, and so M. Vandeloup was left alone. Another thing which happened was that he was socially ostracised from society, and his table, which used to be piled up with invitations, soon became quite bare. Of course, he knew he could force Meddlechip to recognise him, but he did not choose to do so, as all his thoughts were fixed on America. He had plenty of money, and with a new name and a brand new character, Vandeloup thought he would prosper exceedingly well in the States. So he stayed at home, not caring to face the stony faces of friends who cut him, and waited for the trial of Kitty Marchurst, after which he intended to leave for Sydney at once, and take the next steamer to San Francisco. He did not mind waiting, but amused himself reading, smoking, and playing, and was quite independent of Melbourne society. Only two things worried him, and the first of these was the annoyance of Pierre Lemaire, who seemed to have divined his intention of going away, and haunted him day and night like an unquiet spirit. Whenever Vandeloup looked out, he saw the dumb man watching the house, and if he went for a walk, Pierre would slouch sullenly along behind him, as he had done in the early days. Vandeloup could have called in the aid of a policeman to rid himself of this annoyance, but the fact was he was afraid of offending Pierre, as he might be tempted to reveal what he knew, and the result would not be pleasant. So Gaston bore patiently with the disagreeable system of espionage the dumb man kept over him, and consoled himself with the idea that once he was on his way to America, it would not matter two straws whether Pierre told all he knew, or kept silent. The other thing which troubled the young man were the words Kitty had made use of in Mrs. Villiers' drawing-room regarding the secret she said she knew. It made him uneasy, for he half guessed what it was, and thought she might tell it to someone out of revenge, and then there would be more troubles for him to get out of. Then, again, he argued that she was too fond of him ever to tell anything likely to injure him, even though he had put a rope round her neck. If he could have settled the whole affair by running away, he would have done so, but Gollipeck was still in Melbourne, and Gaston knew he could not leave the town without the terrible old man finding it out, and bringing him back. At last the torture of wondering how much Kitty knew was too much for him, and he determined to go to the Melbourne gaol and interview her. So he obtained an order from the authorities to see her, and prepared to start next morning. He sent the servant out for a hansom, and by the time it was at the door, M. Vandeloup, cool, calm, and well dressed, came down stairs pulling on his gloves. The first thing he saw when he got outside was Pierre waiting for him with his old hat pulled down over his eyes, and his look of sullen resignation. Gaston nodded coolly to him, and told the cabby he wanted to go to the Melbourne gaol, whereupon Pierre slouched forward as the young man was preparing to enter the cab, and laid his hand on his arm.

"Well," said Vandeloup, in a quiet voice, in French, shaking off the dumb man's arm, "what do you want?"

Pierre pointed to the cab, whereupon M. Vandeloup shrugged his shoulders. "Surely you don't want to come to the gaol with me," he said, mockingly, "you'll get there soon enough."

The other nodded, and made a step towards the cab, but Vandeloup pushed him back.

"Curse the fool," he muttered to himself, "I'll have to humour him or he'll be making a scene—you can't come," he added aloud, but Pierre still refused to go away.

This conversation or rather monologue, seeing M. Vandeloup was the only speaker, was carried on in French, so the cabman and the servant at the door were quite ignorant of its purport, but looked rather astonished at the conduct of the dirty tramp towards such an elegant-looking gentleman. Vandeloup saw this and therefore determined to end the scene.

"Well, well," he said to Pierre in French, "get in at once," and then when the dumb man entered the cab, he explained to the cabman in English:—"This poor devil is a pensioner of mine, and as he wants to see a friend of his in gaol I'll take him with me."

He stepped into the cab which drove off, the cabman rather astonished at the whole affair, but none the less contented himself with merely winking at the pretty servant girl who stood on the steps, whereupon she tossed her head and went inside.

As they drove along Vandeloup said nothing to Pierre, not that he did not want to, but he mistrusted the trap-door in the roof of the cab, which would permit the cabman to overhear everything. So they went along in silence, and when they arrived at the gaol Vandeloup told the cabman to wait for him, and walked towards the gaol.

"You are coming inside, I suppose," he said, sharply, to Pierre, who still slouched alongside.

The dumb man nodded sullenly.

Vandeloup cursed Pierre in his innermost heart, but smiled blandly and agreed to let him enter with him. There was some difficulty with the warder at the door, as the permission to see the prisoner was only made out in the name of M. Vandeloup, but after some considerable trouble they succeeded in getting in.

"My faith!" observed Gaston, lightly, as they went along to the cell, conducted by a warder, "it's almost as hard to get into gaol as to get out of it."

The warder admitted them both to Kitty's cell, and left them alone with her. She was seated on the bed in the corner of the cell, in an attitude of deepest dejection. When they entered she looked up in a mechanical sort of manner, and Vandeloup could see how worn and pinched-looking her face was. Pierre went to one end of the cell and leaned against the wall in an indifferent manner, while Vandeloup stood right in front of the unhappy woman. Kitty arose when she saw him, and an expression of loathing passed over her haggard-looking face.

"Ah!" she said, bitterly, rejecting Vandeloup's preferred hand, "so you have come to see your work; well, look around at these bare walls; see how thin and ugly I have grown; think of the crime with which I am charged, and surely even Gaston Vandeloup will be satisfied."

The young man sneered.

"Still as good at acting as ever, I see," he said, mockingly; "cannot you even see a friend without going into these heroics?"

"Why have you come here?" she asked, drawing herself up to her full height.

"Because I am your friend," he answered, coolly.

"My friend!" she echoed, scornfully, looking at him with contempt; "you ruined my life a year ago, now you have endeavoured to fasten the guilt of murder on me, and yet you call yourself my friend; a good story, truly," with a bitter laugh.

"I could not help giving the evidence I did," replied Gaston, coolly, shrugging his shoulders; "if you are innocent, what I say will not matter."

"If I am innocent!" she said, looking at him steadily; "you villain, you know I am innocent!"

"I know nothing of the sort."

Then you believe I committed the crime?"

"I do."

Kitty sat helplessly down on the bed, and passed her hand across her eyes.

"My God!" she muttered, "I am going mad."

"Not at all unlikely," he replied, carelessly.

She looked vacantly round the cell, and caught sight of Pierre shrinking back into the shadow.

"Why did you bring your accomplice with you?" she said, looking at Gaston.

M. Vandeloup shrugged his shoulders.

"Really, my dear Bebe," he said, lazily, "I don't know why you should call him my accomplice, as I have committed no crime."

"Have you not?" she said, rising to her feet, and bending towards him, "think again."

Vandeloup shook his head, with a smile.

"No, I do not think I have," he answered, glancing keenly at her; "I suppose you want me to be as black as yourself?"

"You coward!" she said, in a rage, turning on him, "how dare you taunt me in this manner? it is not enough that you have ruined me, and imperilled my life, without jeering at me thus, you coward?"

"Bah!" retorted Vandeloup, cynically, brushing some dust off his coat, "this is not the point; you insinuate that I committed a crime, perhaps you will tell me what kind of a crime?"

"Murder," she replied, in a whisper.

"Oh, indeed," sneered Gaston, coolly, though his lips twitched a little, "the same style of crime as your own? and whose murder am I guilty of, pray?"

"Randolph Villiers."

Vandeloup shrugged his shoulders.

"Who can prove it?" he asked, contemptuously.

"I can!"

"You," with a sneer, "a murderess?"

"Who can prove I am a murderess?" she cried, wildly.

"I can," he answered, with an ugly look; "and I will if you don't keep a quiet tongue."

"I will keep quiet no longer," boldly rising and facing Vandeloup, with her hands clenched at her sides; "I have tried to shield you faithfully through all your wickedness, but now that you accuse me of committing a crime, which accusation you know is false, I accuse you, Gaston Vandeloup, and your accomplice, yonder," wheeling round and pointing to Pierre, who shrank away, "of murdering Randolph Villiers, at the Black Hill, Ballarat, for the sake of a nugget of gold he carried."

Vandeloup looked at her disdainfully.

"You are mad," he said, in a cold voice; "this is the raving of a lunatic; there is no proof of what you say; it was proved conclusively that myself and Pierre were asleep at our hotel while M. Villiers was with Jarper at two o'clock in the morning."

"I know that was proved," she retorted, "and by some jugglery on your part; but, nevertheless, I saw you and him," pointing again to Pierre, "murder Villiers."

"You saw it," echoed Vandeloup, with a disbelieving smile; "tell me how?"

"Ah!" she cried, making a step forward, "you do not believe me, but I tell you it is true—yes, I know now who the two men were following

Madame Midas as she drove away: one was her husband, who wished to rob her, and the other was Pierre, who, acting upon your instructions, was to get the gold from Villiers should he succeed in getting it from Madame. You left me a few minutes afterwards, but I, with my heart full of love—wretched woman that I was—followed you at a short distance, unwilling to lose sight of you even for a little time. I climbed down among the rocks and saw you seat yourself in a narrow part of the path. Curiosity then took the place of love, and I watched to see what you were going to do. Pierre—that wretch who cowers in the corner—came down the path and you spoke to him in French. What was said I did not know, but I guessed enough to know you meditated some crime. Then Villiers came down the path with the nugget in its box under his arm. I recognised the box as the one which Madame Midas had brought to our house. When Villiers came opposite you you spoke to him; he tried to pass on, and then Pierre sprang out from behind the rock and the two men struggled together, while you seized the box containing the gold, which Villiers had let fall, and watched the struggle. You saw that Villiers, animated by despair, was gradually gaining the victory over Pierre, and then you stepped in—yes; I saw you snatch Pierre's knife from the back of his waist and stab Villiers in the back. Then you put the knife into Pierre's hand, all bloody, as Villiers fell dead, and I fled away."

She stopped, breathless with her recital, and Vandeloup, pale but composed, would have answered her, when a cry from Pierre startled them. He had come close to them, and was looking straight at Kitty.

"My God!" he cried; "then I am innocent?"

"You!" shrieked Kitty, falling back on her bed; "who are you?"

The man pulled his hat off and came a step nearer.

"I am Randolph Villiers!"

Kitty shrieked again and covered her face with her hands, while Vandeloup laughed in a mocking manner, though his pale face and quivering lip told that his mirth was assumed.

"Yes," said Villiers, throwing his hat on the floor of the cell, "it was Pierre Lemaire, and not I, who died. The struggle took place as you have described, but he," pointing to Vandeloup, "wishing to get rid of Pierre for reasons of his own stabbed him, and not me, in the back. He thrust the knife into my hand, and I, in my blind fury, thought that I had murdered the dumb man. I was afraid of being arrested for the murder, so, as suggested by Vandeloup, I changed clothes with the dead man and wrapped my own up in a bundle. We hid the body and the nugget in one of the old mining shafts and then came down to Ballarat. I was similar to Pierre in appearance, except that my chin was shaven. I went down to the Wattle Tree Hotel as Pierre after leaving my clothes outside the window of the bedroom which Vandeloup pointed out to me. Then he went to the theatre and told me to rejoin him there as Villiers. I got my own clothes into the room, dressed again as myself; then, locking the door, so that the people of the hotel might suppose that Pierre slept, I jumped out of the window of the bedroom and went to the theatre. There I played my part as you know, and while we were behind the scenes Mr. Wopples asked me to put out the gas in his room. I did so, and took from his dressing-table a black beard, in order to disguise myself as Pierre till my beard had grown. We went to supper, and then I parted with Jarper at two o'clock in the morning, and went back to the hotel, where I climbed into the bedroom through the window and reassumed Pierre's dress for ever. It was by Vandeloup's advice I pretended to be drunk, as I could not go to the Pactolus, where my wife would have recognised me. Then I, as the supposed Pierre, was discharged, as you know. Vandeloup, aping friendship, drew the dead man's salary and bought clothes and a box for me. In the middle of one night I still disguised as Pierre, slipped out of the window, and went up to Black Hill, where I found the nugget and brought it down to my room at the Wattle Tree Hotel. Then Vandeloup brought in the box with my clothes, and we packed the nugget in it, together with the suit I had worn at the time of the murder. Following his instructions, I came down to Melbourne, and there disposed of the nugget—no need to ask how, as there are always people ready to do things of that sort for payment. When I was paid for the nugget, and I only got eight hundred pounds, the man who melted it down taking the rest, I had to give six hundred to Vandeloup, as I was in his power as I thought, and dare not refuse in case he should denounce me for the murder of Pierre Lemaire. And now I find that I have been innocent all the time, and he has been frightening me with a shadow. He, not I, was the murderer of Pierre Lemaire, and you can prove it."

During all this recital, which Kitty listened to with staring eyes, Vandeloup had stood quite still, revolving in his own mind how he could escape from the position in which he found himself. When Villiers finished his recital he raised his head and looked defiantly at both his victims.

"Fate has placed the game in your hands," he said coolly, while they stood and looked at him; "but I'm not beaten yet, my friend. May I ask what you intend to do?"

"Prove my innocence," said Villiers, boldly.

"Indeed!" sneered Gaston, "at my expense, I presume."

"Yes! I will denounce you as the murderer of Pierre Lemaire."

"And I," said Kitty, quickly, "will prove Villiers' innocence."

Vandeloup turned on her with all the lithe, cruel grace of a tiger.

"First you must prove your own innocence," he said, in a low, fierce voice. "Yes; if you can hang me for the murder of Pierre Lemaire, I can hang you for the murder of Selina Sprotts; yes, though I know you did not do it."

"Ah!" said Kitty, quickly, springing forward, "you know who committed the crime."

"Yes," replied Vandeloup, slowly, "the man who committed the crime intended to murder Madame Midas, and he was the man who hated her and wished her dead—her husband."

"I?" cried Villiers, starting forward, "you lie."

Vandeloup wheeled round quickly on him, and, getting close to him, spoke rapidly.

"No, I do not lie," he said, in a concentrated voice of anger; "you followed me up to the house of M. Meddlechip, and hid among the trees on the lawn to watch the house; you saw Bebe throw the bottle out, and picked it up; then you went to St Kilda and, climbing over the wall, committed the crime, as she," pointing to Kitty, "saw you do; I met you in the street near the house after you had committed it, and see," plunging his hand into Villiers' pocket, "here is the bottle which contained the poison," and he held up to Kitty the bottle with the two red bands round it, which she had thrown away.

"It is false!" cried Villiers, in despair, seeing that all the evidence was against him.

"Prove it, then," retorted Vandeloup, knocking at the door to summon the warder. "Save your own neck before you put mine in danger."

The door opened, and the warder appeared. Kitty and Villiers gazed horror-struck at one another, while Vandeloup, without another word, rapidly left the cell. The warder beckoned to Villiers to come, and, with a deep sigh, he obeyed.

"Where are you going?" asked Kitty, as he moved towards the door.

"Going?" he repeated, mechanically. "I am going to see my wife."

He left the cell, and when he got outside the gaol he saw the hansom with Vandeloup in it driving rapidly away. Villiers looked at the retreating vehicle in despair. "My God," he murmured, raising his face to the blue sky with a frightful expression of despair; "how am I to escape the clutches of this devil?"

XVI

BE SURE THY SIN WILL FIND THEE OUT

Madame Midas was a remarkably plucky woman, but it needed all her pluck and philosophy to bear up against the terrible calamities which were befalling her. Her faith in human nature was completely destroyed, and she knew that all the pleasure of doing good had gone out of her life. The discovery of Kitty's baseness had wounded her deeply, and she found it difficult to persuade herself that the girl had not been the victim of circumstances. If Kitty had only trusted her when she came to live with her all this misery and crime would have been avoided, for she would have known Madame Midas would never have married Vandeloup, and thus would have had no motive for committing the crime. Regarding Vandeloup's pretensions to her hand, Mrs. Villiers laughed bitterly to herself. After the misery of her early marriage it was not likely she was going to trust herself and her second fortune again to a man's honour. She sighed as she thought what her future life must be. She was wealthy, it was true, but amid all her riches she would never be able to know the meaning of friendship, for all who came near her now would have some motive in doing so, and though Madame Midas was anxious to do good with her wealth, yet she knew she could never expect gratitude in return. The comedy of human life is admirable when one is a spectator; but ah! the actors know they are acting, and have to mask their faces with smiles, restrain the tears which they would fain let flow, and mouth witty sayings with breaking hearts. Surely the most bitter of all feelings is that cynical disbelief in human nature which is so characteristic of our latest civilization.

Madame Midas, however, now that Melbourne was so hateful to her, determined to leave it, and sent up to Mr. Calton in order to confer with him on the subject. Calton came down to St Kilda, and was shown into the drawing-room where Mrs. Villiers, calm and impenetrable looking as ever, sat writing letters. She arose as the barrister entered, and gave him her hand.

"It was kind of you to come so quickly," she said, in her usual quiet, self-contained manner; "I wish to consult you on some matters of importance."

"I am at your service, Madame," replied Calton, taking a seat, and looking keenly at the marble face before him; "I am glad to see you looking so well, considering what you have gone through."

Mrs. Villiers let a shadowy smile flit across her face.

"They say the Red Indian becomes utterly indifferent to the torture of his enemies after a certain time," she answered, coldly; "I think it is the same with me. I have been deceived and disillusionized so completely that I have grown utterly callous, and nothing now can move me either to sorrow or joy."

"A curious answer from a curious woman," thought Calton, glancing at her as she sat at the writing-table in her black dress with the knots of violet ribbons upon it; "what queer creatures experience makes us."

Madame Midas folded her hands loosely on the table, and looked dreamily out of the open French window, and at the trellis covered with creeping plants beyond, through which the sun was entering in pencils of golden light. Life would have been so sweet to her if she had only been content to be deceived like other people; but then she was not of that kind. Faith with her was a religion, and when religion is taken away, what remains?—nothing.

"I am going to England," she said, abruptly, to Calton, rousing herself out of these painful reflections.

"After the trial, I presume?" observed Calton, slowly.

"Yes," she answered, hesitatingly; "do you think they will—they will—hang the girl?"

Calton shrugged his shoulders. "I can't tell you," he answered, with a half smile; "if she is found guilty—well—I think she will be imprisoned for life."

"Poor Kitty," said Madame, sadly, "it was an evil hour when you met Vandeloup. What do you think of him?" she asked, suddenly.

"He's a scoundrel," returned Calton, decisively; "still, a clever one, with a genius for intrigue; he should have lived in the times of Borgian Rome, where his talents would have been appreciated; now we have lost the art of polite murder."

"Do you know," said Mrs. Villiers, musingly, leaning back in her chair, "I cannot help thinking Kitty is innocent of this crime."

"She may be," returned Calton, ambiguously, "but the evidence seems very strong against her."

"Purely circumstantial," interrupted Madame Midas, quickly.

"Purely circumstantial, as you say," assented Calton; "still, some new facts may be discovered before the trial which may prove her to be innocent. After the mystery which enveloped the death of Oliver Whyte in the hansom cab murder I hesitate giving a decided answer, in any case till everything has been thoroughly sifted; but, if not Kitty Marchurst, whom do you suspect—Vandeloup?"

"No; he wanted to marry me, not to kill me."

"Have you any enemy, then, who would do such a thing?"

"Yes; my husband."

"But he is dead."

"He disappeared," corrected Madame, "but it was never proved that he was dead. He was a revengeful, wicked man, and if he could have killed me, without hurting himself, he would," and rising from her seat she paced up and down the room slowly.

"I know your sad story," said the barrister, "and also how your husband disappeared; but, to my mind, looking at all the circumstances, you will not be troubled with him again."

A sudden exclamation made him turn his head, and he saw Madame Midas, white as death, staring at the open French window, on the threshold of which was standing a man—medium height, black beard, and a haggard, hunted look in his eyes.

"Who is this?" cried Calton, rising to his feet.

Madame Midas tottered, and caught at the mantelpiece for support.

"My husband," she said, in a whisper.

"Alive?" said Calton, turning to the man at the window.

"I should rather think so," said Villiers, insolently, advancing into the room; "I don't look like a dead man, do I?"

Madame Midas sprang forward and caught his wrist.

"So you have come back, murderer!" she hissed in his ear.

"What do you mean?" said her husband, wrenching his hand away.

"Mean?" she cried, vehemently; "you know what I mean. You cut yourself off entirely from me by your attempt on my life, and the theft of the gold; you dare not have showed yourself in case you received the reward of your crime; and so you worked in the dark against me. I knew you were near, though I did not see you; and you for a second time attempted my life."

"I did not," muttered Villiers, shrinking back from the indignant blaze of her eyes. "I can prove—"

"You can prove," she burst out, contemptuously, drawing herself up to her full height, "Yes! you can prove anything with your cowardly nature and lying tongue; but prove that you were not the man who came in the dead of night and poisoned the drink waiting for me, which was taken by my nurse. You can prove—yes, as God is my judge, you shall prove it, in the prisoner's dock, e'er you go to the gallows."

During all this terrible speech, Villiers had crouched on the ground, half terrified, while his wife towered over him, magnificent in her anger. At the end, however, he recovered himself a little, and began to bluster.

"Every man has a right to a hearing," he said, defiantly, looking from his wife to Calton; "I can explain everything."

Madame Midas pointed to a chair.

"I have no doubt you will prove black is white by your lying," she said, coldly, returning to her seat; "I await this explanation."

Thereupon Villiers sat down and told them the whole story of his mysterious disappearance, and how he had been made a fool of by Vandeloup. When he had ended, Calton, who had resumed his seat, and listened to the recital with deep interest, stole a glance at Madame Midas, but she looked as cold and impenetrable as ever.

"I understand, now, the reason of your disappearance," she said, coldly; "but that is not the point. I want to know the reason you tried to murder me a second time."

"I did not," returned Villiers, quietly, with a gesture of dissent.

"Then Selina Sprotts, since you are so particular," retorted his wife, with a sneer; "but it was you who committed the crime."

"Who says I did?" cried Villiers, standing up.

"No one," put in Calton, looking at him sharply, "but as you had a grudge against your wife, it is natural for her to suspect you, at the same time it is not necessary for you to criminate yourself."

"I am not going to do so," retorted Villiers; "if you think I'd be such a fool as to commit a crime and then trust myself to my wife's tender mercies, you are very much mistaken. I am as innocent of the murder as the poor girl who is in prison."

"Then she is not guilty?" cried Mrs. Villiers, rising.

"No," returned Villiers, coldly, "she is innocent."

"Oh, indeed," said Calton, quietly; "then if you both are innocent, who is the guilty person?"

Villiers was about to speak when another man entered the open window. This was none other than Kilsip, who advanced eagerly to Villiers.

"He has come in at the gate," he said, quickly.

"Have you the warrant," asked Villiers, as a sharp ring was heard at the front door.

Kilsip nodded, and Villiers turned on his wife and Calton, who were too much astonished to speak.

"You asked me who committed the crime," he said, in a state of suppressed excitement; "look at that door," pointing to the door which led into the hall, "and you will see the real murderer of Selina Sprotts appear."

Calton and Madame Midas turned simultaneously, and the seconds seemed like hours as they waited with bated breath for the opening of the fatal door. The same name was on their lips as they gazed with intense expectation, and that name was—Gaston Vandeloup.

The noise of approaching footsteps, a rattle at the handle of the door, and it was flung wide open as the servant announced—

"Mr. Jarper."

Yes, there he stood, meek, apologetic, and smiling—the fast-living bank-clerk, the darling of society, and the secret assassin—Mr. Bartholomew Jarper.

He advanced smilingly into the room, when suddenly the smile died away, and his face blanched as his eyes rested on Villiers. He made a step backward as if to fly, but in a moment Kilsip was on him.

"I arrest you in the Queen's name for the murder of Selina Sprotts," and he slipped the handcuffs on his wrists.

The wretched young man fell down on the floor with an agonised shriek.

"It's a lie—it's a lie," he howled, beating his manacled hands on the carpet, "none can prove I did it."

"What about Vandeloup?" said Villiers, looking at the writhing figure at his feet, "and this proof?" holding out the bottle with the red bands.

Jarper looked up with an expression of abject fear on his white face, then with a shriek fell back again in a swoon.

Kilsip went to the window and a policeman appeared in answer to his call, then between them they lifted up the miserable wretch and took him to a cab which was waiting, and were soon driving off up to the station, from whence Jarper was taken to the Melbourne gaol.

Calton turned to Madame Midas and saw that she also had fainted and was lying on the floor. He summoned the servants to attend to her, then, making Villiers come with him, he went up to his office in town in order to get the whole story of the discovery of the murderer.

The papers were full of it next day, and Villiers' statement, together with Jarper's confession, were published side by side. It appeared that Jarper had been living very much above his income, and in order to get money he had forged Mrs. Villiers' name for several large amounts. Afraid of being discovered, he was going to throw himself on her mercy and confess all, which he would have done had Madame Midas come to the Meddlechip's ball. But overhearing the conversation between Kitty and Vandeloup in the conservatory, and seeing the bottle flung out, he thought if he secured it he could poison Madame Midas without suspicion and throw the guilt upon Kitty. He secured the bottle immediately after Vandeloup took Kitty back to the ball-room, and then went down to St Kilda to commit the crime. He knew the house thoroughly as he had often been in it, and saw that the window of Madame's room was open. He then put his overcoat on the glass bottles on top of the wall and leapt inside, clearing the bushes. He stole across the lawn and stepped over the flower-bed, carefully avoiding making any marks. He had the bottle of poison with him, but was apparently quite ignorant how he was to introduce it into the house, but on looking through the parting of the curtains he saw the glass with the drink on the table. Guessing that Madame Midas was in bed and would probably drink during the night, he put his hand through the curtains and poured all the poison into the glass, then noiselessly withdrew. He jumped over the wall again, put on his overcoat, and thought he was safe, when he found M. Vandeloup was watching him and had seen him in all his actions. Vandeloup, whose subtle brain immediately saw that if Madame Midas was dead he could throw the blame on Kitty and thus get rid of her without endangering himself, agreed to keep silent, but made Jarper give up the bottle to him. When Jarper had gone Vandeloup, a few yards further down, met Villiers, but supposed that he had just come on the scene. Villiers, however, had been watching the house all night, and had also been watching Meddlechip's. The reason for this was he thought his wife was at the ball, and wanted to speak to her. He had followed Kitty and Mrs. Riller down to St Kilda by hanging on to the back of the brougham, thinking the latter was his wife. Finding his mistake, he hung round the house for about an hour without any object, and was turning round the corner to go home when he saw Jarper jump over the wall, and, being unseen in the shadow, overheard the conversation and knew that Jarper had committed the crime. He did not, however, dare to accuse Jarper of murder, as he thought it was in Vandeloup's power to denounce him as the assassin of Pierre Lemaire, so for his own safety kept quiet. When he heard the truth from Kitty in the prison he would have denounced the Frenchman at once as the real criminal, but was so bewildered by the rapid manner in which Vandeloup made up a case against him, and especially by the bottle being produced out of his pocket—which bottle Vandeloup, of course, had in his hand all the time—that he permitted him to escape. When he left the gaol, however, he went straight to the police-office and told his story, when a warrant was immediately granted for the arrest of Jarper. Kilsip took the warrant and went down to St Kilda to Mrs. Villiers' house to see her before arresting Jarper; but, as before described, Jarper came down to the house on business from the bank and was arrested at once.

Of course, there was great excitement over the discovery of the real murderer, especially as Jarper was so well known in Melbourne society, but no one pitied him. In the days of his prosperity he had been obsequious to his superiors and insolent to those beneath him, so that all he gained was the contempt of one and the hate of the other. Luckily, he had no relatives whom his crime would have disgraced, and as he had not succeeded in getting rid of Madame Midas, he intended to have run away to South America, and had forged a cheque in her name for a large amount in order to supply himself with funds. Unhappily, however, he had paid that fatal visit and had been arrested, and since then had been in a state of abject fear, begging and praying that his life might be spared. His crime, however, had awakened such indignation that the law was allowed to take its course, so early one wet cold morning Barty Jarper was delivered into the hands of the hangman, and his mean, pitiful little soul was launched into eternity.

Kitty was of course released, but overwhelmed with shame and agony at all her past life having been laid bare, she did not go to see Madame Midas, but disappeared amid the crowd, and tried to hide her infamy from all, although, poor girl, she was more sinned against than sinning.

Vandeloup, for whom a warrant was out for the murder of Lemaire, had also disappeared, and was supposed to have gone to America.

Madame Midas suffered severely from the shocks she had undergone with the discovery of everyone's baseness. She settled a certain income on her husband, on condition she never was to see him again, which offer he readily accepted, and having arranged all her affairs in Australia, she left for England, hoping to find in travel some alleviation, if not forgetfulness, of the sorrow of the past. A good woman—a noble woman, yet one who went forth into the world broken-hearted and friendless, with no belief in anyone and no pleasure in life. She, however, was of too fine a nature ever to sink into the base, cynical indifference of a misanthropic life, and the wealth which she possessed was nobly used by her to alleviate the horrors of poverty and to help those who needed help. Like Midas, the Greek King, from whence her quaint name was derived, she had turned everything she touched into gold, and though it brought her no happiness, yet it was the cause of happiness to others; but she would give all her wealth could she but once more regain that trust in human nature which had been so cruelly betrayed.

Epilogue

The Wages of Sin

Such a hot night as it was—not a breath of wind, and the moon, full orbed, dull and yellow, hangs like a lamp in the dark blue sky. Low down on the horizon are great masses of rain clouds, ragged and angry-looking, and the whole firmament seems to weigh down on the still earth, where everything is burnt and parched, the foliage of the trees hanging limp and heavily, and the grass, yellow and sere, mingling with the hot, white dust of the roads. Absolute stillness everywhere down here by the Yarra Yarra, not even the river making a noise as it sweeps swiftly down on its winding course between its low mud banks. No bark of a dog or human voice breaks the stillness; not even the sighing of the wind through the trees. And throughout all this unearthly silence a nervous vitality predominates, for the air is full of electricity, and the subtle force is permeating the whole scene. A long trail of silver light lies on the dark surface of the river rolling along, and here and there the current swirls into sombre, cruel-looking pools—or froths, and foams in lines of dirty white around the trunks of spectral-looking gum trees, which stretch out their white, scarred branches over the waters.

Just a little way below the bridge which leads to the Botanical Gardens, on the near side of the river, stands an old, dilapidated bathing-house, with its long row of dressing-rooms, doorless and damp-looking. A broad, irregular wooden platform is in front of these, and slopes gradually down to the bank, from whence narrow, crazy-looking steps, stretching the whole length of the platform, go down beneath the sullen waters. And all this covered with black mould and green slime, with whole armies of spiders weaving grey, dusky webs in odd corners, and a broken-down fence on the left half buried in bush rank grass—an evil-looking place even in the daytime, and ten times more evil-looking and uncanny under the light of the moon, which fills it with vague shadows. The rough, slimy platform is deserted, and nothing is heard but the squeaking and scampering of the water-rats, and every now and then the gurgling of the river as it races past, as if it was laughing quietly in a ghastly manner over the victims it had drowned.

Suddenly a black shadow comes gliding along the narrow path by the river bank, and pauses a moment at the entrance to the platform. Then it listens for a few minutes, and again hurries down to the crazy-looking steps. The black shadow standing there, like the genius of solitude, is a woman, and she has apparently come to add herself to the list of the cruel-looking river's victims. Standing there, with one hand on the rough rail, and staring with fascinated eyes on the dull muddy water, she does not hear a step behind her. The shadow of a man, who has apparently followed her, glides from behind the bathing-shed, and stealing down to the woman on the verge of the stream, lays a delicate white hand on her shoulder. She turns with a startled cry, and Kitty Marchurst and Gaston Vandeloup are looking into one another's eyes. Kitty's charming face is worn and pallid, and the hand which clutches her shawl is trembling nervously as she gazes at her old lover. There he stands, dressed in old black clothes, worn and tattered looking, with his fair auburn hair all tangled and matted; his chin covered with a short stubbly beard of some weeks' growth, and his face gaunt and haggard-looking—the very same appearance as he had when he landed in Australia. Then he sought to preserve his liberty; now he is seeking to preserve his life. They gaze at one another in a fascinated manner for a few moments, and then Gaston removes his hand from the girl's shoulder with a sardonic laugh, and she buries her face in her hands with a stifled sob.

"So this is the end," he said, pointing to the river, and fixing his scintillating eyes on the girl; "this is the end of our lives; for you the river—for me the hangman."

"God help me," she moaned, piteously; "what else is left to me but the river?"

"Hope," he said, in a low voice; "you are young; you are beautiful; you can yet enjoy life; but," in a deliberate cruel manner, "you will not, for the river claims you as its victim."

Something in his voice fills her with fear, and looking up she reads death in his face, and sinking on her knees she holds out her helpless hands with a pitying cry for life.

"Strange," observed M. Vandeloup, with a touch of his old airy manner; "you come to commit suicide and are not afraid; I wish to save you the trouble, and you are, my dear—you are illogical."

"No! no!" she mutters, twisting her hands together, "I do not want to die; why do you wish to kill me?" lifting her wan face to his.

He bent down, and caught her wrist fiercely.

"You ask me that?" he said, in a voice of concentrated passion, "you who, with your long tongue, have put the hangman's rope round my throat; but for you, I would, by this time, have been on my way to America, where freedom and wealth awaits me. I have worked hard, and committed crimes for money, and now, when I should enjoy it, you, with your feminine devilry, have dragged me back to the depths."

"I did not make you commit the crimes," she said, piteously.

"Bah!" with a scoffing laugh, "who said you did? I take my own sins on my own shoulders; but you did worse; you betrayed me. Yes; there is a warrant out for my arrest, for the murder of that accursed Pierre. I have eluded the clever Melbourne police so far, but I have lived the life of a dog. I dare not even ask for food, lest I betray myself. I am starving! I tell you, starving! you harlot! and it is your work."

He flung her violently to the ground, and she lay there, a huddled heap of clothing, while, with wild gesticulations, he went on.

"But I will not hang," he said, fiercely; "Octave Braulard, who escaped the guillotine, will not perish by a rope. No; I have found a boat going to South America, and to-morrow I go on board of her, to sail to Valparaiso; but before I go I settle with you."

She sprang suddenly to her feet with a look of hate in her eyes.

"You villain!" she said, through her clenched teeth, "you ruined my life, but you shall not murder me!"

He caught her wrist again, but he was weak for want of food, and she easily wrenched it away.

"Stand back!" she cried, retreating a little.

"You think to escape me," he almost shrieked, all his smooth cynical mask falling off; "no, you will not; I will throw you into the river. I will see you sink to your death. You will cry for help. No one will hear you but God and myself. Both of us are merciless. You will die like a rat in a hole, and that face you are so proud of will be buried in the mud of the river. You devil! your time has come to die."

He hissed out the last word in a low, sibilant manner, then sprang towards her to execute his purpose. They were both standing on the verge of the steps, and instinctively Kitty put out her hands to keep him off. She struck him on the chest, and then his foot slipped on the green slime which covered the steps, and with a cry of baffled rage he fell backward into the dull waters, with a heavy splash. The swift current gripped him, and before Kitty could utter a sound, she could see him rising out in midstream, and being carried rapidly away. He threw up his hands with a hoarse cry for help, but, weakened by famine, he could do nothing for himself, and sank for the second time. Again he rose, and the current swept him near shore, almost within reach of a fallen tree. He made a desperate effort to grasp it, but the current, mocking his puny efforts, bore him away once again in its giant embrace, and with a wild shriek on God he sank to rise no more.

The woman on the bank, with white face and staring eyes, saw the fate which he had meant for her meted out to him, and when she saw him sink for the last time, she covered her face with her hand and fled rapidly away into the shadowy night.

The sun is setting in a sea of blood, and all the west is lurid with crimson and barred by long black clouds. A heavy cloud of smoke shot with fiery red hangs over the city, and the din of many workings sound through the air. Down on the river the ships are floating on the blood-stained waters, and all their masts stand up like a forest of bare trees against the clear sky. And the river sweeps on red and angry-looking under the sunset, with the rank grass and vegetation on its shelving banks. Rats are scampering along among the wet stones, and then a vagrant dog poking about amid some garbage howls dismally. What is that black speck on the crimson waters? The trunk of a tree perhaps; no, it is a body, with white face and tangled auburn hair; it is floating down with the current. People are passing to and fro on the bridge, the clock strikes in the town hall, and the dead body drifts slowly down the red stream far into the shadows of the coming night—under the bridge, across which the crowd is hurrying, bent on pleasure and business, past the tall warehouses where rich merchants are counting their gains, under the shadow of the big steamers with their tall masts and smoky funnels. Now it is caught in the reeds at the side of the stream; no, the current carries it out again, and so down the foul river, with the hum of the city on each side and the red sky above, drifts the dead body on its way to the sea. The red dies out of the sky, the veil of night descends, and under the cold starlight—cold and cruel as his own nature—that which was once Gaston Vandeloup floats away into the still shadows.

FINIS

A Note About the Author

Fergus Hume (1859–1932) was an English novelist. Born in Worcestershire, Hume was the son of a civil servant of Scottish descent. At the age of three, he moved with his family to Dunedin, New Zealand, where he attended Otago Boy's High School. In 1885, after graduating from the University of Otago with a degree in law, Hume was admitted to the New Zealand bar. He moved to Melbourne, Australia, where he worked as a clerk and embarked on his career as a writer with a series of plays. After struggling in vain to find success as a playwright, Hume turned to novels with *The Mystery of a Hansom Cab* (1886), a story of mystery and urban poverty that eventually became one of the most successful works of fiction of the Victorian era. Hume, who returned to England in 1888, would go on to publish over 100 novels and stories, earning a reputation as a leading writer of popular fiction and inspiring such figures as Arthur Conan Doyle, whose early detective novels were modeled after Hume's. Despite the resounding success of his debut work of fiction, Hume died in relative obscurity at a modest cottage in Thundersley.

A Note from the Publisher

Spanning many genres, from non-fiction essays to literature classics to children's books and lyric poetry, Mint Edition books showcase the master works of our time in a modern new package. The text is freshly typeset, is clean and easy to read, and features a new note about the author in each volume. Many books also include exclusive new introductory material. Every book boasts a striking new cover, which makes it as appropriate for collecting as it is for gift giving. Mint Edition books are only printed when a reader orders them, so natural resources are not wasted. We're proud that our books are never manufactured in excess and exist only in the exact quantity they need to be read and enjoyed.

booofinity™

Discover more of your favorite classics with Bookfinity™.

- Track your reading with custom book lists.
- Get great book recommendations for your personalized Reader Type.
- Add reviews for your favorite books.
- AND MUCH MORE!

Visit **bookfinity.com** and take the fun Reader Type quiz to get started.

Enjoy our classic and modern companion pairings!

Printed in the USA
CPSIA information can be obtained
at www.ICGtesting.com
JSHW022215140824
68134JS00018B/1063

9 781513 278360